The Corsairs

Brian Cook

Copyright © Brian Cook 2020

All rights reserved.

The right of Brian Cook to be identified as the Author of the Work has been asserted by him in accordance with the Copyright, Designs and Patents Act, 1988.

All rights reserved. No part of this publication may be reproduced, stored in a retrieval system, or transmitted, in any form or by any means without the prior written permission of the publisher nor be otherwise circulated in any form of binding or cover other than that in which it is published and without a similar condition being imposed on the subsequent purchaser.

All characters and locations, other than reference to the city of Glasgow in general terms, are fictitious and any resemblance to real persons living or dead, is purely coincidental.

For my Mother,
Mary Mitchell Cook
(1941-1986)

And with deep appreciation of those who gave encouragement and support during my first faltering steps into writing. You know who you are and I remain eternally grateful.

Departure

The radio fell silent as he neared Kincardine. There'd been a burst of *A Boy From Nowhere* and the fragmentary chat of someone being up-beat for a living, but the signal, breaking on the limits of reception, had given way to the drone of the engine and the grumbling road beneath his feet. Alec twisted the dial, but it was no use. Auchenbreoch was out of range and reluctant to scan for another he gazed instead at the dark earth of the estuary spreading out before him, a featureless plain stretching towards the Kincardine Bridge, its grey outline framed against the broad sweep of the Ochills, steep-sided flanks splashed with the bright yellow of gorse. Beyond the bridge and hidden by a thick screen of trees, the Scottish Police College, his home for the next eight weeks.

He followed the directions he'd been given and crossing the bridge, drove through the quiet streets of Kincardine until he saw the sign for the police college in large gold letters. Turning up a narrow road, he navigated the manicured grounds to a low-rise building and a broad tarmac'd area, where a small wooden sign declared this to be the Parade Square.

A large number of cars were already parked there. Drawing up to the last he grabbed his bags and joined a queue of young men and women dressed in their Sunday best, like emigres boarding a ship. They looked smart. He looked down at the suit he'd bought for Mum's funeral, his trousers no longer reaching his ankles and he self-consciously pushed down at his pockets. It made little difference and he inwardly cursed Dad's refusal to lend him money for a new one.

At a small entrance door a Sergeant checked in the new arrivals, but progress was grisly and the weight of the bags made Alec's arms ache. It seemed logical to put them down, but as soon as they touched the ground there was a shout from his left.

"Who told you to do that?"

A female Sergeant strode towards him, thin mouth compressed beneath a sharp nose, fistfuls of red hair sprouting from beneath a black checkered hat. Arms locked by her side, body bent forward, she homed in.

"Pick them up."

It was as if she were addressing a child. Alec bit back a caustic reply and braced himself for more reprimands. Instead, she passed by, working her way down the line regaling the other recruits with reminders they could no longer do what they 'bloody well wanted' while her fellow Sergeants, bored with the display, turned away.

When at last he reached the check-in desk the moon-faced Sergeant scored his name off a list and pointed toward the corridor inside, but as he stepped forward he was stopped by another with a red sash across his tunic who moved in close and scanned his face.

"You thinkin' of keeping that 'tache?"

"Yes Sergeant, I've become quite attached to it."

The smirk vanished.

"Smart arse? I'll soon cut you down to size."

Alec stumbled over an apology but it was interrupted by the desk Sergeant shouting 'next' and with the sash Sergeant turning his ire towards someone else he hurried inside, confused and ill at ease.

A group of male recruits had gathered at the bottom of a stairwell and as Alec joined them another Sergeant led them through a series of passageways stinking of gloss paint to a corridor with doorways at regular intervals along one side. They halted at each while the Sergeant read names from a list taped to the wall. Recruits detached themselves and disappeared inside, an exercise repeated until they reached the last room where the Sergeant read out the names once more.

"Munro, Beattie, Primrose, McGovern, Petrie, McAlister, Brown" and finally Alec's own, "MacKay."

The room was an army style dormitory with eight spaces, each containing a metal-framed bed with chain-link springs. Two bedsheets and a thin mattress were folded at the foot of each. A wardrobe stood on one side, a desk and plastic chair on the other. Chest high partitions separated each space, everything replicated down to the last detail. Alec looked around at his fellow inmates. Some raised eyebrows, others shrugged and smirked. They looked as uncomfortable as he felt in the austere surroundings, except for an athletically built lad with blonde hair and sardonic smile who looked around in familiar recognition. Alec put his bags down and sat on the edge of his bed. First impressions weren't great but maybe it was just the unfamiliarity.

As if to forestall further reflection, he was shaken from his thoughts by the return of the Sergeant.

"Right, follow me."

They filed back into the corridor and past an open shower area, white tiled walls resuscitating memories of his first school communal shower, P.E. teacher ordering them to strip and lined up with the others he'd prayed for the steam to hide his skinny frame. He walked in silence, ghosts of awkwardness and trepidation trailing behind him.

There were occasional shouts of "keep left" and "no talking" until they arrived at a hall with parquet flooring where serried ranks of desks were arranged before a large stage. Sunlight streamed through tall windows reminding him of school assemblies and higher-grade exams. There was a barked order to sit and the hall reverberated to the screech of chairs as two senior officers entered. One stood at a lectern and made a short speech about discipline, teamwork and standards. There was a well-rehearsed tone to it all.

A circumnavigation of the college followed. He passed uniformed officers with starched white shirts, trousers sharply creased, all of them clean-cut, confident and relaxed. Alec wondered if they'd experienced the same uncertainty he now felt and whether he'd wear that self-assured look one day. Right now, he didn't feel like a cop; more a child on his first day at a military boarding school.

The Sergeants led the way down a corridor with a panoramic view of the bright world outside. Far away in Auchenbreoch old friends would be gathering for a pint at The Volunteer. Dad would be putting on his suit and tie for evening Mass. Life rolling on with the same slow steady rhythm. Would he be missed? Given the heated exchanges as he left, it was doubtful.

They arrived at the dining hall, air ringing with the ching of cutlery, the crash of crockery and the thunk of metal spoons in food troughs. Alec collected a sub-standard dinner with as much grace as he could muster, sat at his table and poked at a salad of brown lettuce leaves and stale cheese. Someone found a slug and held it up.

"Christ! Will you look at that."

There was muted laughter and someone pointed towards the limp grey lump hanging from the fork.

"That's the garnii."

More laughter, the slug had broken the ice, but none ventured a name; as if they hadn't yet committed themselves and were waiting to see what happened next. And then dinner was over, the exit of the Sergeants at the far end of the hall their cue to follow.

They returned to the dorm through unfamiliar corridors and arrived to a message instructing them to change into uniform and assemble in the laundry room. There were mutters of "fuck sakes" and "bollocks" but they did as they were told, and Alec made his way to a room lit by a naked lightbulb and smelling of bleach. Brown-stained ironing tables leaned against formica worktops where ancient irons stood to attention in neat rows. The Sergeant, dressed in track suit and white trainers illustrated the standards expected of them. Candle wax on the insides of trousers for a sharp crease, the use of spit on the shoe, application of polish, cotton wool and fresh water for a mirror finish. There was a monologue on the subject of haircuts and personal hygiene before announcing they'd be marching on the parade square the next day. Alec found himself with nagging doubts he could adapt to this regimented life.

To a chorus of low groans they were led back to the dorm where the Sergeant selected a bed and demonstrated how it was to be made; sheets tucked under mattresses with paper cut folds, tension tight enough to bounce a fifty pence piece. The Sergeant bounced one off the bed into his outstretched hand. This would be their morning routine, a loose tuck would be punished, sub-standard beds would be torn apart and the officer made to do it again. At that the Sergeant tore the sheets from the bed and dumped them on the floor.

"Ye didnae think it would be that easy?"

The owner of the bed smiled wanly. The word 'prick' formed in Alec's head as the Sergeant scanned the group.

"Anybody ex-forces?"

The blonde-haired lad stepped forward. He had high cheekbones and a small scar across one cheek.

"Scots Guards Sarge."

"Then you'll know the standard. Your job is to help the others reach those giddy heights, ok?"

The Scots Guard gave a curt nod. The Sergeant made his way to the exit and turned to face the dorm one last time.

"Bar is off limits on your first night. Lights out at 2200 hours. Breakfast at 0700 hours in uniform. Sweet dreams."

Alec sat on the edge of his bed and pondered his next steps. He had a bed to make and bags to unpack, but he was dog tired and wanted nothing more than to lie back and take stock.

It had taken a year to get this far. The application process, entrance exam, interviews and a home visit. The nervous wait and the relief of the final acceptance letter, the adjusting perceptions of old friends surprised by his sudden change in direction and the acrimony of a tight knit community who saw his choice as a betrayal of everything they stood for.

And in that moment Auchenbreoch felt further away than mere geography, a grey huddle in a shallow glen beneath the domed hill of Garrioch Law, high moorland to one side, the massive 'A' frame of the colliery on the other, the pit at the tip of a capillary road cutting a seam northward through the town and the rolling green of Ayrshire, toward Kilmarnock and the wider world. Smoke would be rising from the chimneys of a thousand living-room fires, the communal dependence on coal a part of everyday life, defiance as much as necessity in a place down on its luck. A languid pall would be hanging over the town, dirty orange in the last rays of a late spring afternoon, a low-rent Brigadoon resigned to being there the next day, and the day after that. Two years since the strike and the pit still produced coal, but for how much longer? And when the mining stopped and the smoke cleared, then what?

There was his Social Sciences degree of course. Something he'd once viewed as his passport out of Auchenbreoch. 'Mickey Mouse' Dad called it and though it stung he'd been forced to concede it was unlikely to take him anywhere other than a social work career and he'd no patience for that. There seemed few other options. He could hang around a town consumed by slow decay or grab a lifeboat.

There'd been hot words when he'd plucked up the courage to tell Dad and uproar in the town when news got out, but he'd reconciled himself to being the town pariah when he'd completed the application form. The almost inevitable threats of violence came to nothing not because he was feared, but because he was 'Joe's Boy', son of the miner who'd led the strikers back at the head of a pipe band. There'd been disbelief he'd do 'such a thing' to his 'faither', but life was short. Mum's death had taught him that and knowing that simple truth he'd be fucked if he'd spend his days in Auchenbreoch hoping things would get better. The greater the disdain, the more righteous he felt, increasing the hunger to put a distance between himself and Auchenbreoch that was more than physical. He'd be his own man; see life in the raw and decide what was right and wrong for himself; a more honourable prospect than eking the last lump of coal from a dying pit.

So, here he was, lying on a thin mattress, knowing he'd been lucky to escape the drab uncertainties, but the petty officiousness, austere surroundings and squalid food had induced the first stabs of doubt. It was like being led about like a dog on a string. Maybe he wasn't cut out for this new life. Perhaps he hadn't been so smart after all.

A shout from the end of the dorm.

"C'moan look at this!"

He crossed the room and joined his fellow inmates at a window overlooking the vast college grounds. It was dusk, but in the soft light he could make out an expanse of lawn, the access road cutting through it and a sports field beyond. Above a line of tall trees, the pylons of Kincardine power station stood silhouetted against the dying light of the day, their tops marked by flashing beacons.

"There."

The lookout pointed to a cluster of shrubs. Creeping past them were two young men, backs hunched, dragging suitcases along the ground. They looked left and right as they inched towards the access road and a row of parked cars.

One of the watchers laughed.

"What the fuck are they up to?"

The lookout grinned.

"Escaping."

Alec laughed along with the others and watched transfixed as the pair broke into a fast walk, backs straight, legs moving in short quick strides. There was a snort to his right.

"Pair o' mincin' fannies."

More laughter. The escapees broke into a run, luggage bouncing in rhythm until the gap to the car was closed, boot thrown open and cases dumped inside. The men leapt in and the headlights flickered as the engine roared into life. There was a crunch of gears and the car leapt forward, a cloud of blue smoke left behind like the aftermath of a conjuring trick. Alec watched the bouncing lances of its headlights as it crested a series of speed humps and was gone.

"Whit a pair of pricks".

The ex-Scots Guard appeared beside him with a lop-sided smile that reminded Alec of Elvis.

"Imagine getting through all that shite. Gei'n up yer job, getting' yer faimly oan side; jist tae gie up oan yer first day. Fannies."

There were murmurs of agreement and a conversation began. Turned out they'd all come through the same process and experienced the same hurdles. Exams, interview, family misgivings, great expectations, the absence of options. Alec doubted they'd experienced quite the same hostility but he kept that to himself.

Outside, the night grew darker, the pylon lights glowed brighter and Alec remembered his first sight of them as he'd crossed the river. Signposts back to a more familiar world and he wondered where the two escapees had gone to.

"Fuck 'em. Their funeral."

It was the Scots Guard again. There was just the two of them at the window now and Alec found himself talking for the first time that day.

"Can't say I blame them, been pretty shite so far."

The Scots Guard laughed, deep and loud. Big white teeth in a big wide mouth.

"That's how yer meant to feel. It's whit they dae in the army. 'Break ye, then they make ye'. It's so they can build ye in their ain image."

A hand shot out.

"Ah'm Dougie."

Alec accepted the handshake and introduced himself. Dougie gave a sharp nod, a serious look on a hard face.

"Keep the heid doon, play the game. It's just eight weeks of yer life an' it gets easier efter this."

Dougie snapped his fingers and a spell was broken. The escapees and the conspiratorial advice had changed the atmosphere. Chairs were dragged into the middle of the room and a circle formed. Curtains were drawn against the outside world and the warm glow of table lamps filled the room as the travelers sat down to talk about the day with a sense of shared experience. Alec joined them, names were exchanged and it struck him then that he'd never forget them. A radio played in the background, the feint strains of 'Star Treking' rising over the quiet conversation. He'd crossed the universe right enough.

Homecoming

Dougie was mostly right. It did get easier and the weeks passed quickly. The regimen of legal studies, physical training and parade drills became the norm in his life. He'd even mastered the fifty pence bounce off his bedsheets. He was fitter than he'd ever been and had a more upright bearing, partly as a result of his improving physique and partly as a result of a growing confidence. He'd made new friends and there was an emerging pride in the distinctiveness of his new career, but every Friday brought with it the same unease in leaving his unlikely sanctuary to face the communal disapproval that awaited him in Auchenbreoch.

Weekends had so far been marked by an unspoken demarcation, Dad contriving to be out or hunkered in sullen silence in the living room where barely a word was spoken. Alec had no appetite to rehearse old arguments, so he navigated the tiny house on the basis of where Dad wasn't. And yet, despite the air of recrimination his bed was made for his return, the room cleaned and a dinner waiting in the oven. However fracturing his choices had been, there existed between them something which neither had much choice in, nor was completely broken.

It was not something that could be said for the inhabitants of Auchenbreoch and if Alec had become adept at minimising friction at home, he took equal care to avoid the miners welfare and a number of other hostelries where confrontation would be guaranteed. That left only one vaguely neutral venue and the three remaining friends left to him.

The training ended with a passing out parade that Dad refused to attend, but despite this and all that had gone before, Alec left the police college in upbeat mood that final Friday, primed for a new life, the drive home in summer sunshine a prelude to a brighter future. Things were looking up.

It didn't last. It was raining by the time he reached Auchenbreoch and a grunted welcome from Dad. There were some perfunctory questions that barely merited answers before Dad shuffled off to his defence of the sitting room, leaving Alec to retrieve a steak pie from the oven and ponder his next steps at the kitchen table. It would be another hour before he was due to meet his friends, but there seemed little point in hanging about the house waiting for another dispute about his career choice. He cleaned his plate, placed it quietly on the drier and grabbing his coat crept down the hallway, but as he reached the front porch the living room door opened behind him. Dad's big frame filling the doorway, his chin jerking upwards in the universal challenge of hard-working men.

"Where ye off tae?"

"Out."

A snort and a sneer.

"Skulkin' as usual No' even a cheerio."

This was how it always started, a veiled accusation of some kind that he'd feel compelled to defend and one thing would lead to another. Sooner or later the subject of Mum would come up and things would unravel from there. He'd no time for that tonight. He was focused on the future.

"Not skulking. Meeting the pals at seven, so I'd better go."

The taunt followed Alec down the front steps.

"Pals? Sure ye've goat any?"

The door slammed behind him and Alec strode down the hill to the Main Street, zipping up his jacket against the rain, relieved to be free of the brooding house and its ghost, but even as he rounded the street corner he sensed the presence at the living room window behind him, and knowing Dad was watching felt a wave of guilt wash through him.

Auchenbreoch was a small place; a smudge at the foot of a large hill; narrow streets traversing the uneven ground in scribbled lines overlooking a small river, the rows of grey miners cottages like strata breaking clear of the earth. He crossed the ancient two-span bridge to the Main Street, past the red brick Roman Catholic Church and onwards with his hood pulled up towards The Volunteer, giving thanks the rain had emptied the streets and spared him the inevitable caustic comments.

It had been a farming town before the discovery of coal and the Main Street articulated its changing fortunes better than any book. The Bank of Scotland, its portico'd entrance and handsome Georgian façade built to service the needs of mercantile farmers who'd long disappeared. The Co-op, with its individual shops lined along one side, each with their own specialisms, a throwback to a time before the rise of the supermarkets. The rest of the street was made up of the essentials that defined most rural towns. A car mechanic and petrol station, ancient pump complete with ancient attendant and original fifties enameled signs now rusting at their edges. The Lucky Dip Chinese restaurant, Pelegrinni's fish-n-chip shop, the hairdressers with its standing-lamp hairdryers, the austere concrete pill-box of the miner's welfare, an undertakers and where the road forked for Ayr and Kilmarnock, the whitewashed façade of the The Volunteer Arms Hotel. Its last overnight guest had been a coal board manager in the late 70's and now, devoid of visitors, it owed its survival to the public bar beneath its net curtained upper floors.

Through the brown varnished doors stood a bar with faux-rustic plastered walls, blackened beams and horse brasses hanging beside sepia images of bare foot urchins on horse-drawn carts. As if offering an antidote to the ubiquitous history of coal mining, no reference to the pit or its grim history were made in word or picture anywhere. Instead, it had been fitted out with pool table and juke box to entice the 'young team'. And so, despite the kitsch surroundings of faux bucolic idyll it had become the de facto haunt of the youth of Auchenbreoch, desperate to avoid the half-and-a-half mentality of the miner's welfare, but too skint to seek out the thrills of far-off Kilmarnock.

The bar was busy, the pool table lined with the ten pences of those who'd booked their turn, the jukebox pumping out Living In A Box. Some looked up and shook their heads, but Alec knew it would go no further and with pals imminent he ordered a beer before retreating to a quiet corner to wait it out.

It was then he saw Carol at the bar. He'd not seen her since school and there she was all grown up and much more exotic. Turning round with her drinks she caught sight of him. A broad smile. So, he wasn't persona non grata with her then. Alec watched as she headed to the foyer, a surrogate lounge for those wanting to escape the pool players and the jukebox. A catch-up with Carol would be much better than enduring the occasional cold stare in the bar, but when he reached the foyer there was another girl with her. Fearful of intruding, he was turning back when she caught sight of him again.

"Alec! You're looking well."

An appraising look that was more than neighbourly. The other girl beside her was watchful and noncommittal, but Carol put an arm round his waist and drew him closer. She smelled of Chanel and her body was warm beside his. It felt good.

"Julie, this is Alec. Alec this is Julie."

Alec raised his glass.

"Nice to meet you."

He'd put on his friendliest smile and was rewarded with a warm smile in return. The evening was looking up.

"How you been Carol? Haven't seen you in-"

"–Five years Alec. You've changed. Had a beard last time; looked like the Turin Shroud. What's with the crew cut?"

Carol swept her hand over the stubble on his head and grinned. There was a confident casualness about her. Looked like he was on safe ground. Might as well get it out there.

"Ditched the hippy look and joined the police."

Carol laughed.

"The polis? Never thought of you as a cop. Where're you based?"

"Just finished training. Released into the wild next week."

"You'll have learnt how to punch someone without leaving marks then."

Julie had spoken. Alec looked for the signals indicating someone pulling a leg, but instead there were the flat features of someone being deadly serious, the warm smile a distant memory. Behind him, the air was punctured by greetings shouted over the heads of others, the clinking of glasses and laughter. It was in stark contrast to the emotional black hole that opened before him. Carol filled in the awkward silence.

"Alec's an old neighbour Julie. We go back a long way."

She'd put down a marker and for that he was grateful, but the comment had thrown him. Auchenbreoch was a rough old town, but it rarely saw the police. When it did, it was because things had really got out of hand and someone had taken the drastic action of actually lifting the phone. It was a right of passage among the hard of thinking to be lifted when the cops arrived, for only the daft and naive would still be at the scene in the half hour it took the cops to get there. The usual face saver was to claim you'd been beaten up and Alec lost count of the claims of police torture by lads whose features were completely unmarked.

But Julie pressed her case.

"Tam Pearson got the jail the other night. Got a right kicking. Your lot did it. Scumbags."

"'Mad Tam'? You're joking right?"

Everybody knew Tam; a glue sniffing maniac, given a wide berth by anyone with sense. Tam had been in and out of jail since school and spent each time inside developing a huge physique to back up his violent tendencies. The idea of him being a victim was laughable.

"Tam's the local psycho Julie. I'd hate to see the state of the cops after grappling with that mad bastard."

Julie was unmoved.

"Just like the rest, backing each other to the hilt. We've no' forgotten the miners strike here. Should be ashamed of yersel'. Probably a Mason."

He'd been prepared for the jibe about the strike. It wasn't the first time and it wouldn't be the last, but a Mason? Alec couldn't help but laugh. Had she no idea about his upbringing? How unlikely a Roman Catholic boy to be a part of that?

"What you laughing at?"

Julie's voice was raised now. People nearby turned to look and Alec felt under pressure. The last thing he wanted was an argument, but he wasn't going to let a lazy stereotype pass without a challenge. To his surprise, he'd taken her allegations to heart, as if he was guilty of them himself. Carol had stepped back, self-conscious and embarrassed. Fair enough, he was a big boy now, he'd defend himself.

"Laughing at your idea I'd join the masons."

"Isn't that what you do on day one?"

"Alec went to St Paul's Julie."

Carol stepped forward, a pleading look at Julie to calm the fuck down, but Julie had everyone's attention and was enjoying it.

"Pope's got his own branch of the masons. Nothing to stop a Catholic doing the same."

There'd be no talking Julie down. Whatever bitterness she'd saved up, for whatever reason, found its release right there in the hotel lobby. From the sexual anticipation of a few moments before, Alec found himself being interrogated for the ills of the police service, perceived and imagined. It was a shock that the faults of others would be projected onto him, or that he'd be viewed as a proxy for cops he'd never met. He thought himself a good guy, he'd never beat up anyone, but he was having trouble finding the words. With a grace that neither he nor Julie could muster Carol intervened.

"Great to see you Alec, but time we headed. Good luck with the job."

She gave him a kiss on the cheek and with an arm round Julie, led her away. Alec looked around. The Volunteer regulars, smirking with obvious pleasure, had returned to their drinks and conversation. In gloomy spirits he finished his pint and wondered if this would be the new normal in his life. Whatever; two more nights and then he'd be a Glasgow cop, well clear of Auchenbreoch and its small-town shit.

New Start

It took ten minutes to get a response to the bell on the public counter. When it came, it was in the form of a sour-faced old cop with a Mexican bandit moustache and a pendulous gut. He looked at Alec like a tailor with a particularly challenging customer and asked if he was the 'new start'. Alec replied that he was. There was a grunt and a demand to see his warrant card, as if the appearance of con men in full uniform was a regular occurrence at Corsair Street police station and this cop would be damned if he was going to be caught out. Alec held the card at face height. The cop sniffed and pointed to a set of double doors.

"Up the stairs. First floor. Opposite the stairwell."

He climbed the stairs, half expecting to meet someone from his new shift on the way up, but though there was the occasional disembodied voice he saw no one. When he emerged from the stairwell it was to a deserted corridor and the doorway to a long rectangular room. A name plate confirmed this to be the Muster Room.

Raised on police TV dramas, a muster had sounded much like an incident room, a crucible of tension and conflict, a place where activity hummed. A nerve centre where information tangential and oblique, hard won and pivotal, revealed in stages the convoluted origins of the crime. It was an image far from the reality that confronted him. The bare walls, their stark austerity accentuated by the glare of fluorescent strip lights, reminded Alec of the mortuary visit in the final week of training and he gave silent thanks the similarities ended there. Metal-framed windows ran along one side of the room. Some of them were open and vertical blinds, untethered and yellowed by nicotine, flapped in the breeze.

His posting to Corsair Street had been announced on the last day of training: The epicenter of Summerhill, in one of the most violent deprived areas of Glasgow. There was a dark kudos to being sent there and in the initial excitement he'd imagined an office thrumming with activity and battle-hardened cops. So far it had been underwhelming.

There were no complex charts of criminal associations, no magic marker scribbles on Perspex screens. No multi-coloured pins on cork boards, or crime scene photographs. Just four rows of plastic chairs at one end, the back row pressed against the rear wall and at the other, a battered wooden desk behind which stood two swivel chairs, padded seats sprouting tufts of yellow foam from burst seams. Alec looked from one to the other. It was like a furniture 'us and them'.

He pulled at his shirt collar. It was tight and he felt overdressed; a shiny whistle chain between silver tunic buttons, bulled shoes and razor sharp trouser creases, wooden baton inside its special pocket, handcuffs in their leather holder. Like he'd just rolled off a production line, a lanky gawky cop doll, still in its wrapper.

Selecting a seat in the back row he retrieved his notebook and made his first entry. A wall mounted clock indicated twenty minutes to eleven. In five minutes his first muster would begin and a small electric current ran up his spine. The real thing at last. A portly middle-aged cop entered the room. He had black brylcreemed hair and a moustache that curled up at the edges into a laconic smile at odds with the mouth below it. Alec readied himself for a greeting, but there was none. The cop sat in a chair in the same row and produced a notebook from his tunic into which he entered the time and date. Only after he'd completed his entry did he glance over.

"New Guy?"

Alec stuck out his hand and offered the words 'Hi, I'm Alec'. But the hand was ignored and hung in the air held up by nothing other than good intentions. Instead, the old cop jutted his chin in the direction of the seat on which Alec sat.

"That's Tam's."

Alec smiled in an effort to portray himself as light-hearted, but there was no smile in return and he let his hand fall. The older cop waved at the chairs in front.

"You'll need to find another."

Not a joke then. There seemed little point in debating the issue. Before him stood three rows, each containing six empty chairs. He gathered up his hat, stepped into the next row and sat down as two more cops ambled in. Before Alec's disbelieving ears, the first cop morphed into a gregarious raconteur, full of jokes and barbed comments. Alec sat ignored while the three cops traded conversation with easy familiarity. No one spoke to him and no reference to him was made by any of the three. Eventually, banter exhausted, one turned and stared at him.

"New guy?"

Alec kept his hands lowered and confirmed he was. The old cop grunted. There was a hint of pity in his eyes as he cocked his head at the seat Alec had chosen.

"That's Sandy's."

As if to be helpful, he pointed at the two rows in front.

"You can sit there."

No one else had entered the room in the intervening period and Alec felt angry, but anxious to avoid ill feeling he moved forward again. More officers arrived and once more he sat ignored. After a few more minutes, another cop, slightly younger than the rest, sidled up and looked down like a glum child denied his favourite toy.

"That's my seat."

Alec stood and moved aside. The cop sat down without another word and struck up a conversation with the officers behind him. More arrived, each a bird settling onto a familiar roost. There were no women, just men, and they had a clear pecking order.

As each cop took up their positions, Alec was displaced again and again, only discovering by degrees that the only seats available to him were those in the very front row. He chose one and sat down, deflated by the off-hand way he'd been treated; a world away from the police college and the camaraderie he'd discovered there. Behind him, sounds of comradeship washed around the room. Before him lay a sterile expanse of linoleum and the battered wooden desk. He felt multiple sets of eyes on him, but there were no references to his presence and no one said hello.

Two sergeants entered with large files under their arms. The first, a tall man of military bearing, white-haired and grey-moustached; the other, younger, smaller, ruddy cheeked with red hair, shoulders drawn back, gazed about the room as if daring anyone to challenge him. The older Sergeant smiled.

"Alec isn't it? I'm Sergeant Munro."

Sergeant Munro pointed at his fellow supervisor.

"This is Sergeant Fitzpatrick. Welcome to Corsair Street. Everyone introduced themselves?"

Alec opened his mouth to reply but was intercepted by a raucous chorus of friendly affirmations from behind. It seemed that he'd been very well introduced indeed. Very much made welcome in fact. The Sergeant smiled indulgently and swept his hands across the assembly of officers.

"These fine men will keep you right. I see you've been introduced to the seating arrangements."

"Yes Sergeant."

Alec didn't trust his mouth, so kept his answers short. He could feel the combined presence of the cops behind him on their favourite perches. Like crows. A murder of cops. He remembered one of Dougie's golden rules at the police college; mouth shut, eyes and ears open. Files were opened. Shoulder numbers were read out and paired with beat numbers. Alec jotted down the number of the cop who would be his first 'neighbour' and prayed that it wasn't one of the old bastards that had shuffled him forward.

Munro read out the details of the incidents that had occurred in the previous twenty-four hours. Housebreakings, serious assaults, murders, attempted murders, car thefts, shootings and gang fights. An extensive litany of mayhem. The cops commented on likely suspects and possible patterns, their tone conversational and relaxed. Intelligence was shared about dangerous criminals and look-out requests made for missing persons. Alec drank it in. This was what he'd hoped for. It had been a shite start, but with a little bit of luck the next eight hours would bring something exciting and then, eventually, he'd be accepted.

Short and Sweet

His neighbour was Harry, who led him from the muster to the charge bar, issued him a radio and showed how it worked. Ceremony over, they walked from the morose rectangle of brown brick that was Corsair Street Police Station and into the cool night. They'd gone no more than a few yards when a police van pulled up with the offer of a lift and once inside, Harry introduced him to Neil and Jim. There'd been friendly questions and some banter, a world away from the hostile atmosphere of the muster and Alec wondered at the sudden change. Perhaps he'd been too sensitive.

Then, there'd been a burst of radio chatter and the van sped up. In the back, with a restricted view of the outside world, blue lights bouncing off tenements, siren drowning incomprehensible radio updates, he'd quickly lost his bearings. The van rolled around like an old trawler as it careened through a sequence of corners and Alec was forced to sit back and hold onto the edge of the bench seat. Glimpses of red sandstone tenements gave way to grim tower blocks and grey tenements.

Harry leaned forward and shouted over the din.

"Stolen car!"

It was dark in the back of the van and Harry had been no more than a Cheshire Cat grin, but then the car disappeared and radio traffic, increasingly sporadic, tailed into silence. The grin faded, the van slowed and Neil switched off the siren as Harry leaned through the partition door, directing them down various side streets.

"Left. That's it. Motor dumped here a few nights back."

They entered a narrow street lined with grey tenements of the kind he'd glimpsed earlier. None of the street lights were working and the area was submerged in darkness. Harry prodded Alec's boot with his own and pointed to the ink black world outside.

"They sabotage the lights. Easier to get away when they dump the motor."

Alec nodded. Harry's conspiratorial insights created a feeling of belonging, of being allowed into shared knowledge as they edged along the street, lights dimmed, hunting the elusive car. The dull glow from the VHF radio and the instrument panel stood out against the darkness and gave the van a submarine feel, accentuated by the faint outlines of the underwater canyon of tenements slowly passing outside.

"There it is."

The headlights swept the side a Golf GTi, sandwiched between two older cars. Harry looked pleased with himself.

"Wee cunt hoped we wouldnae see it—back for another go later."

As the van stopped, Harry opened the rear doors and leapt out. Alec followed. One or two lights shone behind closed tenement curtains, but the rest were in darkness and the street deserted. Crouching at the front of the GTi Harry shone his torch at the number plate.

"That's it."

His torch off, Harry looked around and having found what he was looking for strode towards the nearest common close. He turned as he walked, a finger to his lips, the other hand making a twisting motion at his radio. Alec felt for the dial on his own and felt a snick as it switched off.

They entered a graffiti covered close and stopped at a badly painted door, lower panels marked by the soles of dirty boots, splintered frame crudely nailed in place. Harry knelt and gently opened the letter box, an ear held to the gap.

The seconds ticked by and unsure what to do, Alec tuned into the unfamiliar world around him. Music played somewhere in the distance and there was the sound of a young couple arguing, but that was it. His new colleague, motionless at the door, seemed oblivious to his presence and desperate to play his part, he crept outside and looked in the front window. There were no lights inside, no sounds of late night TV, no movement within.

Harry appeared beside him.

"Nobody home. Wee bastard's oot there somewhere."

Harry lifted his chin as if searching for a scent and Alec felt the first tentative finger of scepticism. There were at least thirty close mouths in the street. At a rough guess a hundred and eighty flats. More in the streets beyond that. Who'd dump a stolen car so near his own flat? Harry however, was unwavering in his conviction.

"Tell Jim to go on a wee drive."

To Alec's surprise Jim drove off without question and when he returned to the close he found Harry crouched on the first-floor landing. As he reached him, Harry leaned forward and pointed down the stairs to the grubby door.

"Car thief lives there. He'll be back. Cannae help themselves."

And so they waited in silence, Alec slouched against the wall of the stairwell, Harry crouched at the turn of the stairs. The smell of dog piss and fry ups filled the air. Somewhere in the back courts a cat screeched and time stretched out in unfamiliar ways. Alec was about to ask how much longer they'd have to wait when Harry held up a hand and cocked his head towards the stairwell. Then Alec heard it too. A nonchalant whistling, tuneless but jaunty and his heart beat faster as the whistling grew louder. Just as it began to echo up the close the whistling abruptly stopped.

There was a presence in the close; something had disturbed the air and displaced it in a way that sent signals to those capable of receiving. Alec's muscles tensed and a lump gathered in his throat as he fought the urge to swallow, thinking in that unnatural moment the unseen presence would hear him. He held his breath for fear that a cloud would form and drifting down the stairs it would give the game away. Then, the smallest of sounds, the gentle scrape of metal on metal as a key was pushed into a lock. Harry took off like a cat down the stairs, arms out in the act of seizing his prey and even as Alec cleared the first step in pursuit, Harry's shouts were echoing off the close walls.

"Police! Police!"

Harry had a young man pinned against the close wall, one hand on his throat the other on an arm. The prisoner, eyes bulging, lurched to break free, but Harry, fingers clamped hard, forced the man's head upwards and screamed to 'calm the fuck down'. Alec grabbed the free arm and held it. Only then did Harry release his grip and the man regain some composure.

"Bastards! Fuckin' hell!"

Harry grinned.

"Who else wiz in that motor?"

The man shook his head, eyes wide, an expression of complete mystification.

"Whit motor?"

Harry tutted as he pulled the man off the wall and led him out into the street.

"If that's the way ye want tae play it."

Alec kept hold of the arm. The man was thin, but his arms were wiry and strong. An image of a hardy street fighter came unbidden into his head and instinctively he tightened his grip. As if by magic the van arrived and the rear doors opened for the expected guest. Alec felt the prisoner tense up.

"Look, ah wiz jist goin' tae ma flat. Ah've nae idea whit yer oan aboot."

Harry dragged the prisoner that bit harder.

"Fine. This way then."

Neil was standing at the doors and the sight of another cop took any remaining resistance from their prisoner who stepped into the van without further comment. Alec made to follow but was stopped by Harry.

"You'll need this."

It was a torch.

"For what?"

Harry nodded towards the garden.

"Saw him throw a set of car keys there."

Alec stared at the garden. Was that possible? They'd been up the stairwell with no sight of the street. How had Harry seen that? He was going to say as much when Neil patted him on the shoulder and gave a sympathetic smile.

"Best do as he says young gun. We'll be fine."

Alec's last sight of the prisoner was of a pensive young man sitting on the bench seat hands clasped over his knees before Neil closed the doors and walked back to the cab. Alec could hear muffled conversations, but nothing else.

The garden was a patch of rough grass surrounded by a knee high metal fence. It felt like a wild goose chase, but he was the new guy who knew fuck all and maybe Harry possessed abilities beyond his own. Keen to play his part he bent himself to the search through damp grass littered with old toys, household rubbish and empty beer cans. Now and then he came across a bloody syringe and as he plotted his way across the garden, fearful of stepping on one, the verbal exchanges within the van grew louder and more heated. Then, two bangs, accompanied by short-lived, high-pitched scream. The van lurched from side to side and fearful for Harry's safety, Alec moved towards it but as he reached the fence Jim wound down his window.

"Found those keys?"

Alec threw his arms up in the air.

"There are no keys."

The van rocked again, bangs in rhythm with the motion of the van, sides quivering as a succession of strikes impacted on thin metal. Then, as suddenly as it began, the rocking stopped and the street fell into dark silence. Alec scanned the tenement windows. There'd been no change as far as he could see, but he couldn't shake the feeling there were eyes watching behind parted curtains. The van doors opened, thrusting a blade of light onto the roadway. Someone inside shouted expletives and then Harry's head appeared.

"Forget the keys, we're out of here."

Young men had appeared at various close mouths, some edging onto the street. Alec hurried to the van and opened the door to climb in.

Harry hissed.

"Close the fuckin' door!"

The door was the last thing on Alec's mind. The van interior, dented in places, was smeared with blood and a small pool of had gathered on the floor. In the far corner, the suspect cowered against the bulkhead between the rear and the front cab, an arm curled around his head. Blood coated the side of his face and spattered the thighs of his jeans. It matted and gelled his hair. There was not a mark on Harry, except for a large lump now swelling below one eye.

"Get in."

Numbed, Alec did as he was told and Harry shouted to the front cab.

"Nearest office."

The van lurched forward. Alec could hear angry shouts and then, as they picked up speed, banging on the sides of the van. Harry smiled and looked at the prisoner huddled in the corner.

"Yer pals urnae gonnae save ye now."

The suspect remained motionless. His nose, tilted to one side, was bleeding profusely. There was a deep gash above one eye that oozed blood, and more seeped from the back of his head. Harry sat stone faced staring at a section of the van just over Alec's shoulder. There was silence as Jim worked his way up the gears and focused on the road ahead. The easy-going banter of earlier had gone and Alec wondered what the fuck he'd gotten into. Was this the norm? Had the prisoner assaulted Harry and he'd retaliated? Or was it the other way around? As he sat trying to work out what had happened, Stevie shouted through the partition.

"Nearly there."

Harry turned to the prisoner.

"Right. We're going tae get you fixed up. Remember what we agreed."

The prisoner said nothing. A small tic pulsed under Harry's left eye as he leaned a little closer and pointed at the bruise swelling there.

"Remember our wee chat?"

The prisoner stared straight ahead, avoiding Harry's stare, but nodded slowly. Harry looked satisfied.

"Good — we'll say no more."

The van slowed, then stopped and the doors creaked open. They were in the back yard of a police station, the van neatly positioned at a set of open doors. A bright light shone down a ramp that led inside. It looked like the entrance to a space ship. Neil and Jim stood outside the van doors looking pissed off.

"Right, out ye come."

Alec climbed out and turned to help escort the prisoner into the office. It was only then he realized this wasn't Corsair Street and was about to say as much when there was a light tap on his shoulder. Neil smiled a tight smile and nodded towards the office door.

"We'll take care of this."

Confused, Alec walked inside and found a cop standing in the passageway. The cop gestured to him follow and after a walk down unfamiliar corridors led him to a small side room.

"Take a seat young fella. Somebody from your shift's coming for you."

So, he was being removed from the scene. Something passed over the radio maybe, some prearrangement, or coded message. A situation too hot to handle for a new start. He remembered the exchange with Julie in The Volunteer. Maybe she'd been right and he'd no sooner began to digest this wretched possibility when two cops entered the room he recognised from the muster. earlier One of them grinned.

"We've come to take you away from all this."

On the way to Corsair Street they exchanged pleasantries, interspersing these with queries about the incident. The cops who'd come to collect him were Charlie and Stevie. They exchanged glances as he described the incident and he felt isolated, cut off from developments elsewhere. Would he be questioned by detectives, should he be saying anything at all? The worry gnawed at him until he could bear it no longer.

"Am I in bother?"

The front passenger smiled.

"No. Harry is. And don't feel sorry for him. It's his funeral. Getting' a new start involved in something like that? That's shite."

Alec felt some of the weight lift, but the worry kept a holding pattern until they arrived back at Corsair Street. The Inspector was waiting for him as he trudged up the stairs, a dark-haired middle-aged woman who smiled the kind of sympathetic smile Alec had last seen at his mother's funeral twelve months before.

"Alec. A wee minute of your time..."

He'd rehearsed what he was going to say. Whatever technique she planned to use he'd be ready. But no interrogation came. She knew what had happened. Yes, there'd been a complaint and he'd have to submit a statement, but she just wanted to make sure he was ok. It was all very unfortunate and it was unlikely he'd work with Harry again. In the meantime, he'd have to submit a short statement and then go home. The report writing room was just next door to the muster. He could write it there.

Alec turned to leave, but the Inspector called after him.

"One more thing. Was the suspect injured when you first saw him?"

It was a ridiculous question, one that was easily answered.

"No."

The Inspector smiled.

"Just put that in your statement then. Short and sweet."

In that moment the die was cast and Alec made his way to the report writing room as a young man whose preconceptions had been rudely shattered. The excitement of the car chase had been replaced by shock and a dark foreboding that whatever he wrote would have repercussions not just for Harry, but for himself. Far from being his own man, the incident with the car thief had illustrated the painful truth. He was the new boy, there to do as he was told, flotsam to be pulled about by the expectations of others. As he sat to compose the first words, he noted with grim irony that Julie had been wrong after all. They left marks alright.

Consequences

When Alec pulled into Corsair Street the following night it was with a feeling of profound trepidation. In a bid to minimise his commute he'd rented a flat two miles from the office, but the journey to work felt many times more as he agonised over the events of the previous night. When he climbed out the car and scanned the windows of the three-story building, he half expected them to be filled with pointing fingers and grim faces.

He'd endured a fitful sleep, disturbed by violent dreams and the effects of a summer sun through thin curtains. Now, as he walked towards the entrance, it was not the anticipation of an adrenalin filled night that quickened his steps but the desire to reach the muster room before Harry and avoid an inquisition about his statement.

It had taken an hour to write it, during which he'd shuttled back and forth between the report writing room with Sergeant Fitzpatrick insisting on the inclusion of certain facts that Alec was anxious to avoid. He was new but he wasn't stupid. The description of the injuries suffered by their prisoner would be as damning as the events leading up to them. Harry's one bruise hardly indicated the injuries of a victim.

But, as much as he found Harry's actions abhorrent, Alec was desperate to avoid being the singular cause of his downfall. As a result, he became cagier as the statement expanded and the implications of what he was testifying to became more apparent, but with the Sergeant scrutinising every line he'd little room for manoeuvre. When he finally completed his statement Fitzpatrick gave him a curt nod and sent him home.

Alec gave silent thanks that the public foyer was deserted and kept his head low as he headed to the stairwell. A quick change into uniform and then down to the muster room. Once there, he'd wait for the rest of the shift and hope the Sergeants were early. No one would know what he'd put in his statement. He'd keep that to himself.

The locker room was devoid of life, the only sound the traffic passing by outside. Thankful, he made walked to the narrow row where his locker stood and reached in for his tunic and tie.

"A wee word."

Alec jumped and as he turned round there was Harry. He felt sick. He'd been ambushed and the only way out was past Harry who looked in no mood to let him pass. No choice but to play this by ear.

"Hi Harry. What about?"

Harry raised an eyebrow and smiled the kind of smile that said don't try to kid a kidder. Alec's heart sank further as Harry stepped closer.

"You know fine what about."

This wasn't going to be easy. Harry was giving the impression he knew already, but Alec was unsure if this was the same double bluff played by the Inspector, or whether Harry had somehow got wind of some inside information. This alien territory, a place where Harry knew the lay of the land and how the game was played. There seemed little option but to stall.

"Last night?"

"Aye. You got away early; a wee reward for being a good boy?"

The tone was sarcastic and edgy. Harry had lowered his chin so that he looked as if he was staring up from a very low place. There was a palpable sensation of imminent violence and for the second time Alec felt that there was a feline malevolence about Harry so removed from the chatty easy- going guy who'd stepped out of the office the night before.

He tensed his arms ready for whatever came next and prayed others would appear soon.

"No idea what you're talking about Harry."

A sneer.

"Sure you do. Why else would that old goat send you home early? First night and there you are, feted like a king?"

Harry took another step closer. There was the acrid smell of a recently smoked cigarette.

"Out with it. What did you put in your statement?"

Alec took a step back. There was no way he would cough, he'd be toast for sure.

"Nothing much. Just the bare bones."

"What were the 'bare bones' exactly?"

It was like being on the receiving end of an interrogation where every response inevitably led to more questions until you'd spilled your guts and laid yourself bare. He was determined not to let that happen.

"Sergeant says that's my business and it's confidential."

There was a loud bang as Harry struck a locker with his clenched hand. The mesh door quivered on its hinges.

"It's ma business. It's ma heid on the block, no' yours. No' Fitzpatrick's or Munro's, but mine."

Harry was almost face to face. He was smaller, by several inches, but it seemed in that moment that he'd become taller. And broader.

"Here's a heads-up boy blunder. There's gaffers and there's us. They play their game, we play ours. There's nobody looking out for us but ourselves. Your job is to look after yer fellow cop."

Harry pointed to the floor as if the supervisors were directly beneath his feet.

"They don't give a fuck how we catch the neds, as long as we keep trouble from their door. It's all sunshine and flowers, but as soon as the shit hits the fan they're over it like a rash. Some get their rocks off on binning a cop and, one day my bonnie lad, that'll include you."

Alec could see no circumstances in which that would be the case, but Harry wasn't finished.

"Don't forget, you're a probationer - oot the door without a bye or leave if you fuck up. Remind yourself who'll be doing your report cards. That's right. Me and the others on the shift. If you've stitched me up, you're fucked."

"Nobody's been stitched up Harry. I'm sure it'll pan out ok."

Harry laughed. It was a bitter sound.

"You're an expert are ye? Fuck me, they teach ye well at that police college."

Harry jabbed a finger at Alec's chest, right on the sternum. It was surprisingly painful and Alec took an involuntary step backwards.

"Listen up. If you've fired me in, you're fucked, understand?"

There was a cough on the other side of the row of lockers and the large bulk of Charlie appeared, his frame closing off the gap between the rows in which Alec and Harry now stood.

"This a secret rendezvous for star-crossed lovers, or can anyone join in?"

Alec breathed out, only now aware he'd been holding his breath. Harry was all smiles and bonhomie.

"Aye and it's a threesome you'd be intae big fella."

Charlie laughed but there was a dull look in his eyes.

"Aye, but at least I widnae have to pay for my company."

The bonhomie evaporated from Harry's voice.

"Fuck you."

And with that he pushed past Charlie and was gone.

Charlie stepped into the row, a look of concern on his face.

"You alright?"

"I'm fine, just a wee chat."

"I bet. Watch yer step, he's got a dark side."

"Thanks Charlie, Just finding that out."

"He does have a point though."

"What's that?"

"Don't expect help from the gaffers. Fitzpatrick knows fine well what he's doing. Sowing suspicion. Divide and conquer, oldest trick in the book. Don't get caught up in those games."

Alec shook his head; it wasn't as if he had any choice, he was in no position to refuse directions from the Sergeant. He was never more acutely aware than in that moment of the perilous state of being a probationer and he cursed his luck at having been put in such a situation on his first night.

"Last thing I want is to piss anybody off, least of all Harry. Sergeant told me to put a statement in, how could I refuse?"

Charlie nodded.

"Aye, yer fucked there, but here's the thing. The shift'll listen to Harry before they listen to you, so keep yer heid doon ok?"

"Thanks Charlie. I will."

There were other voices in the room, scattered shouts over the tops of lockers as the shift drifted in. Charlie looked around before bending his head conspiratorially.

"We'll see. Expect to be treated with suspicion until you prove yerself to be trusted."

Charlie re-joined the older cops further down the locker room. Alec listened to the communal laughter while he changed into his uniform and made his way to the muster unnoticed through a door at the end, all the while dreading the prospect of Harry waiting for him, but when he arrived in the muster it was empty. Relieved, he chose the seat he'd sat in the previous evening and waited.

The shift were quieter than the previous night and dropped into their roosts with only the occasional comment. Alec could feel eyes boring into his back and there were occasional comments that felt like meanings related to him, but unable to decipher the in-jokes and double entendres he sat with his head up and waited for the arrival of the supervisors.

When the Inspector led them in the mood in the room changed. It was clear that a marker was being put down with her presence and Alec wondered if she normally attended the muster, or whether her absence the previous night had been an exception. She scanned the faces, confident and at ease, as someone who'd thought carefully how she was going to present herself. The supervisors sat down and Alec braced himself for a lecture about the incident.

But there was nothing about the previous night. Instead, the muster took the same form as before. Incidents were read out and comments made. Not as many as there had been previously, but it seemed business as usual. Alec held his notebook open, ready for the announcement of who he'd be working with, reconciled to a tense and depressing night with whoever it was.

His number was read out. A different beat with a different neighbour. Alec looked up at the Inspector who glanced in his direction but said nothing. He jotted down the shoulder number, wondering if this new partner would be on his side, or Harry's.

The muster over, the shift left to collect their radios and hit the streets. He followed them into the corridor hoping to catch a glimpse of shoulder numbers on the way down the stairs and turned to see Harry follow the Inspector to a room at the far end of the corridor. As Harry stepped inside, he looked at Alec with implacable hatred. And then the door slammed shut.

By the time he reached the charge bar only one cop remained. Standing there, spare radio in hand, was Ronnie, the old cop who'd moved him on from the back row the previous night.

Fuck.

Growing Pains

They set off from the station in silence and Alec wondered if this was the usual routine, or whether he was in the doghouse over Harry. He resolved to keep his mouth shut and leave Ronnie to break the ice for fear of sounding desperate.

They walked along the main road before turning into a network of tenement lined streets. After a few minutes, bored with the lack of conversation, Alec turned to ask a question, only then realising there was no-one there. He looked around in time to see Ronnie squeezing through a gap in a high stone wall and cursed under his breath. This was going to be a long night. Walking back he found Ronnie standing on the other side.

"Lesson one. Eyes and ears open."

He ignored Ronnie's smirk and squeezed through the gap to find himself in the estate he'd seen from the muster room the night before; a warren of sixties-built maisonettes and high-rise flats, the buildings a uniform grey, linked by suspended walkways and underpasses.

They walked through overgrown public gardens, past a dilapidated line of flat-roofed shops and a vandalised play-park. Alec saw no-one, other than the odd huddle of hooded teenagers who melted away among the many paths and underpasses, and as he wandered the maze of concrete and cement it struck him just how different this cityscape was from Auchenbreoch. No view beyond the buildings in front of him. No glimpse of horizon or skyline. No open vista to hill or moor, just a jumble of tower blocks and high rises arranged in assorted juxtapositions with no apparent order. It felt oppressive and disorientating.

Ronnie pointed to the numerous small roads intersecting the estate.

"Keep an eye oot for street signs. They're named after Scottish islands. Local councillor was a homesick teuchtar."

The first, daubed with graffiti and crudely drawn cocks, was Skye Court. Alec tried to memorise each as he passed but there were too many and their layouts, seemingly random, made it impossible to remember. He hoped he wouldn't need to chase anyone; he'd have no idea where he was.

Ronnie spoke only when he'd something specific to say, but that was just fine. Talking might lead to questions about the previous night and Alec didn't have an appetite for that, regardless of how it gnawed at him. The radio remained quiet and he was grateful for Ronnie's slow metronomic amble. Occasionally, the old cop would draw attention to the houses and flats of well-known criminals, families with 'history', scenes of notorious events and the homes of those more pleasantly disposed to the police. There seemed precious few of the latter.

The few people he saw crossed the road or changed direction down other footways. Ronnie appeared not to notice and carried on with his tour, highlighting local history, buildings of significance, places where a cup of tea could be had on a rainy day. When they emerged into an area of down-at-heel tenements Ronnie continued in the same vein, drawing attention to streets that were long gone, demolished to make way for a new wave of housing. After a while he seemed to loosen up a little and Alec admired the encyclopaedic local knowledge wondering how long it took to accumulate.

"You worked here long Ronnie?"

Ronnie squinted at the overcast sky.

"Seven years. Corsehill before that. Before that, the support unit. Started in Craigie Street, twenty eight years ago."

"That's a fair bit of moving around."

Ronnie sniffed.

"Don't be stuck in one place. Keep yer nose clean, see the world."

"Must've seen some changes."

Ronnie gave him a serious look.

"Aye. In ma day, probationers kept their mouths shut and spoke only when they were spoken to."

The rebuke left him wrong footed. It was no big deal, but it seemed unnecessary and reminded him of that moment on the parade square when he'd put down his bags. Treated like a child. He walked in sullen silence, deep in thoughts of how he'd navigate a way through his two year probation to a time he'd no longer have to put up with old cunts like Ronnie; though that, and the idea of a world beyond Corsair Street, seemed very far away.

He spent the rest of the night listening to the odd comment from Ronnie and delivering messages on contact cards to dark and silent houses. There was a tension he felt no obligation to ease and Ronnie seemed unwilling to mend so the rest of the shift passed mostly in silence. By four in the morning the streets were deserted and Alec discovered a child-like pleasure in being out and about while the city was asleep. Except that it never truly slept. Somewhere beyond the roof tops was a constant background hum, like a far-off generator, the source of which he couldn't put his finger on. It continued uninterrupted until the first bakery vans appeared, bags of morning rolls casually thrown into shop doorways. And after that the early morning buses, empty save for a scattering of morose and pale-faced workers. Against the backdrop of a rising sun, they checked pubs, shops and factory units, pulled padlocks and checked window grills before the long walk back to Corsair Street and the short drive to another sleep disturbed by a bright summer sun and the sounds of life from the street below his flat.

The rest of the week followed the same pattern. There were occasional calls that never amounted to much. He learned the names of the shift, a group of mostly middle-aged men long in service. The one female was on maternity leave and 'wouldnae be back.' At the police college there'd been equal numbers of male and females and Alec wondered why there weren't more here.

He'd been introduced to the control room so they could 'put a face to the number' and took his first crime report, a break-in to a car in one of the shadowy back lanes that criss-crossed the more affluent part of their beat. Ronnie coached from the side, asking the questions Alec forgot to ask, a helpfulness that Alec put down to remorse for the unnecessary put-down earlier in the week. Whatever the motivation, he was glad of it.

There were no more ambushes in the locker room, no more threats and accusations, but the atmosphere was frosty among the rest of the shift who made little effort to talk to him. He joined in their obligatory card games at tea break, but when it looked like he might win, they'd gang together to make sure he lost. His pride balked at the thought of playing the whipping boy and his status as outsider began to outweigh his gratitude for the temporary truce, but Ronnie for his part maintained a steady neutrality.

"Yer man leavin' you in peace?"

"So far. Can tell he's still angry though. Get funny looks."

A sage nod.

"Yer no' flavour of the month, that's for sure."

There was nothing to say to that. He wasn't prepared to openly admit the fact, but he'd no confidence anyone would lift a hand to protect him when the inevitable complaint investigation got underway and he felt isolated. Ronnie, an old hand who could clearly read a situation, offered at least one consolation.

"Harry's been given the gypsies warning by the Inspector. Ye'll have worked out that she's no' daft and even Harry has to obey the rules sometimes".

"What happens next then? A trial?"

Ronnie snorted.

"There's nothing certain in this life. Seen ropey cases end up with custodial sentences and cast-iron ones dropped before they got to court."

Alec wasn't sure what a ropey case was, but he imagined a scenario where the latter applied. He couldn't condone the injuries on the prisoner and was still troubled by the savagery, but he wished it would all resolve itself without any further involvement from him.

Another night slid by, adding to the seamless transitions as one day merged into another. Time was marked by the twice nightly rendezvous with the Sergeant, the hike to the station for tea break, the religious observance of checking property and the amble back to Corsair Street to hand in his radio and stand down.

Had the week concluded in this vein, he'd would have been convinced that his first night had been an aberration and that despite his posting to one of the roughest areas in one of the toughest cities in Europe, the life of a beat cop was one of strolling about in uniform, taking reports, delivering messages and drinking the odd cup of tea. But that was not how the week ended.

Old School Ties

When the radio burst into life Alec had little idea what was being said. Ronnie answered the squawking black box in his tunic pocket and that meant there was a call, but Alec found it all incomprehensible, his ears not yet tuned to the way speech was corrupted by ultra-high frequencies.

Ronnie translated in his usual brusque way.

"Disturbance, down at the crescents. Pissed up students probably."

The Crescents were an oasis of faded grandeur where large Victorian terraced villas had given way to student sub-lets and shady landlords. They were walking through the Estate of the Isles as Alec now called it and from there it would take them a good twenty minutes to get there.

"Should we shout up a van?"

"Nope. This'll do fine. Give 'em time to cool their jets."

Alec pictured a party gone wrong and a large number of lads, pissed up and hostile. He was in no rush to get involved in a fight; the incident with Harry had spooked him, but all the same he felt an obligation to get there as fast as he could. He began to lengthen his stride but had gone only a few steps when Ronnie tapped him on the shoulder.

"Save yer energy. There'll be plenty to do when we get there."

Reluctantly, Alec fell into the pace set by his tutor. It was Ronnie's call. Frustrating as that was, it was up to him how he dealt with it.

They arrived in a tree lined crescent, the picture of leafy suburban tranquillity, the houses in darkness, the street silent. Alec was unsure whether to feel relieved or disappointed. Ronnie led the way to an ornate wooden door, its centre panel adorned with a brass lion door-knocker. To its right, a metal box with eight backlit glass panels covered by strips of paper with surnames scrawled in cheap pen. A few had multiple surnames. One had no name at all. It was incongruous that a grand looking house would have something as low-rent and basic as this arrangement, but Ronnie ran his finger down the list of names, shaking his head.

"Most of these'll be out of date, just have to take a lucky dip."

A metal button sat next to each panel and Ronnie jabbed at them randomly. Buzzing noises came from within, each different in volume as Ronnie worked his way around the flats above. Eventually, the sound of crying was heard and it came closer until the door opened to a grand hallway of dark wood panels and mosaic tiled floors. In the doorway stood a young woman in her twenties, wearing a short party dress ripped at the shoulder exposing the upper part of her right breast. Both cheeks were streaked with mascara, her skin blotchy and sodden. Beyond her slim frame rose a staircase so grand that Alec expected to see deer antlers and portraits of aristocracy hanging from the walls, but there was a seediness to the place and as he stepped inside he was struck by the smell of damp. The walls were covered in patches of mould and peeling wallpaper and a chandelier, stained and dusty, hung from an ornate plaster ceiling. Some of its crystal pendants were missing.

The woman shook from head to foot and her fists were bunched by her thighs, her arms thin and stiff. As Ronnie quietly closed the door behind him she jerked her head backwards at the staircase.

"He's upstairs."

Alec looked up but could see no-one in the dark shadows of the upper landing. Ronnie didn't as much as glance up the stairs but ushered the woman towards a chair and beckoned her to sit.

"Why don't we start at the beginning."

It was a story of a night gone wrong. A long term boyfriend with a long term drink problem and a short temper. A university sweetheart who'd become violent and bullying. After a night of humiliation at a university reunion they'd come back to recriminations and raised fists. This, apparently, had been the last straw.

Ronnie nodded from time to time and offered occasional encouragements, like 'go on' and 'keep going', until she was spent and had nothing left to say. Alec expected to see a notebook appear, but Ronnie showed no inclination and instead looked up the stairs, slinging a thumb in the direction of the upper floors.

"What do you want to happen now?"

The girl looked upwards, tear stained face angry and bitter.

"I'll get my things and go. He's a total prick and I'm better off without him."

There was a tumbling series of thuds and a young man suddenly appeared on the stairway falling sideways, grabbing at the broad wooden balustrade with both hands. He was drunk and his voice reverberated around the vast hallway as he halted half-way to scream at the girl.

"A fuckin' prick? Yer nothin' but a wee fuckin' whore."

Alec felt foolish. All the time they'd been there, the boyfriend had been up in the darkness and listening. He wondered if Ronnie had guessed as much, or if he'd taken his eye off the ball. Whatever, a drunk young man was making his way down the stairs, shouting obscenities, oblivious to the presence of two large uniformed police officers and intent on restarting hostilities. As the drunk reached the last few stairs Alec stepped towards him. It was only then, as his face drew level, that Alec realised who he was.

Sean Burke had been eighteen when Alec last saw him. A birthday party in the Auchenbreoch Labour Club. Then a law student at Glasgow University, he'd bored everyone with stories of wine bars, wealthy new friends and his newly acquired membership of the Conservative party. He'd been a quiet lad at school, son of a postman, but full of himself he'd told everyone within earshot that he was 'shot of the old dump' and the 'losers' who lived there. He'd been ushered away before the hard boys of the town could get near him; whose lives were preordained for the pit or the dole. True to his word, it was the last anyone had seen him. And here he was, overweight, puffy faced and spitting insults in an alcoholic rage. It was quite a transformation.

None of Alec's training had prepared him for this. He expected Sean to turn his head and recognise him, claim an old friendship and compromise him in some way, but for now, Sean's focus was on the girl and Alec tilted the skip of his cap downwards over his eyes in the hope he wouldn't be recognised. The hall was gloomy and Sean was pissed. He'd let Ronnie do the talking.

It was direct as usual.

"Shut yer mouth son. Yer lucky this young lady doesn't wish to press charges. She'll get her things and be on her way. You can sort this out when you're sober."

Sean's outbursts on the stair had been sufficient grounds for a breach of the peace and Alec had braced himself for the inevitable, but Ronnie had adopted the tone of a patient father. It looked like all might be resolved without further police involvement. Things were looking up. Sean would wake up with only a hazy recollection of what had happened, never knowing how close he'd come to being arrested by someone he'd known from school.

But Sean was in no mood for compromise. A stream of curses followed and as Alec listened to the bile flowing from a white flecked mouth, he realised it wasn't just alcohol that drove Sean's manic behaviour but drugs. Sean lunged toward the girl, neck veins bulging, eyes protruding and it took Alec all his strength to check Sean's advance and push him back onto the stairs. By now the girl was shouting too and as both Sean and girlfriend screamed at each other, Alec looked at Ronnie hoping that there was still some way of rescuing the situation, knowing that they'd gone beyond a tipping point.

It was then Stevie walked in, as casual and unconcerned as the man of the house returning from an evening out. It hadn't occurred to Alec that there'd be back up, that anyone overhearing their call would think to attend it.

Stevie took in the commotion and looked at Ronnie who nodded in the direction of Sean being held at arms-length on the stairs. Sean's fate was sealed and as if sensing it he cleared his throat and with one last lunge, spat across the hall. A thick wad of snot arc'd across the intervening space and struck the girl on the face. As the green ooze slid down her cheek she let out such a wail that even Sean in his maniacal state stopped and fell silent. He was still staring slack jawed as Stevie dragged him off the stairs. Alec took an arm and as they led him across the hall, Sean turned to the girl and began to cry.

"See what you've made me do? You stupid cow!"

As they dragged Sean out through the front door Ronnie finally drew out his notebook and turned towards the now retching girl with a bored expression.

Sean allowed himself to be dragged. He couldn't walk straight and was in no condition to fight against the tall cops on either side, but that didn't stop him mouthing off.

"This how you get your jollies? Arresting a decent guy for a fall-out with his bird? Hope you're fuckin' proud."

When they arrived at the back of the van Sean stiffened and Alec braced for a struggle, but Stevie cut it off at the pass.

"Don't even think about it ya fud, yer under arrest. Any shite and you'll be handcuffed, ok?"

Sean's shoulders slumped and he climbed into the van in silence. Alec sat beside him, head turned away from Sean and hoped Ronnie wouldn't be long. The minutes drifted by. Stevie remained outside; the doors partially open to let in some air.

"Can you no' just let me go?"

The voice was pleading and desperate. Alec wanted badly to avoid a conversation, but stuck in the van with Sean he couldn't ignore him. He lowered his voice and changed his accent a little, feeling embarrassed and deceitful in equal measure.

"Fraid not."

Sean began to cry. Huge lurching sobs and big fat tears.

"I'm going to end up with a criminal record. All because of that wee bitch and you cunts."

It was hard to keep up with Sean's oscillating emotions. The last few words had an edge and Alec got the feeling that Sean remained a hairbreadth away from another violent outburst. He was glad Stevie was nearby. After a few moments the mood changed again and Sean doubled over on his seat, shoulders quaking, dripping fat tears onto the floor. Alec seized the chance to take a closer look.

It was the same guy from school alright, but the intervening years had not been kind. Baggy eyes, a huge paunch, jowls around the jaw, cheeks puffed by drink. He looked much older than twenty-two. He had a Rolex watch, expensive clothes and shoes, and Alec wondered how a newly graduated law student could afford such luxuries. Whatever funded this lifestyle was not from the salary of a trainee solicitor.

Ronnie climbed in and slammed the doors shut. Stevie returned to the cab and the engine clattered into life. Ronnie would do the talking from here.

"Right young man. You're being charged with assault and a breach of the peace. The lassie didn't want to press charges, but yer display back there took that out her hands. Understand?"

Sean stared at the floor.

"Where are you taking me?"

"Corsair Street police station."

Sean's shoulders began to heave again. More tears and deep sobs, but no pity from Ronnie.

"Dry yer tears son. At least be a man about it."

Sean sat upright and for a moment Alec thought this would be a prelude to a violent struggle. Another prisoner injured in the back of a police van. He'd be toast if that happened again. But Sean sat taking deep breaths, composing himself, determined indeed to take it like a man.

There was no doubt Sean deserved the jail, but Alec felt awkward. If Sean recognised him he'd spread the word back home that he jailed old pals and things were bad enough in Auchenbreoch as it was. Alec replayed the scene in his head. Sean's behaviour had been violent and obnoxious, and the grogging had sealed it. Nope. There was nothing he could've done, Sean had sealed his own fate.

The journey to Corsair Street took a few short minutes, during which Sean wept occasionally but otherwise kept his mouth shut. Alec, a bit surer of himself, led Sean from the van to the charge bar and stood him in front of the Duty Inspector.

Sean straightened up to present himself in best order. Ronnie detailed the charges and the Inspector filled out some forms. Tongue thickened by alcohol Sean slurred out his details and the Inspector, a square headed man with silver hair and gold framed glasses, wrote down the names of the arresting officers in an old ledger. Alec saw Ronnie's name, rank and number entered in fine copperplate writing and realised he'd be asked to state his own. The Inspector looked up. His turn. He'd have to blurt it out in Sean's presence. Maybe he could get away with just surname and shoulder number.

"MacKay sir. Yankee forty-six"

The Inspector smiled.

"This'll be your first? "

The Inspector looked to Ronnie.

"This young fella the reporting officer?"

Ronnie nodded.

"I'll give him a hand, but Constable MacKay's the reporting officer."

The Inspector filled more sections of the custody ledger, but to Alec's relief he was not asked his first name and Sean continued to sway beside him, oblivious. A cop arrived and completed more forms, transposing the details from the ledger. Sean seized a chance to make a last plea.

"Can't you let me go? I promise this's just a one off."

The Inspector shook his head.

"You'll be out in a few hours. I'm sure these fine officers told you. A report will be sent to the procurator fiscal and he'll decide what happens next."

The cop with the forms took Sean away and Alec's last sight of an old school friend was of a disconsolate young man wiping snot from his top lip with the back of his arm.

Booking-in complete, Alec followed Ronnie to the report writing room and watched as he rifled through a cabinet containing various forms of stationery.

"Right. You can do the crime report. I'll do the other stuff."

Alec filled out a triplicate form, preoccupied with worries that he'd end up arresting other people he knew. For a brief moment he thought about telling Ronnie his dirty secret but stopped short. He'd signed up to be a cop and all that came with it, but already it was feeling much less honourable than he'd anticipated.

Rules Of The Road

Burdened by the heavy weight of jet lag Alec reported for late shift two days later. Days off had presented the unwelcome challenge of wresting his body clock from its hard-won synchronicity with the night shift, a task he'd found impossible to achieve within the forty-eight hours allowed him. A week book-ended by two nightmare situations and the worst possible start with new colleagues deserved a bender, but there was no-one to share it with. A Monday night in Auchenbreoch held no attractions and none of his friends fancied the idea of getting hammered with work next morning. He'd called Dad and claimed things were going well, a bald lie that served to unsettle him further, but he was dammed if he'd admit the truth. It would simply invite a litany of I told you so's and he was in no mood for that. Out of sorts and under the weather he'd settled for two nights in front of a dilapidated second-hand TV and put his trust in alcohol to ease his body clock back to normality.

The technique was only partially successful for though he was asleep by midnight, he woke at 3am bright eyed and alert. He fared little better the second night and it was an out of sorts Constable MacKay who took his seat at the muster the following afternoon.

Determined to put his best foot forward, he'd arrived before the others and now, as they trudged in, he saw they were no better off. The crows took their seats in silence, ashen faced, dark bags under bloodshot eyes. If these old bastards couldn't manage the transition perhaps there was no formula after all. Alec sat glumly reflecting on the monthly cycles ahead of him, all in a state of near permanent tiredness. It was not a happy prospect. As he pondered this bleak outlook sounds of jaunty whistling were heard from the corridor. Some of the shift looked up, just in time for Harry to stride in bright eyed and fresh faced. He grinned at the silent group before turning to Alec, eyebrows raised.

"Fung's had a rough night. Conscience bothering ye?"

Alec braced himself for mocking laughter, but there were no more than a few grunts, the communal affliction of night shift hangovers suppressing the general mood, even in the face of Harry's unnaturally upbeat banter. Harry looked around at the ghostly assembly and shrugged.

"Suit yersels".

Alec listened to the sounds of Harry making his way along the back row to his allotted place. He wasn't so naïve as to interpret the lacklustre response to Harry's snidey remarks as anything resembling sympathy for himself. No-one had spoken to him as they filed in, so he was still in the doghouse, but he took some heart from the lack of bonhomie for Harry. Perhaps Harry wasn't the star attraction he thought he was.

Alec turned 'Fung' over in his head, trying to decipher its meaning. It wouldn't be flattering, but not knowing made him feel foolish and more at a disadvantage than he felt previously. Harry began whistling again and the tune, made up as he went along, began to grate, so much that even the old timers began to complain, but Harry kept it up right up to the second the Sergeants entered the room. And so began another muster.

It was mercifully quick. The Sergeants had fared no better than their troops and seemed keen to get the business of the day over with. The muster concluded, Alec followed the now familiar routine and joined Ronnie on the front steps of the station. The old cop made a show of looking up and down the busy main road and Alec saw the place in daylight for the first time. Cars buses and trucks thundered by as an assortment of pedestrians, some hunched over with the weight of the world, passed in either direction. Across the busy highway, the skyline was dominated by the high rises of the 'Estate of the Isles', their concrete cladding, grey and austere. To his left, a long line of old tenements, small shops on their ground floors. To his right, a row of single-storey buildings that housed a bookmakers, a pub and a variety of take-aways, behind which a network of tenement streets retreated up a low hill.

Climbing gently toward the distant suburbs, the main road ducked under the broad arch of a canal viaduct through which could be made out the pale blue outlines of the gasworks and more high rises. And between the gasworks and the canal, two hills, each encrusted with squalid tenements; referred to by the shift as 'The Reservation.' The worst housing Alec had ever seen and there was currently no beat man.

Ronnie set off without warning and Alec was forced to catch up. As he strode after the hulking figure, he swore that if he became a tutor cop he'd never be as curmudgeonly as this.

They walked the wide pavement, navigating past old ladies with tartan shopping bags and elderly men with flat caps and patched up tweed jackets. Occasionally, people passed in the opposite direction and Alec soon became uncomfortably aware of how hard everyone stared at him. It was unfriendly. He tried a few hellos and good afternoons but got nothing in response other than sullen looks.

"Don't waste yer breath. This isnae Dixon of Dock Green."

Three young men walked towards them. There was no room for them all and instinctively Alec moved aside to let them pass. Their thin mouths twisted into smirks as they swaggered through and after they'd walked a few more feet there was laughter.

Ronnie brought him to a halt.

"Don't do that again."

"Do what?"

Ronnie pointed to the pavement.

"See that? That's ours."

Ronnie swept his arm around in the general direction of the nearest houses and the city beyond them.

"That's ours too No other fucker owns it, just us. Unless it's a fucking cripple, or a sweet old lady, we move aside for no-one. Understood?"

"Even the Chief Constable?"

Ronnie smirked.

"If it's no' his beat, it's ours."

Alec thought the idea of the chief moving aside for him to be too revolutionary, but he understood the concept. As if to make sure, Ronnie drove another nail into the coffin.

"If the neds think yer saft, they'll take advantage. They'll think yer a total dick, som'b'dy they can push around."

Ronnie threw a thumb over his shoulder.

"Next time you meet those skulls, they're going to try their hand. You'll get some cheek at the very least. They might even take ye on for a square go. Don't put ideas into their heads."

Alec nodded, head filled with dark visions of his next encounter with the 'skulls'. An accurate description, for most of the lads he'd seen looked like this. Thin-faced and furtive, with sunken eyes and prominent cheekbones.

They resumed their walk in silence. Alec had the impression that Ronnie was leaving him alone to absorb the harsh realities of being a beat cop in a part of the city that had seen better days. Perhaps it had never actually seen better days, that it had ever been thus. They passed a red brick factory building set back from the road, gates padlocked, cathedral-like multi-paned windows smashed, walls daubed with sectarian slogans and gang names. The old industries had folded and there was nothing to replace them. A similar story elsewhere, but it seemed to be particularly bad here. No wonder there was an edge to the place. No wonder people looked angry, and for the first time, Alec felt a parallel with Auchenbreoch.

For the rest of the afternoon he held his line down the middle of the pavement. People moved aside, but he felt awkward and self-conscious about it. Only the consequences Ronnie described kept him resolute and he smiled at each passer-by in the way of some compensation. If they didn't smile back, and invariably they did not, at least he'd tried. And so, they spent the afternoon navigating the beat as stately black ships, going wherever the wind blew them, until they got a call that would provide him with an example of the subtler arts of policing.

Spectres At The Feast

Ronnie looked as if he'd been locked in amber. A still life. His left hand cupped his notebook, while his right, pen 'tween finger and thumb, hovered above the paper, frozen in the act of writing. Brylcreemed hair marched in waves across a large head which, cocked to one side, gave him the air of an inquisitive crow. Only his eyes, glinting with stubborn malice, displayed any sign of animation.

Across the room, separated by industrial ovens and stainless-steel work surfaces, a large man with grey shoulder length hair leaned against an American style fridge, chambray shirt straining to stop a pendulous stomach cascading over his designer jeans. Puckered orange flesh shone through the partings between fake mother-of-pearl buttons, the same sunbed orange as the face and hands. He looked like a cheap nightclub owner and his mouth was pulled to one side in sarcastic indifference.

"Don't see why you need a statement. Thieving bastard's in his shitey flat, stuffing his face with my champagne and the contents of this kitchen."

Ronnie sighed and assumed the face of infinite patience.

"We can't breenge into someone's house. Need an account of the facts first. Tell me what happened and I'll get on with investigating the matter."

The restaurant owner snorted.

"Fat chance you keystone cops catching him. Would've stood a better chance myself. I've a good mind to make a complaint, I know your Divisional Commander."

Alec felt uneasy. The call about a theft had sounded straightforward enough, but as soon as they'd arrived at the restaurant there'd been friction between the owner and Ronnie. Now it looked like it would end in a complaint and that was the last thing he needed. The incident with Harry was still raw and Alec glanced at Ronnie, willing him to be diplomatic.

Ronnie teased the ends of his moustache and regarded the chambray shirted man in the manner of a fairground shark weighing up his next victim. After a few seconds he shrugged and smiled a gap toothed smile.

"Brief statement then. But, you'll have to provide a detailed one later."

The restaurant owner looked smug. A concession had been won from a contrary public servant.

"I'm not going anywhere. No food, no restaurant. I'm closed because of that wee cunt."

The 'wee cunt' had been sacked that afternoon. He'd displayed a 'bad attitude' and a 'foul temper'. As Ronnie huh-huhhed, the restaurant owner waved his arms about the kitchen. There was disbelief, a sense of betrayal, of giving someone 'an opportunity' and having it 'thrown in my face'. There'd been a showdown, an argument and a dismissal, followed by the disappearance of expensive food and fine wines. 'Enough to feed an army'.

Ronnie noted the list of stolen food and drink, his dark eyebrows rising higher with each additional item.

"That's some amount. How much would you say that was worth."

The restaurant owner was in full flow.

"At least £5000."

Ronnie stopped writing and looked up. The restaurant owner hesitated before making a show of totting up the damage using his fingers.

"Well, maybe a little less. Let's say £2000."

Ronnie wrote the figure down. When he'd finished, he crossed the kitchen floor and presented notebook and pen to the restaurateur. The restaurateur looked at it and then Ronnie.

"What do I do with this?"

"Sign it."

"Why?"

"In case there are any misunderstandings later."

The restaurateur signed the notebook and handed it back, a wary look on his face. Ronnie slid his notebook into a tunic breast pocket and smiled.

"We'll be on our way."

Alec was grateful to escape the claustrophobia of the restaurant, the clash of personalities had been unnecessary and he couldn't work out why Ronnie was being so difficult. A crime had been committed. Wasn't it their duty to investigate? The suspect's address was miles away and time was against them if they wanted to recover the food and drink but as they emerged onto the Great City Road Ronnie strolled along at his usual glacial pace. A man with time on his hands.

"Will I shout up a van?"

The old cop appeared to give this considerable thought. So much so that many seconds passed without an answer and Alec began to wonder if he'd heard the question at all.

"Will I shout up— "

"—heard you."

"Sorry. Just thinking of the time."

"We've plenty of time."

And that was that. Ronnie ambled on, in no hurry to go anywhere, an old-school cop who thought probationers were to be seen and not heard. A stream of swear words coursed through Alec's head but he held his tongue and fell into step.

The night was humid and the air saturated with a fine rain. The wet pavements, thick with the smell of dog shit and cigarette butts, mirrored the lights of passing cars and glowing street-lamps. The pubs on either side of the road were busy and Alec looked into each with wistful jealousy.

"Ok Ronnie. What's the plan?"

"We go to the boys' flat and chap the door."

"And if he doesn't answer?"

"He'll answer."

"But the restaurant owner…he'll want his stuff back."

"Fuck him. He's a ned."

Ronnie imitated the accent. It sounded like an exaggerated Danny La Rue with a twist of Roystonhill and Alec laughed.

"Yeah, doesn't sound so posh when he's pissed off. Sounds like he's from a council scheme."

Ronnie wrinkled his nose.

"He's a fuckin' drug dealer. Sunk his dirty money into that restaurant. They're all at it. Pubs, clubs and taxis. They think they're the hoi polloi, with fancy houses and flash cars, but they're still fuckin' neds."

Alec recalled the lectures at the police college, about their role as neutral observers and not taking it personally. It was clear Ronnie did, but he felt it too. It was as if they were having the piss taken out of them, that despite all the platitudes crime did pay.

They passed a bar, all plate glass and faux antique furniture, a replacement for a sawdust and spitoon pub that had recently stood there.

Luxury cars and fast hatches sped past on their way to the city centre. Young women in power outfits and Lady Di hair styles tottered along the pavement wearing Hollywood smiles and designer perfumes. In nine months, the city would be opening the Garden Festival and Glasgow was 'Smiles Better'.

Hard to believe it had only been eight years since the winter of discontent and now the wide boys were getting off on money, cars and property. And where there was money, there were neds. The belief that crime didn't pay had been subverted by an excess of cash and aspiration and everywhere Alec looked, pubs, clubs and restaurants, people were getting high on possibilities. Boom time. Except if you lived around Corsair Street or any other sink estate left behind by the new economic order. Alec thought about the easy way in which the restaurateur had assumed the air of middle-class entitlement. There seemed to be more and more like him.

They walked on, two figures charting a path down pavements populated by people who regarded them as an inconvenient truth and pretended they weren't there.

They left the honey-coloured buildings of the affluent neighbourhoods and entered a sequence of terraces lined with dilapidated townhouses; apartments whose hidden grandeur would be revealed in the next wave of gentrification. Alec passed the crescent where he'd arrested Sean Burke and crossed a marble-clad bridge to a run-down area of red sandstone tenements. The brooding presence of grey tower blocks loomed along the skyline. The proximity between rich and poor was striking and Alec marveled at how stratified it all seemed. Honey-gold, red and grey. A city where wealth and deprivation was colour-coded.

After a few more minutes they arrived at a tenement whose entrance door hung off its hinges and climbed to the first-floor landing. There were the familiar smells of stale piss and fried food. Graffiti was scrawled on the walls and anatomical designs stippled onto the ceiling with cigarette burns.

Ronnie found the address he was looking for and pressed his ear to the door. After a few seconds, he stepped back, winked and knocked.

"A wee party within."

There was silence. Then the voice of a young man on the other side.

"Who is it?"

Ronnie lifted his chin.

"Ah think ye know fine. Open the door."

There was a pause.

"No' until ye tell me whit ye want."

Ronnie raised his eyebrows in mock exasperation.

"A wee word. It'll save the damage to your door. Best open up and we'll explain."

Another pause.

"Ye need a warrant."

Ronnie smiled at the spy hole on the door.

"Would you like to put that to the test?"

Time stood still and then, after the slow turn of a key, the door opened.

Alec had expected someone hardy and streetwise, like one of the skulls that hung about the local off-licence. Instead, a skinny boy of seventeen stood before him, shoulders dripping with defeat. His face, wan and tired, looked like it was sculpted from a bar of white soap.

"Ye'll be wanting to see what's left."

The boy retreated into the flat and Alec followed him to a tiny room where a young man and woman sat at a makeshift table constructed from a wooden cable drum. An assortment of dishes overlapped each other, empty save for thin scraps of salmon and venison. In whatever spaces could be found amongst the car crash of dishes stood plastic tumblers half-filled with wine. An empty bottle of champagne lay under the table. The diners sat with cutlery at the ready, but at the sight of Alec they put them carefully on the table, as if laying down their weapons. There was a pregnant silence.

Ronnie spoke first.

"Anything left?"

The boy looked miserable and shrugged.

"Some trifles in the fridge."

Ronnie looked convincingly disappointed.

"Shame. If we'd arrived sooner, we could've returned some of it."

Alec gazed around the wreckage of food and drink. There'd been a lot, but not enough to feed an army. At a rough estimate there was a few hundred pounds worth, and most of that was alcohol. A months wages for a kitchen boy in a busy restaurant. He sensed Ronnie staring at him.

"Be so good as to obtain the details of our friends."

Alec took out his notebook.

"Please. There's no need to bring them intae it. They didnae know."

The boy had stepped forward but was prevented from coming closer by the outstretched arm of Ronnie. He looked pleadingly at the old cop.

"Look, I'll take the 'derry'. They had nae idea."

Ronnie smiled and muttered a common law caution. It was like a Latin mass. A soft incantation that cast a spell on the room. The boy looked at Alec and then Ronnie.

"It's fine. Four months ah worked there. He was a fuckin' wanker. Widnae pay me. Ah just took in kind what ah was owed."

Alec jotted down the boy's details, the caution and the comments. Ronnie turned to the guests.

"Right. Party over. Toodle-pip."

The diners required no second invitation and left in haste. Alec opened his mouth to protest but was met by the upturned hand of Ronnie.

"Boy's admitted it. There'll be no court case."

"What about the grub? Do we take it to the station?"

Ronnie looked forlorn.

"Perishable goods sadly. The most we can do is retrieve some of the drinks."

Brandy and whisky bottles stood against a far wall. Alec selected the few that were still full. Ronnie sat the boy down and spoke on his radio. A van arrived, the flat was locked up and the boy, quiet and respectful, was transported along with the drink to Corsair Street.

Alec guessed he'd never encounter an arrest so underwhelming. Once the formalities of fingerprint and photograph had been observed, their prisoner would be released, and knowing that he'd soon be going home the boy chatted amiably. Alec rolled each inked finger onto the fingerprint form as Ronnie teased out a life story with practiced ease. It was like being in a brightly lit confessional.

It was a story of abandonment, squalor and neglect. Absent father. Alcoholic mother. A life on the street, avoiding school and avoiding home. No qualifications and no prospects. A story of school friends on 'smack', of suicides and overdoses, of life on the dole and a dream of earning his own way. It was all told with off-hand sincerity and when they were done Alec led the boy to the front door and watched as he walked off into the night.

"What now Ronnie?"

"We make a phone call."

They went to the report writing room where an ancient bakelite phone sat in a corner. Ronnie sat, composed himself and dialled a number. Alec could make out the pompous voice as the phone was answered. Ronnie gave an update, a tale of success mixed with regret.

"Yes sir…appreciate that. Seems he'd help in consuming the food. Ahhh…sadly not much…just a few bottles of whisky and brandy."

A vocal explosion on the other end. Ronnie removed the receiver from his head and flashed a Terry Thomas grin before replacing it to his ear.

"Appreciate that. A lot of money…the boy will face the full might of the law. Indeed… I'm sure the court will treat him most severely."

More ranting.

"The spirits? Sorry. Evidence. Probably a year. You can write to the P.F., he might look kindly upon the request of an honest businessman, (theatrical wink). Not at all. Here's the address."

Ronnie read it out, bade the restaurateur a good night and hung up. He looked quite satisfied.

Alec saw Ronnie in a new light. The training at the police college was no match for the Machiavellian instincts of an experienced cop determined to maintain some decency in a world of impersonal rules and regulations, and for the first time since setting foot in Corsair Street Alec felt that perhaps he'd made the right choice after all.

"What'll happen to the boy at court?

The old cop shrugged.

"If it goes to court...Depends on how you write up the case."

"How do I do that?"

Ronnie smiled a pirate smile.

"I'll show you."

Rites Of Passage

The week turned out to be a noticeable change in tempo from the night shift. Alec's workload rapidly expanded as Ronnie went about introducing him to as many situations as possible in a nine-hour period. Ronnie took his tutor role seriously and prompted only when Alec teetered on the edge of embarrassment, manfully trying to recall the things he'd been taught at the police college.

"Best way to learn is by yer mistakes and thinking for yerself."

He knew one day he'd appreciate this tough love, but mistakes were the last thing he wanted, given his precarious reputation with the rest of the shift.

The Sergeants turned out to be just as hard-nosed and to Alec's dismay his carefully crafted police reports came back festooned with scored out sentences and red ink annotations. He'd laboured over the Sean Burke case only to find it in his in-tray, butchered and heavily critiqued by Sergeant Fitzpatrick. He began to believe the Sergeants hated him and that he was beset by enemies in all directions.

Ronnie simply laughed.

"No-one's saying you cannae write a great story but the P.F. disnae have time to read War and Peace. He's got to wade through thousands of these each week."

Ronnie lifted up Alec's latest report, flipping from one page to the other.

"P.F's got seconds to decide whether it's worth his while. He wants to see the charges and a neat wee summary on the next page that supports the fella getting the jail. One day, when yer a fancy detective, ye can flex yer writing muscles. Till then, it's bare bones. There's an art to that too."

Alec accepted the explanation, but it was disheartening. A university education counted for little here. Writing the words that would seal Sean Burke's fate was daunting and it was troubling that one day he'd have to stand up in court and testify against him. It occupied his thoughts so completely that he forgot about the incident with Harry, but as he began his last day of late shifts Alec was confronted with a stark reminder that the latter was still much in play.

The muster ended and he was putting his notebook away when Alec heard his name called. He looked up to see Sergeant Fitzpatrick motion with his head to follow him out the far door. He'd thought at first that it was the return of yet another butchered report, but when he caught up in the corridor Fitzpatrick merely beckoned him to follow and without explanation led him straight into the Sergeants room.

"There are two gentlemen from Complaints and Discipline here to see you."

Alec was in the room before he'd had time to absorb the news and the sight of the two immaculately dressed middle aged men in business suits dropped his heart to the pit of his stomach. They smiled, but the smiles did not extend to their eyes. They sat quietly in the middle of the room, opposite an empty plastic chair and looked at him with a mixture of curiosity and intent.

Fitzpatrick, normally puffed up and bullish was deference itself.

"Constable MacKay for you Sir."

Fitzpatrick gestured towards the older and taller of the two, a thin patrician man with long bony fingers.

"This is Chief Inspector Brown. The other officer is Chief Inspector

Thompson."

Alec wasn't sure how to respond and with heart racing decided it best to say little other than a polite hello. The two men nodded back. There was a heaviness to the atmosphere only broken by Brown dismissing Fitzpatrick from the room in a manner that spoke of comfortable seniority. Fitzpatrick looked glad to leave and glanced fleetingly at Alec with a look that seemed to say, be careful.

The door closed and Brown motioned Alec to sit down. It was a simple movement of the hand, but it did more to convey who was in control more than words could. Alec sat and braced himself, cursing the lack of opportunity to refresh his memory from the statement he'd written two weeks before.

Brown reached into a leather briefcase and pulled out a sheaf of papers. It was a copy of his statement, parts of it circled in pen with notes in the margins. While Brown made a play of studying his notes, Thompson lit a cigarette, sat back and relaxed a forearm on the Sergeants desk watching Alec with a steady gaze. After a few minutes Brown looked up and smiled his unsmiling smile.

"You'll know why we're here, but for the sake of formalities, and to ensure there are no misunderstandings later, we're investigating an allegation of serious assault against Constable Millar and which relates to the arrest of a suspect some few weeks back."

It sounded strange to hear Harry's surname. The official speak and the formal nature of the Chief Inspector's opening remark felt intimidating. Alec cleared his throat and replied that he understood, hoping he sounded confident and composed. Brown read over some words about the obligations of a police officer and the role of the Complaints and

Discipline department. In a declaration that sounded eerily familiar, Brown announced that he knew everything, had read all the statements and spoken to the key witnesses. There were just a few points to clarify, some tidying up. Alec gave silent thanks for the way he'd been seduced by that line before, knowing full well this particular interview would be far from simple.

The Chief Inspector returned to the statement, seemingly engrossed. His sidekick sat and watched. Cars whizzed by on the road outside, but otherwise there was silence. After a few minutes Brown raised his head and looked directly at Alec. There was intelligence in his gaze that told you he was not the kind of guy to be fucked around with.

"Ok Alec. I'm sure you don't need me to remind you that an assault to severe disfigurement is a serious crime indeed."

Alec felt a lump in his throat but resisted the instinct to swallow. He didn't trust his voice so nodded vigorously.

Brown continued in a measured almost casual tone.

"I'm certain you don't need me to stress just how precarious your own position is, as a probationer, in such circumstances. Should there be any shortcomings in the standards we rightly expect of a Constable of Strathclyde Police, your services will be dispensed with at any time within the first two years. And that applies to your cooperation in this investigation. I hope I've made myself clear."

So that was the angle. Dirty bastards. He was all too aware of his status, but to have it used as a means to coerce felt cheap. Maybe Harry had been right. He looked at the senior officers opposite and wondered if they'd ever been where he was now. Perhaps they'd risen without contact with the realities of the frontline and looked down their noses at cops like him.

Maybe it was just a game to them. He felt galvanised, he'd done nothing wrong, and though he was afraid of what they might do if he didn't 'play ball' he was determined to hold his ground.

"I'm very much aware Sir, yes"

"Good. Let's begin with what you've written in your statement…and what you may have left out."

As if on cue, both investigators looked at Alec at the same time. It felt as if he was being pinned back. Brown read out Alec's statement, pausing now and gain to ask if there was anything Alec wished to reconsider. Alec replied that he did not. And so it went on, section by section, each new excerpt jogging Alec's memory further. It was pedestrian and uncomplicated until they reached the point at which the struggle had erupted inside the police van. At this, Brown slowly put aside the statement and looked directly at Alec.

"A bit convenient wouldn't you say?"

"In what way Sir?"

Brown sat back and stared at the ceiling for a few seconds. When he levelled his eyes at Alec once more they were implacable.

"It really is best if you don't play games son. I've been doing this job for a long time."

Brown jerked a thumb over his shoulder to the world beyond the windows. He looked pissed off.

"I know fine what goes on. I was a cop too. Thing is, I stayed on the right side of the law."

Alec believed him. He looked the churchy type, but for all the righteousness there was something about Brown that Alec disliked. He had the air of a man who was best bib and tucker at the local Kirk A man who did all the right things in all the right places, saying all the right things, at the right time, to all the right people. He spoke like an elder, sententious and full of his own self-importance.

Brown leaned backwards and looked at Alec as if he was a specimen in a biology lecture.

"Here we have a young Constable, his first night on operational patrol. To his great surprise and excitement he's involved in a vehicle pursuit. Catches a car thief! Something to tell his pals in the pub. The excitement of the chase, the pride in catching the bad guy."

Alec waited for the question, but there was no sign of it. Brown had found his rhythm.

"He arrests his man. Puts him in the police vehicle. But the prisoner doesn't go quietly and puts up a struggle. Of course, it's tight inside that van, there's little option but to grab hold of something, anything, and things get confused. The young officer and his colleague get things under control, but it's not without some violence. That's when he sees blood everywhere and the suspect's badly injured."

A heavy pause. Alec hadn't been asked a question, so there didn't seem any need to respond, but as he waited for the next instalment it occurred that this scenario had an uncomfortable ring of authenticity to it. He almost believed it himself and would have nodded along had it not been profoundly untrue. Doubts crowded in. Is this what Harry had claimed? If he'd been Harry, is this what he would've said? It was only then Alec began to realise the reason for the hostile cross examination. Brown was evidently sceptical.

"But here we have the new probationer, conveniently out of the picture. Not yet trusted. Or did you take fright at the blood?"

Alec tried to orient himself. He was simply a witness, yet here he was, an object of suspicion and veiled accusations. He wanted to explain, to lay it all out in uncertain terms, but there was something of the night about Brown and Thompson, something about them he didn't trust and this wasn't the time for blabbing his mouth off. It was a time to tread very carefully indeed.

"There was nothing to be frightened of."

Synchronised eyebrow raising.

"Really? First night on the street, with officers you don't know…next thing there's a bloodbath and it's not what you'd signed up for. Your colleagues would've been glad to write you out. I'm quite sure it would be something of mutual benefit. You're off the hook, they remove the weak link."

Alec bristled at the idea of being considered weak. It was difficult not to lash out in some way, but the way he'd been given a fools errand by Harry lent truth to what Brown had said and it was unnerving. His pride was wounded and he felt his face flush.

Brown sat back and smiled, satisfied that he'd gotten a reaction.

"Why don't we back up a little. There's no rush. Myself and Chief Inspector Thompson have all day."

Thompson reached into his packet and drew out another cigarette, lighting it with a crisp strike of a match. He inhaled deeply and offered the open end of the packet in Alec's direction.

"Thanks sir, I don't smoke."

The cigarettes were withdrawn with a shrug but Brown, ever watchful, nodded his approval.

"Quite right. Dirty habit."

The Chief Inspector appeared to have arrived at some sort of decision. A different tone followed; fatherly and conspiratorial.

"It might not look it Alec, but we're on the same side. Myself and Chief Inspector Thompson were beat cops once. It's a messy old business. Mistakes are made, things go wrong in the heat of the moment. We're only human. If made in good faith we can put things right, but only if you help us. Understand?"

The change of tack had done nothing other than raise Alec's suspicions. He nodded and readied himself for the question. Brown continued onwards, calm and reasonable.

"I'm going to ask you simple questions Alec. Remember, we're just here for the truth and we'll help you in any way to achieve that. Remove any worries about your colleague, he's a big boy who can look after himself. Just concentrate on doing the right thing and leave the rest to us."

He had to hand it to Brown. It was hypnotic and soothing. The voice of a helpful man, saying reasonable things, someone you could trust. But the truth was, he didn't trust Brown one bit, and this realisation made 'doing the right thing' a little more complicated. The Chief Inspector leaned forward in his chair. Alec remained upright and waited, but when Brown spoke again the tone had changed, more authoritative and businesslike.

"Let's get to the heart of it, then everything else will fall into place. Now. You were in the van when the suspect was assaulted, weren't you?"

This at least was easy enough.

"No Sir, I was not."

A brief flash of irritation.

"I'd think very carefully on this Alec. Remember we have the statement of several eyewitnesses."

Alec pictured the dark street, the young men at the doorways, the thuds on the side of the van as they drove away. What had they seen and heard? Easy to be caught out in a lie. But it was the Chief Inspector who was lying and in that moment the mystique fell away. Brown had nothing up his sleeve other than bluff and coercion. There was no doubting the Chief Inspector believed he'd been removed from the scene, but it hadn't happened in the way he'd supposed and Alec, still fearful of repercussions, was in no mood to elaborate.

"I think your witnesses may be confused."

"And why is that?"

"I wasn't in the van during the commotion sir. I had been told to search a garden for car keys."

Brown snorted.

"How convenient. And who told you to do that?"

"Harry. Constable Millar sir."

Brown threw his arms up and smirked at Thompson who shook his head in a show of shared disbelief.

"Did you really believe there'd be keys in the garden? Or did you simply take the easy way out, knowing what was coming next?"

Another sting to his pride, but Alec was immune. It was all just a game. Like the attempt to unsettle him at his job interview, when a fat Sergeant had asked him if there was a yellow streak up his back that the panel couldn't see. He'd bristled then, but hadn't bitten. This was just old-fashioned baiting, and he'd pass this too if he kept his cool.

"Sir, I'd no idea what was going on. It was my very first night on duty and I just did as I was told."

Another smirk. The tone had shifted to one of sarcasm.

"Just following orders? Think that one's been used somewhere before."

The comparison with the Nazis wasn't lost on him. It hadn't been so long ago he'd laughingly deployed the epithet himself, chanting out insults at student demos. Now, squirming on a hard plastic chair in a claustrophobic room with two old sharks circling, it wasn't funny anymore.

Brown reached into his attache case and drew out another sheaf of papers. To Alec's surprise, Brown produced the form he'd filled to join the police. That it was retained and kept in his personnel files surprised him. A lifelong dossier it seemed. Brown opened it out.

"Says here that you were a student. Glasgow. Sociology and Politics. Impressive."

Brown dropped the form on the desk on top of the witness statements.

"You've a great future ahead of you. University education, bright young man. You'll pass your promotion exams, work your way up the ranks. It's a rewarding career if you play your cards right."

There was a quick backwards nod of the head towards the world outside.

"Don't waste your life away plodding around in the pissing rain, rolling in the gutter with the neds on a Friday with the Constable Millars of this world. You're much better than that."

Another pause.

"The question is: are you your own man-or simply a stooge for the likes of Harry Millar?"

It was an unfair question. Cops had no authority over each other, but everyone knew the line was blurred as a probationer. He did all the crap jobs and took directions from the older cops. It wasn't a simple situation and Brown knew it fine.

"I'm my own man sir, but I'm also part of the team and as a probationer. I'm here to learn and listen to the guidance of my fellow officers."

It sounded prissy, but he no longer cared. He was playing a straight bat and had no intention of allowing Brown to pick him off.

Brown looked unimpressed.

"Wonderful answer. Right out of the police college handbook. The training staff would be proud."

Brown sagged backwards into his chair and turned to Thompson.

"Anything you'd like to ask our upright young officer here Chief Inspector?"

Thompson shook his head. Brown stared at Alec for a moment before speaking again.

"One more then. I'd think carefully before you reply, because once you've answered it, there's no going back. If there's something you need amended in your original statement before my report goes to the P.F., now's the time to do it, while the Chief Inspector and I are still in a position to help. Beyond this, you're on your own. Understood?"

Christ, he was laying it on thick, but he had the measure of it now. He'd been unprepared for the interrogation, the suspicion and veiled accusations, the unsettling mixture of coercion and false camaraderie, but the longer the interview had gone on the more he'd adjusted to it and the more he was determined to avoid pouring petrol on an already combustible situation. He told Brown he understood and waited, more a sense of curiosity than trepidation. Brown leaned forward again, as if doing so would get him nearer to the truth.

"Ok. On the night you and Constable Millar arrested the suspect, where you inside the police vehicle when he was alleged to have been assaulted by Constable Millar?"

It was all Alec could do to suppress a smile. Was that it? The big finale? A rehash of the question he'd been before? He checked over in his head for any potential pitfalls to his imminent answer but could find none.

"No sir. I was outside the whole time. Only when I got in the van did I see the injuries. I didn't see how they came about and I wasn't present when they occurred. It's all in my statement and there is nothing I want to change."

"And yet you also state that there were no injuries before the suspect was placed in the van?"

Ah. The real question. The incrimination of Harry that could not be avoided. His stomach lurched with the knowledge that he was still the smoking gun and there was no way out of it.

"Yes sir. That's correct."

Brown looked hungry for more.

"So, articulate, well-educated, smart young man that you are. How do you think our suspect came about these horrific injuries?"

Alec had no answer. It seemed painfully obvious that Harry had inflicted them, but he'd no idea why. He'd no desire to step into that particular minefield. There'd be enough evidence against Harry without his amateurish speculation.

"Sir, I honestly have no idea what happened. I only saw the aftermath."

Brown made a play of shaking his head slowly in sad resignation as if he, Alec, had passed up a golden opportunity. But there were no follow ups, no tough questions or raised voices. Just a pedestrian round up of what was in his statement and a request that he sign to confirm that he stood by what he'd written there. The interview was over.

The investigators packed away their files and cigarettes. They no longer appeared interested in the young officer sitting there, tense and alert. It was only when he stood up that Brown, looking tired and detached, spoke to him again.

"Let's see what happens next. In the meantime, stay here until your Sergeant comes for you."

They left, leaving Alec to slowly exhale and his pulse return to normal. His mouth was dry, his armpits wet, but though he felt grubby he was in one piece and hadn't cocked it up. But, he'd not done the right thing exactly. He'd been seduced by the 'us and them', sticking to the line of least controversy. He'd not been the honourable man he thought he was and in recognising that there was a feeling of loss, of an innocence he'd never regain. He was still coming to terms with that when Fitzpatrick returned.

"Well? How did it go?"

He wasn't sure and the last thing he wanted was to say something he'd come to regret. He'd done his duty, up to a point and hadn't escalated the situation between him and Harry. For now, that would have to do.

"Fine Sarge. I think."

He readied himself for a post mortem but Fitzpatrick just nodded, stood to one side and pointed to the open door.

"Back on the street then. Your neighbour's waitin' downstairs."

Glad to be free of the suspicion and stress, Alec walked toward the stairwell and caught a glimpse of a grim-faced Harry disappearing into the Inspector's room. As the door closed he heard the voices of Brown and Thompson inside. So, he'd been questioned first to see what could be used against Harry. Alec felt the sickening lurch again. Big boy games in a big bad world.

He found Ronnie and they left the office by the front door, striding down the main road in silence. Only once they were a half mile away did Ronnie slow down and speak.

"Well, they'd need to run hard tae catch ye now. How'd it go?"

Ronnie could be an old bastard, but he was discrete and it was a relief to have someone to confide in. He'd hardly covered himself in glory, but what he wanted most was a sense of validation, that what he'd said was within the rules of the game and he hadn't cemented a reputation to be distrusted. When he finished Ronnie looked satisfied.

"Don't be so hard on yersel. Those guys aren't daft. Ye need to keep tae what's in yer statement and no' get caught out with any of their wee games. Sounds like ye did just fine."

They reached a junction and as usual Ronnie paused for a while taking in the movement of people and traffic. He looked pleased with himself, as if Alec's rite of passage was something he'd personally overseen and was therefore within his rights to take pleasure from it. He nudged Alec in the arm.

"I reckon we'll make a cop out you yet."

Alec very much wanted that to be the case, but he had reservations about Ronnie's assessment of the stance he'd taken at the interview and Brown's question played on his mind. Was he his own man? Life didn't seem so simple now his was inextricably bound with the others. His vaunted principles now felt compromised, but there was no going back on what he'd said and he'd have to make the best of it.

A strong wind swept the street. On the opposite footpath, pale-faced figures competed with empty crisp bags and torn newspapers past a line of shops huddled at the feet of a row of tenements. Some were empty, their windows smeared with Windolene, a visual testament to the rise of the supermarkets. Bucking the trend, someone had opened a second-hand furniture store and it was doing a brisk trade. In every shit situation lay an opportunity for someone else it seemed.

They ambled past a children's home and an abandoned church, weeds sprouting from a stiletto spire, past vacant plots of grey-brown earth where factories and slums once stood. Nothing remained but the scarified earth, the mounds of dusty bricks and twisted metal; only the narrow cobbled roads, their granite sets still intact, spoke of the communities that once existed there.

The streetscapes changed as they neared the city centre. New red-brick houses lined both sides of the main road, Saltire Society plaques screwed to their walls. An old cinema, freshly renovated and converted to a community centre. An old tobacco warehouse undergoing conversion into yuppie flats. All around were the tentative signs of change, but it was still a bleak place, deprived and far removed from the affluence of the West End and the rejuvenating effects of an economy built on cheap money and brass necked opportunism.

Ronnie threw in the odd sobriquet. About things that once had been and now gone, about a city that was always in flux. Recession and renewal, destruction and construction, metamorphoses and reinvention. It occurred to Alec that he was going through a similar process, one that had begun at the police college and was nowhere near complete, as uncompromising as the changes in the city around him. It was a rough ride, but he was glad he'd made it this far, glad he was in a job when so many were not, glad he still had a chance to prove himself.

Adrift

If he approached his days off in a more optimistic frame of mind, it was because the week had ended no worse than it started. The issue with Harry remained unresolved, for it was clear from Harry's sullen demeanour at the stand-down things hadn't gone well in his own interview. Alec kept a discrete distance and put faith in Ronnie to spread the word that he'd at least held his own.

But, if he had, there was no instant thaw in relations to show for it. Later that week Alec listened to the banter in the locker room about a football match with another sub-division. His ears had pricked up. A game would be a chance to show he was a team player and he waited quietly for an invite. But it never came and as the last of their voices retreated down the stairs, he knew there was still some way to go before acceptance. It was a measure of how far he'd travelled that he took the rebuff with quiet stoicism, hopeful that somehow it would turn out alright in the end, something owed to Ronnie's quiet confidence that he'd make a cop yet.

In any case, his days off presented the same solitary options as the last. He was an outsider in an organisation who's culture he struggled to assimilate, in a city that was a stranger to him. It was tempting to take a drive to Auchenbreoch and seek comfort there, except there'd be none and Alec balked at the idea of running for cover or confessing to anyone just how rough a start he'd made, or the compromises already made to his high ideals, or to consider even momentarily that this was no life for him. For the time being he was in a no-man's land, with numerous obstacles before him, the landscape littered with casualties, but determined to avoid retreat at all costs.

He phoned Dad. A listless conversation full of heavy pauses, where he maintained the same pretences as before and where the highlight was an invitation to a wedding on his weekend off. Cousin Margo was getting hitched, so there was no way he could avoid Auchenbreoch now. Still, silver linings. There'd be a chance to catch up with the gang the night before and see cousin Margo on her big day.

And so it was, on a Wednesday night on a late summer evening, Alec contented himself with another bottle of wine in front of the TV, consoling himself with the prospect of a quiet week where enquiries acquired on the late shift would be concluded and his first weekend off begin. A chance for some breathing space. After all, as Ronnie had assured him, nothing much ever happened on an early shift.

Toast

The knock came just as Alec put the toast to his mouth. For a moment he thought it was a kid playing a prank, but it was followed by a succession of hammer blows so thunderous he worried whether someone was trying to break in.

Ronnie, squeezed into an easy chair in the corner of the room, tie unclipped, collar unbuttoned, brushed the crumbs from his moustache and shrugged.

"Go and see. Somebody wants yer attention."

Alec drew the bolts on the outer doors, his plate in one hand and so it was he swung them open to a bright summer morning, presenting buttered toast like a waiter to a well-dressed middle-aged woman with lilac hair and a pearl necklace. She stared up, eyes wide, pale face drawn.

"You need to come, my nephew has shot himself."

Alec had expected some kind of emergency, but not this. He'd enough presence of mind to put the plate on the shelf containing crime prevention leaflets and was about to ask the lady inside when Ronnie appeared beside him, uniform buttoned, hat in perfect alignment and carrying Alec's tunic, hat and tie.

"Please lead the way."

The woman departed without another word and Ronnie fell into step by her side. Alec was still trying to get his head into gear. Someone had been shot. Did that make it a firearms incident? Images of armed response vehicles and tactical firearms units rose up in his mind as he wriggled into his tunic. Maybe the guy with the gun would be waiting for them. Maybe it was a trap. Such concerns did not appear to trouble Ronnie who'd disappeared down the street with the woman. Alec tipped his hat onto his head, closed the doors of the police box and set off in pursuit.

The police box. That's what Ronnie had called it as they'd left the muster. Alec had pictured a blue Tardis, like the ones still dotted around the subdivision, but when Ronnie led him along the canal to this obscure part of the beat it was to a tiny brick-built building with a flat roof, a report writing room, kettle, toaster and toilet. Built on the periphery of a 1930's housing scheme and across a busy road from an industrial estate, it was a place intended for the prevention of unnecessary trips back to Corsair Street.

Once there, Ronnie'd introduced the early shift custom of tea and toast, a ritual to be enjoyed before the day began in earnest, where the probationer fetched bread and milk from the local shop and made breakfast. Except this day had started early and very much in earnest.

Alec caught up as Ronnie and the lady entered a small cul-de-sac, at the end of which was a large wooden gate. She led them through and down a narrow lane to the canal tow-path where she turned left and there, overlooking the canal, stood a row of whitewashed cottages, each with a well-tended garden. It was half past seven on a Friday morning on the last day of August and the sun was rising. Alec could feel it's tentative warmth on his face. The canal, it's still waters thick with reeds and ducks, was as peaceful a scene as you could expect to see and Alec wondered if the woman was mentally unwell, that the whole thing was a result of a fevered imagination, or some well-meaning misunderstanding.

She continued up the gravel path of the middle cottage and was about to open the front door when Ronnie grabbed her arm.

"Before we go in, ye'll need to tell us what you heard."

The woman pursed her lips and shook her head. She looked on the cusp of crying, but Ronnie was resolute.

"If there's a gun involved, we need to know what we're getting into."

She nodded and took a breath.

"This's my oldest sister's house. Her son moved in last week. Lost his job—split from his wife. They've got two boys."

Ronnie nodded sympathetically but Alec knew he'd want something more up to date.

"What happened this morning?"

"I come every day, make breakfast, do things round the house. She's got dementia you see. I'm making tea when I hear a big bang."

The lady looked up to an upstairs bedroom window, it's curtains firmly closed. Ronnie pressed on.

"How long as he had a gun?"

"I didn't know he had a gun. But I'm sure that's what I heard."

"Did you hear anything after that?"

"Nothing."

"Did you look?"

The woman began to tremble, her eyes wide again.

"I don't want to see what's in there."

It occurred to Alec that they'd not heard the man's name.

"Your nephews' name?"

"Fergus."

Ronnie nodded. He'd heard enough. The aunt led them into a narrow hallway that opened into a tiny sitting room, where Alec saw an old lady rocking back and forth in a high backed chair. The aunt pointed up a stairway to a small landing and a white door.

"That's where the bang came from."

With that, she walked into the sitting room and closed the door.

Ronnie led the way, but when they reached the bedroom he turned and held out his hand as if to say 'after you'. Alec knew the drill and listened at the door, but there was no sound inside. Perhaps Fergus was injured and needed help, or maybe lying there with the gun, waiting for them. It seemed only right to check.

"Fergus? It's the police. You ok?"

Nothing. Alec reached for the handle and turned it clockwise. The door opened reluctantly, as if there was an obstruction on the other side so he put his shoulder to the door and applied more pressure. It opened some more and that was when he saw the smear on the carpet, grey and glistening. Like fish paste. It widened into an arc as the door opened further and he was so troubled by the sight he stopped to point at it.

Ronnie shook his head.

"Not good."

Reluctant to push wider, Alec squeezed into the room through the gap he'd created and looked down to see what had been resisting his attempts to enter.

Pinched between the thick nylon carpet and the bottom edge of the door sat a human brain. The sight of it stunned him, but there was no sense of revulsion or horror. The brain, bloody stem trailing behind it, was so abnormal that there was no emotion in his arsenal to draw upon. It looked cartoonish, but at the same time just as Alec imagined a brain would look like, complete with folds and lobes, wet with blood and fluids. If anything it was smaller than he'd expected but then he'd already smeared some of it across the carpet.

Ronnie's head appeared and Alec pointed to his discovery. The old cop arched his eyebrows in response but said nothing. They were both struck dumb. Alec moved back to let Ronnie into the room and turned to see what else lay in store for them.

Beside him was a single bed, it's scalloped headboard pressed flat against a papered wall of roses and bluebirds. A chintz duvet cover and chintz pillows matched the chintz curtains at the window. There was a faint smell of Parma Violets, the bedroom of an elderly woman, quite at odds with the dead man lying there. Alec was pretty certain it was a man, but it was hard to be sure given the catastrophic destruction to his head.

The body lay on top of the duvet, feet splayed at the bottom edge. A pair of shoes sat side-by-side on the floor. Alec's eyes travelled from the black socks on its splayed feet and along the dress trousers on its legs. Held between the knees was the carved butt of a double-barrelled shotgun, the silver plate above the trigger guard engraved with hunting scenes and the ornate script of the gunmaker. It looked new and expensive. At the trigger guard, the two hands had fallen away to each side, fingers curled inwards. The barrels of the gun rested on a smart business shirt, muzzles nuzzling a thick and swollen neck.

Until this moment the only shotgun that Alec had seen was the one an angry farmer pointed at him when he was a boy. It was obvious they were deadly. He'd watched enough films to cement the fact that guns killed, but he'd no comprehension of their real power until he looked at what remained of the man's head.

The deceased had done his research. Thrusting the muzzles under his chin he'd sent the contents of both twelve-gauge cartridges through his mouth and into the centre of his head. The explosive power had not only blown the top off his skull, it forced jaws, face and anything behind it outwards. Like someone had pumped up the man's head until it'd finally burst. Except the result had been as instantaneous as it was catastrophic and Alec had no doubt he'd died instantly. The exiled brain was testament to that.

Ronnie looked ashen and Alec wondered, despite a weird feeling of serenity, if he looked the same. He returned to the dead man and wondered what it had felt like in those last few seconds before he'd pulled the trigger. What had he felt when the superheated shrapnel had shredded flesh and bone? What could drive someone to this? He remembered the priest at Sunday Mass banging on about suicide. It was a sin, an act of selfishness. Life was a gift.

Despite the horrific damage, or perhaps because of it, Alec was drawn to the face of the dead man. It was the eyes that affected him most. Displaced by the force of the explosion, they dangled over the grossly swollen head, held in place by the gelatinous strands of their optic nerves. It was like the joke shop glasses of his childhood, with their pop-out eyeballs. This wasn't funny either.

The sockets, empty and bloody, were grotesque but they paled in comparison to the broken rim a few inches above them. Here, the row of jagged bone formed a perfect circle like a crown of white thorns. Within the white bowl of bone that remained a small pool of blood had gathered. If anyone had wondered what the contents of the human skull looked like, it was there for all to see, from the jagged remains still attached to the body, the brain on the floor and the huge arc of blood, skin and splintered bone adorning the headboard and wall above it. Fragments were beginning to peel away from the wallpaper, while pieces slid downwards leaving red snail trails across the bluebirds and roses. Alec tried to express his disbelief but found that he'd lost his power of speech.

Ronnie cleared his throat, the first sound either of them had made for several minutes and Alec turned to see that Ronnie was now looking at him with an expression of the gravest solemnity.

"You want to try mouth-to-mouth, or will I?"

It was like pulling the stopper from a bottle. Alec found himself trying in vain to suppress laughter. It caught hold of Ronnie and they stood at the foot of the bed, shoulders shaking, half laughing, half crying, snorting with the effort to bottle it up. Alec felt confused and ashamed, but he was powerless to stop. It was a catharsis, a reaction to the horror on the bed. Had it not been for the querulous voice on the stairway it might have continued for a minute more, but the sound of the aunt brought them back to their senses and Ronnie, wiping his eyes, called back that he'd be down shortly. He turned to Alec.

"Pull yersel together while I break the news. Look around and see if there's a note or anything suspicious. But don't touch anything."

Alec felt the hysteria ebb away. He'd thought the very least he could do was back Ronnie up for such a horrible task and he offered to go with him, but Ronnie was adamant.

"Mammy won't have a clue, Aunt knows fine he's dead and I need to radio this in. Soon as I do, the circus'll come to town."

Alec nodded. The death would be regarded as suspicious until the casualty surgeon and a post mortem put it beyond doubt. The CID would be called and then Uncle Tom Cobley and all would descend, but looking at the corpse and the arms stretching down, it was clear that the dead man had pulled the trigger just fine.

After Ronnie left, Alec made his way to the other side of the bed. There, on a small dresser among bottles of perfume and hairbrushes, lay three envelopes, one addressed to a female, the others for two males. There was an empty bottle of whiskey and a note written in a barely legible scrawl. It was addressed to 'Whoever Finds Me' and as that was undoubtedly him Alec began to read.

He'd expected suicide notes to be poetic, or at the very least dramatic, but here was a calm explanation expressing remorse for what was about to follow. The redundancy the aunt had mentioned and sorrow for a marriage long finished. The revelation of an illness. Symptoms that began as flu and ignored until the appearance of ulcers and swollen lymph nodes. Of a hidden sexuality and a secret lover who'd passed on something fatal.

Alec looked to the corpse. The AIDS campaign was still running on the telly. Most feared disease on the planet and a death sentence all on its own. He looked at the sprayed arc of fresh blood and worried if there was a chance he'd catch it. He examined his hands and though he hadn't touched anything other than the door handle, rubbed his palms down the sides of his trousers just in case.

The note finished by summing up the shame he'd bring to the family and the worry that he'd passed something to his wife. To Alec's surprise there were concerns aimed at whoever would find his body. For the distress his mangled remains would create. For being unable to find a less messy way out. The note scrawled to its end, the writing increasingly shaky, finishing with the hope that someone would pray for him.

It had been a long time. The last had been at his mother's funeral and he was out of practice. At first he couldn't find the words, but in the dim light of the tiny bedroom he said a prayer for a man he never knew. He'd just whispered a quiet Amen, when Ronnie reappeared at the door.

"Cavalry on its way."

"Better tell them our man had AIDS."

Ronnie's eyes widened and he left the room to pass the word.

Alec began taking notes. Ronnie's prediction was all too accurate as first the Inspector and the Sergeant, and then the on-call CID descended on the house. Cops from the shift were detailed to stand at either end of the row of cottages, some did door-to-door. Scenes of crime arrived, taking photographs and measurements from various angles. Swabs were taken with the greatest of care. To Alec's surprise the sub-divisional Superintendent arrived.

Superintendent Currie was a bull necked man who could be heard most days roaring at any hapless cop of who happened to pass his office. The more savvy found ways of navigating the various floors without passing his door, but here he was quiet and formal, just a nod as he made his way up the stairs and he stood patiently while Alec entered his details in the notebook. Currie had an unflinching stare and a face like stone, so it was a surprise when he spoke with a degree of compassion.

"You ok?"

The initial shock had worn off and Alec was keen to show that he was on top of it, especially to someone as senior as Currie.

"Yes sir."

"Good lad. Not easy these things, but you'll get used to it."

Currie squeezed his barrel chest into the room and exited a minute later as a subdued pale-faced man who gave a short nod with glassy eyes. He passed on the landing and descended the stairs without a word.

The casualty surgeon came and went, muttering that any damned fool could see the man was dead. Evidence was gathered and bagged. Sergeant Munro, looking tired and grey, arranged for someone to stand-by the body so that Alec could return to Corsair Street and submitted the report. A car waited for him in the cul-de-sac.

He made his way down the narrow stairs and stepped blinking into a sunny afternoon, glad to be away from the abnormality. Across the canal lay a small housing estate partly screened by an old hawthorn hedge that bordered the far side towpath. Behind it, two men in raincoats watched with bored expressions. One had a camera and was taking pictures.

Ronnie snorted.

"Didn't take them long."

Alec recognised them. There was something cliched about the way they dressed.

"How did they know?"

Ronnie looked surprised.

"You didnae listen on the radio when ye were wee?"

Of course he had, scanning police frequencies, picking up the odd garbled message, it just hadn't occurred to him the press did the same. Ronnie nodded in the direction of the journalists.

"These guys have professional kit. There before us sometimes–it'll be in the glove compartment of their car.'

Alec felt an instant dislike. Creeps who'd be knocking on the old woman's door after they had gone.

"Should be a law against that."

Ronnie smiled.

"The scanning? Isnae worth yer while. They'll run a shite story about you and make yer life a misery."

"Still doesn't make it right"

The now obligatory shrug from Ronnie.

"That's life."

On their return to Corsair Street Alec found a quiet corner and wrote the story of the day while Ronnie lodged the gun and suicide note. It was a story shorn of emotion, a description of a life pronounced extinct in clinical language, brief and to the point. There would be a post mortem, though one aspect of that had been performed by the deceased already. An overworked Procurator Fiscal would ask some routine questions and that would be that. There would be a quiet funeral for a man named Fergus who would be forgotten by everyone except two small boys and an ex-wife worried about her own fate. Alec finished the report and handed it to Munro who put it in his tray and sent him home.

He checked in with Ronnie on the way out, anxious to make sure he hadn't left him with things still to do, but Ronnie was being sent home too and as they walked across the car park Ronnie patted him on the back.

"That'll be yer first sudden puddin'."

Alec was taken aback by the expression. Another one to add to his ever-expanding vocabulary of police speak.

"Went to the city mortuary last week of training. A few bodies, but nothing like that."

Ronnie grunted.

"I doubt you'll see anything as bad as that again."

Alec hoped not. Human carnage was one thing, but it was the words of the dead man that weighed most on his mind, that someone could think there was no option other than to blow their head off. He swore to himself, no matter how bad life got he'd hang on, right to the bitter end.

Like his mother had done.

The journey home was slowed by the stop-start pulse of rush hour traffic. Kids, fresh out of school, tugged the arms of harassed mothers forging paths through groups of liberated office workers. A billboard advertised beer refreshing parts that others couldn't reach, while a newspaper seller held aloft the Evening Times and shouted something incoherent about the headline of the day. It wouldn't feature a shotgun suicide. Not until the next day.

As Alec trudged up the stairs to his flat he realised he hadn't eaten. His toast would still be on the shelf at the box, but he was too tired to care. Instead, he sagged onto the sofa and despite his hunger succumbed to sleep, his last thoughts; Ronnie's words of reassurance that at least he'd seen the worst of it, that no matter what the rest of the week brought, he'd never have to deal with anything like that again.

Assumptions

He drove to work the next morning in subdued mood, partly because he'd woken at three in the morning on the sofa with a crick in his neck, and partly because the trudge to bed hadn't ended in sleep as he'd hoped but with mental replays of the suicide and the dead man's face.

Spirits weren't improved by the revelation that Ronnie had taken the day off and he'd a new neighbour for the day; Ricky, a loud mouthed scouser who'd muttered 'fuck sakes' in the muster when the pairing had been announced. The news hadn't filled Alec with joy either. Ricky had a reputation as a lazy bastard and if confirmation were needed it came in the form of a declaration on the front steps of the station.

"I've got a stinkin' hangover. Could do with a cuppa. Where's yer dosses?"

The smell of stale beer wafted over Alec. He thought of the police box, but the idea of being cooped up in that small space with Ricky was too horrific to contemplate.

"There's a twenty-four-hour garage."

Ricky's face scrunched up like chip wrapper.

"Ron not showed you his dosses? Probably thinks you'll grass 'im in."

It was said with a leer, but Alec ignored it and waited. Ricky looked at the sky as if weighing up his options.

"Old folks it is. C'mon."

The 'old folks' was an elderly care home tucked down a back street near the Crescents that Ronnie had pointed out on the late shift. A three-storey white-harled rectangular block, stark simplicity incongruous among the leafy gentrification. A place the shift went to for early morning tea, a routine that irritated Ronnie immensely as this was his beat.

When they finally arrived there were several police cars and a van parked within the walled courtyard. Why Ricky hadn't shouted for a lift when others were going there was a mystery but, in any case, Ricky didn't give them a second look as he opened a door and stepped inside.

The first thing Alec noticed was the smell. A heady mix of bleach, boiled cabbage and something else he couldn't quite put his finger on. It intensified as they walked past a humid laundry room and into a large kitchen where women in blue tops and slacks cooked breakfasts while others carried trays to a large hatch in the far wall. Beyond the hatch, old people sat silently at formica tables. From somewhere behind, the sounds of laughter and Alec turned to see Ricky enter a smoke filled room where the shift sat en-masse at a table set with plates of toast and large metal teapots. Ricky spread his arms wide to a hail of welcomes. Alec followed to indifferent silence.

At least Charlie and Stevie were there and when he found a space beside them, a cup was pushed in his direction. He filled it with stewed tea while the others traded gossip and insults. It was a polis tea party and Alec wondered what the staff made of Corsair Streets' finest on their large backsides tucking into a free breakfast, the streets all but abandoned. He felt embarrassed but could see no similar emotion on the faces of his colleagues who were very much at home in their de facto cafe. An older woman stuck her head through the doorway and asked if they needed more. A volley of affirmations and a voice asking if there was marmalade. A laugh from the woman who looked like she enjoyed the presence of uniformed men in her workplace. There was a wink from Ricky and an invitation to sit beside him.

A few minutes later a younger woman brought more toast and tea. There were attempts to engage her in banter, but she was made of different stuff and scowled at the assembly before leaving without a word. It left Alec feeling uncomfortable. Surely these women had better things to do than be at the beck and call of this bunch of chancers.

"Turn yer radio off. Control room knows where we are."

It was Ricky, who made himself at home, tie unclipped, tunic unbuttoned, slice of buttered toast in one hand, cigarette in the other.

Alec made a play of twisting the dial but didn't switch it off. He wanted a call, anything that would force Ricky and the others off their arses and onto the streets. He wasn't a Puritan, no point in aimlessly walking about all day if there was nothing happening, but there was something crass about this mass freeloading and he understood Ronnie's irritation now. Oblivious, the shift exchanged pleasantries while Alec sipped his tea and prayed for a shout.

It was answered immediately, in the form of Bob's voice in the control room. A fire at one of the newly built flats on their beat.

There was a chorus of surprises and condemnations from the tea party. Ricky put his mug down and stared.

"Thought I told you to switch that fucker off."

Alec felt his face flame up, but he was past giving a monkeys. In his peripheral vision Charlie and Stevie grinned as Bob's voice continued to press its way into the awkward silence. No one wanted to be heard dyking a call. That would invite an enquiry by the Sergeants and a raft of early morning notebook signings that would put a stop to the breakfast club.

Ricky threw back his seat, clipped on his tie and answered the call. As he made for the exit he grabbed another slice of toast and stuffed it in his mouth. Alec sunk the last of his tea and followed, glad to be away from the source of his discomfort and content to take his chances with Ricky.

Another update as they walked towards the call. The fire brigade had arrived, the flats evacuated, but it did nothing to cheer Ricky who walked in silent fury, occasionally scowling at the young cop beside him. Alec pretended not to notice, happy that he'd stuck one on Ricky.

As they neared the fire, Alec scanned the rooftops for a pall of thick black smoke, but when they emerged onto the broad reach of City Road it was to the sight of thin grey wisps over the roof of newly built low-rise flats. The smoke looked anaemic. Other than the odd passing car there was no sign of life. No fire service. No residents. No curious onlookers. He was just about to say as much when Ricky spoke, his voice terse with recrimination.

"There's a building site behind. They'll be round there."

They rounded the end of the block to a large area of waste-ground with security fencing, assorted machinery and a small portacabin. A fire engine was parked in the middle, red paint gleaming in the early morning light, 'Summerhill' in gold letters on a wooden plaque along its side. Assorted people in nightclothes, newly woken up from their beds, stood pale faced around a young sub-officer, his black-striped yellow helmet visible in the middle. Two firemen hoisted oxygen cylinders onto their backs while others looked on. Smoke wafted from a broken window on the top floor. It looked a little thicker and darker now.

Alec scanned the refugees trying to pick out the tenant, but none of them had a sooty face or looked up to the flat with anxious glances. The only signs of discontent were from the residents as Ricky barged them aside to reach the sub-officer.

"How long have your crew been here?"

It was a question shorn of the niceties usually observed between the emergency services. The sub-officer, startled by Ricky's lack of grace, pulled his head back and looked down his nose at the fat cop standing before him.

"You'll get that from your command and control surely?"

Ricky stood his ground. The sub-officer shrugged and checked his watch.

"We've been here about…five minutes."

Ricky stared.

"And you're not in the flat?"

Alec groaned. These guys knew their job, they didn't need direction from a lazy cunt like Ricky. He edged closer, ready to placate the sub-officer if things went pear shaped, prepared to endure the wrath of Ricky for the loss of face that would cause, but he needn't have worried, the sub-officer, young and self-assured, announced all was in hand.

"Flats've been evacuated. Dropped cigarette most likely, we'll be in shortly."

A few feet away two crewmen were checking their face masks. The sub-officer turned to walk towards them but was stopped by Ricky who'd taken a firm grip of his arm.

"Who cleared the flats?"

The sub-officer wrenched his arm free and pointed towards a small man wearing a flat cap and donkey jacket in the doorway of the portacabin.

"Night watchman, speak to him."

Ricky carved a course through the muttering crowd towards the cabin.

It was so unnecessary, Ricky stomping around, taking his hangover and a missed breakfast out on this call. Alec vowed to take this as an example of how not to handle the public.

The watchman, eyeing their progress, began to retreat inside. Alec winced as Ricky shouted, his voice echoing off the surrounding buildings.

"You! Stay still."

The old man grimaced but did as he was told. Ricky lumbered up to the cabin, throwing an arm backwards in the direction of the burning flat.

"You cleared the folks out?"

The 'watchie' stank of beer, his eyes bloodshot. Another man with a hangover. He lifted his chin and drew his shoulders back.

"Aye. Checked each door ma'sel."

Ricky stepped closer. The old man took a step back.

"What d'ye mean, 'checked each door'?"

The watchie wore the look of a man who knew all the facts and took great comfort in them. He spoke to Ricky in the manner of a patient and wise man in the presence of a small child.

"Nae need to worry. Ah chapped each door, goat ev'ryb'dy oot."

The men with the BA kit were giving the thumbs up to their crew mates. Alec looked up at the thickening smoke. Little tongues of orange flame licked at the inside of the window sill. He turned to the old man, keen to be involved.

"That top flat, the one on fire. Where's the tenant?"

The old man shrugged.

"Naebody in son. Chapped it a coupla times. Nae answer."

Alec was still digesting this as Ricky turned and broke into a hard run. It took Alec a few seconds before he realised the significance of the comment. As the horror struck he began running after the charging form of Ricky who was now approaching the back door to the common close. The fire crew, spooked by the sudden activity, began moving towards the building. Alec, path converging on the firemen, pointed at the smoke.

"Someone inside!"

The firemen broke into a run. Alec reached the close and hammered up the stairs through a grey haze to where Ricky was throwing himself at a red door. As it crashed inwards a dense black cloud exploded into the stairwell. Ricky, head lowered, arm over face, disappeared into the funnelling smoke just as Alec threw out an arm and caught his tunic collar. They were in the doorway, the heat so intense that Alec's face began to burn and to his horror he found he couldn't breathe. Ricky had sagged against a wall and Alec beginning to tug drag him backwards when a pair of gloved hands grabbed hold of his own shoulder and they staggered backwards onto the landing. Alec was dimly aware of the shapes of two firemen running past them into the furnace.

Desperate for air, Alec sank to his knees, but no matter how he tried, he could not get a breath. Ricky slumped next to him, coughing and gasping, face blackened by soot. Knowing they'd collapse there if they stayed, Alec grabbed Ricky's arm and dragged him down the stairs as more firemen ascended. Somewhere up above someone called out for signs of life.

No one answered.

Once outside, Ricky, face smeared with soot, coughed blackened spit onto the bare earth. Alec's throat burned savagely and he sucked at the cool air grateful to have escaped the smoking cauldron above. The tenants, huddled at the fire engine, gazed up at the flat, a look of communal worry on every face. Flames had burst through the window and a thick column of black smoke rose into the clear blue sky. Over at the fire engine the sub-officer issued orders to his men. Not once did he look in the direction of the two cops hacking up their guts at the close mouth.

It took a few minutes before Alec could speak. There was something thick and claggy catching at his throat. He hacked and coughed until he finally cleared it, gobbing thick black mucous to the ground.

"What now?"

Ricky drew his hand across his eyes, smearing the soot with his tears. He could barely speak, his voice a whisper.

"Radio for an ambulance. Tell the control room what's happened."

Alec radioed the update. The smoke from the flat turned from black to light grey, dwindled to small eddies and then stopped. After a while the crew returned with the hose and a fireman raised a finger to the sub-officer. One person. The look of resignation on the sub-officer's face was all the confirmation Alec required. Ricky jerked his head at the close mouth and together they walked back into the building.

In the acrid atmosphere of the stairwell Alec's eyes began to smart. Water cascaded down the stairs and the walls were coated with a thin layer of soot the colour thickening as they climbed upwards. The air was angry and sticky. The smell of burned plastic caught at his nose and throat and he breathed in short shallow breaths in a vain attempt to limit his exposure. There was another smell too.

They stepped into the hallway, it's walls radiating heat like an oven. There was a charnel smell, greasy and cloying that hung in the air and filled his mouth and nostrils. He could taste it thick on his tongue, like the smell of pork mixed with the electric taste of sulphur. There were other smells, repellent and repulsive, but they hovered at the edge of his senses beyond recognition.

Two firemen stood in the bedroom. They'd opened the windows and taken off their masks, their two-tone faces darkly comic in the tiny room. One of them pointed at a double bed with his axe.

Only the outline remained. The mattress and carcass, reduced to scorched bed springs and melted plastic had sunk to a congealed mass on the floor. Lying on the charred remains, form bent inwards, was a blackened corpse. It looked for all the world as if it had fallen into a dark chasm, arms and legs reaching upwards in surprise, black curled fingers grasping in vain for the edges of the pit. Alec searched for recognisable features, but apart from feet and hands there were none. Just a crisp blackened shape glinting in the light of the firemen's torches, face distorted, flesh burned away to reveal a grinning set of smoke tainted teeth.

The floor and bed were sodden with water but apart from smoke damage to the ceiling and window, the room was relatively unscathed. It was incredible that such a fire could reduce a human being to charcoal yet be confined to such a small space. A glass ashtray sat beside a packet of Capstan cigarettes on a small bedside table. Alec looked for matches, or a lighter, but there was neither. He had his own theory, but it seemed only proper to ask.

The fireman who'd pointed to the bed, shrugged.

"Dropped match. Old fella has a few, falls asleep, bed goes up and he's too far gone to wake."

They all looked solemn and nodded. It wasn't rocket science. Ricky took over, but it was a measured Ricky this time. The fire had gone from him too.

"Smoke inhalation?"

The fireman nodded.

"Too early to confirm, but most likely. Post mortem to be sure.

Ricky searched the flat and found a name on some documents. Alec radioed for the services of a casualty surgeon and photographer. An ambulance crew arrived and to no-one's surprise pronounced life extinct. The firemen filed out and Ricky, pointing to the sub-officer, prodded Alec in that direction. Some animosity would remain and Alec was happy to play good cop.

The sub-officer turned out to be helpful and looked Alec in the eye when his statement was done.

"The guy was dead by the time the watchman raised the alarm. Smoke builds up a long time before anyone sees it."

It was probably the truth but it sounded like the sub-officer was rehearsing something to himself. They'd never know for sure and it was sometimes kinder for the living to think that way. There was nothing anyone could do for the dead man now.

Alec found the night watchman in the portakabin, hunched in an armchair likely salvaged from a derelict tenement cleared to make way for the new builds. The place stank of cheap wine. A plastic bin filled with crushed cans and empty bottles sat under a Pirelli calendar displaying a topless woman in mechanics overalls, the pages well-thumbed and grubby. Alec stood at the door while Ricky grabbed a milk crate and sat down. There was silence for a few seconds.

"Don't blame yerself. The fire brigade say the fella was dead by the time you saw the smoke."

The old man stared at the floor, the permanent stain of blame in his eyes. Ricky looked up and held his palms out at each side. Alec pulled out his notebook and took a statement, the watchman recounting the sequence of events in a low, tired voice. When he'd finished, Alec helped the old man to his feet.

"Nothing else to be done. Go home, get some sleep."

The watchman nodded and left, head bowed, back hunched.

Alec followed him outside. The fire service were packing up, the residents filing back to their houses as the paramedics reversed their ambulance onto the road and drove away.

He'd be there for a while yet. Casualty surgeon to eliminate suspicious circumstances and the 'shell' to take the body to the city mortuary. House to be secured. The gaffers would be on their way.

Ricky looked up at the broken window.

"Think the old fella was alive when the watchie chapped his door?"

"Got to assume he wasn't."

Ricky hacked more black gunge to the ground and grunted.

"That's the thing – never assume."

The gaffers arrived, Sergeant Munro at the wheel, Inspector in the passenger seat like a small potentate. Alec watched as she ran a hand through her short dark hair and put on her hat. She stepped out, straightened her black woollen skirt and strolled across the waste ground to where he and Ricky stood waiting.

"All done?"

Ricky looked around.

"Almost ma'am. Deceased inebriated - set his bed on fire - dropped light. Waiting on the casualty surgeon, photographer and shell."

The Inspector looked over to the fire blackened window before turning back to Ricky.

"Dangers of drink eh?"

The look was direct and it caught Ricky off guard. He forced a smile, but for once he was stuck for words. The Inspector held her gaze and Alec felt the tension rise. She was no fool. Ricky looked away and pointed to the portacabin, as much to show he was on top of things as to change the subject.

"Interviewed the watchie. Failed to raise the occupant when clearing the flats. Thought there was no one in. He's away home to bed."

The Inspector raised an eyebrow.

"Not the only one who could do with a lie down."

She turned to Alec.

"On a roll aren't you? Any more and I'll have you down as a suspect."

There was mischief in her eyes and Alec gave thanks that he wasn't in the bad books with her at least. She turned to Munro who'd stood silent behind her.

"Sergeant. Do we need both these men here?"

Munro looked at Alec with an appraising look.

"I'm sure Alec'll be fine. Just radio for a lift back to the office when yer done."

A bit of responsibility. Trusted. It felt good.

The Inspector returned to the car, Munro in her wake. Ricky began to follow, but as he did she turned and shook her head.

"You're walking, exercise'll do you good."

Ricky waited until the car had disappeared and spat more black phlegm onto the ground.

"Fuckin' Queen of Sheba."

Alec braced himself to catch Ricky's ire, but it's was a mellower cop that turned towards him now.

"Listen, thank's for grabbing me. Shouldn't run into a fire when the brigade's there to do that for ya."

Alec wondered if Ricky had inhaled something that had altered his brain chemistry.

"I'm sure you'd do the same."

There was a hard look, like this was being seriously weighed up.

"I guess. Even if ye are a scrote."

There was smile made more comic by the soot around his eyes and mouth.

"Remember, get the names of the undertakers and the photographer. I'm off to get me' breakfast."

Ricky strolled towards the end of the building and disappeared, leaving Alec to ponder the vagaries of human behaviour. How someone could be a complete prick one minute, but courageous and tenacious the next. How something straightforward could be anything but. Nothing was to be taken at face value and nothing to be assumed. Ricky had pissed everyone off, but he hadn't given a fuck and there was something about that Alec admired. Like Ronnie's unbending command of the pavements. It wasn't pretty, but it came with the territory.

He wandered over to the flat. He'd have to stand by the stench of charred human and burnt plastic till the undertakers came, but it was no more than was expected and he was being trusted to get on with it. Right now, that was all he could ask for.

Blue Rendezvous

It rained for the next three days. Introduced to the porous qualities of his nylon raincoat, Alec was glad when Ronnie returned, reluctant to tramp the sodden streets no matter how noble the cause. A sheaf of arrest warrants handed out at muster were folded away and their execution delayed until the weather broke. Instead, they'd cadged lifts to various 'dosses' around the beat, only venturing out when the odd call came their way, or tea break beckoned.

Their visits to cafes, schools and youth clubs came as a welcome change. Ronnie, normally Calvinistic about the whole idea of dossing, had apparently been on a road to Damascus, albeit one submerged beneath a North Atlantic weather system. Alec thought it no more than a practical response to the elements, but after a few days he wondered if something else was at play.

The answer came behind the closed doors of Giacomo's Cafe. Sipping cappuccino's in the back shop, Ronnie regaled old Alberto with polis war stories from an earlier time; tales of safe crackers and house breakers, of streets long knocked down and the characters that once lived in them. Stories of dodgy pubs and old cops who cleared them in return for beer. Of wily old foxes and some who'd been part cop, part ned. Surrounded by the smell of coffee and ice cream, separated from the world by the frosted glass façade of the café, it was warmly nostalgic. Alberto who evidently loved a good yarn had slapped Ronnie on the back and shouted through to Alec from the front shop.

"You watch out, this man'll get you into trouble!"

Alec'd been thinking up a reply, but Ronnie cut him off.

"Ach, tell ye the truth, I'm too old for this shit."

It caught Alec by surprise. It wasn't simply the remark of a cop in a low mood, there'd been something in the abrupt way it had been declared; like Ronnie had stumbled into an epiphany, the consequences of which were yet unclear, but in which a cog had turned in his mind and soon there'd be another turn, and another and before you knew it the big hand had swung to midnight and something would come to an end.

Alberto had noticed it too. Ronnie's hang dog expression and his crumpled frame had thrown the old Italian for a moment, but then another big smile and another friendly slap.

"Too old? Big Ronnie? No, you go on forever. Summerhill go to the dogs. I get another coffee, you'll feel better."

And Ronnie did brighten up, so much that Alec thought he'd mistaken the mood, but when the subject of the fatal fire cropped up a pall fell over him once more and Alec felt compelled to ask.

"How many dead folk you seen?"

A shrug.

"Hundreds — in every way you can think of."

"Such as?"

"Murders, accidents, suicides, stupidity. Seen 'em shot, drowned, stabbed, poisoned, crushed and burned. Old age cot deaths, overdoses, falls from buildings, hypothermia. You name it, I've seen it. You will too."

Alec accepted the fact he'd see dead people. All part of the job, and grizzly as the two deaths had been he'd bounced back, cocooned by youthful immortality. But it seemed different for older guys like Ronnie and Superintendent Currie. It was in their glassy eyes and ashen faces, as if death inched nearer at every new exposure, raising questions of their own mortality. Alec wondered if there came a time you'd seen too much.

Ronnie gazed at the gauzy world outside the frosted windows. Probably a trick of the light, but to Alec his tutor looked older in that moment. Tired and beaten.

They'd have continued their watch of the shadows passing the cafe window, each lost in their own thoughts, had it not been for Fitzpatrick's voice on the radio. Ronnie swallowed the last of his coffee, threw a thanks over his shoulder and pulled on his raincoat. It was still wet. They'd been in the café an hour, but the coat had been folded so that when Ronnie stepped outside it looked as though he'd never left the street. There was a shout for a rendezvous, followed by Ronnie's selection of an obscure street name and a long wait while the Sergeant criss-crossed the area in a vain attempt to find them, unwilling to admit his ignorance and unable to locate it in his well-thumbed A-Z. By the time he requested an 'alternative cross reference' they were clear of the café and satisfied the Sergeant had been humiliated, Ronnie finally offered something recognisable.

When the panda drove into the street, it was to find two beat cops whose sodden raincoats were evidence of dedicated policing. The Sergeant smiled the smile of someone who couldn't help but admire the chutzpah of an old hand, but beside him the Inspector sat poker faced and watchful.

Fitzpatrick pulled the car in to the kerb and shuttled it back and forward a little until he was satisfied that it was precisely aligned with the kerb. Ronnie smiled a plastic smile.

"Supercilious wee ginger cunt — gets right on my tits."

Fitzpatrick climbed out and put his hat on with great care. It was like watching a self-coronation, the slow donning of the hat essential to the solemnity of the proceedings, it's presence the beating heart of the discipline code. Satisfied that he'd positioned it perfectly, he strode towards them, a man happy at his work.

"Yet another street I hadn't heard of…building up quite a collection of dead ends and building sites Ronnie. Trying to tell me something?"

Ronnie smiled. You could almost believe it was sincere.

"Not at all Sarge, though I'm surprised you didn't know this place given the presence of that fine building behind you."

Fitzpatrick swivelled. Behind him stood a nondescript single storey building with white cement walls and a grey corrugated asbestos roof. It looked unwelcoming, an effect accentuated by the mesh grilled windows, the heavy padlocked doors and the high metal railings around the perimeter. A flagpole leaned over the doorway, limp Union Jack hanging from the tip. It was a building that possessed the ubiquitous architecture of many others like it, but in case the onlooker had any doubts, thick blue lettering above the door proudly declared this to be the Summerhill Memorial Orange Hall.

Alec tensed. Ronnie was skating on thin ice. Fitzpatrick wore his Protestant credentials on his sleeve and the subject of Rangers football club was the one topic guaranteed to light him up, but to suggest that he was a member of the Orange Order was surely going too far.

Fitzpatrick turned back, smiling and not the least put out.

"A fine lodge that — never gives any trouble."

"Indeed Sarge. I'd guess a few members at Ibrox on Sunday?"

Normally Ronnie would've confided his intentions in advance, all the more to illustrate the cleverness with which he laid conversational traps for the sergeant, but this time he'd pulled a red, white and blue rabbit from the hat and set Fitzpatrick in motion with the subject of the next old firm game. Alec tensed. A warning would've helped. Too late now.

The Sergeant grinned.

"We'll ride the Fenian bastards rotten, nothing better than seeing their fuckin' manky faces trippin' them."

Alec had expected some banter, but not quite this. He made to say something, to steer the conversation somewhere else, but Fitzpatrick had hit the ground running.

"Taigy cunts stink, ever smelled them? Rank rotten."

Ronnie shook his head.

"Can't say I've noticed, maybe I've been upwind."

The Sergeant laughed, a row of crooked teeth capped with nicotine.

"Should fit Parkhead with sprinklers – only time they'd get a wash."

Happy on his favourite subject, Fitzpatrick took advantage of the limitless stage that only a captured audience could provide. Chest puffed out, he addressed them like a bible belt pastor, white-flecked lips and shining eyes, a martinet with trim ginger moustache and whisky-burned face. Religion, it turned out, was his favourite subject.

"The papish cunts can fuck their Pope."

Alec held his notebook open. Maybe the Sergeant would take the hint and sign it, but Fitzpatrick hadn't yet signed Ronnie's and waving it about for emphasis, continued to give the little gathering the full force of his deeply held convictions in relation to Scotland's West Coast Roman Catholics. And Ronnie was happy to steer him along.

"Always some fine communal singing Sarge."

"You've got to be jokin'; that Soldiers Song pish? If the Republic's that precious, they can get on their tattie boats and fuck off back where they came from."

Fitzpatrick brayed like a donkey. Ronnie smiled his polite smile. Alec tried, but his face didn't seem to be working. A few feet away in the patrol car, window wound down, the Inspector watched proceedings with a bored expression.

The Sergeant, ruddy face now lit by the incandescent fire of righteousness, stood at the gates of the Orange Hall preaching to the seemingly converted, eyes shining with the faraway look of a zealot gathering wood for a brightly burning bonfire.

There was little that could be done. It was obvious to Alec that Fitzpatrick had assumed he was Protestant. His surname probably, and as the Sergeant ranted on, Alec came to the conclusion that any intervention now would just cause embarrassment all round. Prospects of completing his probation hung on good reports written by this man and though his silence felt deceitful, almost complicit, there was nothing to do but hope the Sergeant ran out of steam and soon.

It was the Inspector who brought matters to a merciful stop. Wrapped up in his true blue soliloquy, Fitzpatrick had forgotten her and stumbling onto the theme of 'party tunes' had begun to sing The Sash.

"Oh the colours– "

"– John!"

To Alec's relief the Sergeant stopped and pirouetted towards the car. The Inspector wagged a finger.

"John, you've entertained these officers enough."

The look was of disappointment, but the tone respectful.

"Right you are Inspector."

Fitzpatrick signed Ronnie's notebook and passed it back. He winked at Alec as he took his and signed it.

"Right lads, see you at the office."

Fitzpatrick returned to the patrol car and confident that the Inspector couldn't see him, rolled his eyes. They were part of his gang. All together in a protestant world.

The Sergeant ducked into the driver's seat and Alec switched his gaze to the Inspector who wore the same inscrutable expression she always had, but as the car pulled away she looked at him with a curious directness, as if mulling over a discovery and pondering how valuable it was. Alec wondered now if something had given him away and whether anything would come of it.

"That was entertaining. Who knew he was such an arsehole?"

Ronnie pulled at his moustache and grinned a gap-toothed grin but Alec felt wary. The subject of religion and the team you supported hadn't come up in conversation so far and though he'd braced himself for the 'what school did you go to?' query it hadn't happened yet. Ronnie hadn't shown any interest and Alec had been happy to keep it that way. Maybe best to keep the tone neutral.

"Sure was…so…where now?"

Ronnie gave him a funny look.

"Don't take up poker lad, you'll lose yer shirt."

Not for the first time Alec felt wrong-footed. He readied himself for the question, but Ronnie simply sniffed and looked around. The rain had eased and a tattered ribbon of blue sky appeared in the broken clouds above.

"Time to give somebody the jail."

Ronnie pulled a sheaf of warrants from inside his tunic and flicked through them, muttering names as he went. Most were for the Estate of the Isles and hopeful of some action, they set off in that direction, Ronnie whistling a jaunty Gaelic tune as they walked along. Alec was glad the subject had been dropped and Ronnie was his old self again, but he couldn't escape the notion that his Catholicism would be outed eventually and there'd be hell to pay from the Sarge. He looked forward to the warrant enquiries, a chance to show his worth and bank some goodwill.

The incident so preoccupied him that he walked several yards into the estate before he saw them. A line of young men, fifty yards apart, shoulders hunched, walking in the same direction. Another appeared and then a few seconds later a girl in her late teens. They possessed an identikit thinness, heads bowed like penitent monks, faces hidden in tracksuit hoods, hands deep in pockets. The nearest looked haggard beyond his year, emaciated pockmarked face stretched over razor-sharp cheekbones, eyes deep in dark bruised pools. The others looked no better.

Ronnie snorted.

"Junkies parade."

Yet another appeared from around a tower block heading in the same direction. Alec expected to hear a bell and the chant of 'unclean, unclean' echo from the grey concrete canyons around them.

"Where are they going?"

"Tenner bag somewhere up the flats. Back to bed — shoplifting in the afternoon — cash for another tenner bag. Round and round it goes."

The heroin disciples continued on their pilgrimage. Someone somewhere was doing great business. How many lines like this were snaking through the streets of Glasgow that very moment? Patrols of lost souls marching to the same soporific beat. Smack and AIDS and

Hepatitis... Smack and AIDS and Hepatitis...

As ever, Ronnie had a less than philosophical take.

"Lad in the middle looks like one of my warrant enquiries."

Ronnie never pointed. Pointing was strictly forbidden and Alec'd been given a slap on the wrist in the first week for this transgression. Instead, there'd be a warning that someone of interest had been seen and a brief description would follow. A fleeting look was allowed, and then a subtle acknowledgment that the message had been understood.

"Blonde hair, black bomber jacket, white tracksuit bottoms."

Alec scanned the high rises, keen to give nothing away.

"See'm."

"Paul Anthony McGroarty. Two apprehension warrants."

Ronnie gave the neds their full names. It reminded Alec of Porridge and the sententious pronunciation of 'Norman Stanley Fletcher' in the opening credits.

"This's what ye get paid for. Go get him."

The path was curved, its apex drawing close to where he and Ronnie stood, before arcing away across the open ground to the next tower block. McGroarty had long passed that point and was moving further away with each step. It was now or never.

Whether he knew of the warrants, or finely honed instincts picked up the intent, McGroarty chose that moment to look up. Their eyes met for a split second and then McGroarty was off, head back, heels striking his backsides.

There was no starting gun, no whistle, or 'on yer marks'. Alec was still absorbing McGroarty's transformation from deadbeat to athlete as he himself broke into a run, feeling slow, heavy and stupid in comparison.

By the time he'd lurched across the muddy grass and onto the path McGroarty was haring over the open ground to a gap between two high rises and was a sizeable distance away.

It took several strides before he found his rhythm, but as he picked up speed a feeling of elation built, a euphoric fizzing through his arms legs and chest, and with it a hunger to catch McGroarty that was visceral. Each stride launched him faster and faster until he was sprinting at full tilt, the wind rushing in his ears. His vision sharpened, he'd eyes only for McGroarty and nothing else mattered in the whole wide world. Something slid from his head. His hat. He jabbed out a hand and caught it. Up ahead, McGroarty rounded the base of the nearest high rise and Alec raced after, certain he was closing the gap, but when he cleared the corner McGroarty was as far away as ever and sprinting hard.

He dug in, but as they weaved between parked cars, past startled mothers with buggies, it became increasingly clear that this was no sprint and catch and several hundred yards passed with no sign of letting up. They hammered round the foot of another high-rise into a labyrinth of lanes and walkways, feet spanking concrete, the sound magnified by the narrow passageways. Alec's radio squawked with raised voices. Ronnie must have put the balloon up and Bob's voice sought updates, but breathless and lost Alec could do no more than shout he was among the high flats.

They battered through the estate, McGroarty twisting and turning in a desperate attempt to shake off his pursuer, but Alec, heart hammering breath rasping, cursed his quarry and hung on. Multiple voices on the radio, cops nearby, but Alec saw no one; the only cop on planet earth on a mad foot chase after a random junkie around a random housing estate.

McGroarty turned down another alley, this one lined with high wooden fences. Life became a diorama of fragmented images and sensations. The smell of creosote, a lane flanked by tall hedges, terraced houses, teenagers with prams, a barking dog, graffitied walls and 'Fuck The Polis'. An old woman with a tartan shopping bag, a row of shops, some 'skulls' shouting support to McGroarty and obscenities at his pursuer.

He lost all concept of time. A sprint over a few yards had turned into a desperate slog. His lungs ached and his heart felt fit ready to burst. The heavy tunic dragged his arms downwards and his woollen trousers, damp with sweat, clung to his burning thighs. The soles of his feet felt like they'd been whacked with a bamboo cane. Knackered, he caught sight of McGroarty's training shoes and tracksuit bottoms. Lightweight running gear. Wee bastard.

They burst from an alley onto the access road. On the other side lay the boundary wall of the estate and beyond that an ever expanding network of city streets. McGroarty was going to leap the wall and on they'd fuckin' well go, a perpetual footchase around the peripheral deprivation of Glasgow. Fuck.

It was the Number Thirty-Two that changed the course of events. McGroarty, eyes fixed on the high stone wall, hadn't seen it. Alec glimpsed an ashen faced driver and the Strathclyde Passenger Transport logo as McGroarty, belatedly aware of impending doom, desperately checked his course to avoid it. He struck the bus a glancing blow and for a second Alec's heart was in his mouth. There was a brief image in his head of a dead boy on a pavement, but that was something for a parallel universe, for in this one McGroarty bounced off the windscreen and executed a wide parabola that took him back into the estate.

Whether it was the contact with the bus, or a natural consequence of running hard for several minutes, McGroarty finally slowed a little and Alec allowed himself a small hallelujah. Time to try a shout.

"Stop! Yer under arrest."

A raised hand. A prominent middle finger. Wee prick.

From somewhere in the estate, squealing tyres and screaming engines. Police cars, had to be, but Alec only had eyes for the boy in front. They leapt iron railings into a play park, ducked through swings, passed a children's slide and over a see-saw. More railings. More leaping. It was the Summerhill Grand National. He'd be put down at the end of it. His legs felt like blocks of wood and he was close to throwing up, but he was inching closer.

As they ran around another tower block, McGroarty threw out a hand to grab the corner of the building, slipped, missed, righted himself and disappeared up a stairwell. Alec followed the hoarse breathing up several flights of piss-scented stairs onto a veranda that stretched along the face of a high maisonette. McGroarty was still jogging, but he was spent. There was nowhere to go but along the veranda, or onto another flight of stairs and neither had the strength for that.

From far below, the sound of vehicles skidding to a stop. Alec managed a grim smile. His first chase, his first capture. He'd only to close the gap, reach out, bring the boy down and it would be over.

It was then he noticed the doors. Spaced at regular intervals along one side, each recessed within a small porch. McGroarty fished inside his jacket. A key? Did he live here? Alec tried to speed up, but could do no more than put one foot in front of the other and his heart sank with the dread that his quarry would disappear through one of them.

McGroarty never saw what sent him crashing to the deck. To Alec, the sudden appearance of a black trousered leg and highly polished boot was no more surreal than anything else offered by the preceding ten minutes, or indeed the way in which the portly body to which it was attached stepped from porch to veranda and looked down upon the prostrate body of McGroarty with an air of feigned indifference. Ronnie placed a foot gently upon the back of his kill and striking the pose of a big game hunter, twirled his moustache. Alec would've laughed if he'd breath left to do it. Ronnie cocked a thumb at the next porch.

"I'd work on yer fitness–wee shite nearly made it."

Alec, doubled over, hands on knees, heaved air into fucked lungs. The polyester shirt beneath his tunic was soaked. He'd stink later but was past caring. He'd run the boy to ground and that's all that mattered. Desperate to avoid throwing up he staggered to the balustrade, leaned over and drew in the cool air. Thirty feet below, a crowd had gathered round a huddle of police cars. Some of the shift were pushing people away, one or two had their sticks out. It looked hostile.

There were footsteps on the veranda and Alec turned to see Stevie and Charlie appear from the stairwell. Stevie grinned. Charlie looked relieved.

"Thought we'd lost you there."

Ronnie nodded in Alec's direction while he dragged McGroarty to his feet.

"Aye, but we'll need a new probationer. This one's burst."

More cops. Sandy the big Ayrshireman and behind him, Harry. Both slowed when they saw it was over, but it was clear from Harry's flushed face that he'd been running for some time. Sandy smiled and gave a thumbs up. Harry sniffed and turned his attention to the mob gathered below.

Keen to get their prisoner to the van, they led McGroarty down the stairs. His mother, a skin and bone woman with thin lips and a high-pitched voice appeared above them, jabbing a finger and shrieking obscenities. Harry and Sandy stayed to hold her back, but her voice followed them down the stairwell.

"Fuckin' bastards, leave that boy alane. He's done fuck all - whoremaisters that's whit ye's ur!"

More people had appeared in the street and there were faces at various high windows. The odd profanity was shouted from a safe distance and a nappy thrown from the top storey of the block opposite. There was a huge bang and a wet brown crater on the van roof, followed by sporadic chants of 'black bastards', but for the most part the onlookers stood with sullen expressions as one of their own was put in the van and taken away.

McGroarty for his part was sanguine. The warrants for his arrest had been live for several months and when Ronnie read over their contents in the relative tranquility of Corsair Street's charge bar he shrugged.

"Dae the crime, dae the time."

For Alec, there was a strange feeling of anti-climax. The thrill of the chase had dissipated and looking down at the thin figure beside him he felt no joy at having arrested him. McGroarty was a prolific thief, the warrants were for a series of housebreakings and he deserved the jail, but as Alec removed his prisoner's jacket with leaden arms it was hard to get the feeling that he'd made the world a better place.

The Custody Inspector read over the rights. McGroarty, standing in tracksuit bottoms and Celtic top, answered the questions before they were finished. He'd heard it all before. Formalities concluded they were about to lead their prisoner to the cells when Fitzpatrick appeared at the counter and leaned over.

"Another Taig bites the dust. Plenty of room here for shite like you."

The transformation was instantaneous. Alec had a good grip of McGroarty's arm, but the sudden lunge seemed to have caught Ronnie off guard. McGroarty's hand lashed out like a snake and struck the Sergeant just below the eye. Fitzpatrick let out a cry and fell back. Ronnie quickly regained control of the wayward arm and they wrestled the screaming McGroarty down the cell passageway as Fitzpatrick screamed obscenities behind them.

"I'll see you later ya wee fucker!"

McGroarty writhed and twisted all the way down the passageway. Ronnie talked in his soft low voice but it had no effect and it was with some difficulty they cast their prisoner into his cell and slammed the door shut. Alec made his way back towards the charge bar to McGroarty's echoing screams and the loud bangs as he threw himself at his cell door.

Ronnie was angry.

"Like I said. Hate that wee bastard. A supercilious fuckin retard."

"Me too."

Fitzpatrick was back on his feet at the charge bar. A red lump had appeared below his left eye and there'd be a peach of a bruise later. Alec suppressed a feeling of satisfaction. Never rile a prisoner, was one of Ronnie's maxims. If the battle had been won, there was no need to rub it in. Fitzpatrick could've done with a few days working with Ronnie.

The Sergeant looked rattled and his lips were flecked with white.

"I want that wee shite charged with police assault and Alec, you're doing the case. Have it on my desk by end of play. Ronnie, have more control of yer prisoner, you should know better."

Ronnie held up his hands in a show of contrition.

"Sorry Sarge."

Alec watched the Sergeant disappear into the back office. Fucking great. Two hours to do a custody case because the twat wanted to play the big man. Beside him, Ronnie leaned on the charge bar and shook his head.

"That's us off the street till the end of the shift."

Alec skipped tea break and bent himself to the task of writing the report. It was simple enough, but Fitzpatrick would want it perfect. He'd almost finished when Ronnie appeared, a mug of tea in one hand, a bacon roll in the other and some sage advice for good measure.

"Remember, Fitzpatrick's pride's been hurt and he'll want to overdramatise it. He'll no' want references to what kicked it off. Leave that out."

"But—"

"Never mind the buts, just hold yer nose and hand it in."

Alec wrote the report as Ronnie directed, but it stuck in his craw and every now and then the conversation at the rendezvous echoed in his mind. The words of a bigot. And he himself a Roman Catholic too. Was he really going to be complicit? As he mulled over the injustice of it, a plan formed. It was risky, but what the fuck, it took at least a year for most cases to get to court. And if it never went ahead at all?

Fitzpatrick was in his office, a wet cloth held against his face. Munro, cigarette in hand was reading a paper, a mug of coffee on his desk. Alec handed over the paperwork and stood back. The Sergeant read the report line by line. A few words were crossed out and some others put in, but he looked pleased.

"Excellent. Take it to the typists. Case management will send this off with McGroarty in the morning. You've done well."

Alec took the report and left. The typists were just along the corridor and there wasn't much time. A few yards short of their door he ducked into an empty room and extracted a sheet from the case papers. He crumpled it to a small ball and from inside his tunic produced another, sliding it carefully in place of its predecessor. Another summary of events, one that described the situation exactly as it happened. Heart thumping, Alec walked into the typist room and placed the report in the in-tray and that was that. If Fitzpatrick found out, there'd be dire consequences but in that moment Alec felt that he'd changed the world in a small way and it felt good.

Ronnie was in the canteen, cigarette in one hand, mug of tea in the other. Alec took a chair opposite. It felt strange to be there when the room was empty. Normally it was full of noise, cigarette smoke and the cut and thrust of a card school. A well-thumbed pack of cards lay on the table.

"Was surprised to see Harry."

Ronnie looked confused.".

Why?"

"Well, what with the complaint, just thought he'd be the last guy to show up."

Ronnie just shook his head. He looked weary.

"For someone quite bright ye can be quite thick."

The old cop heaved himself around and pointed his cigarette towards the window and the city beyond.

"Anytime, out the blue, you could be up to yer neck in shite. A moron with a knife, pub rammy, gang fight, young team givin' you a kickin'. There's only you, me and a few others coverin' thirty square miles of Glasgow. If the public knew how few cops there were they'd shit themselves. It doesn't matter whether somebody hates you, or you hate them—when the chips are down, we all weigh in. There's nobody else."

Alec looked out to the tower blocks of the estate, silhouetted against the late afternoon sun and thought back to Harry's rant in the locker room weeks before. Then, it felt like the words of a bully. Now, it sounded like a universal truth and it had been a relief, despite the bad blood, that he'd still help when it was needed. If there was a sense of honour lost in the interview with the complaints investigators, some had been regained in the chase with McGroarty and the realisation he wasn't alone after all.

They made their way downstairs to the de-brief, Alec reflecting it hadn't been a bad day if you discounted Fitzpatrick's rant at the rendezvous. In any case the wee prick had gotten his comeuppance. That was some whack McGroarty gave him. It was surprising Ronnie hadn't been in control of the prisoner, for an experienced hand like him to be so lax. Alec replayed the moment in his mind's eye. The sudden flash of the arm, the lightning-swift strike, the absence of struggle preceding it. An arm free to move in a powerful jab, an old cop with his hand by his side.

Surely not.

If there'd been an opportunity to quiz Ronnie it was lost in the friendly chaos of another stand-down and the quick exit of Corsair Street's finest into a Summerhill afternoon. Ronnie left before Alec had hung his tunic, leaving his protege to work out for himself that there was more than one way to skin a cat.

Saturation

If the incident with McGroarty had provided some unexpected excitement, the remainder of the week proved an anti-climax, although not altogether fruitless. Alec had learned some new tricks. The art of whistling bird calls as they entered each common close, a technique used by the neds to signal the presence of a friend and a series of secret knocks on tenement doors that were mostly guesswork. To Alec's surprise one rat-a-tat guddled another fugitive into eager hands, but that had been their only success. For the most part Ronnie had resorted to threats to kick in doors because 'we know you're in there', but no sound ever came, no key in lock, no pale face presented themselves for arrest.

"They'll get a weekend lie-in and they know it. No point flogging a dead horse."

The warrants were put away and when they stepped onto the beat that Thursday morning, it was to have breakfast in the box and see out the last day of the early shift in peaceful harmony with the world. Some ambling around, some chat with the few locals willing to chat back and a coffee at Giacommo's.

That'd been the plan, but they'd no sooner reached their first port of call when they were directed to another, Ronnie cursing the uncivilised hour and Alec resigned to the familiar twists of fate as Bob's perpetually weary voice relayed the concerns of an old lady who'd got no reply at a neighbours door.

Ronnie groaned.

"You know what that means."

He knew fine what it meant, but he made his way to the house hoping it was a misunderstanding. Deafness perhaps, away visiting family, there could be all sorts of reasons.

The house was a four-in-a-block cottage flat, one of hundreds huddled round a small but steep hill, the quiet streets arranged in concentric rings, neat gardens of trimmed lawns, heather rockeries, borders of rhododendrons and azaleas. Alec made his way up the incline to the sound of lawnmowers and Ronnie's laboured breathing.

An old woman waited for them up a short flight of steps. She wrestled one hand over the other as she talked about her downstairs neighbour, an old friend not seen for three days and who'd not been 'keeping well'. Alec looked over to the front door. A stuffed letterbox vomited junk mail onto bottles of milk, their foil tops pecked by birds. Ronnie, still out of breath, pointed to the drawn curtains of the downstairs windows.

"Any lights last night?"

The old woman looked glum and shook her head. Alec felt the nudge at his arm.

"Give the door a knock."

"And if there's no reply?"

Ronnie pursed his lips.

"Kick it in."

Alec tried the doorbell, but there was no response and when he removed the mail from the letter box he was confronted with a dark smell that made his head jerk back. Ronnie, noting the involuntary reaction, led the neighbour away, suggesting she make a cup of tea. When he returned, his face was set in resignation.

"Might as well get on with it."

"Do we have permission?"

A snort.

"I've just given it."

Alec was still getting used to the difference between the procedures taught at Tulliallan, and the semi-autonomous habits of old-school cops like Ronnie, but in this case it was clear cut. No Sergeant would tell them to walk away from this.

He stepped towards the door and landed a heavy kick on the centre panel. The door shuddered, but the only change was the appearance of a dirty shoe print on the white PVC surface.

Ronnie shook his head.

"Two steps back - big step forward - kick above the handle."

This was harder than it looked. Alec took a deep breath and struck the door with malice. There was a loud bang and it burst inwards. The ching of something metal hit the floor and then silence. He stood aside to let Ronnie past, but the old cop smiled.

"You seem to have it well in hand."

Alec had only gone a few steps when it overtook him. In all the years that lay before him he'd never describe it adequately. It's putrid uniqueness, it's corruption of the senses, an alien stench that filled nose and mouth and wakened a primal urge to retreat, to heave, gag, retch and vomit. A thick cloying miasma of rancid meat, rotten fish guts and sour milk. A viscous musk of Satan's shit regurgitated by a parliament of maggots and embroidered with a beguiling syrupy scent that seduced the senses into tasting the corruption again and again, teasing them into the irredeemable foulness so that the retching longing to retreat would return with vengeance in a never-ending loop.

He stopped, bent over and tried to gather himself as his breakfast lurched around his stomach, but as he drew breath the waves of nausea struck again and he was forced to suppress each violent heave with Herculean effort. He inhaled in shallow sips, hoping to limit his exposure somehow, but this failed and his next steps were a triumph of will over instinct. It was hot. Someone had left the heating on and as he entered the living room the putrid stench intensified, though he could see nothing to explain it. At the far side, a door opened to a small bedroom, bed empty, bedsheets cast aside. On the other, a closed door with a square panel of dimpled glass in the upper half. A light shone inside.

He reached for the handle and turned it.

The door swung open to a small bathroom, complete with standard fixtures and fittings. Alec guessed it had been floored with linoleum, but it was impossible to be sure for it was submerged beneath a thick layer of blood, set like rust coloured jelly. Here and there, ragged chunks of flesh broke a gelatinous skin shining dull beneath the wan light of a naked bulb. The surface was undisturbed save for two ragged arcs, like the wings of bloody snow angels, thrashed side-to-side at the toilet bowl sending thick splatters of blood onto the side of the bath and the skirting boards. Within this bloody mess, frantic motion stilled, a pair of blood-soaked feet splayed at the ends of two stick-thin legs, each leading upwards to a cheap dressing gown it's faded cotton hem matted with blood. The thin form of an old woman was huddled over a toilet bowl filled to overflowing with the same visceral stew of flesh and blood that covered the floor. Her bone-white skeletal hands gripped the blood soaked rim. Bluebottles crawled over her fingers. She kneeled, slumped to one side, held upright by the toilet and the wall next to it. Alec couldn't see her face, for in the moment of death her head had slumped forward and lay submerged in the bloody soup. At first he'd been convinced it was a murder scene, but the contents of the toilet and the desperate tableau of thrashing feet told Alec clear enough that she'd died vomiting up the contents of her own internal organs. He was still coming to terms with this when a hand pulled him back and Ronnie stepped forward to take a look.

"Jesus Christ – what a way to go."

Alec was struggling for words. The obvious seemed easiest.

"Poor old cow."

"Aye…She could've flushed though."

Alec looked down at the thick expanse of gore. He'd no desire to intrude upon it but felt the question needed asked.

"Shouldn't we at least check — just in case?"

Ronnie shook his head.

"Be my guest, but the average woman has nine pints of blood and she's donated most o' that to the floor."

Alec felt Ronnie's arm across his chest, guiding him away.

"C'mon, it's fuckin' horrendous in here."

They opened the windows and left in the hope the smell would dissipate. Alec had little confidence it would.

Ronnie updated the control room with his usual sardonic wit, while Alec spoke to the neighbour, as much to get enquiries started as remove himself from the horror. There were no expressions of surprise when he broke the news, though he'd taken care to leave out the grim details. The deceased had been ill for years and on medication for a stomach ulcer. She'd drunk too much and smoked too much. There'd been a husband who'd died of cancer and a daughter in New Zealand who never wrote.

He noted the depressing details and returned to the house. The smell was less intense, but it was still there and the reacquaintance renewed his gagging reflex so that he had to stand in the hall for a few moments before going inside. His tutor raking through the drawers of an old bureau had evidently acclimatised. Piled on a coffee table were various certificates and assorted medication. Ronnie pointed to the bottles and cardboard boxes, head still buried in the bureau.

"It's no' a wonder she died, it's a wonder she lived."

"Neighbour says the same. Massive ulcer."

Ronnie grunted.

"Ye can add angina, rheumatoid arthritis and a stroke to that."

The bathroom door lay open and Alec's thoughts returned to the body draped over the toilet, the desperate convulsions and thrashing legs, the fear and loneliness of her last moments. What had she felt as her body convulsed again and again and helpless to stop it, blood hot in her mouth, choking and gasping, she'd spent her last minutes in terror? Alec didn't think himself religious. Any sense of that died the day they'd buried mum, but the same questions returned to him now. Was there really a God, and if there was, why was He so cruel? Was He bored with immortality and turned to dark invention for self-pitying amusement?

The rest of the day played out much the same way as the others. The casualty surgeon, a man who'd seen it all, pronounced life extinct from the bathroom door, but busy with other deaths across the city the shell would take longer than usual. Ronnie went back on patrol with a promise to get the report started, leaving Alec to wait for the undertakers arrival.

Several hours passed before an anonymous black transit van pulled up at the house. The undertakers, black suits and black ties, polite but reticent, pulled covers over their polished shoes and retrieved the body of the old woman with quiet efficiency. Alec watched as they straightened the stiffened limbs before placing the body inside a thick plastic bag sealed with a heavy zip. He felt undeniable respect. What a job.

A council joiner arrived and Alec watched him secure the front door before joining the undertakers in the waiting van. As they navigated their way off the hill, Alec tried some conversation, but the undertakers placed no value in small talk so he turned his attention to the world outside his passenger window.

The route to the mortuary took them through the city centre. It was a sunny afternoon and Alec gazed at the new restaurants and bars, designer clothing stores and upmarket hi-fi shops. Young women peered through plate glass windows at the latest sales, while sharp dressed men, chins up, strode to upmarket offices on Blythswood Square. Buskers played Dylan to the indifference of material girls, while men in flat caps sold the Evening Times on street corners, their calls unheard by loping students wired to Sony Walkmans. A bearded man in a filthy suit slept in a doorway, piss coursing from splayed legs, while far above on a domed rooftop a neon sign advertised the delights of Bell's Whisky. The town looked threadbare in places and the mixture of old and new gave the city a schizophrenic quality. It was in a state of transition and Alec could see that it was incomplete. Would it ever be? The van glided past renovated buildings with sandblasted stone and smoked glass facades, past abandoned department stores with trees in the gutters and 'To Let' signs on the upper floors. At the Tollbooth Bar a group of men jabbed incoherent fingers at each other for the benefit of a toothless audience, while beyond them stretched the Gallowgate and its sullen congregation of low rent pubs and pawn shops. Through it all, in plain sight but unseen,

Alec and the undertakers drove onwards with their cargo of the dead like the secret police of the underworld. They turned down towards the High Court and through the gates of the single storey red brick building that was the City Mortuary. A smartly dressed woman appeared at the rear door and directed Alec to a small room lined on two sides with uncomfortable chairs. A vase filled with fake flowers sat at a frosted glass window and there was the smell of cheap air freshener. After a few minutes a pale young man, hair in a pony tail, King Crimson t-shirt half hidden under his lab coat, led the way down a broad corridor and through a doorway draped with the thick clear plastic strips seen in abattoirs. The post-mortem room, cold and austere, clad to shoulder height in white glazed tiles. Three post-mortem tables were spaced at regular intervals down the centre of the room, each made of stainless steel. Manufactured of the same material and taking up the length of one wall, large metal doors rose from floor to ceiling. Alec remembered his previous visit when, with other recruits, he'd watched a pathologist open one at random and selecting a drawer from a tower of three, slid out a tray containing the naked body of a young woman. A suicide who'd drowned at the suspension bridge. In his mind's eye Alec could see her still. The room smelled as it had done then; of the dead, mixed with the chemicals and fluids used by the morticians. It was unpleasant in a way he couldn't put his finger on, but then, it was a world removed from what he'd endured earlier.

The old woman lay on her back on one of the tables. Alec was surprised to see that her face had been cleaned. A pale green cover had been draped over her body and her washed feet lay astride the fluted channel down which fluids would drain when her post-mortem was performed. Not that there'd be much left to drain. The attendant removed a wedding and engagement ring from a wrinkled finger and placed them on a tray. Alec put them in a clear plastic bag and produced a label for the attendant to sign. And that was that. No fanfare, no minutes silence, no pause for effect. Across the room, a cat with glossy black fur and sleepy eyes stretched on a tiled window sill while wraith-like figures shape-shifted window-to-window beyond the frosted glass.

It was mid-afternoon by the time Alec made it back to Corsair street. The shift had gone, their weekend already begun and Alec changed in cloistered silence, a far cry from the earlier pre-muster banter and the chat about a shift night out; Sandy and Ricky trading insults with Harry about his shagging prowess and the low rent nightclub they'd end up in. There'd been no invitation to join them and unwilling to embarrass himself by asking he'd kept his own counsel. He'd be heading to Auchenbreoch the next day and despite the downsides that entailed there'd be a night with the gang and Margo's wedding to look forward to. In fact, he was relieved there'd been no invite. He was in no mood. The death of the woman had affected him in a way the others hadn't and in a reflective state of mind he made the journey home in a state of exhaustion that lent itself to auto-pilot driving, only briefly interrupted by a stop at the local supermarket. Had they been interested; the casual observer would've noted the pale young man in black trousers leave the shop with a laden carrier bag. The trained eye would've counted the wine bottles within it.

Dislocation

Alec dropped his bags on the floor of his old bedroom. His head hurt and his shoulders ached, not from the weight of the bags or the frenetic drive down winding country roads, but from the accumulated abnormalities of the past four weeks. The bottle of red the previous night hadn't helped either. He'd intended a quick hello and out again, but instead of Dad's antagonistic welcome there'd been the offer of dinner. The rich smell of steak pie wafted through the house and with it a memory of Saturday dinners with mum and dad, plates perched on knees, watching the 'A Team'. It would be home made, and though he dreaded another stilted conversation there was no way he could refuse.

Two places had been set at the dining table, complete with cork mats and wine glasses. Quite the occasion; though once Alec sat to eat there was little interest in how he was doing. Instead, he got the benefit of Dad's abridged updates on the various happenings and occurrences since he'd last been in Auchenbreoch, as if to remind his boy where his roots lay. There was initial comfort in the familiar, of small town life going on as it ever had, but there was also a sense of loss and a feeling that he was a non-combatant observer in the affairs of others. It surprised him that such a sense of dislocation should happen in such a short time and he tried putting into words what'd happened in his new life, but however hard he sought an opening gambit it eluded him and bereft of the words to explain the awful start he'd made, or the gross abnormalities he'd witnessed, he left the stories where they lay. Another time perhaps. Over a pint maybe. It was time they put aside their differences and set the world to rights over a beer.

And then the moment slipped away. Dad gathered up the plates and declared 'you're doing the washing up, it's no' a free hoose', rough humour lost among the gruff words. It was hardly a ticker-tape welcome, but as he stood at the kitchen sink Alec wondered at the subtle change in atmosphere, consoled by the effort Dad had made in making a meal, knowing it was one he'd enjoy. There were all sorts of ways you could call a place home and in that moment perhaps he'd found another. He was still mulling this over when there was a shout from Dad that he was 'going out' and the front door slammed shut. Oh well. He put the last of the plates away and contemplated his own plans, a night out with the gang at The Volunteer and a chance to get some things off his chest. He looked at his watch. An hour to kill. Keen to avoid the town until his rendezvous, he struck out for the end of the street, a dead-end marked by a dry-stane dyke and a wooden stile. It had been the border between street football and bigger adventures when they'd been kids and, ignoring his mother's warnings to stay away from the fields, it had been his first act of rebellion, of pulling away from her orbit, childhood games giving way to long walks across the moors and fishing the lochans. It was where they'd smoked their first cigarettes and at fifteen drank their first illicitly procured lager. Buoyed by nostalgia, Alec climbed the broad flank of the Garrioch Law, past hawthorn hedgerows, up through a sprinkling of rowans and sleepy faced cows to another dry-stane dyke that marked the line between pasture and moorland. The hill had been his Everest and Wild West and though it seemed smaller now, as he looked down on the town, once the epicentre of his life, it still looked miniature. Though now, it wasn't just a reflection of distance but perspective. Auchenbreoch no longer held what he needed and the sun around which he'd once orbited now gone, he was spinning outwards unsure of direction or destination.

Across the glen, on the far side of the town, the giant 'A' frame of the pit stood silhouetted against a setting sun. A muscular construction of iron, four broad feet planted over the hole in the ground marking the entrance to Auchenbreoch colliery, the spoked wheels at its apex hauling men hand-over-fist from the bowels of the earth where they'd hacked out the coal that fired Longannet Power Station. Within the hour, fresh from the showers, their cars would appear on the road from the pit, most no longer living in Auchenbreoch they'd be pedal-to-metal towards the bigger towns further out.

In the way that a mariner seeks out familiar landmarks, he scanned the rooftops of the town, seeking the house in which he'd been raised. In a place where the roofs all looked the same, it was a case of finding the street and counting chimney pots until he got to the seventeenth. Checking the back garden for the greenhouse confirmed it.

Seventeen Bevan Place and a childhood marked by continuity and stability, until the night Dad brought darkness into the house with the news of mum's cancer. 1984. The longest year, where he'd been forced through some cockamamy mawkish idea of Dad's to protect Mum from the truth, the stress of living that lie, watching her fade away, determined to get better and full of hope 'til the obvious overtook her and a light that once burned brightly, guttering when the brutal realisation dawned. A year in which Dad pulled strikers from the earth while Mum, a dying star, fell toward it, her last breath drawn as the strike ended. Death and defeat in equal measure, a period of recrimination and consequences in more ways than one.

A chill wind blew up the slope. It drew Alec back to the present and looking at his watch realised he was going to be late. Retracing his steps down the hillside he passed the house without once looking toward it and deep in thoughts of a recent past, headed into town where for a nice change only two people crossed to the other side of the street on seeing him. One of them shouted 'wanker' though.

The gang had arrived in The Volunteer before him. Waves to show he'd been seen and a synchronised raising of half empty glasses to indicate what was required. Alec ordered a round and squeezed into the booth. Andy, Tam and Mick, a miniature Mount. Rushmore of heavy rockers with majestic long hair and black leather jackets. Alec passed the palm of a hand over his crew-cut stubble. Three months ago he'd looked just like them, an easy-going scruffiness that was part natural and part affectation, his tight jeans, baseball boots and tour t-shirts a gentler kind of uniform.

He'd arrived in the midst of a competitive conversation about the family trees of rock bands and as he listened to the familiar jousting he leafed through the card index of police stories in his head looking for the best one to start with. He'd leave out the incidents with Harry and Sean Burke, but there was plenty to tell. All it needed was some curiosity on their part, some casual question about the job and then it would tumble out and he'd get things off his chest. Sitting amid the fog of cigarette smoke and the rumble of communal conversation in a busy pub, Alec realised how badly he wanted to receive the wisdom of old friends.

There had been the usual chorus of 'hi's' and 'great to see you's' but there were no follow ups, or eagerness to hear what he'd been up to. The chat moved onto who was shagging who and the subject of jobs, or the lack of them, something that particularly exercised Tam who stared into his pint and announced that he'd been 'let go' from a factory in

Kilmarnock. The round of commiserations received a shake of the head from Tam.

"They're no' bust, they're uppin' sticks to England."

A raised eyebrow from Andy.

"Ye moving south?"

Tam looked like he'd been accused of eating babies.

"Nae chance. Price of rents doon there? Jist have tae see whit comes up."

An exchange of looks between Mick and Andy. There were few jobs left. Certainly not in Auchenbreoch. Tam's, like so many others had gone south or overseas, the state sponsored economics of the labour years washed away by the new ideology of the free market.

Andy had fared no better. A degree in chemistry but now washing windows after the nylon plant had closed, waiting for an 'upturn' that was never coming. Alec felt uncomfortable. Mick was unusually quiet.

The conversation lingered on the depressing subject of sticking it out or moving away, but Auchenbreoch was all they'd ever known. They'd grown up in a town where the only change had been the decline of the once busy Main Street. They'd gone to school together, explored the moors behind the town, gone through the same rites of passage, but now forces they couldn't see or control were moving them in different directions and a gloom settled among them.

Mick chose that moment to make his big announcement.

"I'm moving out."

Tam, mid-pint, wiped the froth from his beard.

"Fae yer folks hoose?"

Mick's eyes moved from face to face, looking uncertain.

"London."

The sounds of the pub rushed in around them. London. Four hundred miles away. The other side of the world. Andy stared at Mick with a look of bewildered incomprehension. Tam looked sceptical.

"Christ, that's desperate."

Mick looked like he didn't believe it himself and was still coming to terms with a giant leap for mankind.

"Everything's fucked. You can stick it oot and hope something happens, or take destiny into yer own hands and seek yer fortune elsewhere."

Andy laughed.

"You getting' on yer bike?"

Raised eyebrows all round and a sour look from Mick. They all recognised the Norman Tebbit speech. The only time folks had moved away before this had been to serve in the war, and here was Mick the living embodiment of the brave new age. He drew his shoulders back, offended by the reference and keen to justify his reasons.

"Ah've got a job in the stock exchange."

That hung in the air for a few seconds. It sounded impressive, outlandish even, and Alec worried that Mick was making it up to cover embarrassment for something more menial. Tam clearly thought the same.

"Stock exchange? The place where guys jump up and doon, holding bits of paper?"

Mick nodded.

"Ah've an uncle in Gravesend works in a bank. He's got a mate who works in the city and he'll show me the ropes."

Stunned silence. Hard to believe Mick would be a guy in a striped shirt, like the ones jumping about on the telly, a nightly fixture on the 6 o'clock news. The stock market, the new drama in a world fixated by money. Boom and bust, rise and fall, a new age of opportunity and speculation. It seemed implausible that a boy from a quiet mining town could be part of that.

Tam raised his glass.

"Well, if yer goin' to be one of thae yuppie pricks, ah'll have a double whisky and coke."

Mick's response was to say 'fuck you', but he went to the bar anyway while Alec listened to the post mortem between Tam and Andy with a feeling of shame. He'd thought himself the main event not realising he'd not be the only one going through change. They all were, and with a sinking feeling he recognised that life was moving onwards and outwards, and nothing would be the same again. The idea that Auchenbreoch would always be there, a touchstone and source of reassurance, like a lowland Brigadoon, was simply that, a fantasy.

Someone put money in the juke box and there was a communal groan as Ghost Town began to play. Tam muttered something about 'reggae shite' and there was a whip round so that he could 'right a wrong' by ensuring the pub would be entertained by Motörhead and Deep Purple for the next hour. Mick returned with the drinks. It was only then that Andy looked up, as if suddenly remembering Alec was there.

"Awright for you, one of Maggies boys. Beat up any prisoners?"

Had it come from anybody else Alec would've taken offence, but it was Andy's way of making sure you didn't get above yourself, something that Alec didn't mind. Kept you grounded.

"Maggie disnae pay my wages Andy. And before you start, I didn't swear an oath to the queen either."

Andy raised his pint. "Amen to that brother."

Tam returned looking gleeful.

"Never guess what ah jist learnt?"

Mick raised a brow.

"Yer ten times table?"

This was ignored, Tam knew something they didn't and he wasn't going to be derailed. He looked around expectantly but said nothing. Alec threw his hands up. Tam could be infuriating.

"We're all ears."

Tam hunkered down, head drawn into his shoulders as he leaned over the table.

"Remember Sean Burke fae school?"

Alec's insides took a tumble. Mick was first to reply.

"Used to be good mates wi' yersel Andy."

Andy looked sour.

"'Til he fucked off tae uni. Never heard from again. A decent wee spud though."

Tam bobbed up and down like a puppy.

"Well, ye'll never guess what happened to him."

Alec had no idea how he was supposed to react. There was no way he could discuss the case and admitting he knew something would open up an almighty can of worms. Across the table, Mick and Andy were taking the piss, determined to make Tam work for their attention.

"He's grown another cock."

"Joined the galactic federation?"

"He's found Shergar."

Tam let it all wash over him satisfied he had their attention. As the suggestions petered out he moved in for the kill.

"Sean's been given the jail."

Andy went wide eyed.

"Sean? No way. What for?"

Tam grinned. This was the best part.

"Serious assault — on some lassie… and assaultin' the polis."

A sip of the pint. A wipe of the lips.

"But, it's a fit up. He wis in the wrong place, wrong time and they arrested the wrong guy. Sean defended himself fae wrongful arrest and mair polis arrived mob-handed and he got a kickin' fur his trouble. Hospitalised."

Mick looked grim.

"Didn't have much time for Sean I've got tae say, but that sounds terrible."

Murmurs of discontent around the table. Alec sat dumfounded. That the subject had cropped up in the first place was tricky, but that it had become this bent out of shape was unbelievable. Andy, as ever, focused on the most salacious aspects of the drama.

"Who was the lassie Tam?"

Tam shrugged.

"His burd…going to her rescue or something."

It was all Alec could do not to laugh. Sean's violent outbursts, the big gob of snot he'd spat at the girl. A knight in shining armour right enough.

Tam spun on. Apparently, the girlfriend had tried to intervene and prevent Sean's arrest, but Sean had insisted she stay out of it. For Alec, there was no longer any surprise in the story. Sean had been bright enough to know word would get out and he'd got in first with his own version. A bit of him applauded the creativity. He was lost in his own thoughts when someone gave him a nudge. It was Andy.

"What do you reckon Alec? Sounds bad. Fitted up like that."

Hell's teeth, what can you say? Too much and it looks like you know too much, avoid the subject and it looks like you're hiding something. Best play a straight bat.

"Sounds a bit exaggerated. Folk make things up to save face don't they?"

Mick nodded. He'd never been a fan of Burkey, but Tam wasn't about to let his scoop fall flat; this was big news, it had to be true.

"Nae offence Alec, but a bunch of violent bastards they Glesga cops. Widnae think twice. Burkey wis awright; no' everybody's cup of tea, but he'd never harm a fly."

Mick produced one of his sage nods, a man of the world who could see the truth in all things.

"Got to say I'm with Tam on that. That'll be you in a few years Alec. Once a cop and all that."

All three looked at him as if picturing that eventuality. It stung. Alec gripped his pint and smiled back. The need to tell the true story grew strong, but he resisted. It was more than his job was worth. Instead, a more spiteful thought took hold. Let them wallow in ignorance, with their small town attitudes and small minds.

Andy stepped into the momentary silence.

"Ah think yer being a wee bit rough there Mick. We've known Alec for how many years? Seventeen? There's no way ye'd dae a thing like that, would you Alec?"

Alec gave Andy what he hoped was his best death stare.

"Do you really need to ask?"

Andy smiled.

"Naw. Still the same Alec. Shame about the G.I Joe haircut though."

Alec passed his hand over his head again.

"Saves on shampoo."

Some banter broke out. A slagging match over haircuts and music. The ice had broken and though there was a bad taste in his mouth Alec wanted very much not to lose his friends. He got up to buy another round, but when he returned Tam and Mick had gone leaving a subdued Andy alone in the booth. As Alec rested the pints on the table Andy pointed to the back of the hotel and the pool room.

"Mick's challenged Tam for a game."

Alec eased into the booth. Andy slid around beside him.

"Never mind thae two. Just pumping their gums, they mean nae harm."

"I know that Andy. No harm done."

Silence. There was something else coming. Alec waited.

"Alec. Was wondering if you could help me oot with something."

Here we go.

"Oh aye."

For a moment Andy looked uncertain and Alec thought he was going to change his mind, but then fishing inside his jacket pocket Andy produced a torn square of paper and having smoothed it out, slid it towards him. A line of letters and numbers was scrawled across it. Alec felt his stomach tighten.

"Is that a car reggie number Andy?"

Andy nodded.

"Ah've been offered a wee motor, dirt cheap, but it's one of the McGill's that's selling it."

"McGills? What the fuck Andy—"

"— ah know, ah know."

Andy's face went pink and he looked down into his pint.

"Ah'm rooked Alec. Ah need a motor if ah'm going to get a job and this is really cheap."

"Probably cos' it's a ringer. It'll be a two-for-one."

Andy didn't need telling. In a town as small as theirs just about every act of thievery or thuggery could be put down to one of the McGills. Now they were moving up in the world and ringing cars. But Andy, hooked on the idea, wasn't letting go.

"I'm sure it's fine Alec. Black XR3i, in good nick and if it's legit, it'll be a steal."

The irony of the last words weren't lost on Alec who had a sinking feeling that what was going to be asked of him was potentially illegal and definitely compromising.

Andy, who'd had come this far, wasn't for turning back.

"Ah was thinking you could do a wee check on the police computer. If it's legit, nae harm done, but if it's stolen, you've solved a case and you'll be in the good books."

Andy pushed the paper closer.

"All I need is the keeper's address. My lips are sealed."

Alec wasn't sure what to say. There was no way he was checking this car on the PNC. He'd been left with no doubts at the college the penalties for contravening the Data Protection Act. He wouldn't be so much out of a job as in the jail. He looked at the scrap of paper for a few seconds before shoving it back. There was no way of sugar coating this.

"Sorry Andy. It's more than my job's worth."

Andy looked up, hurt and betrayal in his eyes. The paper was scrunched up and shoved back in his pocket. Another big gulp of his beer and he was standing up.

"Mick's right, once a cop, always a cop."

With that he shouldered his way through the crowded bar and disappeared towards the exit.

Alec slumped into his seat. The tension of earlier returned and he was surprised to find that his heart was racing. He was still turning over the event in his head when Mick and Tam returned, broad smiles falling from their faces as they noticed the absence of Andy. Mick nodded at the half-finished pint.

"Away to the bogs?"

"He's fucked off."

"Something you said?"

"That would be one way of putting it."

They sat down, a look of confusion on both faces. Tam slid in but not quite as far as Andy had. The physical separation was telling.

"What happened then?"

Alec wondered if it was fair to tell them but given the atmosphere over the Sean Burke affair the last thing he wanted was another issue to put a further wedge in their friendship. Anyway, they were used to confiding in each other's fuck ups.

"Andy asked me to check out a motor. I'd get sacked, so I told him and he stormed out. Obviously the car means a lot, but there's no' much I can do."

Mick and Tam shared a conspiratorial look and smirked. So, there was more to Andy's story than met the eye.

"Ok, enlighten me."

Tam was more than happy to oblige.

"Andy's got girl trouble."

"What's that got to do with a motor?"

Tam had that 'fuck's sake can ye no' guess?' look on his face and all at once Alec got it.

"It's not for sale is it?"

Mick grinned and gave a slow hand clap.

"Well done Sherlock."

"And by girl trouble, you mean she's fucked off with somebody else."

"You'll be a detective yet."

"And the new boyfriend drives an XR3."

Mick nodded.

"A black one. Very nice too."

Alec shook his head. Thank christ he hadn't taken up the request. A scene flashed in his head. Andy on some blokes doorstep, a black XR3i parked outside. An argument, a punch, a screaming ex-girlfriend. And then questions. How did Andy know? A quick audit of the PNC and bingo, Constable Alec MacKay.

He should've felt angry, that an old friend would compromise him for something so banal, but it was sadness he felt most. His job was asking questions of friendships in ways he'd not expected.

Mick and Tam filled in the rest of the story. A long-term girlfriend

Alec had never met, a cooling down, arguments and a bust up. Rumours of a guy in a nice car and Andy's obsession with finding where he lived. Tam thought it hilarious.

"Andy's turned into a fuckin stalker."

Mick laughed.

"He'll grow out of it."

There was a shout of last orders and Mick looked at his watch.

"The Crown's open till one. Anybody fancy a stroll?"

They drank their pints and left. The Crown was busy and though he bumped into some old faces Alec's heart was no longer in it. It hadn't helped that one of Dad's old buddies had staggered in pissed and sought him out in the crowded bar. A jabbed finger in the chest and the immortal words 'ye'll never be half the man yer dad is.' But he'd heard that stuff before and out of loyalty to Mick and Tam he'd stuck it out til last orders and then made his excuses, promising Mick he'd be there for his leaving do.

The route home took him by the river. It was raining again and the unlit path, potholed and uneven, was pitted here and there with deep puddles. It turned a routine walk into a watery Russian roulette. He lost. Twice. And so it was a cold and sodden Alec who stripped for bed, thoughts consumed by the strains in a once seamless life.

Compromise

The Glen Garrioch Country House Hotel, three miles out of town, was the place to have your wedding. Set in acres of manicured grounds and surrounded by mature woodland, it had once been the grand Georgian residence of a wealthy Glasgow tobacco merchant, but with a rectangular block added to the rear, it was now a spa hotel with an all-purpose function suite, containing a very large bar and parquet dance floor.

Alec had lost count of the number of times he'd been there. Eighteenth birthday parties, anniversaries, retirements and weddings, though he hated the latter, especially when only invited to the evening reception. He felt like an intruder gate-crashing a party in full swing, everyone in a happy equilibrium that his arrival disturbed in some way, like a ripple in the force.

He'd not seen Margo for years. Not since her first love, Kenny had died. A soldier who'd survived two tours in Belfast to be killed by a sniper on his third. Kenny had been one of the quieter ones who'd sat in the assembly hall during careers week in fourth year when an army major tried to sell the positives of being a soldier in the British Army to shouts of 'Up The Ra' from the dafties in the back row. But Kenny saw the writing on the wall when rumours about the mine began to circulate around town and he'd signed up to the Royal Highland Fusiliers, an outfit described by Dougie at the police college as a 'bunch of fucking nutters'. For Kenny, it had been a one-way ticket and Margo had been in bits, but here she was, a year later, hitched to someone from Kenny's platoon. Alec wasn't sure who Margo was marrying, a lad from Pollock, or the ghost of Kenny. As he slowly made his way among the circular tables he saw the groom surrounded by skinhead boys in parade uniform, their laughter cutting through the din of the wedding band, faces flushed, collars unbuttoned.

Alec scanned the function room for Margo. He had a present to offload before he found his feet among the hundreds assembled around the hall. He found her making her way through the tables, pretty but harassed, casting occasional glances at her man. Any other time he'd have got a huge hug and that typical Margo grin, but tonight there was only a quick thank you and a peck on the cheek. As his cousin made her way onwards, stopping at the occasional table on a trajectory that would take her towards her pissed-up man and his pissed-up buddies, he felt sorry for her. Every table was full except for one at the back in which friends of Margo's side of the family sat in conspiratorial familiarity. There was an empty chair and a brief look of interest but in essence he didn't fit the company and after a few minutes of small talk Alec made his excuses and headed for the bar. He passed Dad sitting with aunts and uncles, jacket off and tie discarded. He looked well oiled, but it wasn't so much the large whiskey and empty pint glasses that gave the game away, as the rosy cheeks and cigar. He only smoked when he got drunk. Alec waved but, glassy-eyed, Dad hadn't seen him and happy to escape a meaningless catch up with his aunts Alec pushed on, promising himself that he'd have a couple of beers, chat to one or two cousins and then sneak away.

When he reached the bar, it was four-deep with flush-faced men jostling for position, each shouting orders over the heads of others. A wiry frame squeezed through, sharp elbows and a solid shoulder that wedged openings through the press of bodies like an arctic icebreaker. A cheeky wee bastard skipping the queue. Alec tapped him on the shoulder.

"Whit's yer hurry?"

Alec realised his mistake as soon as the queue jumper turned. The uniform he'd missed in the gloom, but the broken nose, scarred cheek and army haircut telegraphed the presence of one of the squaddies well enough. He was a foot smaller, but of the kind that viewed a taller opponent as a fair challenge. He looked up with glazed eyes and a slack mouth.

"What of it, Jock?"

Straight into challenge mode. And the Jock word, in a cockney accent, guaranteed to piss you off. Alec felt the danger and so did those around him. It was a thing of wonder that no matter how tightly packed a crowd, room was always made for a psycho and from being wedged too tight to do anything stupid, the squaddie suddenly had all the room in the world. Still, no point in backing down. Just encourages them.

"Calm doon. You'll get served soon enough."

A finger jabbed at his chest. Intensely annoying.

"I'll do as I fucking well please. Jock."

Alec wasn't afraid, his new friend had enough second prizes to suggest he'd more bravery than skill, but he didn't want trouble either. It was a long shot, but maybe some kidology would work. He tried a winning smile.

"It's the bar staff you want to watch out for. Piss in yer pint if ye piss them off."

The squaddie's head performed a quick swivel towards the bar. When it snapped back he wore a smirk.

"Maybe they need some discipline".

The last word was accentuated, in a way that left no doubt what discipline meant and a dull weight nestled into the pit of Alec's stomach. There was no reasoning with the victim of a humour by-pass. For this guy everything was a challenge.

It was hot, a sticky oppressive heat that added to that pressure cooker feeling of hovering on the cusp of fight or flight. Alec's body thrummed and with a sickening feeling he realised he was on the edge of lashing out. There was the added spice of all those squaddies in the far corner in his peripheral vision, standing like Meerkats and facing his direction. This wasn't going to end well.

Help often comes in unexpected forms. There was a waft of floral perfume and then Margo, a vision in white, appeared between them. She put an arm around the squaddie who, flummoxed by the affection of a woman, looked confused and uncomfortable. As if to drive home her advantage a light peck on the cheek was administered before she pointed to Alec.

"Tony, you lovely boy, I see you've met my favourite cousin, Alec?"

It was all that Tony could do to admit he had. Margo, warming to the task of making introductions, carried on as if they were at a tea party at Holyrood Palace. A very loud one, with a rock band in attendance.

"Alec this is Tony. Tony's in the RHF, aren't you Tony?"

Tony nodded glumly.

"Tony, this is Alec. Alec's a cop in Glasgow."

Oh shit. The hate re-surfaced on Tony's face. Probably a ned who'd escaped a life of crime to join the army. Back to square one then. Tony was keen to emphasise the point.

"Old Bill are hated down my way. Useless cunts. Paki's and Dago's do what they fucking like. Bill's scared to touch em - race card every time." Great. Racist and a psycho. Margo smiled her best smile, but Tony was locked on. Target acquired. It didn't stop Margo from trying.

"Now Tony. Not like that here. Alec's cut from different cloth, isn't that right Alec?"

Conscious that Margo was desperate to avert a confrontation he nodded, but never took his eyes off the squaddie. There was a feeling that a punch was imminent and he badly wanted to miss it. Tony smirked and pointed to the door.

"Fancy a word outside?"

It was funny to hear the universal invitation for a 'square go' couched in that way. Almost polite. Suppressing the urge to smirk Alec almost accepted, but a more forceful Margo put a lace covered arm between them. Even above the din, there was no mistaking the change in tone.

"Right. That's enough. This's *my* day and I'll be dammed if you two fuckwits are going to spoil it."

She'd inserted herself between them and turned her head towards Alec with a quick jerk of her head towards the bar. It was less busy now.

"I'd get that drink."

Alec took the hint. The hunger to fight had ebbed away and he wanted nothing more to do with it. Looking down into the glazed features of rat faced Tony, he understood where the term cannon fodder came from. It was there, in the form of a violent wee bastard who probably picked a fight wherever he went because he was useless at everything else. An empire had been built on brainless fuckwits like him. Alec extricated himself and got his pint. As he wound his way back from the bar he saw that Margo had cajoled a reluctant Tony onto the dance floor and there, among the swirling masses, the spasmodic jerking figure of a pissed cockney danced in a vain attempt to replicate the graceful steps of his white clad partner. Alec watched the carnival of excess and gave thanks that a small disaster had been averted, but he couldn't escape the conclusion that he'd have to calm down in future; find a way of dealing with guys like Tony. The idea was a gloomy one, but he'd have to turn the other cheek from now on, anticipate trouble and steer clear, for encounters like this seemed to go with the territory. The incident with Andy had driven home the differences that could open up between old friends, but the spat with Tony revealed the social minefield that lay before every meeting with a stranger. It occurred then, that with the tensions in his old life and the new one unfolding in Corsair Street he was accepted in neither.

The band segued into a medley of songs that provided the signal for a mass invasion of the dance floor and the execution of ragged line dancing. Tony, attempting to escape and evade the ranks of pissed up women was dragged into the heart of the square and his obvious misery gave Alec a brief feeling of satisfaction. There was a lounge bar somewhere in the old building. He'd head there to escape a similar fate.

He'd just reached the exit when there were shouts and a crash from somewhere behind. The band stopped and Alec turned to see a group of men in a circular melee of arms and fists. As women screamed and others tried to prise the men apart, the band stacked their instruments and rushed forward as men from surrounding tables did the same. But, with a sense of the inevitable, those arriving to stop the fight got struck by wayward punches and they too became embroiled, so that the small nucleus got bigger until a western saloon bar brawl was in progress, with more screams and upturned tables. For a moment Alec thought it had been Tony in the epicentre, no doubt starting his ritual conflagration, but as the group momentarily disassembled Alec saw to his horror that it was not

Tony who'd kicked it off.

Centre stage, staggering amid a knot of drunken middle-aged men, the broad-shouldered figure of Dad held his own, blood trickling from the corner of his mouth, fists taking lumps out of whoever was within reach. Somewhere in the mix were the squaddies, Margo's man leading the way.

The fight had now assumed the power of a black hole, sucking people towards it. A scattering of women stood on the periphery, among them Margo, mascara running down her face, her mother, hat battered and torn, leading her to the exit.

Alec looked over to the bar. The staff were young, no more than nineteen and he felt sorry for them as they cowered behind the counter. One, a bit older than the others had reached for a phone and was dialling a number. Time to leave.

There was no possibility of extricating Dad. Men peeled away, noses and mouths bleeding, but those that remained looked like Custer's last stand as others in the wedding party circled in a vain attempt to pick others out and pull them from the battle. Alec downed the rest of his pint, collected his coat and left.

As he walked across the car park he pulled his collar up against the rain and left the bright lights of the hotel behind for the pitch darkness of the country road. Three miles away, half obscured by the downpour, the dimmed sodium streetlights of Auchenbreoch shone through the murk. Then more lights, imperceptible at first but growing brighter, twinkling blue, swinging left and right in tune with the scalloped contours of the land. As they came closer, Alec could make out the sing song tone of sirens. There'd be more coming from the other direction.

He almost turned back. Maybe he could pull Dad clear, perhaps explain away his behaviour, that he hadn't been right since mum's passing. But in his heart of hearts he knew it was too late and he'd likely get arrested too. As the first police car roared past, he kept his head low and pressed on.

When he woke the following morning, it was to the smell of whiskey and the acrid reek of cigars. There was no need to check the bedroom, the smell was enough to confirm Dad had escaped arrest somehow and unbelievably had returned to the house without disturbing anyone. Alec silently opened the door to find Dad spreadeagled on his double bed, face down, fully clothed, the occasional snort the only proof of life. Satisfied he'd survive, Alec closed the door, made breakfast and packed his bags. There seemed little point in waiting to hear the skewered version of events. There'd be recriminations for not backing him up when the 'chips were doon' and Alec wanted to be spared the tenuous excuse for why the fight started in the first place.

He stuck his head in the living room to make sure the fire hadn't been left on and saw the large manila envelope on the coffee table. His course photograph from the police college. It had lain there unopened for a month. Oh well. Gently closing the front door, he climbed in the car and eased away from the house glad to be free of it.

The streets were quiet as he drove along Main Street and along the winding road out of town, upwards past the reservoir to the low-lying hills and moors behind Auchenbreoch. Ahead, a series of winding country roads that would converge on the main road to Glasgow and an uncertain future. As he crested the final rise above the town he took one last look in his rear-view mirror. A narrow strip of housing, compressed between hill and colliery, Auchenbreoch shrank and then disappeared.

Transition

If the weekend proved a depressing disappointment, it was nothing compared to the ongoing trials and tribulations of life at Corsair Street. Archaic forms and procedures reminded him there was still much to learn and much to be corrected. Battling against piles of paperwork, it felt as if he was stuck in a never-ending flow of low-level crap while his radio bristled with the kind of calls he longed to be part of. Housebreakings, stolen vehicles, robberies ongoing. There were also days when he trudged about with Ronnie making small talk while the radio stayed silent and the world took a break away from death, violence and thievery. On those days he felt his little boat had not yet joined the river of life; caught in an eddy, circling around and around and going nowhere.

But there were other times, when he stood on the steps of the station and felt a low-level tingling anticipation of the unexpected and unforeseen; when the calls came thick and fast as soon as he'd stepped onto the broad pavement. Then, time was liquid pouring through his fingers, an ocean swell of drama that threatened to inundate him. There was an intoxicating randomness to it all. No guarantees that any day would turn out as expected.

The overt hostility of the shift had receded to some degree, but he was little more accepted than before and he wondered if that would ever change.

Auchenbreoch remained a part of him, but Summerhill was becoming an ever more intrinsic part of his life. Its streets and the faces of those who lived in them formed the background hum of his existence as each new incident revealed a hidden corner or peeled back a façade to reveal lives hidden from the everyday. And though the city remained in general a foreign land, he knew this would change and that at some point he'd be expected to take on his own beat and stand on his own two feet.

Ronnie had less than a year to retirement and among the fatherly advice and old cop war stories there was an increasing preoccupation with overtime and the effect it would have on his pension. The lugubrious Ronnie of a few months back became the guy at the head of the queue for football duties and a willing witness to all kinds of incidents as long as they gave him a 'speaky' at court. Court citations preoccupied the whole shift for they generated overtime. A quick leafing through diaries to check if they were 'payers' and groans when they were not. There had been the arrest of Sean Burke and many others; street brawls, gang fights, family disputes and domestics, but none had yet yielded him a citation, leaving him unblooded in the arts of giving evidence. A question mark therefore remained over his ability to 'speak to things'. It was right of passage he'd yet to pass and for that reason, as much as the bad start with Harry, he remained an outsider, the butt of occasional jokes and the victim of the card shark mentality at tea breaks.

There'd been a university reunion, but to his dismay the few months as a cop had put clear blue water between his new career and the emerging professional lives of old friends. They'd been friendly, but he was no longer one of them and while their onward journeys in life represented continuity, his was a radical departure from a future they'd once shared. He'd struggled with the anti-police rhetoric when the drink flowed and as the evening drew to a close he felt as if he was looking through the plate glass window of a department store, and on display was an alternative life, one he could've been part of if he'd made a better choice. There'd been hugs and waves when they'd parted and cries of 'we must do this again!', but as Alec waved through the steamed-up window of his taxi he knew this would be the last time he ever saw them.

The social circle that emerged was that of his fellow recruits, scattered about the force, who came together every few months for probationer training at the force training centre. A chance to enjoy the camaraderie of those in the same boat. Stories of their own trials and tribulations helped support the idea that it was a case of keeping his head down and ploughing on. But there'd been troubling news too. One of their number had been assessed as 'unsuitable' and shown the door via the dreaded 'Regulation Twelve', confirming the journey to permanent cop was not a foregone conclusion and added to the feeling that his own situation was a minefield to be traversed with caution.

There were occasional phone calls to Dad as much to confirm they both still existed. And the once-a-month Friday night with the gang that reinforced how much he was peeling away from Auchenbreoch like old paint. Mick left as advertised, his night out coinciding with a Saturday late shift for which Fitzpatrick refused time off, something that resulted in an off-hand 'cheerio then' when he'd phoned Mick to explain.

Sergeant Munro retired. There were sarcastic comments from many who'd thought he'd retired years before, but Alec was sorry to see him go. Munro had been a quiet man who'd kept things ticking over with a steady hand, a counterweight to the abrasive Fitzpatrick. How would Fitzpatrick behave without the steady hand of Munro?

His worries were given added spice by news the Inspector had passed a promotion panel and awaited her next posting. Nothing stayed the same it seemed, an observation given further credence by the arrival of a new probationer, a rugby playing law graduate from a private school who rejoiced in the name Stewart Duncan, a back-to-front name that cemented his middle-class credentials. Alec had given thanks to the gods. Someone new, who'd stick out like a sore thumb amongst the grizzled old cunts on the shift who'd hoot and laugh at the mangled vowels and snotty attitudes. He'd would no longer be the whipping boy.

But, to his dismay, the new guy fitted in just nicely. Despite his toffee nosed and mangled enunciations the shift loved him. He was a curio to be metaphorically turned over in their hands and examined. Tea breaks morphed into the Duncan show as he was verbally prodded by all and sundry about what it was like to be posh and Duncan. And Duncan laughed along with the humorous insults and sarcastic jibes. He took everything thrown at him with good grace. Duncan was a good sport and Alec watched with growing bitterness as the love-in spread to the supervisors who reflected in the glory of having a law graduate with the right social credentials in their midst. Here was a go-getter destined for greater things, someone who was just 'passing through'. To add insult, Duncan was put in the fast response car, the better to accrue the maximum amount of experience before the inevitable grooming for stardom. Alec didn't get it. Glory had been bestowed on Duncan simply because of the way he spoke and the circumstances of his upbringing. He'd thought class differences had been swept away by the new order and its suggestions of success for those who worked hard enough. It was all bollocks. With a degree of bitterness he recalled Dad's rants at the dinner table about class. Back then he'd written them off to the inverted snobberies of a disappearing world, but now he could see that it still very much counted and his growing ire was cemented by his continued status as the 'boy' despite Duncan's arrival. He was man enough to acknowledge this was no fault of Duncan Stewart, but the subservience of his own class, so easily seduced by those who possessed the social qualifications of their 'betters'. A public school education, a plummy voice and a law degree from Glasgow University was all you required to make good. That, and a Dad who was local councillor on the Police and Fire committee. But the unfairness was a spur. If he was going to make a success of this policing life it would be through hard work and competence. He'd earn his way. He'd show the world how great he was.

The chance would present itself, but not in the way he'd imagined

Repercussions

It was an early shift and the muster was packed. Alec walked into a thick smog of acrid cigarette smoke, and the sight of every seat taken bar his own. He'd expected the usual raucous atmosphere, but instead there was an air of hushed expectancy as if waiting for a performance to begin. He sat and waited for the supervisors to arrive with a sense of unease he couldn't quite place.

At seven precisely the Inspector entered, confident in her authority, smiling at the packed house. Fitzpatrick followed, folders under each arm, full of his usual self-importance. They sat, Fitzpatrick placing the files before him in their proper order and then with exaggerated solemnity opened the file that contained the shoulder numbers and the beats assigned to them. In preparation for the usual, Alec wrote Ronnie's number in his notebook and was poised to enter the beat details when Fitzpatrick looked up for the first time and made an announcement.

"The Inspector and I have decided it's time for a few changes."

There was murmuring and shuffling in the chairs around him, but Alec was relaxed. This wouldn't apply to him.

The new arrangements were read out to a rapt audience. A change of scene for Ricky and Sandy who were now 'neighboured' together. Some cursing from Sandy but it was apparent both welcomed the arrangement, though it was hardly good news for the residents of one and two beats. Three and four beats. Alec began to write the numbers down, but the numbers that followed were not his, but Ronnie and Stewart Duncan's. Someone snorted.

Fitzpatrick read on, working down his list in monotone. More beat numbers and new partnerships, some welcomed with sarcasm, some with stony silence. Charlie and Stevie kept the van but the other mobile patrols had new crews and as a consequence some beats had ex-drivers. An outbreak of hilarity when Harry was paired with Gerry who'd a reputation for doing things entirely by the book, something Harry deemed worthy of comment.

"Don't worry Gerry. Ah'll make a cop of you."

Barbed comments from Gerry. Others joined the joust; this was the pairing of the day and there was something salacious about the neighbouring of two cops so different from each other. A pairing guaranteed to produce sparks and Fitzpatrick would know it. Alec wondered why he'd put oil and water together like that. More beats, more shoulder numbers, but still no sign of his own. With growing unease Alec realised that of the beats as yet unallocated, two lay in 'The Reservation' the most deprived area of Summerhill. Four beats. Three cops. Who'd be his new neighbour? Who'd get the reservation? A puff of cigarette smoke wafted past his left shoulder and the voice of Harry whispered.

"Brace yersel."

Someone sniggered and when Fitzpatrick announced the pairings for the next two beats, it was to confirm what Alec had begun to suspect in those final few seconds. With five months on the street, barely nine months in the job, he was the beat officer for the reservation, and he was on his own.

Fitzpatrick looked at the bemused assembly. Happy with the effect he'd produced, he selected a file containing the crime reports and incidents of the past twenty four hours and began to read them out.

Stunned by his sudden change in status Alec began noting down the beats he normally walked with Ronnie, a habit that he'd only recently cemented. Harry's voice came snaking over his shoulder again.

"They urnae yours anymore."

Stifled coughing from a few places in the back rows.

Alec's face grew hot, but he kept his head down, scored out the entries and waited for the stats on his new fiefdom. But nothing much was said about the reservation. Nothing much seemed to have happened there and Alec wondered if its reputation had been exaggerated. Maybe it was a quiet corner to cut his teeth, a place to find his feet. If he could avoid making an arse of himself, he'd get one of the better beats next time.

The post-muster air was thick with chatter and casual insults, but Alec was in a bubble, preoccupied with the day ahead and how he'd cope on his own. Some of the old cops gave him a pat on the shoulder and there were words of encouragement from Ronnie and Stevie, but there was the odd shake of the head from others who considered it an affront to the sacred status of the beat man that someone so young should be elevated so soon. And then of course there was Harry, smirking as he left for a day of mixed personalities with Gerry, throwing a comment in Alec's direction as he passed through the front door.

"Good luck young blood. Yer gonnae need it."

Alec smiled back and gave a thumbs up, determined to look like he'd taken it as sincere goodwill, knowing it would annoy Harry no end. Fitzpatrick appeared, as much to chase the stragglers onto the street as anything else, but he took the chance to slip some words Alec's way as he too made for the outside world.

"Last time Celtic won the league the Reservation was awash with tricolours. You'll be right at home there…"

And in that moment Alec knew he'd been outed but there was nothing he could say. His elevation to beat man would be represented as an acknowledgment of good progress, even if it was anything but. Sink or swim, it was up to him. But how had Fitzpatrick found out? His thoughts must've betrayed him outside the Orange Hall after all. Had the Inspector spotted something? Whatever. He had no intention of asking. That would only make things worse. Alec met Fitzpatrick's gaze, nodded, and walked out into the cold damp of a late autumn day with a growing sense of determination. If this was Fitzpatrick's idea of a laugh, then bring it on.

The reservation was an amalgam of two areas known as Barnhouse and Woodmill, covering two low hills to the north of Corsair Street, notorious for gang fights and drug dealing. He'd heard it talked about often enough; the squalor of the housing, jokes about wiping your feet on the way out, female and child unit visits to daughters being shagged by their fathers. An area besieged by rampant alcoholism and drug abuse. Not a month went by without a shooting, or a knifing for a drug debt. Alec had often poured over the beat map in the muster room, the war stories of older cops in his head as he traced the outline of the area wondering whether the bold beat numbers superimposed on the street grids would've been better marked as 'There Be Monsters Here'.

It was a dark cold morning and by the time he reached the reservation an icy wind had needled its way through his nylon raincoat. A bruised sky had given way to a thin rim of orange on the eastern horizon, the world below it cloaked in many shades of grey.

Keen get a better perspective he climbed the main road into Woodmill through quiet streets of drab housing to the summit of a small hill where slum clearances had left an open area of mud and coarse grass. A small flat-roofed building with bricked up windows and heavy metal doors stood in the clearing looking orphaned in the emptiness. From here, the rooftops of the tenements descended in giant steps, street by street, to a small valley where the main road from the suburbs ran through a deep cut in dark rock. A steep embankment rose on other side, on top of which ran the same canal that passed the house of the shotgun suicide many miles to the south. Here, it descended a series of lock gates, dropping in giant steps before straightening for its journey West to the Clyde estuary.

On the other side stood Barnhouse. Across its broad flanks, long rows of tenements staggered upwards in disorderly ranks towards a dark gothic church whose enormous spire caught the first rays of the winter sun.

Mary of the Immaculate Conception. Built out of all proportion to the tenements around it and beneath its soot-stained honey sandstone there was no doubting the old time Catholicism it represented, or the religious make-up of the area it dominated. It didn't so much sit in benevolent splendour as glower down on Barnhouse with brooding disapproval at the sinners around its feet. The church and the grim village of tenements looked more a medieval township than a housing scheme. If it hadn't been for the brutal architecture and the shit weather it could've been a hillside town in Tuscany. Built on the highest spot for miles it looked down upon a land that fell away in gentle folds towards a city had once resented the flood of Irish immigration to their Calvinist world of factories and filth. From its position on the skyline, it could be seen for miles around, a statement of bullish papal intent. Fuck you it said. Fuck your hostility. Here we are and here we'll stay.

Below him, the main city road struck out for the affluent suburbs, the city bound traffic already reduced to stop-start monotony. Behind, the brick strewn streets were empty save for stray dogs with whip-thin tails. There were few cars in Woodmill and those that were scattered about looked old and battered.

With nowhere in particular to go and no routine to fall back on, Alec wandered around in haphazard exploration. Woodmill was mostly tenements and old cottage flats. There was an abandoned Baptist church, an area of weed choked scrubland where a factory once stood, a row of flat roofed shops and the Woodmill primary school. No old folks homes, no Italian cafes, no police box, no welcome of any sort.

He crossed the rubbish choked canal via a ramshackle lock gate and climbed toward the gothic monstrosity of the Immaculate Conception. It was a similar story in Barnhouse, an area were the tenements had outlived their usefulness, paint peeling from rotting window frames, close doors smashed and vandalised. The gardens, uniformly fenced with metal railings, reminded Alec of that first night with Harry, a dumping ground for wrecked baby buggies, household appliances and needles.

Alec snuck through graffitied common closes in the forlorn hope of surprising someone up to no good, but other than sporadic sightings of early morning junkies and teenage mums dragging kids to school there was nobody about. It was as if the reservation had been leafleted about his arrival and closed shop. The novelty of having his own beats soon wore off and he was no more enthused when he set off after tea break to do it all again. With little option than to restart at the beginning, he retraced his steps to the summit of Woodmill.

This time he found the doors opened at the white building he'd seen earlier. Sounds of Radio One wafted out through the gap. Curiosity piqued, he walked into a small vestibule with posters on the wall about the dangers of drugs. He pushed through more doors to a large square room, cream coloured breeze-block walls lit by fluorescent strip lights. A battered pool table in the centre was surrounded by a group of hard looking young men watching another pot a ball. A Pet Shop boys song blasted from a cheap Amstrad hi-fi. What Have I Done To Deserve This. It pounded out for a few seconds before the only long-haired male in the room walked towards the hi-fi and with deliberate slothfulness, switched it off.

There were groans from the skulls. One of the gang, pool cue in both hands, made the feelings of the team known.

"Fucksakes Robbie, it's just the polis."

Robbie, older than the rest and better fed, raised his hands up by his sides as if to say what else could he do and walked up to Alec a look of weary concern on his face.

"What can we do for you officer?"

The politeness threw Alec for a moment. The lad was well spoken, fresh faced and healthy, in stark contrast to the emaciated boys in cheap tracksuits behind him. Had to be some kind of youth worker, so this had to be some kind of youth club. Best foot forward, could be a place for a cuppa on a wet Monday night and a chance to meet some of the locals.

"Constable MacKay. The new beat man, thought I'd say hello."

Alec held out his hand, but in a throwback to his first night at Corsair Street, none rose to meet it. Belatedly realising that shaking hands with a cop would damage Robbie's street cred Alec withdrew the gesture and turned to the watchful skulls. They hadn't moved an inch since he stepped inside the room and there was something menacing about the frank stares and confident silence that made him wary. Maybe they didn't trust cops.

Maybe break the ice with a game.

"Pool? Used to be a dab hand myself."

Silence. The faces continued to look impassive and remote, and their unity of purpose felt unreal. Most of them, fair-haired, looked like Woodmill's Village of the Damned. Alec scanned their faces determined to show that he wasn't intimidated, hoping they couldn't read his thoughts. He wasn't for giving up yet.

The one with the pool cue looked familiar, as did two of the boys at the back and as they locked eyes it was then Alec remembered; the morning with Ronnie when he'd stood aside to let the smirking skulls past. It was them and Alec's heart sank. Maybe they wouldn't recognise him. All polis looked the same under their hats.

"What's up lads, cat got yer tongue?"

Pool cue boy switched hands so that the cue was in his right hand, the tip pointed towards Alec.

"Yer no wanted here."

So. Leader of the pack. Robbie shifted on his feet but said nothing. Cue boy was in charge. A face appeared behind cue boy's shoulder and a thin nasal voice buzzed over the top of it.

"Like the man says, yer no welcome. We're here to get away fae the likes of you."

Murmurs of agreement around the table. One of the gang shifted his pool cue from hand to hand, a broad smile beneath an unwelcoming stare. Another tossed the cue ball up and down in the palm of his hand. Smack. Smack. Smack. Alec felt the cold empty air behind him. There was no one to bail him out now.

And then, the cue juggler grinned, a row of rotting teeth and a look of recognition in slitted eyes.

"Hey Beanie, it's the lanky polis fae months ago. Hen Broon! How's it gawn?"

Laughter all round, but 'Beanie' wasn't happy his nickname had been revealed. It didn't marry up with his carefully crafted persona.

"Fuck up. Nae names in front o' the polis."

The grin disappeared from the juggler's face and the perpetual motion of the pool cue stopped.

So, he had a nickname. A badge of honour. But the skulls were getting confident and if he let the insults go unchecked the greater the chance one of them would try it on. There'd be no help from Robbie. It was clear the club was run by the gang. Beanie returned his attention to Alec.

"You've seen the place n' we're no doin' nothin'. You can fuck off now."

There was something about Beanie's confident swagger that wriggled under Alec's skin. He'd heard this shit before, a long time ago in the playground of a rough school, the arrogant entitlement of the scuzzer at the top of the food chain. Well, they weren't in school now.

"I'm going nowhere Beanie."

Alec had enjoyed putting the emphasis on Beanie – it would rankle. He pointed at the others.

"And I'm not in the least bit fazed by this bullshit. First to try it on gets the jail."

Beanie smirked and pointed his cue somewhere over Alec's shoulder.

"You and whose army?

Beanie took a step forward. There was less than a foot now between the cue tip and Alec's face. A wintry smile.

"Better toddle off before something bad happens."

The village of the damned closed behind their boss, chins lowered, eyes locked-on under hooded lids, fists bunched at sides. Crunch time. Alec had to admit he felt very exposed, but if he walked away he'd lose these beats forever. If he stood his ground, he'd get a beating. Not a great choice. He wondered if Robbie would at least phone for an ambulance once it was over. There was his radio of course, but as soon as he reached for that they'd pile in. Even if they didn't, what would he say to the control room? Some bad boys weren't being nice? His body thrummed with adrenalin and he focused on stopping the shakes knowing it would be a green light for these pricks and something he'd never live down.

And then, a feeling of separation, of seeing the world from within a capsule in his head, of an inner confidence founded on nothing. He felt the weight of the tunic on his chest and thought of the hard-won reputations built by those who'd gone before him. It brought with it a sense of expectation. Of being compelled. There could never be any possibility of backing down. He'd meet this head on, whatever the consequences. Fuck these wanks, fuck Corsair Street, fuck Fitzpatrick.

"Ok then. Who's first?"

His voice boomed in the room with an angry rasp that seemed to catch Beanie off guard. The others lifted their chins like they'd woken up and Alec turned his attention to Beanie pointing his arm at him as if it too was a pool cue, pleased to see that it was rock steady.

"Acting the big man cos ye've got an army of munchkins behind ye?" Beanie stared back, face flushed, lips pursed, the pool cue poised in his hands as if weighing up his options. Any second now…

"Excuse me, I really don't think this is an appropriate way to engage officer."

All eyes swivelled to Robbie. Alec caught out by the intervention was about to reply but Beanie got there first.

"What the fuck would you know?"

Beanie swept the tip of his cue around the room.

"Is this what we are? Engagement? Some wee tick box on yer CV?"

Robbie, a young man who recognised a mistake when he saw one, had both hands in the air palms outwards, voice soothing and slow like he'd been taught in a training course.

"Now. You know that the council are trying to put something back for the local youth. You should be grateful for that."

Unfortunately, the training course hadn't supplied the warning about pouring petrol on a fire. Beanies eyes bulged, the veins on his temples prominent in the glare of the fluorescent strip lights.

"Local youth? Fucking grateful? There's fuck all here. Nobody gives a flying fuck! Grateful for a fucked pool table in a shitey wee cabin? Get yersel to fuck ya poncy prick!"

Beanie's lips were flecked white. The adrenalin stored up for a fight had found its outlet in Robbie and Alec wondered whether this was the first time Robbie'd experienced Beanie's hair-trigger temper. The blood drained from Robbie's face, evidence enough he'd been here before. No wonder the gang were in charge with this spineless twat in charge. Still, someone had to bail him out.

"Poor timing Robbie. Beanie and I were just beginning to form a beautiful friendship there."

A laugh from the back. Beanie looked confused for a moment before his smirk returned and some of the old swagger too.

"Ah'm picky about who I call a pall."

Alec made a point of looking over the faces around the room.

"I can see that."

A nod. He was being sized up again, but the storm had passed and though he was still very much the enemy the fact he'd not backed down had changed things. Still, best to give Beanie a way out that would save face, the boy had an on-off switch that spoke of psychopath.

"How about a game. You win — I never set foot in here again."

A glint in the eye and a broken toothed grin.

"And if you win?"

It was Alec's turn to smile.

"I come whenever I like, get the benefit of your dazzling wit and a cuppa from Robbie."

Robbie eyed them both, uncertain and confused, trying to play catch up but relieved the prospect of being smacked over the head with a pool cue had receded. Beanie looked at the others who nodded in enthusiastic anticipation. They were keen to see their champion beat the polis.

It was a quick game. Neither were any good and it took a few lucky ricochets for Alec to stay in the game. In the end, a mistake by Beanie left the black hovering over a corner pocket. It crossed Alec's mind to miss it, but such an act would be condescending and worse, the gang would know. Everyone needed a little bit of honour in their lives. Alec sunk the black and waited for the angry retort, but to his surprise there were murmurs of well-played and as he turned to face Beanie a hand was extended in his direction. Something that Robbie had singularly failed to offer. They shook hands, a truce, though Beanie was keen to have the last word.

"No' bad, Hen Broon."

Laughter around the room, but Alec laughed with them. He did look a bit like the cartoon character and he admired the imagination behind the nickname. He'd been called far worse in Auchenbreoch.

"You'll beat me next time."

A smile.

"We'll see."

Others clamoured for a shot at beating the new cop, but Alec sensed it best to get out while he was on top, there was plenty of potential for something to go wrong still. He picked up his cap, said a brief goodbye and turning down the offer of tea from a bemused Robbie, headed into the pale grey light of the afternoon, feeling lighter than he'd done all day. When he arrived back at the station Fitzpatrick was ticking off the shoulder numbers on his sheet. The Sergeant looked up, the flicker of a smile.

"Enjoying your new beats?"

Alec placed his radio on the counter.

"The natives seem very friendly Sarge. Think I'm going to like it there."

He turned away before Fitzpatrick could react, but climbing the stairs to the locker room he pictured the Sergeant's florid cheeks and bunched hands on the charge bar counter.

Last In Line

A quiet week was followed by a quiet weekend, in which he decorated the flat and flushed with achievement, hit the city with Dougie and the others on his probationer course. The next day was spent nursing a hangover at the Kelvingrove Art Gallery, a cultural dip of the toe Mum would've loved and for a moment the pain of her absence resurfaced only to be tucked away again among the stuffed animals and Glasgow Boys. Sunday was a day spent reading books, the peace broken by a call from Dad and an awkward conversation that telegraphed his struggles to broach a difficult subject. Guessing what that would be, Alec tried to steer the conversation to small talk about his weekend. It didn't work.

"About the wedding…"

"Dad, it's ok. Glad you got home in one piece."

"Aye. Well…it should'nae have happened."

A pause.

"When ye comin' doon?'

'Comin' doon'. Shorthand for Auchenbreoch. Where he'd have to endure excuses for what had happened. Fuck that.

"Sorry Dad, it'll be another month til my next weekend off. I'll come down then."

A long sigh and an attempt to regroup.

"Aye well. You know where we are. Don't be a stranger."

And then he'd hung up.

A feeling of guilt rolled into the gap. He felt bad about pushing Dad away but he'd had enough of the past and the awkward social situations with the denizens of Auchenbreoch. He was moving on.

On, to a night shift that revealed the reservation to be a place that hid from the world when the street lights came on. The occasional gang fight dispersed to the sound of approaching sirens, leaving only sticks and broken bottles to prove they'd been there at all. After midnight he had the place to himself bar the odd stray dog and scrawny fox. He wasn't quite ready to admit he was bored shitless but wandering the streets with nothing to do induced a state of ennui. A feeling only relived by the kindness of Stevie and Charlie who occasionally drove through the area to offer a hurl in the back of the van for a while. At times like those he appreciated the camaraderie and the sense of belonging it brought. Nights gave way to 'lates' that began with a wild day in which dark clouds scurried over Summerhill, dumping torrential rain so hard that rivers of brown water tore down steep paths and cascaded over stairways to an unsettled canal. Trudging beside swollen gutters, Alec was transported back to childhood and autumn walks from school, racing lollipop sticks into leaf clogged drains; a warm memory dispelled by the dampness seeping through his raincoat and waterproof trousers. His only respite was a weak cup of tea with an upbeat Robbie at the youth club, who relayed the news that Beanie's gang had moved on and younger kids had taken their place. The council had given money for play equipment. There was a second-hand TV and an Atari console in the corner. There was talk of a bingo night for the old folks and musical instruments for the club.

Tea break brought relief from the weather, but despite attentiveness with a hot radiator, his waterproofs were still damp when he returned to the sodden streets. The radio remained silent, and with there being little point in aimlessly trudging through a wet evening, he resolved to go in early and catch up on paperwork. A day to get over with.

He was passing the hulking edifice of the Immaculate Conception, thoughts on the steady descent to the office, when he got his only call. Thirty minutes till finish time. What was so urgent he'd get a call as late as this?

A death message. Something usually handed out to the early shift. The idea of breaking bad news at this late hour seemed wrong somehow.

"Roger that. Could this wait 'til the early shift?"

The response was predictably unsympathetic.

"Negative. To be delivered without delay."

The address lay within a tenement overlooking the canal and like the rest, bordered on unfit for human habitation. The reinforced entrance door hung on one hinge and Alec wondered whether anyone had bothered to tell the council. It was unlikely. Few had a phone and most relied on the vandalised phone box at the top of the hill.

He walked into the usual smells. In the dim glow of the close light drawings of spurting cocks adorned the walls alongside venerations of the I.R.A. and Bobby Sands. The grit of unwashed stairs ground beneath his feet as he climbed to the first floor.

Alec raised his hand to knock the door, but then hesitated. How did you break such life changing news to a stranger? How would they react? Ronnie had talked about keeping it simple and playing it by ear. That everyone reacted differently. There was only one way to find out how this would go.

Alec gave the door three solid raps. No reply. For a moment he thought of heading back to the office and requesting a delay till morning but having only tried once that felt cowardly.

Another knock. Fairs fair.

His second knock was heavier and painful to the knuckles, but after a few seconds he became aware of a presence behind the door. There was a spy hole and there seemed to be movement on the other side. Then a reedy voice, hesitant and uncertain, with a distinct lilt of the isles.

"Who's there?"

"Mr Gillespie? It's the police."

A pause.

"Yes?"

Alec was impressed by the economy of the question. Why use a whole sentence when one word would do.

"I have a message — but I'm afraid I can't deliver it out here. Can I come in?"

The sound of a chain being slid, a key turning in a lock and then the door opened to a thin old man no taller than five foot four, dressed in black trousers, a crew necked jumper and brown tweed jacket. He gazed upwards with rheumy eyes and a face that had been beaten, not so much by the weather or a local, as by life.

"I suppose you'd better come in Constable."

It was spoken in an accent that emphasised the three distinct syllables of his rank; the slow deliberate speech of a bye-gone age. Alec felt instant sympathy for the old man as he followed him along bare floorboards to a tiny living room lit by a solitary table lamp that cast Dickensian shadows on bare walls.

The flat was cold and the presence of a single bar electric fire did little to take the edge off. Its grill was blackened here and there with what Alec guessed to be the tips of cigarettes lit on the bar behind it. Right on cue, the old man drew out a packet of cigarettes and offered one before kneeling slowly in front of the fire and lighting another. As Mr Gillespie coaxed his cigarette into life Alec looked around.

The room was sparsely furnished, a threadbare couch on bare floor boards, stained here and there with drink and food, so absorbed by the wood they were no longer identifiable. A small table was squeezed into a corner by the window complete with two wooden chairs. The lamp sat on the table, nicotine-stained shade askew. The smelled of damp and cigarettes, of fried food and neglect.

Gillespie sat at the table and drew on his cigarette. A gust blew the smoke in Alec's direction and for the first time he saw the broken window pane through half-shut curtains. A piece of card had been taped across the break, but it had been blown loose and the bottom half moved in-and-out like the gill of a fish.

The old man gestured to the other chair.

"Take a seat Constable."

Alec politely declined. To sit across from the old man would be too convivial, a loss of gravitas, but as Gillespie stared up at him, Alec felt like a child about to perform his best Halloween trick and he'd forgotten something to put his sweeties in. The old man simply nodded.

"I'm guessin' it's bad news."

It was the opening he needed and Alec was grateful for it.

"Afraid so, but first I need to confirm you're James Gillespie and that you've a brother in Vancouver, John Gillespie."

Gillespie nodded again but displayed little emotion other than put the cigarette in the ashtray and his hands on his knees.

"John moved there after the war. Used to write, but I've no' heard for a while."

Ok. There was no other way of couching it. Alec recalled Ronnie's advice and stuck to it.

"I'm very sorry to tell you Mr Gillespie, but we received bad news from John's family that he passed away today."

He readied himself for tears, questions of how and where, background confirmation that his brother had been ill for years, or something of that kind. Instead, there was a long impenetrable silence as Mr Gillespie retrieved his cigarette and stared at the floor.

The response had thrown him. He'd done as he'd been asked and strictly speaking there was no requirement for anything else, but it didn't seem right to walk out on the old man.

"Is there anyone can I get in touch with, maybe keep you company?"

Mr Gillespie looked up as if from a dream and then over his shoulder to a framed sepia photograph on the wall above him. A beach scene with a plump woman in a floral pinny beside a thin moustached man in a flat cap and three boys in shorts and thick woollen jumpers. They stood at the water's edge with islands dotted behind them, a fierce wind blowing the woman's hair over the top of her head, the man pressing his flat cap to his with one hand.

"My mother, father, me; my brothers John and Robert. Arisaig before the war."

Alec took the picture off the wall so the old man could see it better.

"Where's Robert? I could get in touch with him."

A sad smile.

"Unless ye can raise the dead I doubt yer chances. He was killed in action. Italy, 1944."

Alec scanned the wall for pictures of children, or of Gillespie with wife and family, but there were none.

"No children of your own Mr Gillespie?"

A shake of the head. The old man was lost in the photograph, in a place far removed from Summerhill. Alec imagined Gillespie was on a beach in Arisaig, the wind tugging at his clothes, the sun bright upon his face, the smell of seaweed and salt.

"Wife died twenty years ago Constable. Cancer. A son in Australia, but we don't speak. Got his address somewhere."

Alec sat down. His place wasn't at the office, or supplying a brief update to the control room, or heading back to the flat for a cold beer.

"I'm not sure what else I can say Mr Gillespie. I'm reluctant to leave you like this. Isn't there som'bdy in the close who could keep you company for a while?"

A snort.

"Half them are junkies. The rest would steal the shirt off yer back soon as look at you."

Alec took in the bare walls. He'd never seen a place so devoid of furniture or material things. There was no TV and the only concession to the outside world was a copy of the Daily Record and an old Philips radio on the window sill. He'd imagined a kindly old neighbour who'd sweep in, put the kettle on and make the old man a nice cup of tea, but that obviously wasn't happening.

"How about I make a cuppa. Warm you up a bit."

A sour look, another draw on the fag and quick shake of the head.

"If it's alright with yerself, I'll have a whisky. There's a bottle in the kitchen."

The kitchen turned out to be nothing more than a stretched out broom cupboard. An old canvas bag filled with tools lay just inside the doorway, a sledgehammer propped up against it. Along one wall, a few basic kitchen units in fifties shades of cream and turquoise, an old cooker and a small fridge that buzzed in the corner. It smelled of Fray Bentos puddings and lorne sausage. A frying pan sat on the cooker, congealed fat within, grey and opaque.

Gillespie's voice floated in from the living room.

"Up in the wall cupboard son."

Alec swung the doors open. Behind packets of sugar, tea bags and rich tea biscuits stood a quarter bottle of Whyte & McKays and two glass tumblers. They looked clean enough but Alec held them up to the light anyway, the greasy worktops and the linoleum sliding beneath his feet made him squeamish in a way many sudden deaths had not. Again the voice floated through, as if Gillespie could see exactly what he was doing.

"Bring both tumblers."

It was said with a kind of old-time authority, as if the generosity implied by the request would be badly insulted if refused. Alec hesitated. It would be simpler to take one glass, but perhaps it was easier just to play along. There'd be no chance he'd drink anything. Some of the shift took a drink, but he had a feeling Fitzpatrick was waiting for a mistake like that and a return to the office with whisky on his breath would be suicide. Alec placed the whisky and the tumblers on the living room table and sat down. He'd wait for the offer and turn the old man down with rueful apologies.

But Gillespie made no move to pour a drink. He continued to stare at the photograph, his cigarette a burned-out stub, the light from the fire casting shadows across the folds and hollows of his face. A Glasgow Rembrandt.

"Used to be a decent place. When Margaret and I settled here I had a job in the shipyards and she was a pay clerkess in the locomotive works. We took turns at cleaning the close and there was Saturday night dances in the Labour club. There were three picture houses and the city a tram ride away. And a dog track, at the back of Barnhouse, though I never liked the dogs. Gambling's a sin that's ruined many a life."

Gillespie looked up, eyes narrowed with suspicion.

"Tell me yer no' a gambler."

"I'm no gambler Mr Gillespie. I've seen what it can do. Had an uncle with the addiction."

Gillespie held up a hand, like an act of benediction..

"It wasn't all chocolates and roses. Some drank too much, gambled their wages, treated their wives badly, but it was a damn sight better than it is now."

Alec knew the story. He'd heard it often enough from Dad and the news headlines of the last eight years had simply corroborated it. There'd been the miners strike of course. The decline of heavy industry, British Steel and British Leyland, rising unemployment, the need to go elsewhere for work and with it the decline of cohesive working class communities and their sense of belonging. Sitting across from the old man, Alec had no doubt he was looking at one of the last surviving relics of the post war dream.

"Did you miss your brother when he left?"

A nod.

"Broke ma heart. We'd made the move to Glasgow together, the whole family, the whole shebang, squeezed into a tiny flat in Yoker. Saw out the war, but then John found a lass and she wanted out. You couldnae blame her. They offered cheap tickets on the boats - jobs a-plenty, away from the smoke and the grime and the hard times. Would've gone too, but I'd just met Maggie and well, she didnae fancy it."

Gillespie's eyes welled up.

"Would you mind pouring that drink Constable, my hands are no' so steady."

Alec unscrewed the cap and poured a large measure, the liquid glowing amber in the light of the lamp. Gillespie nodded his appreciation and waited, but when Alec put the bottle down without pouring another he looked up with surprise.

"Will ye no' have one?"

The rain renewed its assault on the hillside above. Driven by the wind, it beat a tattoo on the panes of the window. The cardboard flapped and rainwater found its way inside and trickled down the frame. Above, in a corner where the walls met the ceiling, a cloud of black mould and Alec felt a deep sense of sadness. That the old man's life had come to this. In poor health, no friend to comfort him, a son estranged on the other side of the world. He looked at his watch. The shift would be on their way home and it was a wonder Fitzpatrick had not chased him up for an ETA. The thought had no sooner entered his head when Fitzpatrick's voice burst from the radio. Alec imagined him leaning over the controllers shoulder, face burning with retribution.

"ETA Constable MacKay."

Alec counted to five in his head. Keep it professional.

"Still at that call Sarge. Elderly gentleman on his own and no family support. I'll be a few more minutes."

The reply was curt.

"You're no' the social work. Yer on yer own time, understood?"

Insensitive wee prick.

"Roger that. Back soon as I can."

There was no reply. Fitzpatrick would be heading for the exit. Alec looked at the old man and shrugged. Fuck it.

"Maybe just a wee one."

The old man smiled and raised his glass. Alec poured himself a small drink and together they saluted John Gillespie and his brother, and his mother and father too. And with the whisky hot in his chest and warming his stomach, Alec listened to Gillespie talk of an old way of life in Arisaig, a crofter's life, of hard work on poor soil, swimming off the white sands of Morar, collecting shellfish in the summer and fishing beyond Rum and Eigg. Of people he'd known in the shipyards and the friends in Summerhill who'd passed away. And of a wife who was a good woman, who would've loved a new life in Canada, if only she'd seen what his brother John had seen. And in the light of an electric fire and old table lamp, Alec found to his surprise that he was talking too, of his mother, the sense of loss and the uncertain nature of life, of whether he'd made the right choice in joining the police. Mr Gillespie listened, his eyes fired by whiskey.

"Make the best of what you've got Constable, life seldom gives you second chances."

And then, a strong grip on his wrist.

"Don't turn yer back on family. They're all you ever have."

Alec kept his own counsel about family, the old man had no idea about how bad it was with his. He finished the last dregs of the whiskey with thoughts of second chances, knowing he could blowing his first, but he was past the point of caring. The unexpected encounter had taken him outside himself. Nothing like a discussion about life and death in the company of a stranger to open your eyes.

Gillespie finished his drink and reached for the bottle.

"I heard what your sergeant said, there's no point in hanging round here. I'll be alright."

There was some colour about the old man that hadn't been there before. No doubt there'd be private tears, but in his heart of hearts Alec was relieved that Gillespie had ushered him to the door.

"Sure you're ok Mr Gillespie?"

"I'll be fine. You get back to the real world."

Alec placed his cap on his head and reached for the door. As he opened it onto the common close, he felt a tug at his raincoat pocket.

"That's for you."

Alec felt the weight as it slid in and he was impressed by the speed in which Gillespie done it, but there was no way he could accept the gift and he retrieved it with a show of regret he didn't feel. He took hold of one of the old man's calloused hands and pressed the bottle back into it.

"That's very kind, but I'll get my jotters. Raise another to your brother when I'm gone. I've got a beer in the fridge back home and I'll raise one to you."

Gillespie accepted the return with a smile. It was likely an old-fashioned test of some sort anyway and he raised the bottle in salute.

"Can't thank you for bringing me bad news, but I appreciated the company."

With that, he closed the door leaving Alec to follow the light of the street-lamps into a wet winter's night.

When he reached the office he eyed the car park nervously, but the shift had gone and so had Fitzpatrick. He changed in an empty locker room before stopping at the public counter to shout that his radio was there. As the night shift cop walked towards him, Alec gave a wave and headed for the exit. Only when he reached the safety of his flat did he relax and berate himself for taking such a stupid risk. But he followed through on his promise and taking a beer from the fridge, raised a glass to the old man and to families everywhere however bruised and imperfect they might be.

First Cut

There was little said the following day. Fitzpatrick showed more interest in whether overtime had been incurred than the circumstances of Mr Gillespie. Instead, the focus was on the standard of Alec's paperwork, which had 'gone down' and 'was causing some concern'. It was laughable, for his paperwork had improved to the point of needing little supervision at all, but Alec could laugh all he liked. In the following days his reports were returned with petty criticisms and Alec began to worry that Fitzpatrick was engineering a path towards a bad appraisal. It weighed on him throughout the rest of that week as the consequences of his deployment to the Reservation became more and more apparent. Urgent calls, the kind that led to arrests, went to the pandas, leaving him with messages and low-level crap. As a consequence, there were no arrests, or charges to report and his work rate took a dive. Further criticism would surely follow, something he raised with Charlie and Stevie on one of their occasional run-abouts, prompting a solution from Charlie.

"Look. When you hear a shout that needs someone to speak to it, call us up, we'll pick you up en-route — boab's yer auntie."

"What if I come across a fight in the street and there's no call. What then?"

"Just lay hands on them Alec. Folk need to get the jail, ye cannae just stand there like a plum watching folk kick seven shades of shit out of each other."

Alec was certain he could handle himself, though he'd stop at intervening in a Barnhouse gang fight. It was the steps after that were the problem. Once you'd laid hands on someone they were under arrest, but with no witnesses it would be for nothing and maybe even a malicious complaint for which he'd have no support.

"I know Stevie, but no corroboration - case goes nowhere."

An exchange of glances and a sigh from Charlie. A look of admonition and an imperceptible shake of the head from Stevie. A shrug from Charlie. Stevie leaned closer.

"Look. Just shout as soon as you see something. There's a good chance we'll be really close and we'll see most of what you see."

Alec was grateful, but what was being inferred just wasn't worth it and to his relief the subject changed to shift gossip, but when a call for the van brought the pit-stop to an end, Alec recommenced the circumnavigation of his beats reassured that at least Stevie and Charlie were on his side. As the van reversed onto the main road, Charlie wound down his window and gave a thumbs up.

"Remember. Here if you need us."

Alec watched the Cheshire Cat grin disappear down the road before crossing over into Barnhouse. A walk about, a brief stop at the youth club to see how things were going and then tea break. Maybe the second half would bring something better.

He'd just began the steep climb towards the club when his radio erupted into a riot of shouts and strangulated sentences. Bob's voice cut through the melee, his bored tones abandoned.

"Code Two-One! Stations, a Code Two-One! Yankee 42 what's your position?"

Nothing.

Alec stood transfixed. The shoulder number was Harry's. There were incoherent snatches of someone shouting, then muffled and cut off by the voice of another. Screams and curses, and then Harry's voice again, as if coming up for air.

"Gray Street! Gray Stree—"

Harry's voice was cut off again, replaced by a squabble of voices declaring attendance at Gray Street. Bob's voice rode over the top of it all.

"All stations — get off the radio. That's a Code Two-One, Gray Street. Code Two-One, Gray Street."

From time to time Harry's voice burst through only to be cut off again. At times it sounded as if he was underwater. A male in the background shouted obscenities over sounds splintering and smashing. Gray Street was over a mile away, by the time he got there the whole thing would be over, but as Alec listened his heart quickened and he felt an overwhelming desire to go. He was trying to work out his best route when a black cab emerged from a side street.

He'd thought no further than sticking out an arm, he'd no idea what he'd say or if the cab would stop but he needn't have worried. The taxi veered into the pavement, an old man behind the wheel wound down his window and leaned out.

"Officer in trouble?"

"How did you know?"

"Only time I've ever been stopped by a cop. Jump in."

They sped down the city road to the sound of sporadic chaos on the radio. There were several junctions and traffic lights but Alec, carried away by the moment, announced that he'd given permission to break every red. The driver relishing the chance did just that and when they careened into Gray Street less than a minute later Alec shouted his heartfelt thanks and leapt out, the driver's voice faint behind him.

"A pleasure!"

There were police cars everywhere. An eye watering cacophony of blue lights and at first Alec thought he'd been too late, but as he jogged along the street cops emerged from common closes shrugging shoulders and cocking their ears to radios. There was no trace of Harry and the radio had gone silent with only Bob's voice trying to raise him from the dead.

Gray Street was not the simple street Alec had imagined. It was a melange of old tenements, low-rise tower blocks and a clutch of new build red brick houses at its far end, the start of an urban regeneration scheme that had petered out.

Bob continued his attempts to raise Harry without response and with every passing second anxieties grew. Someone asked if Harry had a call in the area, but there'd been none, the 'two-one' had come out of the blue.

Desperate to break the stasis, he stopped at each common close, craning his head to pick up any sounds. It was the only solution he could think of, but it was a long shot and he feared missing the one clue, the one muffled shout or sound that would lead him to Harry. Someone had seen him and a voice shouted across the street to others.

"Check each close! Work yer way down one at a time."

Alec cleared the line of tenements and was crossing the spare ground to the tower blocks when he heard the sound of someone behind him. Gerry, his face beetroot, beads of sweat trickling down his forehead onto a long sharp nose. He was breathing hard.

"I'll join you. Everybody else's checking closes or running about like headless chickens."

"Weren't you two supposed to be neighboured up?"

Gerry looked up at the first tower, brows knitted with worry.

"Harry does his own thing. I take one beat he takes the other."

Alec left it at that. What they did was their own business and the only thing that mattered now was finding Harry.

There were forty-eight flat numbers at the first block. Alec pressed the silver buttons on a large metal plate until someone on the upper floors buzzed them into a foyer that smelled strongly of bleach. Twelve floors in total, they'd have to check each one and his heart quailed at the prospect of having to repeat this at the other blocks. Gerry radioed in their location and their intentions.

"In case we walk into something."

Alec stored Gerry's common sense away for another time while Gerry walked over to the sign with the flat numbers.

"Ok. Lift to the top. Search each landing. Walk down the stairs to the next."

Alec pursed his lips. There was a better way.

"We leap-frog each other going down. One in the lift the other the stairs."

Gerry gave a thumbs up. The lift rattled up to a common landing with a brown door on each side of a communal square. Alec listened at the two he'd picked. Nothing. Gerry shook his head. Alec bounded down the stairs while Gerry took the lift and so it was they began their leapfrogging descent.

On the third floor down Alec sensed something different in the air. It felt heavier. An unnatural stillness that raised the hairs on the back of his neck. Across from the lift a brown door just like all the rest, but with feint boot marks on the lower half. Then a woman's voice, high-pitched and nasal on the other side.

"Tommy, fur goad's sake, put it doon. Let's talk aboot this."

A low growl in response.

"Shut the fuck up. You're next, after 'ave sorted this smart arsed cunt."

Alec held his ear against the door. It gave a little and he tentatively pressed his fingers against it. The door opened further. His fingers trembled with pent up energy. Was this the house, or had he stumbled across something else? And then another voice, lower and calmer. Harry.

"C'mon Tommy, it's a wee misunderstanding. Put the knife down and we'll sort this out."

A coarse laugh.

"Ah understand alright and you're gonna pay for it, polis or no polis."

The female voice again. Sobbing.

"Yer goin' tae end up in the jail, jist let the man explain."

"Whits tae explain? No' a big man now. Nae radio fur help. Jist you and me."

Alec held his breath. He could retreat and shout in his position, but the thought of Tommy attacking Harry while he whispered in a stairwell felt shameful. And he didn't have the luxury of time. He pushed the door open a little further and thanked god that the hinges were silent. A narrow hallway led to a small sitting room. In its doorway, a large broad shouldered man with a long kitchen knife in one hand and a police radio in the other. Beyond the knife man, back to the wall crouched Harry, tunic half open, top buttons missing, police baton up and ready. It looked no match for the long blade in Tommy's hand.

Tommy held the knife higher and took another step toward Harry.

"Let's see who's the big man noo."

Harry moved from foot to foot and readied himself. Tommy's attention was on Harry, sizing up his angle of attack. Alec crept further down the hall, but though Harry must've seen his advance, he gave no sign. Instead, he put on a show of waving his hands, voice raised higher.

"C'mon Tommy. Yer better than this! Let's sort this out another way."

Tommy took another step and knowing time had run out Alec launched himself forward, but as he took that first stride his radio burst into life and cat like, Tommy turned, mouth open, blade raised. It was too late to change course and with Alec's mind lit up with thoughts of knife! knife! he crashed into the solid torso of Tommy and in a mess of arms and legs they toppled over. As they hit the floor Alec felt a heavy shock to his left arm and then a sharp pain before the world dissolved into punches and curses as they lashed out at each other with both fists. And then there was Harry landing his own blows and a flash as the knife spiralled across the room. Supercharged by the sight, Alec punched Tommy in the face with as much force as he could muster. There was an odd feeling of mush and bone as he connected with Tommy's cheek, a gasp of air and then Harry pinning Tommy down, voice growling and triumphant.

"Right ya fuckin' prick. It's over."

Tommy bucked beneath them, legs thrashing the air, but it was no use. It was over and he knew it. As a last hurrah he looked up, eyes blazing, and with unbridled fury spat in Alec's face.

Across the room in a far corner, a young woman sat on a sofa and wept, her thin dressing gown pulled tight across her chest, small breasts obvious through the thin material, mascara running down her cheeks. She looked wretched and shook uncontrollably. The room was a disaster zone of wrecked furniture and broken crockery, wallpaper stained with an arc of tea or coffee. The knife lay on top of the shattered remains of a glass coffee table. The woman stared at it for a moment before making to retrieve it. Harry's response was immediate.

"Touch that knife and it'll be you too."

She drew back as if stung and her face wore a look of betrayal, but she said nothing while Alec and Harry wrestled Tommy onto his front where, with difficulty, they placed handcuffs around his thick wrists. Alec's radio burst into life again. Gerry looking for his location. Harry stepped over Tommy and retrieved his radio lying on the floor.

"Yankee Forty Two. Sixty three Gray Street. Flat 7/3. I have Constable MacKay. One male arrested."

A tsunami of voices acknowledged the update as they dragged Tommy to his feet and Harry searched his pockets, while their prisoner stared hard at the woman who refused to meet his gaze. Alec wiped his face with the back of his sleeve. The adrenalin was fading and his legs began to tremble. The struggle had been short but explosive and the shock of the near miss had shaken him. There was a sharp pain in his left upper arm that really hurt and as he moved his arm white heat lanced through it.

"Christ."

Harry's head snapped up with a look of concern.

"You ok?"

Any sign of weakness would give Tommy confidence to kick off, handcuffs or no. Whatever was causing the pain could wait. From the voices on the radio it was clear others were on their way.

"I'm fine."

Harry looked sceptical but said nothing. There was the sound of footsteps coming up the stairwell before the large figure of Gerry crashed through the door with a look of relief that was almost comical. He took one look at Harry and shook his head.

"You're a mad cunt."

Harry, his composure now restored, smirked and pointed to Alec.

"That's the mad cunt."

More of the shift arrived and any sense of Tommy resuming a struggle went with them. Ricky and Sandy led Tommy away but as Alec followed onto the landing, he felt sick and lightheaded. Harry took him to a corner.

"There's no medals for playing John Wayne. What's up."

Alec looked at his upper arm. The material of his tunic was ripped and the black wool looked damp. Harry's fingers brushed the tear and when he held up his finger it was smeared with blood. It hadn't been a punch. He'd been stabbed. Alec felt sick again but held it back and bent over to stop his head swimming.

Harry shook his head and pursed his lips.

"C'mon. Down to the hospital. I'll shout up Charlie and Stevie, the others can sort this out."

Harry pressed the button for the lift and then, as if forgetting something, disappeared through the doorway of the flat where a number of cops had gathered. Alec watched Harry take the girl to one side. He talked rapidly and she nodded. She looked worried. Some finger pointing from Harry and some words with the cops and he was back again.

"Some loose ends. Nothing for you to worry about."

And then they were out in the fresh air, Charlie standing at the back of the van, the door opened in anticipation. As Alec climbed in Harry gave him a pat on his good shoulder.

"You did well. That's a story to tell the grandweans."

There was a quick mumbled conversation between Harry and Charlie before the door slammed shut. The van picked up speed and Stevie's face appeared at the partition door.

"You alright big yin?"

It felt good to be called big yin. It helped keep the waves of nausea away. Alec slumped against the side of the van his feet braced against the bench seat opposite.

"I'll live."

A smile from Stevie, but also a look of worry.

"We'll be at the infirmary in a few minutes."

Alec gave a thumbs up and the van lurched around a series of corners before straightening up. As the world outside shot by, he caught glimpses of blue lights in shop windows.

They sped through city streets, past a tree lined park and under a broad gate its metal arch painted black and yellow. The hospital. The back doors opened and light flooded in. He felt unsteady and Charlie walked alongside chipping in jokes and comments while Stevie went ahead. They were met at reception by a nurse who led them past curious onlookers into a corridor lined with booths. There was a swish of curtain and as Alec sat on the edge of a trolley bed, a doctor arrived and closed the curtains around them. It was impressively efficient. Charlie's voice came through from the other side.

"Just shout when yer clear. Yer in good hands."

He'd enough time to shout 'thanks' before the doctor and the nurse were peeling the tunic off and dumping it on a chair. The doctor held up his arm. The same lancing pain. Another wave of nausea. The nurse produced a paper mache bowl and thrust it under his chin. Almost by magic he vomited and the bowl caught it just in time. The doctor wrinkled her nose and stood back nodding in recognition of the obvious.

"You're in shock."

She waited until the retching stopped.

"Better?"

He did feel a little better and he managed what he hoped would be a nonchalant smile.

"Better out than in."

The nurse returned with another bowl and placed it on the bed. Alec hoped he'd not need it. The doctor examined his upper arm and for the first time he saw that his shirt sleeve was soaked with blood and now free from the constriction of his tunic it oozed downwards to his fingers. Another wave of sickness but he held it back. He didn't want to undo his heroics by acting like a schoolboy.

A pair of scissors appeared and without ceremony his shirt sleeve was cut off and thrown in a bin. He'd been about to mutter something about official police uniform, but the sight of the gash in his arm shut him up.

There was a tsk tsk from the doctor and the nurse wiped the wound. The wipe stung and smelled of iodine. A pause while the doctor looked closely at the tear. He shook with gentle tremors that oscillated up and down his body. The doctor appeared not to notice and he was grateful.

"Good. It's beginning to clot. We'll wait a bit, but I don't think anything major's been damaged."

A look directly into his eyes.

"You've been lucky. Don't know what gets into you lot. Knives are dangerous."

Alec almost laughed out loud.

"No shit Doc."

A thin smile. Alec felt as if he was a schoolboy being reprimanded by a teacher for misbehaving. What else did she think he was supposed to do? The doctor disappeared through the curtains leaving Alec with the nurse, a coal eyed Irish girl with the kind of smile that had a spark at each end. Alec felt warmed by it.

"Never mind her. She cares really. I'll make you a nice cup of tea after."

A wink and a smile and she was gone too.

Alec shivered. It was more than just the shock. He was down to a thin shirt that as now missing one arm and a cold blast was whistling under the curtains from the world outside.

The doctor reappeared. The wound was checked again. Another wipe and a nod of satisfaction.

"Right. I think we're ready. When was the last time you had a tetanus?"

Alec thought hard. It had been a long time. A curt nod from the doc.

"Stitches and a tetanus nurse."

The nurse re-appeared through the curtains carrying a kidney shaped metal dish containing a syringe and a number of needles. The doctor reached in with her latex gloves hands and brought out a needle, threaded with thin black thread. She looked at the wound and then Alec directly.

"This may hurt a little but I'll make it quick."

It didn't hurt as he'd imagined. He was still in shock and she was a deft seamstress, for in a few seconds he was able to look once more at the wound where neat little loops had drawn it tight. He'd no sooner smiled at the professionalism when he felt a sharp jab in his other arm. The anti-tetanus. And that *did* hurt.

Navigation

He returned to Corsair Street a week later. In truth he should've been off longer, but hanging about the flat held no attractions and there was an ache to return bigger than the one in his arm. Besides, he'd done good. There'd been mention of a commendation from the Inspector and he hoped it had gained him some acceptance with the shift and Harry in particular.

He'd hardly expected a ticker tape welcome, but the response was in fact underwhelming. Ronnie's first reaction was to ask why he'd returned and Alec's explanation of missing his beats had drawn a shake of the head.

"Sure it wasn't a blow to the head?"

It was the same in the muster. There were mutters of 'yer aff yer heid', but he took some consolation that behind the cynicism was an element of concern and that was progress of a kind. As it happened Harry was off and there seemed little appetite from anyone to update on what had happened in Gray Street, other than Tommy had gone to court and released pending a trial date.

Fitzpatrick and the Inspector launched into the established routine of shoulder numbers and beats, crimes and missing persons, incidents of note and intelligence. It was the usual litany, but as he left the station and merged with the ebb and flow, Alec knew in his heart of hearts that he'd rather be there than anywhere else.

Autumn lurched into winter and the twinkling lights of the first Christmas trees added some colour to the drab reservation. They also signalled a spate of housebreakings as junkies kicked in doors for ready cash and cheap electronic toys. There was an increase of punters at the public counter claiming that they'd been robbed of their giro. Junkies with debts to pay and alcoholics who'd drunk the Christmas money. Press-ganged to help, Alec denounced them as liars, but it made no difference. On they came, with predictable regularity, something that produced a rueful smile from Ronnie when Alec complained.

"Nothin'll stop them claiming they've had their broo money stolen. The DSS will sort it oot."

He'd been forced to work Christmas Day so that cops with family could get away. A tradition he couldn't usurp, but it had drawn a cold silence from Dad when he'd phoned to explain. As reward for his generosity he inherited a sudden death from the early shift, his only break a hastily consumed Christmas dinner in the cell block. The rest was spent waiting for an undertaker, watching the world from the eighteenth floor of a tower block, an elderly woman dead in a high-backed chair behind him.

He drove to Auchenbreoch on Boxing Day. There was no mention of Margo's wedding and he was happy to keep it that way. A day in which potential recriminations were shouldered aside by the presence of aunts, uncles and cousins. There was an exchange of presents, but the manila envelope with his course photograph lay where he'd last seen it and it remained unopened.

There'd been a catch-up with the gang and Mick, who'd returned from London with news that the streets were indeed paved with gold. An awkward start with Andy dissipated over a drink and the evening ended with a mumbled apology and a shake of hands. New Year came and went with relief that 1987 was over. Surely the next would bring better fortune.

It brought change. The Inspector got her promotion, an occasion marked by a crate of beer and bottles of whisky one Sunday morning off the night shift, the troops sitting in awkward silence in the senior officers dining room consuming enough alcohol to stun an elephant, after which they'd all driven home. Navigating deserted streets, Alec wondered at the absence of traffic cars and wondered if they'd been warned to stay clear.

A new Inspector arrived. Eddie Harkness. Transferred from the drugs squad he was a large man with crew-cut hair and a boxers jaw. The chair groaned when it took his weight in the muster and he announced that if you played his game they'd all get along. A new sergeant arrived. Andy Bell, fresh faced and newly promoted from community safety who'd smiled nervously, the shift staring impassively as he'd said hello. There'd been dark mutterings of being supervised by the Tufty Club and Alec felt sorry for him.

Alec had hoped the new arrivals would blunt Fitzpatrick's pettiness, but it only increased. Paperwork was returned with monotonous regularity, but Alec swallowed his pride and made the changes. Nothing stayed the same it seemed, so maybe Fitzpatrick would be shuffled onwards too.

The incident in Gray Street faded from his mind as other incidents and experiences settled on top. He'd developed a thirst for knowledge and his tea breaks were now spent leafing through intel reports and the pictures of local neds. He got better at spotting them as they disappeared like will o' the wisps up common closes and he'd whisper to himself their full Sunday names as he wrote them in his notebook. The smallest things became important. Who was seen, when, where and with whom. And gradually, he became the go-to guy for anything happening on the reservation.

With the old Inspector gone, the promise of a commendation went with her. Ronnie gently reminded him that some senior officers were old enough to have seen combat in some part of a disintegrating empire before joining the police. His stabbing would be considered small beer and there'd be a reluctance to award someone so young in service. Still, it would've been nice, and the only opportunity he'd ever get of earning one.

Thin Ice

January brought a period of prolonged cold weather so intense the canal froze and Alec found to his bitter dismay just how inadequate his police clothing was. The t-shirts he wore under his shirt and the boots bought from an army and navy store barely improved things.

Harkness made a big impact, front and centre at every incident, rolling about the streets with the best of them. The old Inspector became the subject of disparaging remarks, especially from Ricky who'd not forgotten her comments at the fatal fire. She was now 'Miss High and Mighty', not like Inspector Harkness who 'wasn't afraid to get his hands dirty', an assessment that won widespread agreement. But there were soon misgivings. Harkness's ubiquitous presence became claustrophobic and the older cops complained they couldn't move without their new Inspector there to direct proceedings and decide everything, right down to who'd do the paperwork. It particularly incensed Charlie who didn't need anyone to lead him 'by the nose'.

"Fuckin' micro manager. Thinks we're all donkeys."

They'd parked up on a piece of spare ground alongside the canal its surface, thick as plate steel, spread before them like sugar glass. Stevie stared at the wintry scene and looked as glum as Alec had seen him.

"Name's on every case, disnae matter what it is. Witness, arresting officer, rights of accused, lodging evidence. You name it, he's on it."

Alec's ears pricked up. This didn't sound like your average Inspector.

"Why would he get involved like that?"

Charlie leaned around the partition.

"Seen the car he drives?"

Alec had seen Harkness in a new car. It attracted admiring glances.

"The Beemer?"

"Yep. And the watch he wears?"

Alec had no idea, he wasn't as observant as Charlie, but Charlie was happy to oblige.

"Rolex Oyster."

"Nice."

Charlie smiled, but it wasn't a friendly look.

"And do you know where our fine Inspector lives?"

Charlie wasn't looking for an answer, he was on a roll.

"The Lochdrum Estate out by Drumgeddie. Where the posh folk live."

Alec had seen the adverts in the Glasgow Herald. One of many purpose built estates springing up around the periphery of the city. Lochdrum came with a duck-filled pond, trendy shops, sporting lodge and a golf course. An imposing stone entrance discouraged the casual visitor. It looked like a pastiche of an upmarket village, without the road running through it. That Harkness could afford this lifestyle was incredible, even on an Inspectors wages.

"His wife got money?"

Charlie shook his head.

"Used to be a nurse but gave it up for the kids."

"Nice life if you can afford it."

Charlie winked.

"Maybe he cannae."

Alec pictured Harkness playing golf with Pringle clad men of a certain social bracket, leading a life of conspicuous wealth at odds with old

Presbyterian Scotland and an Inspectors salary. It smacked of trying to be something you weren't, a form of social neediness Alec found embarrassing. Harkness was as rough as a badgers' and it was hard to imagine him being accepted in wealthy company unless he acted like them and spoke like them; scheme vowels mangled into private school Scots, humble origins a bottom rung to climb up from. The questions bubbled up. There was more to Harkness than met the eye and Charlie seemed to know something.

"How did he end up at Corsair Street?"

Charlie adjusted his large frame.

"When Harkness was in the squad they tore up half of Glasgow, big names in jail, high court every other week. Everybody making big bucks, driving nice cars. Squad was tighter than a tight thing, in a tight competition in the village of Tight, on Tight World."

"And then?"

"Rumour has it he tried it on with a female D.C. Grabbed her arse. She complained but didnae want to press charges, so he got punted here to cool his heels."

Alec scanned Charlie's face. If his eyes weren't sparkling at something as salacious as this, then Charlie didn't believe it himself.

"So, the true story?"

Charlie looked as if he was preparing a death message.

"I knew Harkness when he was younger. Flew close to the wind, but a decent enough guy. In the drug squad he found his feet and built a big reputation."

"So, what went wrong?"

A shrug.

"Results dried up. They hit house after house and nothing. Neds opened their doors with a smile - houses clean as a whistle."

"All the drugs gone?"

Alec knew the question was daft, but he could think of no other reason why such a successful operation could turn so unlucky.

A laugh from Stevie. Charlie snorted.

"Aye. That'll be it. All that smack and cocaine just ran oot."

A pause.

"Somebody was giving the neds a heads up. Suspicion fell on Harkness sometime around the time he bought his townhouse out at Lochdrum."

Alec was amazed that hadn't ended up in the papers. This was dynamite.

"How do you know all this?"

"That would be telling."

It sounded outrageous. Harkness touting for the neds? Surely it wasn't possible to stay in the job under those circumstances, let alone keep your rank. The more Alec thought about it, the more it sounded like gossip, it had to be. His thoughts returned to the story of the female D.C.

"I think I believe the other scenario now."

Stevie nodded in agreement.

"Either way, our Inspector has a taste for money and the good life."

Charlie laughed.

"He'll find neither here."

"That's why he wants to be the professional witness. Court overtime."

Alec turned the revelations over in his head. Cops keen on getting a 'speaky' wasn't anything new. Finding a screwdriver was enough for a citation in a stolen car case and many of the old cops had survived the lean years because court overtime made their pay half-decent. Old habits had stuck and though wages had risen a court citation was still a big deal. But, Harkness was an Inspector. He was already on a decent wage.

The glum voice of Bob drew them back to the present. Another round of notebook signings had begun. Stevie grunted a random street name into his radio and started the engine.

"Ok Alec. See you around."

Jumping into the chill air, he called out his thanks for a warm half hour. The van rolled off the frozen ground and sped off to another part of the sub-division where Fitzpatrick would make small talk about the weather.

He stood for a while, his breath slowly rising in the frigid air. Beside him, the canal, its ice encrusted surface littered with stones and the odd boulder, and a shopping trolley on its side where someone had tried to break into the dark waters beneath. The ice looked impenetrable but looks were deceiving.

An insipid cup of tea with the insipid Robbie seemed the best bet among a shit list of options and pulling the collar of his raincoat higher, Alec turned his back on the canal and taking the long route set off up the hill to the youth club. Robbie welcomed him with a smile and put the kettle on, but Alec'd no sooner sat when his radio burst into life.

"Stations, child in the canal. Canal lock at Berry Street."

The spot where they'd parked the van. Alec grabbed his hat and bursting through the club doors, sprinted across the spare ground. The hill was steep and there were moments when he almost ended up on his backside on the icy pavements. His legs wearied with the constant checking and adjusting of his stride, but it took him less than two minutes to reach the canal.

A large crowd was gathered at the boundary wall. Chest heaving, Alec pushed his way through the onlookers and looked over. In the middle of the frozen lock, within a circle of water black as ink, a boy clung to the jagged edges of the ice. Cracks radiated outwards. There was no sign of the shopping trolley.

Some men were gathered on a crescent of dark grit on the bank below, an unlikely beach from which barges had once been launched. One of them was inching onto the ice, arms wide, spreading his weight through the air around him. A twang reverberated across the ice and a large crack snapped across the surface. The man retreated in quick shuffles to a low moan from the crowd and from somewhere among them a woman cried. Alec pushed through the spectators. Some began shouting 'the polis is here!' as if the solution to the crisis had been found and Alec ran to where the wall had collapsed and clambering down a rough causeway made it onto the shore.

The boy had stopped thrashing. The only movement were from his hands which occasionally slipped and pawed at the ice. Water slopped over the edge of the hole as the boy, eyes blank as death, stared at nothing.

Alec looked around for something reach out with. He had a primordial fear of water and though he'd passed his lifesaving at the police college, each class had been preceded by the vomiting of his breakfast, the sessions more an exercise in drowning by numbers. It was therefore a surprise to find himself discarding his raincoat, tunic and tie. A scene from an old survival programme came to mind and throwing his hat to the ground he lay on the ice and edged his way forward.

He'd gone no more than three feet when he felt it flex. Ominous pings rang across the ice and he shouted that he'd need a ladder. Someone clambered up the rubble and disappeared through the gap in the wall.

The boy was six feet away, but it might as well have been six miles. Alec inched forward again. Another crack appeared and became more pronounced the further he went. The boy looked through him, eyes marble-black and Alec wondered if he could see anything or was in some other place.

Through the glassy opaqueness he saw a twig trapped between water and ice. It wasn't thick at all. The sense of dislocation that eased his way onto its surface faded and a shocking cold seized hold of him. This was mental. He was merely delaying the inevitable, or even hastening it and he'd end up in the water too. Alec looked up and fixed his gaze on the boy.

"We'll get you. Just hold on."

A nod.

Sirens coming closer, doors slamming, police radios. On the opposite bank a small crowd stood like cardboard cut-outs. Words of encouragement from behind, and then silence.

He crawled a few more inches. The ice flexed some more and Alec wondered just how much he could push his luck. Then a snap, a crack and the sensation of icy water under his stomach. He slid to the side, but another snap and a gush of freezing water across his chest made him gasp. There was a communal intake of breath behind him. Alec tried reaching out, but the boy two feet across the crazed surface simply stared back. A shout from behind.

"We've goat a ladder!"

Something scoured the ice and the prongs of a wooden ladder

appeared at his shoulder.

The boy was talking.

"Mister, ah cannae hold on. Cannae move ma fingers."

And at that, the boy slipped backwards.

Fuck!

Alec darted towards the boy but the ice, weakened by weight and movement, opened like a trapdoor and he was through into the black waters below, an icy iron maiden compressing chest and limbs. For a moment he sank paralysed into the murk before fear took him and he began thrashing in blind panic, kicking and flailing, eyes closed against the impenetrable darkness.

His hand struck something. Soft. Slippery. Clothing? He cast his hand around and caught a bony arm. Alec gripped it tight and struck out, legs kicking hard, unable to tell which way was up. Fear gripped him, that he was pulling the boy to the bottom and there'd they'd die. He kicked and kicked, lungs bursting, panic taking hold, convinced it was all for naught and then, a lancing pain across his forehead, broken ice and water cascading over his face. Holy Christ, he'd made it. He opened his eyes and treading water looked for a way out, the boy limp by his side. But it all looked so different down here in the water. Where the fuck was the ladder? Shouts from the bank. Arms pointing. There it was, a foot away. Alec reached for it but his fingers, numbed by the icy water, slipped from the wet wood.

Ricky stood at the water's edge, jabbing his finger.

"Grab the ladder. Grab it!"

Alec cursed and reached out again. He grabbed the rung and was instantly dragged through broken ice and brown water, but his fingers had lost all feeling and as the canal bank drew close, they lost power, the ladder slipped from his grasp and the boy, a dead weight, began to drag them under again. They'd drown after all.

And then hands around him, hauling him to the shoreline. A roar went up around the valley. Chest heaving, beached like a prize catch, Alec looked up and saw that hundreds had gathered on both banks, clapping and shouting.

A blanket was draped around his shoulder, the voice of Ricky soft in his ear.

"Well done. Give yerself a moment, and then take the applause."

He didn't want the applause. He wanted the boy to be ok. A few feet away on the shore the boy lay on his back, his chest being compressed by an ambulance crew. Silence descended, the initial joy stilled by the prospect of defeat, but then a retch and the boy turned onto his side, the contents of the canal vomited onto the bank.

Somewhere above, someone shouted.

"Thank christ."

Low level grumbles, mutters of 'lucky boy' and 'they'll no listen' rippled among the onlookers as relief gave way to recrimination. Alec got to his feet. His legs felt like jelly and he shuddered violently, but he wanted to know the boy was alright.

Wrapped in a coarse woollen blanket, the boy sat upright, colour seeping into his cheeks. His mother, who'd given him a passionate hug, was now shouting at his bowed head.

"Wee bastard. Ah've telt ye about this canal umpteen times! Whit a fright you've given me."

Sensing his approach she'd turned, eyes bloodshot, face drawn with worry. A simple smile.

"Thank you."

In any other set of circumstances the absence of fine words would've been underwhelming but in that moment the simplicity was golden and Alec was so touched by the sincerity behind them that he could think of nothing in response other than to say that he was glad the boy was ok.

And then the moment was gone. The boy was carried to the ambulance, his mother hanging onto the stretcher and together they disappeared up the slope and through the wall. The crowd, satisfied that they'd extracted every last iota of excitement melted away into the late afternoon leaving Alec on the canal bank unable to process what he'd just done. Ricky led him up the slope. He was exhausted beyond speech and he longed for a hot cuppa. The thought had evidently crossed Ricky's mind too.

"Need to get something hot down ya. No doubt they'll give you plenty down the hospital once you've been checked over."

Alec wondered if the Irish nurse would be on duty. He was pretty sure the sight of her would warm him up for sure. And the tea, however bad, would taste much nicer than the canal.

Brief Encounter

The following week was spent in bed. He'd swallowed some of the canal and a bout of gastroenteritis followed. It took another week before he could reasonably claim he'd recovered and it was a thinner Alec MacKay who reported at Corsair Street in time to begin a week of night shifts.

This time there were smiles and affirmative nods when he entered the changing room. A shout of 'here's Marine Boy' and laughter among the clanging locker doors. There was banter with Ricky about figure skating and though he'd balked at the comparisons with Torvill and Dean someone in the muster hummed Bolero anyway.

There was a brief chat with Harkness after the muster. Something about the finest traditions of the service and a commendation. Alec couldn't think of anything to say other than it had been spur of the moment and he was glad it turned out ok, but deep inside he hoped it would come true.

He was re-united with Ronnie. Duncan Stewart was on annual leave and the arrangement was presented as a chance to ease himself in before he took up his beats again.

The first few hours were, however, awkward. Alec no longer considered himself 'the boy' and the trials of the past few weeks had instilled a sense of independence that chafed against Ronnie's patriarchal attitudes. Ronnie bristled at the impertinence of someone younger answering calls for his beat, as much as Alec resented Ronnie's insistence that he take the lead whenever they got there. And so, he found himself having to accommodate Ronnie, as much as Ronnie had to accommodate him. Their temporary arrangement settled into something workable when

Ronnie realised a competent neighbour allowed him to sit back and relax, but all the same it took several nights before Alec felt confident enough to broach the subject of Harkness.

They were walking one of Ronnie's 'wee shortcuts', an abandoned railway track, one of many that'd intersected Glasgow before the Beeching cuts and whose disconnected sections were all that remained of a network that once trundled through congested landscapes of houses and factories. Most of the route had been swallowed up by housing, but other sections had grown wild, their embankments flanked by tall trees and rhododendrons; perfect escape routes for house-breakers and discrete thoroughfares for wily cops. They'd walked along the track, past upmarket townhouses and new build apartments, before arriving at an elegant sandstone viaduct spanning a deep gorge whose steep sides were filled with beech and sycamore.

Alec peered down at the river, its dark waters tumbling over stepped ridges in the rock, trees draped in a fine mist. In the distance, the orange glow of streetlights and the first towers blocks of the Estate of the Isles. Civilisation of a kind, but suspended above the wooded gorge it felt like he'd a bit of wild countryside to himself. As good a spot as any for conspiratorial conversation.

"Hear the Inspector's causing waves."

A grunt. A response Alec knew well enough to indicate a reluctance to comment but a cautious signal to proceed.

"Said I'd get a commendation for the canal thing, so I guess his heart's in the right place."

A sideways look.

"Thought I'd taught you better than that."

A bite. Perhaps a change of tack.

"Tryin' to give him the benefit. Charlie and Stevie are pissed off. A few others too."

Ronnie resumed his slow advance across the bridge neither looking one side or the other, eyes fixed on a distant objective. After a few seconds of rumination he declared his hand.

"Don't get on the wrong side of Harkness. If you're no' on his bus, yer under it."

Alec shook off the image of Harkness driving a bus.

"Hear what yer sayin', but he'll no' be a witness in my cases if he's done nothin' to justify it."

Ronnie turned in his tracks. The old cop pointed a finger at Alec's heart as if the answer lay there.

"That's up to you, but if you want my advice, and I think you do, you'll need to bend with the wind from time to time."

"That's what Stevie said."

Ronnie gazed at the night sky as if picturing Stevie using those words, testing them in his head to see if they rang true. He looked wary and Alec belatedly realised how much a test of trust this was. Speaking ill of a gaffer in the wrong company was a sure way to find yourself in deep trouble.

"S'ok Ronnie. I'll keep my head down."

Alec met Ronnie's probing gaze and smiled. Ronnie looked unconvinced, but as he opened his mouth to speak there was a shout from the other end of the viaduct, and then another. Alec quickened his step but was stopped by a hand on his shoulder.

"You might be a beat man, but yer no a Jedi yet."

"Sounds like somebody in trouble."

"Aye, but not the kind you're thinking. They're cops."

The shouting subsided into a kind of call-and-response with a third voice, the familiar nasal band-saw of scheme Glaswegian. There was anger in the voice and an additional harmonic of fear that bordered on hysteria, but Alec couldn't see where it was coming from.

Edging further along the viaduct revealed two black figures who seemed fascinated with something over the edge of the parapet. They spent their time looking at it so intently they seemed unaware of his approach. The third voice rose clear from the other side.

"Ya fuckin' mad bastards. Get me up!"

It was answered by a Liverpudlian voice, unnaturally reasonable and controlled. Ricky.

"Wouldn't want ye to fall, but ye haven't told us, and ma fingers are getting tired."

The 'band saw' responded from the other side.

"Ah'll tell ye when ah'm back on the bridge."

Alec could hear a tsk tsk and then the Ayrshire lilt of Sandy. The same reasonable tone as Ricky but with added brutality.

"No one knows yer here Frankie. A wee slip and down ye go."

Frankie's voice rose an octave.

"Ye's widnae fuckin dare! Let me up ya cunts — then ah'll tell ye!"

Alec edged closer. The crouched figures wore police hats tipped backwards on their heads and each held a leg in a tight embrace, chests pulled onto the parapet by the weight of the body below them, knees braced against the stonework. A pair of trainer clad feet, heels hooked over their broad shoulders, waggled as the voice rose from the dark depths beyond.

"Please, honest tae God, ah don't want to die."

Ricky was looking down the length of one leg as if aiming down the barrel of a gun. His voice sounded laboured.

"The name Frankie. Give us the name."

The sound of the river deep in the gorge and then the voice, thin and hesitant.

"Zippy…Zippy Morrison."

"Willie Morrison? Bendyke Street?"

Silence. Sandy and Ricky exchanged a look and then lowered their prize with a jolt, producing a scream from the other side.

"Fuckin pricks!"

Sandy chuckled.

"Fingers getting' sweaty Frankie. Answer the question."

"Willie Morrison — Bendyke Street — pull, me, the, fuck, up!"

Ricky and Sandy hauled at the figure of a skinny young man. It wasn't easy. Somehow, he'd been lowered backwards and there was no way he could assist in his ascent. As he reached the top of the parapet his back scraped across the stonework to a cacophony of curses until his shoulders cleared the topmost edge and he collapsed with a grunt on the stone chippings. Sandy and Ricky stood above him, breathing laboured, plumes of vapour rising into the air. Ricky looked up and put on his best grin. If he'd been surprised by the company, he was doing a good job of hiding it.

"Come to see how it's really done?"

Frankie pushed himself into a sitting position, back against the parapet, knees pulled to his chest. In the diffused light of the distant housing scheme, Alec saw the fear in his thin face. There was no doubt that he'd been convinced by Ricky's threats and he sat in furtive silence watching for clues to what would happen next.

Ronnie looked down with mild interest.

"Still dealin' smack Frankie?"

Frankie scowled in return.

"Never touch the stuff."

Sandy prodded Frankie's thigh with his boot.

"Don't tell lies."

Frankie scowled and rubbed his thigh but said nothing.

Ricky peered into the darkness around him, as if making sure there were no further witnesses. Alec could almost see the wheels whirring as he worked out his next move. After a brief pause he smiled, jerked a thumb toward the figure at his feet and began talking as if he was a children's TV presenter.

"Frankie here works in an ice cream van, don't you Frankie?"

Ronnie stared at Frankie as if the news was a thunderclap of some kind, but Alec was confused. Working in an ice cream van was no crime as far as he knew.

Ricky continued in his best Jackanory voice.

"Frankie's route is Summerhill."

At this Ricky turned and pointed beyond the desolate scrubland at the end of the bridge to the jumbled skyline that was the Estate of the Isles.

"But the best bit for our Frankie, is the estate aaannd, the reservation."

Alec knew the ice cream van. An Italian sounding family from somewhere in the north of the city, their name painted in fifties style pastel colours along the sides. The chime 'Whistle While You Work' echoed among the tenements twice a day, afternoon and evening, kids and teenagers queuing for ice cream and crisps. Alec looked down at the gaunt face of Frankie who dug his heels into the chippings. He looked an unlikely ice cream seller.

Ricky gave the sole of Frankie's foot a kick.

"Frankie loves his job, don't you Frankie? Nice wee earner."

Ronnie stepped forward for a closer look. He looked angry.

"How long you worked for Donatelli?"

Frankie shrugged.

"A couple a months."

Alec had no idea what was going on, or where the conversation was heading, but so far there was absolutely nothing to explain why Ricky and Sandy had threatened to drop a young man off a bridge. Ricky, timing impeccable as ever, supplied the first clue.

"Tell the nice officer what yer selling the kids Frankie."

Frankie looked from Ricky to Ronnie, thin mouth twisted into a sardonic smirk.

"Ah sell the weans ice cream."

Another kick from Sandy. Frankie clutched his thigh and cursed. Alec watched, with mounting anxiety. He'd travelled through a portal into a parallel universe, where local criminals were routinely tossed over bridges. Now there'd be another complaint and Frankie would have the bruises to prove it. He looked about, convinced an onlooker was taking notes somewhere beyond the gloom and he'd be viewed as an accessory. Now was the time to intervene and put a stop to it, but Ronnie had no such worries. His attention was solely on Frankie.

"You're the prick selling smack to the weans. There's teenage junkies on my beat thanks to cunts like you. Lives fucked, mammies in tears".

Frankie stared off into the night and shrugged.

Sandy and Ricky stepped back to give Ronnie free rein and Alec understood now why Frankie was of such interest. From the initial shock of seeing him being dangled over a parapet he began to see things in a different light and his thoughts turned to the early morning ghosts on the reservation. His heart shrank at the memory of how young they were. And here was the dealer with the niche clientele. Get 'em young, get 'em for life, however short that life would be.

Frankie was pulled to his feet. He adjusted his tracksuit bottoms, eyes darting between Ricky and Ronnie, a hunted animal trying to guess the next steps. Ronnie shrugged, he'd had enough and Ricky, hands in pockets, nodded sideways at the distant housing estate, voice returning to its normal state of languid boredom.

"Right Frankie, fuck off. Don't let me see you hangin' round here again, or I might drop ya next time."

A dark cloud passed over Frankie's face. A look of loathing that replaced the nervous look of moments ago and he spat at Ricky's feet.

"Maybe I'll just go up to Corsair Street and tell 'em what you did."

Not for the first time, Alec was surprised by the speed of Ronnie's reactions, of how a fat middle-aged man could strike like a snake. Before Frankie had registered the movement Ronnie had him by the face, his momentum carrying them onto the bridge parapet and Frankie's torso over the abyss. Ronnie's meaty hand gripped Frankie's jaw so tight his lips puckered into a tortured approximation of a kiss, rotten yellow teeth bared like a snarling dog.

Alec moved to stop Ronnie, but Frankie was so far over the edge that any intervention could tip the balance the wrong way. Sandy was making calming noises, but Ronnie was oblivious, focused solely on Frankie, head inches from Frankie's face whose eyes bulged as if the pressure on his cheeks were squeezing them from their sockets.

"Listen ya wee shite. Take a step inside that office or speak to anyone and I will personally hunt you down. I'll bring you here and toss you in that fuckin' river and no one, and I mean no one, will give a fuck that you're gone."

Frankie's feet scrabbled across the broken ground trying in vain for some sort of purchase, but Ronnie continued in his calm surreal tone.

"If I see you in that fucking ice cream van just once I'll give you a '99 you'll never forget."

Alec had to turn away and hide the grin. Ricky and Sandy found something of interest at their feet as Ronnie eased Frankie back onto the track and let him go.

Back on solid ground, Frankie massaged his jaw before raising his hands in a show of contrition. He was shaking but trying his best to control it.

"Ah wiz only jokin."

Ricky smiled.

"We do the jokes around here Frankie. Now, fuck off before my colleague does something he'll never regret."

Frankie took a look around to make sure no one had objections, then hurried towards the scrubland and the housing estate beyond. After a few yards he broke into a jog and then a run as he disappeared among the trees. Ricky looked at Ronnie with keen interest.

"Thought you were going to throw him over."

Ronnie looked sour and grunted.

"For a second, so did I."

Sandy grinned.

"Doubt we'll see him for a while."

Ronnie stared at the distant scrubland and shook his head.

"He'll be in that van tomorrow. He doesn't give a fuck."

As if that was all the explanation that was required, Ronnie announced they were overdue their tea break. Ricky chatted about where he and Sandy were headed next and they parted as if nothing much had happened, other than a chance rendezvous in which banal pleasantries had been exchanged.

But the encounter had left Alec with a deep impression. He'd seen a man dangled over a bridge for information. There was no way he could condone it, it was banana republic stuff, but as he walked beside Ronnie his thoughts strayed to the events of the past months and how deeply he'd become embedded in this new life. How much his fate had become entwined with others. Like when he'd saved Ricky from the fire and had the favour returned at the frozen canal; of Ronnie's fatherly tuition and his intervention in the capture of McGroarty; of how he'd put his life on the line for Harry despite the bad blood between them. Bound together in mutual dependency, just as Ronnie had described.

More than that, the incident solidified something that'd hovered on the edge of his thoughts since the theft from the restaurant. He was much more than an impersonal observer and recorder of facts, there was no such thing as detached neutrality. The stuff they'd taught at the police college was indeed bullshit, it was very personal indeed. How could it be otherwise when every day you recorded the despair of others and heard in their voices the hope you'd do something about it?

Alec pictured the huddled groups he'd seen at Frankie's ice cream van, the furtive looks as they disappeared into the common closes. He'd written it off as the looks he'd seen elsewhere in Summerhill, but now he saw it for what it was and his loathing towards Frankie grew, and all those like him. It hurt that the Frankie's of the world were getting away with it and he was beginning to understand where Ronnie, Sandy and Ricky were coming from. But this Frankie wasn't a big fish. If they knew he was dealing smack from an ice cream van, why hadn't he been caught?

Ronnie, still hot from the confrontation, was happy to explain.

"He's been turned three times in the past month. Fuck all found. The Donatelli's are pals with local councillors. There'll be letters flying about with claims of harassment and the Div Comm gets the gypsies warning."

"And that's that?"

"Yup. Frankie thinks he's one of the untouchables. A few more years and he'll be breaking into the big time. It's how they start."

They found a hole in the boundary fence and entered the streets of 'The Isles', the rabbit warren of passages and paths deserted and silent. In a few hours the sun would rise on another grey morning and the junkie parade would start again. Alec's thoughts drifted to the reservation. He felt protective of it, that it was down to him to make a difference and as he climbed the steps to Corsair Street, he vowed he'd do whatever it took to put Frankie where he belonged. And in that moment the seeds of his own addiction were sown, that there was honour at least in throwing yourself at the wall, even if there was little chance of breaking it.

Whistle While You Work

To Alec's disbelief Frankie made no complaint and the rest of the week passed without incident. Nights gave way to lates and the encounter at the viaduct, like the boy in the canal and the stabbing before it, took on a dream like quality, but as he returned to his beats on the reservation one thing remained crystal clear. He'd get to the bottom of how Frankie was dealing heroin and expose him.

It was a mission that was easier to accept than execute. As predicted, Frankie was unfazed by Ronnie's threats. The familiar chimes rang around Barnhouse and there was the Donatelli van parked in its usual spots around the hill, with the usual furtive disappearing acts of the thinner clients as they scurried up the nearest close. There was definitely something hooky going on but Alec was presented with a number insurmountable obstacles. One was the obvious problem of being a tall man in a police uniform who stood out a mile no matter how he casually approached. There was the additional challenge of evading the window-hangers and close mouth meerkats who populated every street and whistled warnings as soon as neared. He tried being more circumspect by crossing back courts unseen and emerging where the van had stopped. Except there was always someone at a rear window raising the alarm, or a tail end Charlie assigned sentry duty. There were times when he'd no sooner approached his objective than he'd get a call from the control room and the chance would slip away. It was an object lesson on why covert operations were conducted in plain clothes and Alec began to experience real doubts about his ability to shut Frankie down. No wonder drug dealing was so rampant.

Near the end of the week, while crossing over the canal to Barnhouse, he saw Gillespie hunched over a tartan trolley-bag, jacket covered with dust. The trolley looked heavy and Alec offered to help, but Gillespie had politely refused and offered an alternative.

"It's they drug dealers you want to be lifting."

Alec shook his head.

"Harder than ye think. There's plenty making sure they're not caught."

They'd reached Gillespie's flat. The old man turned with a sideways nod to the streets on the hill.

"It's no' the van you should be bothering with. It's they flats over yonder."

At that, Gillespie hauled his trolley up the steps and disappeared into the close. Alec didn't look in the direction Gillespie had indicated for fear of giving the old man away. In any case, he knew what was being hinted at; the semi-derelict streets earmarked for demolition on the hill behind him. Empty for months, they'd been pillaged for copper boilers and piping, water cascading down the stairwells and onto the streets, their empty rooms used as junkie 'shooting galleries'.

Curiosity piqued he approached the streets by degrees until he reached a terrace overlooking a bend in the canal, windows meshlighted, close mouths shuttered. They were secure at the front, but it was a different story at the back where doors had been jemmied off their hinges and internal doors busted. Like tunnel rats, the kids had knocked holes in adjoining walls so the block was a network of connecting rooms from one close to another. An architectural Swiss cheese. Making his way over the rubble Alec found a door that had been forced open and squeezed inside.

The air smelled of plaster dust and urine and from somewhere above the odour of burnt plastic. Only a matter of time before some enterprising pyro set the whole lot alight. He stood for a while making sure he was alone and then made his way upstairs 'til he reached the top landing. No shooting gallery, but the door to one of the flats had been forced open. Alec passed through to a hallway where a water boiler lay flattened on the carpet, left in preparation for uplift by an enterprising thief. It was then he remembered Gillespie's dust coated jacket, the bag of tools in his kitchen, the heavy dusty shopping trolley, the sly hint of things afoot inside the abandoned tenements. You'd have to be on the inside to know.

He'd need to have a quiet word with Mr Gillespie.

A large hole had been made in the living room wall. Intrigued, he climbed through into another hallway, water running along the floorboards from burst pipes and onto another landing where he was confronted by the familiar smell of vinegar. At his feet, a dessert spoon, the silver bowl burned dark by the flame of a lighter. Next to it, a bloodied swab and empty syringe, but what interested him more was the small cardboard box in the corner and the cartoon of Superman on the cover. Sweet cigarettes, the kind he'd bought as a kid, 'puffing' on them with his pals, laughing at the joke.

Alec picked up the empty packet. The insides smelled faintly sweet. He put it in his pocket and moved through the ruined building where he found more bloody syringes on other landings and at each another empty packet. By the time he'd emerged into the crisp air of early evening Alec had six of them folded flat in his raincoat, certain he'd discovered Frankie's secret.

But if he thought the CID were going to be just as excited, he was to be disappointed.

"Just a bunch of sweetie boxes."

The D.S., a decent guy burdened by a huge in-tray and a career laced with disappointments had taken one look at the boxes and laughed. Alec wasn't without his own doubts, but with little else to go on he was determined to push his case.

"I know, but next to each used syringe is one of these. Same each time. Sweetie cigarettes with Superman on them. Got to be the Donatelli's van. We could have them fingerprinted, Frankie's dabs might be on them."

The D.S. shook his head as someone who'd love to believe but had been round the block too many times to take anything at face value.

"I'd love to see Frankie get the jail, but you need more than that. The co-op down the road sells them. Is there a law against selling sweets? Anyway, the lab won't touch 'em unless there's a crime number."

Bottom line, he'd have to catch one of the junkies right after he'd bought a packet from the van, with the smack still inside. Fat chance.

It was Harry who supplied the answer over the now ritual humiliation at the tea break card school.

"Get the plainers to turn the junkies after they've made their purchase. Find some smack and Section 23 the van. Boab's yer auntie."

There'd been vigorous nods and murmurs of 'aye, plainers' as if that was all there was to it, but when Alec found their hideaway in an old storeroom next to the recreation block, the plain clothes unit were just as sceptical.

"Turned that van twice. Fuck all in it."

There were four of them. Identikit looking cops with long hair, who stuck out like a sore thumb because they were well fed and healthy. Each sported a thick stubble and a subtle patina of defeat that came with trying to please a hierarchy who believed denim jacketed men in unmarked Ford Escorts were a crime busting solution. The room was festooned with intel reports and photographs of various targets. One or two had darts hanging from their faces. Alec'd no doubt that the plainers looked upon him as a green romantic and were keen to keep him in his place. Some flattery was required.

"Only you can do this guys. They packets are on every landing and they're from the Donatelli's van I'm sure of it. And the D.S. says he'd love to see the prick in jail."

Nothing interests a plain clothes cop more than the approval of a Detective Sergeant, each holding out hope they'll be a detective one day. A favourable appraisal from the DS was a pathway to glory and a Ralph Slater suit.

The questions became more constructive. Times and places. Registration numbers, look-outs and descriptions. They were in. He'd only one more favour to ask.

"Can you involve me in some way?"

There was a synchronised intake of breath and the tight pressing of lips. This was a tall order apparently.

"One whiff of you and the baw's on the slates."

The jungle drums on the reservation were the finest in all Summerhill, but he figured his complete absence from the scheme would also be viewed with suspicion. It was his only card, so he played it.

"I can be a distraction. And if Frankie bolts on foot I'll catch him."

It was a promise he'd no confidence in fulfilling but if Frankie should blunder his way there was always a chance. There was a short conference and with a show of reluctance that bordered on the theatrical, he was in.

Alec's nerves jangled throughout the muster the next afternoon, but the plainers confirmed the turn and gave one of their sets to listen on. It was all he could do to stop from running to the reservation, but as the hours ticked down and with time on his hands, doubts crept in. What if Frankie was days off, or changed routes and timings? He was hit by a succession of calls and spent the first hours striding about his beat, dealing with each as fast as he could, fearful he'd be elsewhere when the turn went down. But as the hour approached, the calls petered out and it was a wired young cop who made his way up to the Immaculate Conception to keep his end of the bargain. He passed a battered transit van parked in a side street. It looked as shabby as anything in the area and he made a note to check it out. But it could wait. Eyes on the prize.

The next half hour was spent trying to look nonchalant and failing. He circled the chapel, saying hello to the same people, until finally fed-up with his own impatience, he took up a spot at a street corner like a Scottish Dixon of Dock Green, and waited.

The city hummed and droned. Dogs barked. Children screamed and shouted as they fought and played. Now and then a siren wailed in the distance. Time ground onwards. And then, the sound of distant chimes growing louder in fits and starts until finally, they were in Barnhouse. Glory be. Alec listened to the stop-start twinkling and pictured the locations during the silences where the van would be parked; Frankie dolling out the boxes, 'clients' disappearing into closes. He wondered where the plainers where and whether they'd shown up at all, but their radio stayed painfully silent.

And then, as the sound of the chimes moved up the hill, a shout of 'Go Go Go!', a pause and then confirmation that a 'customer' had been caught. Alec muttered a small hallelujah.

The ice cream chimes began and stopped again. The next pitch. There was a chance Frankie would be alerted to what happened at his last stop and Alec edged downhill. He'd be better use if he was a little closer.

The chimes again, but quieter now and Alec made a quick mental calculation. Frankie was headed to his last stop, at the bottom of the hill near to the main road. It was now or never, but the plainers radio remained silent and with a feeling of growing unease Alec made his way towards the distant van convinced something had gone wrong.

It was at that moment his own radio burst into life with the sound of Bob containing his excitement.

"Foot-chase, Barnhouse. Plain clothes in pursuit of a male."

Shit. Alec ran towards the next junction and listened for the next update. Was it Frankie? Uphill or down? The canal or the exit road? Another shout. Inverie Street. He was coming his way.

He reached the next corner in time to see a black clad figure dart into a close opposite, but even as he threw himself through the battered door in pursuit Frankie had cleared the close and was crossing the back courts, leaping dividing fences and making for the next block. Alec sprinted after, ducking clothes lines, leaping the fence, praying that Frankie wasn't made of the same stuff as McGroarty.

Frankie reached the other side and made for a door only to find it locked. He gave it several kicks and then seeing his pursuer, cleared a metal railing and ran for the next close. Alec narrowed the gap as Frankie stumbled inside. It wasn't much, but it was enough, and leaping headlong through the closing door he caught Frankie by the shoulders and they fell headlong to the concrete floor.

There hadn't been time to think how he'd bring him down and Alec landed badly. Frankie had taken the brunt but he was back on his feet and for a moment Alec though he'd lost him, but as Frankie reached the exit something sent him flying back onto his arse and there, standing over him, was one of the plainers. Alec got to his feet and rubbed his arm as Frankie was lifted against a wall, the plainer jerking his chin in a rough approximation of a polis James Dean.

"You alright?"

Alec confessed himself to be more than alright. Another plainer arrived and Alec followed them downhill to the exit road from the estate where the Donatelli ice cream van was parked, half on the pavement, front offside bumper nestling against a lamppost. Flanking at an angle, back doors open, the battered Transit van. Well, well, well. Not just Ford Escorts then.

Frankie was led to the serving hatch and a plainer climbed inside. Frankie spat at the ground as the fourth, a broad-shouldered cop with fair hair, leaned against the side and pointed to the impromptu vendor within.

"I'm afraid the van's under new management Frankie. But, since you've been a loyal servant to the Donatelli's you can have any one of the sweeties on the shelves behind my lovely colleague here. Free of charge."

A game show hostess from hell, the plainer inside the van made a show of waving his hand along the shelves. The lead plainer winked.

"Any one you like."

Frankie's face was a picture of twisted malevolence.

"You cunts better have a warrant — Donatelli's goin' tae waste you."

The lead plainer's eyes went wide and his mouth formed a small 'O'.

"Language Frankie. The offer's a generous one, don't you agree boys?"

They nodded solemnly. A once-in-a-lifetime it seemed, though it held no attractions for Frankie who stared at the serving hatch without a word.

The lead plainer shrugged.

"Frankie's shy. He's been brought up a nice boy. Let's help Frankie choose."

Friendly smiles all round. They were only there to help. The lead plainer straightened and made a play of looking around the insides of the van like an overgrown child craning his neck to see the bottom shelves.

Frankie had stopped twisting. There was a tense watchfulness that added to the moment, while the lead plainer stroked his chin in mock consideration.

"I'm thinking that Frankie's not an ice cream guy. Too delicate a confectionary, looks a bit homo-erotic on a drug dealer. Am I right Frankie?"

Frankie looked at the faces around him, trying to read the runes, but the plainers stared back in silence, eyes fixed absolutely on their prisoner. It was like being in a circle of hyenas sizing up whether this was the right to time to kill or wait until their prey was a little weaker. The fair-haired tormentor continued as the calm game show host.

"What about a sherbet dip Frankie. A wee snort of the white stuff?"

Frankie shook his head. Alec wasn't sure it was an indication that he didn't like sherbet dips or something had gotten inside his head and he was trying to shake it off. A crowd had gathered up the street and Alec wondered if there'd be trouble but for now they stood like curious animals watching one of the weaker ones being picked off.

"C'mon Frankie. Yer no' playing. How about my colleague inside the van giving a helping hand. Yer the helping type aren't you?"

The vendor nodded solemnly. Yes he was, and to prove it he stepped to one side, the better to show off the shelves, one stacked above the other. Each displayed a cornucopia of sugar in various forms. Toffees, chocolates, boiled sweets, penny chews and jelly babies. The plainer ran his fingers seductively along and down, stopping from time to time to look at Frankie as if sizing him for a suit. He continued down the other shelves until he reached the lowest at the back. There, in a small cluster, was an assortment of little boxes, each depicting a cartoon character. Some had footballers jumping to head a ball. Some had Spider-Man cartoons. Behind these, a row of yellow boxes each with the Superman image. Bingo.

Frankie tensed. The plainers tightened their grip, knuckles white around Frankie's biceps. Alec felt his mouth go dry. Frankie kicked the side of the van and began shouting.

"Ah'll see ye get done for this, fuckin cunts!"

The lead plainer smiled the smile of a priest.

"You don't have to say anything, but anything you do say will be noted down and may be used in evidence. Do you understand?"

Frankie bucked and twisted in an effort to kick out but his flanking escorts were strong. Instead he turned towards the watching herd.

"Ah've been fitted up! Cunts ur plantin' evidence!"

The crowd looked on. There was the odd shout of polis bastards, but Frankie would get no help from them. The lead plainer turned to his colleague in the van and jutted his chin upwards in a gesture of 'let's get on with this.'

"Ok Frankie. Let's see what you might've won."

The Superman packets were extracted from the rack and placed on the counter, while Frankie snorted like a bull. The lead plainer turned to Alec, a funeral undertaker handing out a cord for a coffin.

"Constable, would you like to reveal today's star prize?"

Alec stepped forward and took one of the packets. He was shitting himself. What if there was nothing inside but sweet cigarettes? He could hear Frankie's braying laugh, the bitter look of betrayal on the plainers faces, the condemnation of the shift as he went from hero to zero.

He lifted one of the packets, opened the top and tipped the contents out. A part of him expected to see the little white candy cigarettes with the red tip but instead a tiny polythene bag plopped onto the counter, insides filled with powder the colour of Demerara sugar. Alec had anticipated a volcanic eruption from Frankie, but instead, he sagged between his detaining officers as the lead plainer read over the next steps from a laminated card.

The ice cream van was driven to Corsair Street, while Alec hitched a lift in the battered van with the others, his smile as wide as the Clyde. There'd be a further search and no doubt they'd find more. Two junkies had coughed up their guts in a darkened close in exchange for their liberty and then slipped away to score tenner bags elsewhere. There was no customer loyalty when it came to addiction.

He was standing at the charge bar basking in the afterglow when Fitzpatrick strode in, face red, shoulders back.

"Where the fuck have you been? I've been shouting you on the radio the last half hour!"

Alec reached for his radio and realised he'd turned down the volume after they'd caught Frankie. Shit. He'd missed a notebook signing, but he'd made a great arrest, surely that should cover it.

"Helping the plainers Sarge. Caught Frankie Campbell. Van full of smack."

The response was instantaneous.

"Upstairs. My office."

What the fuck. The petty wee bastard probably had his nose put out of joint because he'd made a good arrest. Alec trudged upstairs after the retreating figure of Fitzpatrick kindling an undying hatred for the man.

When he reached the Sergeants office Fitzpatrick was waiting for him. Andy Bell sat at his desk in the other corner.

"Perhaps you'd like to explain why involved yourself in a plain clothes operation without our permission."

So, there it was. Choking back sarcasm Alec described the arrest of Frankie and the kids who'd be spared heroin for a while, but Fitzpatrick wasn't listening and like a schoolboy being chastised, Alec watched as Fitzpatrick drew out his notebook and begin to write.

"I cannot emphasise how seriously I take this. This is a formal warning. Any future transgressions may see you out of a job."

Fuck right off. He wanted to shout the words, but impotent in his anger he looked to Andy Bell hoping he'd intervene. Bell, unable to meet his gaze looked down at a report on his desk. 'Tufty Club' right enough.

He was then dismissed, to walk the last hours of the shift as a shipwrecked mariner, cast adrift on an ocean of anger, dumbfounded that something so good could be turned into shit. That such a high could quickly turn into a low. But what struck him more than anything was the realisation of how much enmity there was in the heart of Fitzpatrick and how real the danger there was of him orchestrating his dismissal.

Stick or Twist

The sour taste was still there at the start of the early shift. A late winter's day where the wind dropped and the rain fell like stair rods. His mood further deepened when he was directed to help Ronnie and Duncan with a sudden death. It reached black hole levels when Fitzpatrick announced he was to take over entirely and let Ronnie and the golden boy return to patrol duties.

There was just enough time for Ronnie to pass what little information they'd gleaned, before they were whisked away in the supervisory car like VIP's, Duncan Stewart waving his friendly entitled wave. Cunt.

Alec watched the rain hammer the pavement before closing the door and retreating down a gloomy hallway to the bedroom. The orange glow from a streetlight shone through the thin curtains and Alec could make out the rough shape of Mr Bannerman on his bed, stick thin and ramrod straight, a candlewick blanket over his face. The casualty surgeon had been and gone. A suspected heart attack and no suspicious circumstances. Next of kin unknown. Little else to do but wait for the shell.

He retreated to the sitting room in which a ceiling light, stained yellow from decades of cigarette smoke, produced a sickly pall over a space that was filled with junk. A storm tossed sea of clothes, books and bric-a-brac broke on islands of cardboard boxes, some marked for charity shops, others simply labelled 'books'. In the eye of the junk storm, two high backed chairs faced a formica topped coffee table. Alec pursed his lips and shook his head. He was yet to find Carmichael's birth certificate and there was the issue of valuables. Somewhere in the chaos would be a small sum of money. The old folks didn't trust banks. He was pondering where to start when there was a knock on the front door.

Thinking it was Fitzpatrick returning to gloat Alec swung the door open. But it wasn't the Sergeant, it was Harry. And over Harry's shoulder was Gerry in the driver's seat of a panda, the sound of the engine drowned by the drumming rain on its roof. Harry smiled and teased the end of his black moustache.

"Thought you might need a hand."

And with that he brushed past, his disembodied voice calling from the darkness.

"Where's the old fella?"

Alec followed. He felt strangely protective of the dead man and resented Harry's casual intrusion, but he felt obliged to answer.

"Bedroom. On the left."

By the time he'd caught up, Harry was in the doorway of the bedroom giving the corpse no more than a cursory glance as his torch beam swept the furniture.

"You've searched in here?"

Harry had an unerring ability to make him feel stupid. Now that he'd asked the question it was obvious this is where he should've started.

"Was just about to."

It sounded lame and he knew it. There was the sound of the front door closing and Harry called over his shoulder to the hallway beyond.

"Bedroom's no' been searched Gerry. We'll start here."

Alec bristled. He was grateful that Harry had volunteered to help but this was his call and he resented his relegation to bit player. He was about to say as much when he felt Gerry tap him on the shoulder, his voice a whisper.

"He's here because he's been telt to. Him and Fitzpatrick don't see eye to eye."

So, Harry had been sent as a punishment. Alec felt the tension ebb, but what transgression had Harry been guilty of?

"He could be nicer about it."

Gerry smiled and patted Alec on the shoulder. Harry was already rummaging around, opening cupboard doors and pulling boxes off shelves. With the body a few feet away, the casual approach made Alec feel uncomfortable but Gerry simply winked and eased his way into the bedroom.

"Let's do this right Harry. We'll start in one corner, Alec in another. That way we'll no' miss anything."

They searched the room, Alec working his way through a cupboard piled high with shoe boxes containing documents, letters and photographs. Little stepping stones across a river of life. Harry, hunched over a mahogany dresser, pulled out heavy drawers with a grunt, sweeping the clothes from side to side.

"There's money somewhere here. I can smell it."

Gerry jabbed a thumb at Harry with a 'get the state of him' look. Alec smiled at the conspiratorial cockiness but Harry, oblivious, continued to rifle through underwear and folded shirts.

"Ah ha!"

Harry stepped back triumphant, torch aimed at the bottom drawer.

"Gentlemen. I have struck the motherlode."

There, deep within the recesses of the drawer, small polythene bags had been bundled in tight rows. Within each could be seen the rough outlines of banknotes bound by elastic bands. Harry pulled the drawer out and shone his torch into the void beyond.

"And there's more..."

Gerry knelt on the carpet and shone his torch in the direction of the find. In its glare Alec saw the gleam in Harry's eyes and his vulpine grin. The floor inside the dresser was carpeted with bundles of money. Lots of it.

"The auld fella must have robbed a bank. There's a few thousand there at least."

Harry snorted.

"Not a bank Gerry. A bookies."

"Eh?"

Harry sat back. He looked bemused.

"Bannerman's Bookies? *'Bet With Bannerman's'?*"

Gerry shook his head.

Harry tutted.

"He was a big deal round here. Filthy bastard took my father's wages every Friday. Should've had 'Sponsored By The Millars" above his shop. There were days we starved cause of this old tosser."

There was silence. Harry stared at the money with a look of anger and shame. It sounded a familiar story. A memory of his oldest cousin extracting money from his dad before he blew his Friday wages rose up towards him and in that moment he saw Harry in a different light. Is that where the anger and aggression came from?

Harry shook his head as if to dislodge a memory.

"Let's get this lot into the sitting room and get it counted. Might take a while."

It took several trips, arms folded over their chests, bundles of cash like swaddled babies. When the coffee table was overwhelmed they placed the rest underneath and after the final bundle had been deposited they stood staring. Alec, realising how big a task it would be, looked at Gerry.

"Shouldn't we count this at the office?"

Harry spoke first.

"Here. Less chance of being interrupted."

Harry turned to Gerry, his back to Alec who felt like an Edwardian servant in the presence of his masters.

"The boy should get back to the office. He's got a report to do — we can take it from here."

Gerry looked at the money and then shook his head.

"Needs three…there's too much for two."

When Harry turned back to the money the smile had disappeared and he looked petulant.

"Better get started then."

Alec found an old poufee and they sat around the table, their torches pointing upwards lit their faces in a ghoulish parody of a late-night card school. The notes were old, but dry and Harry counted with crisp efficiency.

"Ten, twenty, thirty, forty, fifty, sixty, seventy, eighty, ninety, one hundred."

As each hundred was reached Harry laid the notes to one side and started again. When he reached the next hundred, the notes were laid across the previous at right angles until a crisscross tower of notes formed.

The towers multiplied. Gerry sat back, face deep in shadow and conscious that no one was recording the totals, Alec reached for his notebook. Harry, eyes still locked on the money, stopped counting.

"You'll no' need that yet..."

Alec stared at the top of Harry's head and wondered if there were eyes hidden there. They all knew the importance of recording the seizure of money and he looked over at Gerry, but his face was impassive as Harry began counting again.

"Ten, twenty, thirty, forty, fifty..."

Alec took his notebook out anyway and vowed that he wouldn't leave the flat until every last note was accounted for. But not yet, something was afoot and he wanted to see where this was going. Harry's metronomic voice continued hypnotically onwards as he counted the money into three distinct groups, each containing five towers of cash. Five thousand pounds in each, fifteen thousand in total. Alec looked at the bundles on the floor. It was a rough guess, but there was a similar amount there.

"..sixty, seventy, eighty, ninety, one hundred."

Harry stopped and looked up, eyes bright, a thin trace of a smile and not for the first time Alec thought there was something of the night about him.

"No next of kin?"

Alec shook his head and hunched his shoulders against the chill. There was something rapacious about Harry's demeanour, but he answered anyway.

"No kids. Wife died years ago. Neighbour says he lived alone —so no visitors."

Harry pursed his lips. When he spoke, it was slow and deliberate.

"Sad. All goes to the government then. Total waste."

Harry sighed and looked down at the money, shoulders slumped, hands clasped, head lowered.

"Five thousand in each pile, maybe another fifteen on the carpet."

He then looked at Gerry, voice velvet soft and measured.

"Nobody would miss this."

Alec was young, but he wasn't stupid. Five thousand each. The rest counted out and lodged. No-one to claim the money. No-one to show up at the station, shouting 'where's the rest?' Alec looked at Gerry willing him to say something, but Gerry just stared at the money and Alec felt compelled to intervene. It was stick or twist.

"There'll always be someone Harry. The neighbour, a friend of a friend, a distant second cousin. Word gets out."

Harry shrugged and waved a hand over the money. There was jokey tone, but it had an edge.

"There's nobody. Just a pile of notes that'll take hours to count, pin to a card, record in a book, put in a safe. And for what? Goes to the tax man."

Harry winked at Gerry.

"Tell him."

Alec cut in. It was bad enough trying to face down Harry, he didn't need the burden of taking on Gerry too.

"What would it buy you Harry? New car? Sofa and a washing machine? For that you get the worry there's someone out there after all? Then, one day, two senior detectives waiting to interview you at work."

He tried to maintain an air of jocularity. After all, no one had suggested anything concrete, but he was conscious of a tension in his voice as he pointed the piles out to Gerry.

"How much do you get paid? Four times this and a nice pension when it's all done. Who'd gamble that?"

He'd expected a sarcastic response from Harry, an escalation of some kind, but the room was silent. Gerry and Harry looked at him without comment, but it felt as if he was being weighed and assessed. Gerry leaned forward as if to study him closer and then turned to Harry with another wink.

"Let's get this counted and down the road. There's tea waiting for us at the old folks home."

Harry smiled ruefully and shook his head as if an opportunity had been lost but he counted the rest of the money. When he finished, he sagged in his chair, reached in his tunic and pulled out a pack of cigarettes. He lit one, took a deep draw and exhaled, a smokers satisfaction on his face. After a few seconds he looked at Alec.

"Better get that notebook open. You've got some writing to do."

Alec wrote the details down. Thirty thousand pounds. Harry made a show of perusing the entry before scribbling his signature below it and with that he stood up, reached for his cap and left the room. Gerry signed the notebook and gave a curt nod.

"You did well. Give me a shout when you're done and I'll give you a lift to the office."

Gerry gathered up his hat and walked towards the living room door, but Alec couldn't let him leave without asking the question.

"Gerry?"

"Yeah?"

"Was Harry serious…about the money?"

Gerry opened his mouth to reply, but at that moment there was a shout from the front door.

"Move yer arse Gerry! I'm gasping!"

Gerry put on his cap and smiled.

"See you later Alec."

Gerry vanished into the hall and after a few seconds the front door slammed shut.

Alec sat befuddled, unable to decide whether whether it had been an elaborate test or if Harry had been serious. He was still replaying the conversation in his head when there was a knock at the door and this time it was Harkness with Fitzpatrick.

"All done?"

"Yes Sir."

A curt nod.

"I hear some cash recovered. We'll take it to the office while you wait for the shell."

It was an unexpected kindness and the offer was a good one. It would save the hassle of lodging it and anyway, it wasn't a request, it was an order.

He handed the money over and watched Harkness and Fitzpatrick drive away. He'd have a long wait for the shell. Plenty of time to get his notes in order. Plenty of time to reflect on the strange behaviours money brought out in his fellow human beings.

Connection

Over the following weeks Alec had cause to reflect not only on the personalities of his colleagues, but on the vagaries of his existence. Estranged from Auchenbreoch, seldom in touch with Dad and persona-non-grata with his Sergeant, he took consolation from the fact the canal rescue had finally initiated a thawing of relations with the shift, though his relationship with Harry remained tense. Despite his heroics at the stabbing the complaint remained a black cloud hanging over them. Harry's contradictory behaviour with the money at the sudden death hadn't helped and then, on the last day before another weekend off, an order from Harkness at the end of the muster.

"Harry. My room please."

Harry stubbed his cigarette on the floor and followed the Inspector into the corridor. Ronnie muttered something about the complaint. Was Harry going to be charged? There'd be real trouble now. Harry would go on the warpath and the shift would side with him. Again.

Alec went to the radio room in a gloomy frame of mind, but when Harry appeared minutes later he looked younger, the creases on his face gone, a broad smile on his face. Harry reached out and Alec braced himself, but the slap on the back was friendly.

"Yer off the hook. Complaint's been dropped."

"You're joking."

"Never joke about a thing like that. Yer man dropped the complaint."

Alec was speechless. Had something gone wrong with the investigation? He was about to offer half-hearted congratulations but Harry, keen to spread the good news, had left the room and it was tea break before he could tap Ronnie for information.

"Happens. Complainer gets compensation from the criminal injuries people and they're happy with that."

Cash for scars. Was that all it took? He remembered the lads from school who worked in the abattoir, each missing a finger in an industrial 'accident', the compensation buying them a hot hatch. A funny old world.

Harry was the life and soul at tea break, not even a losing streak at cards dimmed his general satisfaction with life. Alec watched from the sidelines in disbelief. It was never over 'til the fat lady sang right enough.

A corner might have turned with Harry, but nothing had diluted Fitzpatrick's enmity and each time Alec came into the orbit of his malice it sealed the impression that his Sergeant was hell bent on sectarian cleansing. Alec doubled down on doing the best he could; bulling his shoes and pressing his tunic, so that every day was parade day. With the help of Charlie and Stevie he kept his case load up without resorting to the kind of chicanery hinted on the day of the stabbing, but with a year till his probation finished Fitzpatrick could play the waiting game and so the sword of Damocles remained suspended. Thank Christ for the weekend. A chance to regroup. Maybe a trip to Auchenbreoch. He'd not spoken to Dad for some time and as each week passed the guilt pressed ever more heavily.

He was still weighing up his options in the locker room when the portly figure of Ricky appeared at the end of the row.

"There's a race night at the Bellevue Club tonight. Partners evening but it doesn't matter. There'll be other shifts — you might meet one of those female cops they keep talking about. Fancy it?"

Bloody hell. He'd enough grace to accept the invite without it seeming like the earth had just shifted on its axis, but it surely had. In a far lighter frame of mind he headed home for a nap and a shower. Auchenbreoch could wait.

The Bellevue was a former gentleman's club, one of many with associations to army regiments long disbanded or merged within the ever-contracting footprint of the British Army. It had been owned by a small Scottish regiment whose last battle honour had been in a far-flung quarter of the dying empire and since former combatants were now dying of old age rather than battle, they'd sought clientele from something considered to be similarly hierarchical and embattled. And so it was an enterprising committee member found the one true source of guaranteed income for a decaying west end Victorian villa, an organisation populated with near alcoholics more than willing to spend cash on cheap beer every day of the week.

An elderly doorman greeted him in a vestibule the size of a small house, the ceilings ornate and impossibly high. The whole effect was of a small embassy, dusty chandelier suspended from the ceiling, grand staircase wide enough for ladies with ballgowns to descend two-by-two, a detailed and colourful regimental crest complete with Latin motto on the tiled floor. The doorman, probably an old soldier, pointed down an oak panelled corridor to the rear of the building from where the muffled sounds of Agadoo could be heard. Oh well. Onwards and downwards.

He'd never been to a race night, but Ricky had been enthusiastic.

"Horses racing on a big screen, buffet and some dancin'. Cheap booze, you only have to reach into yer pocket for the gee gees."

It sounded fair enough but as Alec opened the panelled doors to a small hall, it was not a disco that came to mind but the Auchenbreoch

Labour Club functions of the early seventies his mum and dad used to go to.

Under the spinning starscape of a cheap mirrorball, men in tan suits and thin ties chain smoked cheap cigarettes between swigs of beer and glasses of whisky. In keeping with the 70's zeitgeist their wives had all, to a matriarch, adopted the same mode of dress and hairstyle. Some wore the kind of arched frame spectacles from the sixties that his school pal Tom had called 'angry specs'. It gave them the same look of suspicion and scepticism as their men who periodically shuttled back and forth to a small bar for vodkas and orange. The wives, wreathed in cigarette smoke, chatted in huddles that spoke of established social circles beyond which nothing else existed. Alec could guess the talk. Shift gossip and things their men had seen and done. Well, the version their men told them anyway.

Around the hall, in squares Wellington would've been proud of, sat the four divisions that'd signed up to the nights entertainment. At the far end, disco equipment perched on a trestle table, a fat bald man trying to fire up the crowd with Rick Astley. It was going be different if nothing else.

A solid phalanx of Corsair Street's finest sat midway down the hall. A chair had been kept free and Alec was relieved it was beside Ronnie and his wife who he half-expected to whistle Gaelic tunes just like her man. She did have an accent straight from Benebecula but Agnes, a solid name straight out of the forties, went on to smash his preconceptions through the simple fact of being lively company, much more approachable than the old sod himself, who added to the conversation only when it was strictly necessary.

There were nods from the other wives, but there was no attempt to engage him in conversation. It gave the impression that they followed the same hierarchical rules as their husbands and that as a probationer he was not to be much bothered with. The saving grace was the absence of Fitzpatrick and Harkness; their non-appearance explained by Ronnie as if he'd just descended from Mount Sinai with a tablet.

"Gaffers don't come to night outs. Cannae let yer hair down with them taking notes."

Alec looked around the hall. Most of the men looked repressed, as if the regimented nature of their work had crushed the impulsive sides from their natures. In what ways did they let their hair down? If Fitzpatrick had stuck his head in, he'd have left convinced his men were still on duty, such was the watchfulness around the room.

The volume levels increased and with the drink dissolving their iron clad reserve, the men became more animated. Risqué jokes and old war stories emerged, funny and sharply observed and Alec found himself in a pocket of real enjoyment, the men relaxed, the women with the indulgent smiles of wives who saw again something of the men they'd married before death, violence and despair had taken their toll.

It was the same all around, except that in the other tables there were young women and men wearing the same bemused expressions as he. A slim red-haired girl looked around and their eyes met. An exchange of smiles before the intervention of a drunken colleague took her attention away. Maybe a chance of a dance there. He slowed his drinking and found ways of shuffling his unattended pints under the noses of those willing to accept them.

Disco gave way to horses and having lost some money for a good cause, he sought solace in the buffet, which turned out to be a mountain of luncheon meat sandwiches and sausage rolls. He'd been in the process of filling his plate when a well-spoken voice appeared at his side. The girl from across the floor. She had a beautiful smile and pale sapphire eyes that contained a glint that was altogether too intelligent.

"I'm guessing this isn't your normal Thursday night."

Alec swallowed hard. He'd just bitten a sandwich and from her smirk guessed she'd chosen that moment deliberately. Funny girl.

"God no. I mean it's ok, but reminds me of the functions my mum and dad used to go to. Same fashions."

An enthusiastic nod.

"Me too. Only came because they said there'd be dancing and an extensive buffet."

Alec laughed and held up his plate of sandwiches. She held up hers. They'd been fed the same line.

"Well, there's always the dancing..."

It had been said impulsively, but now he realised how much he hoped she'd agree. So much hinged on simple moments.

She layered more sandwiches onto her plate, face hidden from view and when she looked up the smile was dialled back a little and there was a look of curious assessment.

"Hope you can wiggle those hips as well as you can eat."

Before he could think up a reply, she crossed the empty dance floor to join the raucous company of the men on the other side.

Alec returned to his table discombobulated. He'd expected nothing of the night, but things had taken an unexpected turn. He tried to concentrate on the conversations around him, but his mind was no longer in the company and when he looked round he found she'd turned to look at him at the same time. There'd been a theatrical roll of the eyes and he'd grinned, but conscious he could only do that so often he returned to the sight of Harry making balloon shapes. This one looked decidedly sexual and the women hooted and shrieked in faux outrage as Harry made the final twist. A cock and two balls. Who'd have thought that possible with two party balloons.

But the next piece of entertainment didn't come from Harry. It was provided by Ricky who, lager in hand, weaved his way among the constellations cast by the mirrorball towards the red-haired girl. Ricky made a theatrical bow, lager slopping on the floor and extended his free hand. The girl smiled as polite a smile as a young woman could when faced with the likes of Ricky, but shook her head. And that should've been that, but Ricky too pissed to take a hint placed his pint with great care at the edge of a now silent table and began to pull her to the dance floor. The men at her table rose to their feet but Ricky, oblivious to their protestations, continued to drag the girl from her chair. Alec was about to ride to the rescue when one of the younger cops at the girl's table stepped between Ricky and the object of his desires, pushing them apart and sending Ricky onto his backside.

It was a replay of the wedding and any other social function in any town or city the length or breadth the country where drunk men fight over young women. Ricky staggered to his feet and swung a punch that struck his rival's shoulder and sent him spinning to the floor. Men swarmed to restrain Ricky, but all was lost in the chaos as Sandy, Charlie and the others rushed to Ricky's aid and as they collided in the middle of the floor one punch led to another in an almost nuclear chain reaction.

Above the sound and fury the DJ called for calm but as other tables emptied onto the floor it was clear the evening was over.

A voice appeared at his side. It was Harry.

"Let's get the fuck out of here."

Alec felt his jacket pressed into his hand as Harry tugged him in the direction of the exit. Ronnie and a few others were doing likewise. There was no sight of the girl and Alec hoped she was doing the same. A fullscale fight was underway and with the disco switched off the air was rent with the screams and curses of fighting men.

He weaved through a throng of old gentlemen in the reception area and into the street where Harry turned towards the city and Alec fell into step beside him, head lowered against a fine rain, hands deep in pockets. Behind them, the wailing of sirens and they quickened their steps to put as much distance between themselves and the Bellevue. Only when they'd reached the next junction did Harry pause.

"This is where we part. Go home, unplug the phone, stay low for a day or two."

Alec was still trying to get his head around the fight. He felt as if he'd betrayed the others by running away. He could imagine the looks of condemnation in the locker room on Monday night and it depressed him.

"What about the others? Shouldn't we go back and help?"

Harry laughed.

"You'll only get yerself in bother. They're big boys and can look out for themselves."

Harry waved down a taxi and as he climbed in, he shouted.

"Go home. There'll be hell to pay on Monday. Keep yer phone off the hook!"

The taxi disappeared into the smir, leaving Alec on the pavement, a fine drizzle soaking his jacket. The excitement of meeting the girl had gone, replaced by a sense of foreboding and anxiety. Back at the Bellevue he imagined the shift handcuffed, with torn shirts and black eyes and wondered what would happen next. Fucking hell, what a life.

Another cab drew into the kerb beside him. He was just about to congratulate the driver on his clairvoyant powers when the passenger window slid down and the face of a beautiful woman with red hair and blue eyes appeared at the opening.

"Don't just stand there. Get in!"

Retribution

Her name was Emma. And as she explained in the taxi home, she'd seen Alec at the last second, her mind preoccupied with the events at the club. When they arrived outside his flat he'd hoped she'd come in, but she'd smiled and shook her head.

"I don't know you well enough."

"Maybe a coffee sometime?"

It felt like a last throw of the dice, but it was worth a try. He was rewarded with another smile and the sight of her rummaging in her handbag for a scrap of paper. She couldn't find a pen but determined that there'd be no fall at the first hurdle he'd cajoled one from a recalcitrant taxi driver. When she handed the slip over it was like the golden ticket for Willy Wonka's Chocolate Factory and Alec folded it carefully before stepping from the cab.

"Glad I bumped into you — only good thing that happened tonight."

Her look told him she felt the same but there was a sadness there too.

"Coffee. But don't phone for a few weeks. There's going to be a shitstorm and I've things to sort out at home."

With that enigmatic farewell Alec slipped some money to the driver and closed the door. The taxi sped off, Emma briefly waving through the back window as the cab disappeared into the night.

He thought of her a lot, moods alternating between the possibilities of a first date and a black despondency that she'd change her mind. He'd barely talked to her, what chance did he stand with a girl like that? The rest of the weekend was spent moping and with night shifts approaching, his thoughts increasingly turned to the Bellevue, the fate of his colleagues and the repercussions to follow. Thank god he'd got out in time.

The muster was a morgue on the first night. Some of the shift sported the second prizes they'd picked up at the Bellevue. There was no Ricky. Harry sat behind and just before the entrance of the supervisors whispered a stern warning.

"Burst tae fuck all."

Alec acknowledged the message with a quick nod. He knew what Harry meant. There would be an inquiry. Whatever he was asked, he was to say absolutely nothing. He'd heard about stuff that'd happened on other shifts where those who'd kept their mouths shut often escaped censure. Those that blabbed dug their own graves. His heart sank with the prospect of another complaints interrogation.

Harkness strode in. He didn't sit, but instead leaned his knuckles on the table and tilted his head so that he looked at the assembly beneath hooded eyes. Alec braced for a furious tirade, but what came next was measured and filled with remorseless intent.

"I received a phone call over the weekend from the Deputy Chief Constable."

Alec felt the air escape his body and those around him visibly sagged. The Dep was a puritanical zealot in all matters conduct. If Corsair Street was the Wild West the Dep was the hanging judge looking for the nearest tree.

"Ricky is suspended and the Dep has made clear more heads will roll. Some of you think you've got a job for life and can do as you bloody well please. Those days are over. You're well paid and the public expect higher standards. This is now a criminal enquiry and each of you will submit an operational statement by close of play."

The muster got underway to a tense silence. It concluded with a communal scraping of chairs as the shift made with haste for the door. Alec had just gathered up his raincoat when Harkness called his name.

"Constable MacKay. My room."

Constable MacKay. Very formal. Alec caught Ronnie's warning look and tried to respond but Fitzpatrick was having none of it.

"Quick about it."

A chair had been placed in the middle of Harkness's room. The careful preparation further cemented the feeling that something bad was going down. Alec felt the familiar sick dry-mouth tension and Harry's whispered warning echoed in his head.

He sat and waited for the inevitable questions about the Bellevue, thanking his lucky stars he'd not been part of the punch up. He'd been drunk, his recollections would naturally be hazy. He was thinking through the angles when Fitzpatrick produced a folder and retrieved a sheaf of papers. He looked at Alec with a thin lipped stare.

Alec's heart hit the pit of his stomach as Fitzpatrick asked the question he knew was coming.

"Recognise this?"

Of course he did. The McGroarty case. He was in real trouble now. Why hadn't he just rolled with the punches as Ronnie told him? Here were the consequences. He braced himself for what was coming, knowing he'd handed Fitzpatrick all the ammo he required, on a silver plate.

Harkness took a seat while Fitzpatrick leafed through the case papers. Having found the summary, he pressed the pages flat, all the better to read out the selected passages picked out with highlighter pen. Very organised.

"Do you know what insubordination is Constable MacKay?"

That formal thing again.

"Yes Sarge."

"Then explain why you disobeyed a lawful instruction and altered this case without my permission?"

There were no words. Not the kind he really wanted to say, like the fabrication of evidence to suit your world view was never a lawful order, so no insubordination there you bigoted prick. But Alec's deceit weighed on him, he'd acted the dutiful Constable and his secret alteration of the report now felt like low-life deceit. He'd been congratulated on his report and then stabbed his Sergeant in the back. And now, bizarrely, he felt dishonourable. The pious attitudes that'd gripped him that day had been no more than mere self-indulgence. The reply felt mealy mouthed.

"I just wanted it to be accurate."

Fitzpatrick exploded.

"Accurate! That fenian fucker punched me in the eye and you took his side?"

Harkness hadn't batted an eye at the fenian reference. There'd be no help there then. Fitzpatrick waved the case papers in the air.

"This's an attempt to sully my good name. To embarrass me in court and damage my hard earned reputation."

Alec wanted to say his reputation had been easily enough earned but said nothing. There was no way he'd get a word in and there was an inevitability about where this was going next. Holding up a hand, Harkness brought Fitzpatrick's ranting to a close. If the Sergeant was the prosecution, Harkness was judge and executioner. The tone was somber, the regret, fake.

"Alec, you've done good things, but by the same measure there's been sides to your personality that have given the Sergeant and I great cause for concern. Sergeant Fitzpatrick has drawn my attention to your yearly appraisal. It makes very bad reading."

It was so well choreographed. Harkness drew the appraisal from an envelope and Alec saw the boxes for A, B, C, D, E. The ticks were all in the D's. What kind of fucking stunt was this? It flashed through his mind to get up and walk straight out, go home, go sick. But he stayed, pressed to his seat by a sense of honour and the invisible weight of the discipline code as the Inspector methodically read over a damning appraisal.

What now? He'd received a warning already. Harkness pulled another form from the envelope and Alec's eyes welled up. He'd seen one just like it presented on his police college course by a Chief Inspector from the Complaints and Discipline Branch. The Regulation Twelve form; a one way ticket out the service. So it had come to this. Harkness drove on, a man whose mind had been made up, who spoke to prevent protestation or plea from stopping what he had to say.

"Alec. It's not just this case, or the poor appraisal, it's the inconsideration you displayed for

Sergeant Fitzpatrick in leaving your duties to assist the plain clothes unit. You're a law unto yourself and this is a disciplined organisation that relies on teamwork and respect for rank. You displayed neither. And now we have Thursday night, a shambles of an evening in which the good reputation of the force was damaged by a bunch of drunken officers of whom you were one."

Alec began to protest. He'd done nothing wrong, but Harkness held up a large hand.

"You'll have your day in due course. I take no pleasure in this, but there're thousands queueing to join and we can't carry passengers."

Overwhelmed by the moment, Alec lost the power of speech and as Harkness read over the contents of the form he began to fall in on himself, so that he didn't hear the last few sentences and had to be brought back to the present by Harkness.

"Is there anything you want to say before we conclude Alec."

There was. Fitzpatrick's blind hatred of Roman Catholics for a start, but riddled with doubt and stunned by the suddenness he sat paralysed as his mind wandered punch-drunk over the possibilities. Harkness hadn't balked at Fitzpatrick's fenian reference. Was he in the Orange Lodge too? If Fitzpatrick was the idiot with the red hand on his sleeve was Harkness the one who kept it under wraps? Would an allegation of sectarianism pour petrol on the flames? As ever, when faced by unreasonable men, the victim falls back on reason.

"I'm sorry if I've caused upset sir, but I'm willing to learn. Can't you reconsider?"

He hated himself, but what else could he say that wasn't full of retribution and revenge. While there was hope, however, slim, he'd stay composed. The fat lady hadn't sung yet. Harkness shook his head. Alec hoped for a glimmer of remorse but when he looked to Fitzpatrick there was none. Just implacable determination and a hint of triumph.

"If you want to use some annual leave Alec I'm sure the sergeant and I can accommodate that. After all, your thoughts may be elsewhere until the matter is concluded."

A flicker of defiance flared within. Fuck that. Whatever time he'd left he'd spend it as a cop. With a brief thanks, but no thanks, he left for the radio room, grabbed a radio and headed for the street, tears welling, fists clenched.

He carried the burden for an hour before Charlie and Stevie found him wandering around Barnhouse. Harkness's summons had caused a communal raising of eyebrows and as Alec climbed into the van the question from Stevie was immediate.

"What did they pricks want with you?"

He told them everything. There was no point in sugar coating the role he'd played in his own downfall. Charlie frowned, but said nothing until he'd finished.

"That's the basis of the reggie twelve? They can fuck right off."

It became the focal point of the tea break, eclipsing even the events of the Thursday night and the usual cut and thrust of the card school. Alec was heartened by the support, but kind words and outrage weren't going to save his bacon. He'd retreated to write his operational statement in the report writing room when Ronnie appeared.

"It'll never stand Alec."

The sentiment was welcome, but he was already beginning to feel different, set apart like the man in the condemned cell.

"I don't hold out hope of changing anybody's mind."

Pursed lips and a shake of the head.

"Don't assume those clowns are held in high regard. Get yerself into Currie. Raise a complaint. Do a bit of shit stirring."

Ronnie's advice dominated his thoughts on the way home and after fitful three hours in bed, he showered, breakfasted and putting on his best suit and tie, headed back to the office. He'd have it out with Currie and a see what happened next. What had he to lose?

But Currie's office was empty, a scribbled note declaring he'd be back in an hour. Except that it wasn't an hour, it was two, and by the time Currie clumped up the stairs Alec was dead on his feet. He must have looked it, for the first question was 'are you alright?'

"I'm hoping you can make it right Sir."

Currie wrinkled his nose and signalled to follow. The Superintendent rounded his desk and with the accuracy of a man who'd been office bound for years, sat without having to check where his seat was. He tapped a large manila envelope sitting on his desk.

"If it's about this report from Inspector Harkness, I'm afraid it's out of my hands. Very disappointing. After you pulled the lad from the canal I thought there'd be a commendation."

Shit. Harkness had beaten him to it. Now, more than ever, he needed that commendation, his case for the defence.

"My commendation sir, will I still get it? It would make my dad proud."

Currie sat back, shoulders slumped.

"Your Inspector has withdrawn it. Given the circumstances I'd think that's the least of your worries."

Bastards. He'd have no cards left when this reached Force Headquarters. A written warning, a bad appraisal and the coup de grace, the Regulation Twelve. Done like a kipper. He'd no other options. Just tell it as it is.

"Sir, this is all wrong. I must tell you I've been the subject of anti-catholic prejudice by my supervisor."

His heart made valiant attempts to burst through his rib cage as he braced himself for the questions, but there were none. Instead, Currie was up and round the table before Alec could draw breath. He stepped back as the barrel chested Currie bore down on him, eyes gleaming with furious indignation.

"Get out!"

Alec retreated a few steps, unable to think of a way to calm the old bastard down but Currie was just warming up.

"How dare you come in here and fabricate this shit to save yer own skin?"

He tried to cut in, that this was no fabrication, there was proof and holy fuck why didn't the old fucker just listen? But Currie kept up this torrent of condemnations as Alec backed into the corridor, colliding with a female cop who stood transfixed, mouth wide open.

"I've heard this crap from every jackanape come to play their last card. You're not the first to drag their accuser through the dirt and I'll have none of it!"

Alec felt his eyes smart. He felt belittled, like a snotty schoolboy. Everything he'd gone through had been for nothing, hopes he'd turned a corner, up in smoke. Angry for being so naïve, so stupid, he bounded down the stairs, fists clenched, muttering 'fuck this', wheel spinning from the car park a beaten man.

By the time he reached the sanctuary of the flat he'd calmed down, but the embarrassment of his encounter with Currie and the feeling of defeat weighed heavily. So much for Ronnie's advice, so much for the low esteem Harkness and Fitzpatrick were held in. It was just as the old timers said; the gaffers stuck together. And Harry was right after all, it was 'us' against 'them'. Except there was no us. Just them.

He reached into the fridge and opened a bottle of beer. As the cap hissed and spun to the floor his mind was made up. He'd take some time off. He'd no appetite for keeping the company of Harkness and Fitzpatrick, but in turn it presented another problem. What would he do with himself?

Retreat

He'd not been to Auchenbreoch since Margot's wedding, the events of that weekend cementing the notion his future lay in Glasgow and his new career. Going back, even for a few days, would be an embarrassing admission that he needed the place and tail between his legs admit that Dad and half of Auchenbreoch had been right after all. There was no way he was ready to admit that. Far easier to pass his reappearance as an overdue reconnection with family and friends, a pretence that barely survived crossing the threshold, Dad greeting him in time honoured fashion.

"If I'd known I was getting royalty, I'd have put out the red carpet!"

Gruff love. Alec put on his best smile. In response, there was a narrowing of the eyes.

"What's up?"

You can't kid a kidder. A half truth would have to do for now.

"Some minor trouble on the shift. Time off till it's sorted."

Dad looked sceptical.

"You can tell me when yer ready. Have ye had yer tea?"

Alec shook his head. Appetite dulled by anxiety he'd not had breakfast, or lunch, but when the familiar smell of steak pie wafted from the kitchen it returned with a vengeance. Just what the doctor ordered.

It was a meal consumed to the background hum of small talk and Alec gave silent thanks that Dad had taken his arrival at face value for now, even if he was undeniably sceptical. There'd been no recriminations for his failure to keep in touch, or his long absence from Auchenbreoch Instead, there'd been gentle acceptance of his reappearance, as if he'd.

never left in the first place.

Alec gathered the plates and did the dishes. Ordinarily he'd have sought solace in The Volunteer but it was Tuesday and it would be like the Mary Celeste on a school night. Accepting it as a blessing he made himself at home in his old room and had an early night.

He spent the next two days walking the hills and moors, fishing the lochans with his old fly rod. He caught nothing but it was meditative and in the serenity of the high moorland, among the cries of lapwings and the baa-ing sheep, the wind whipped away earthly worries and a sense of perspective returned. He climbed the Garrioch Law, this time to its summit and looked over the rolling hills to the distant Firth of Clyde and Ailsa Craig. Life was filled with possibilities. He was young. Maybe fate had played a hand and there was something better round the corner. Que Sera Sera. The thought of leaving something he'd only just learned to love lanced his thoughts from time to time, but he was far removed from it and for the first time he blessed the anchor that was Auchenbreoch.

There'd been a call from Ronnie, offering encouragement and the surprising news that many of the anachronistic assembly were asking for him. The consensus was that he was getting a raw deal and they were rooting for him. The words were welcome, but he couldn't escape the irony of becoming accepted just as the journey was ending.

It was a feeling that dominated his walk to The Volunteer on the Friday night. A reunion with Andy, Tam and Mick who'd flown up from London. A night of quiet beers and a chance to unfurl his troubles. There had been the usual small talk by way of catching up but he had time on his hands and had learned to be patient. When it was his turn he bought a round and placing the pints around the table, took his chance.

"I've got some bad news."

Mick drew the pint back from his mouth.

"Pope's no' a Catholic?"

The inevitable round of competitive quips began.

"Thatcher's immortal?"

"Michael Foot's a zombie."

"Bigfoot's a man in a suit."

"Souness is a lady in drag."

"That'd be good news…"

"It widnae be news at all."

Alec let it wash over him and as the jokes tailed off, he took another sip of beer and launched in.

"Might be looking for another job."

Looks exchanged between confused young men. Mick was first to react.

"I'm guessin' there's a story."

He told it, from start to finish. Another round was bought, a chance for questions and comments, but for the most part they listened as Alec spilled his guts.

Andy rotated his pint glass, tracing a spiral down its dewy surface.

"It's 1987, no fuckin 1690."

Alec hadn't the heart to tell them that most of the cops he worked with lived in the 50's, but he'd said his bit. All he wanted now was the company and to get pissed. He was about to ask if they fancied another when Tam cut him off.

"I was chuffed you'd joined the polis Alec. It was good to see one of us getting on. You too Mick."

Mick waved a dismissive hand as Tam slapped his palm on the table.

"You've got to fight this. Go up the tree. Write a letter to the chief."

Nods all round.

Alec shook his head. They didn't understand how it worked. How, once you were labelled an undesirable it was impossible to turn that over. Anyway, there was a big world out there. More to life than the police.

"Might go back to uni. Study law this time. Become a solicitor."

Andy laughed.

"You could defend Wee Burkey!"

Grins all round and then Tam raising his eyes to the ceiling in self-recrimination.

"I'll forget ma own name. You've no' heard?"

They hadn't.

"Burkey plead guilty. Sixty quid fine."

Waves of relief swept over Alec. He'd avoided the discomfort of giving evidence against an old school friend and Burkey had risen a little in his estimation for putting his hands up. Time to come clean himself.

"It was me who arrested him."

He braced himself for the disappointment, but it never came. There was laughter. This was a sensational piece of gossip to be traded on. Alec was quizzed about it all the way to the next pub and was glad when they'd pushed their way inside. He'd told all that he decently could without damning Sean to hell, but they thought it a big hoot, Burkey the girlfriend beater and Alec the night in shining armour. A nice image. Not remotely how he felt at all.

He got blind drunk. The first time since his eighteenth when rounds of Pernod and blackcurrant had followed several ales in the Volunteer.

He'd emptied the lot into the sinks, toilets and floor at the school disco, after which he'd been taken home in disgrace. There'd been a solemn vow of never again, which he'd meant, but he'd broken it now and would pay the price.

Unable to face breakfast he'd risen late and took a walk along the river, thick tongue in a gummed up mouth, eyes smarting in the bright sunshine. The fresh air and stiff wind cleared his head a little, but he still felt grim. He'd crossed the river via an old cattle bridge a mile upstream and was on his way back when Dad's old Austin Montego drew up on the road above and his head appeared at the window.

"Jump in."

Tired and out of sorts it was a welcome offer. The interior was warm and the seat comfortable. He could go to sleep there.

"Fancy something to eat?"

Thinking they'd be going home he'd nodded gratefully.

The car turned onto the road, but not for Auchenbreoch. Instead, they headed over the moors to the coast road and having nodded off for a while, Alec woke to a pleasant drive through seaside villages, the road hugging the contours of the land where it kissed the sea, Bob Dylan on the tape deck.

"When did you start listening to Dylan?"

"Before you were born."

They reached a small village overlooking a low lying island, just as the ferry slowed to hit the concrete slipway and Alec began to suspect the timing was no accident.

"We're going over there?"

A nod and a smile. There was a time when Dad had smiled a lot more.

"Used to take your mum in our courtin' days. Wee café did ice cream sundaes like those American places in the fifties."

The café no longer existed but that didn't matter, what mattered were the memories and Alec realised he'd been blind to his father's love for his mother and that the old man missed her far more than he ever let on. Typical of his upbringing, it came out instead as stories and recollections of better times. A succession of anecdotes filled the journey till they stopped at a café on the far side of the island where Dad yanked up the handbrake.

"They do great bacon rolls."

Alec'd just wiped the ketchup off his lips when the questions started and he admired the sleight of hand being played. He'd been softened up with lunch.

"So, what's up?"

Dad gazed out the window as he told him about the deaths, the boy in the ice and the stabbing. He winced and smiled by turns, but his face turned to stone at the story of Fitzpatrick's bile filled rant, the banishment to the reservation, the petty vindictiveness over Frankie's arrest and the Regulation Twelve.

"It's winging its way to Pitt Street. I'll get a call into HR in due course."

"And then?"

"Dunno. Hand in my warrant card and leave a free man."

"Is that what you want?"

Alec sat back in his chair and stared at his old man. Hadn't he been listening?

"I don't get much say."

Dad interlocked his big knuckled fingers on the table.

"I heard you, but is that what you want?"

A meaty index finger was pointed at his chest. Just like the night with Ronnie on the viaduct. In truth, he felt confused. What was the point in staying somewhere you weren't wanted? And anyway, that boat had surely sailed.

Dad returned his gaze to the scenery, his thoughts elsewhere.

"Your mum would've been proud to have seen you in uniform."

What? This was news.

"You said she'd be disappointed!"

Dad looked down at the table, a little colour in his cheeks.

"That was me. Polis is full of masons and wee shits like yer Sergeant. Didn't want you exposed to that crap, not after all you'd achieved at uni."

"And now?"

Dad struggled to find the right words, but as ever, he was succinct.

"Ah want ye tae stand up for yourself."

"Like you did, at Margo's wedding?"

It was a low blow, but who was Dad to tell him what to do when he'd caused such embarrassment?

Dad looked directly at him then. It was unnerving.

"Want to know what that was about?"

It would be something melodramatic, something about honour, however tenuous, but yes, he wanted to know.

"I'm all ears."

"You know yer uncle John did time when he was younger?"

Alec sat forward. He did not.

"Well, it's ancient history now, but he got snidey when he heard you'd joined the police. Pigs this, pigs that, pork on the menu, all that shit. You walked by and he was going on about smelling a sty. He can be a wanker. When he saw you square up to that squaddie and walk away he decried ye for a coward."

It hadn't occurred to Alec that any of that confrontation had been seen. It came as a shock that there'd been a running commentary.

"What happened?"

Dad grimaced and shrugged as if it were no big deal.

"I walked around the table and punched him."

The simplicity was funny, but that it had all been about him came as a shock.

"Sorry Dad. Joining the police probably wasn't my greatest hour."

A shake of the head.

"It's your life. Lead it as you see it, but at least stand up for what you believe in. There's honour in that. The shame is in walking away."

They ordered more tea and Alec had another bacon roll. There was no more said about Corsair Street. Instead, they talked about the view, Dad's wartime childhood and the changes there'd been, and for the very first time about Mum and how much they both missed her. And it would've been easy to pick at the wound again, to sink into 'what if's' and recriminations, but Alec knew that whatever had been in Dad's head then had been motivated by love, and who was he, such an imperfect human, to cast judgement on all that.

They travelled back to Auchenbreoch the way they'd come, through lush Ayrshire farmland and small villages. Dad threw in anecdotes as they passed places that jogged his memory, while Alec sat alone with the choices only he could make.

Turning Point

It was tempting to take more time off, but Dad was right, that would be running away and he wasn't going to hide. The conversation had galvanised him and he set off with stiffened resolve for Glasgow, but as the city neared doubts multiplied and by the time he reached Corsair Street his situation seemed irretrievable again.

The atmosphere was funereal in the locker room. Looks of concern and the odd pat on the shoulder, but he'd decided to treat it as any other day. He didn't want their pity.

At the muster Fitzpatrick raised an eyebrow but read out the detail as if it was just another shift. There was the usual round of handouts. Fiscals memos, cases to be amended and a large envelope. Fitzpatrick sniffed as he handed it over.

"Your first and last."

The remark was greeted with stony silence around the room and Alec took some comfort from that. He opened the envelope expecting it to be a date for his disciplinary hearing, but found instead a cream coloured sheet, typed with the words 'P.F. V. Anthony Donatelli, High Court of Justiciary, Glasgow.' He hadn't arrested any Donatelli's. Surely some mistake.

Harry leaned over and whispered.

"Three days time. Nice one. A payer."

Alec nodded his appreciation, but he was none the wiser.

"I haven't arrested a Donatelli."

Harry pointed a nicotine stained finger to the case number.

"Headquarters number. Frankie's probably burst to who he's been working for. The Drug Squad will have turned the Donatelli's. You'll be supporting cast."

His first court case and it was the High Court. Not for him the three ringed circus of the District, though it was a surprise it'd come so quickly.

Ronnie provided the explanation in the radio room.

"They'll be on remand and they've fast-tracked the trial out of fairness to the accused."

The days passed without incident. Fitzpatrick seemed keen to avoid him, so there were no notebook signings, or caustic remarks. The shift acted as normal, but steered clear of conversations that featured future events of which he might not be part. Everyone kept the banter light, though it felt artificial and only added to the sense of impending doom. Something confirmed by Fitzpatrick as he watched their radios being booked in at the end of the last shift.

"Alec. A word."

Here's one. Prick. It would've been satisfying to say it out loud, but Fitzpatrick was still the Sergeant and he was still a cop, so he followed Fitzpatrick into the corridor where he was presented with an official looking envelope.

"This arrived tonight."

Sick with dread, Alec found a quiet room and opened it. Inside was a memo directing him to attend a hearing at Force Headquarters in three weeks time. A week after that and he'd have been at the police college for his second year course. Fat chance now. Eyes brimming with hurt and frustration he stuffed the envelope in his tunic. He'd cross that bridge later, there was the Frankie Campbell case to navigate first and the next two days were spent looking through his statement in anticipation of the questions he'd be asked. By the day of the trial he could recite the case backwards, but even so, he could hardly face breakfast and his toast tasted like cardboard and so it was an anxious cop who climbed the well-worn steps of the High Court, through grey colonnades, into a world of polished tiled floors, dark wood panels, frosted glass and dense clouds of cigarette smoke.

A lugubrious court cop pointed down a corridor of black and white tiles, walls echoing with court ushers shouting the names of the accused and the next witnesses. At its end Alec found a room filled with men and women in ill-fitting suits. Their haggard expressions telegraphed the presence of drug squad officers and they spoke very little, other than in coded quick-fire comments that cemented their otherness from the rest of the room. In the far corner, the plainers, delighted to be in company to which they aspired and next to them, Harkness. Alec executed a discrete double-take, such was his shock to see him. How had he wangled a part in a drugs squad operation? Maybe Harkness had friends there after all.

Alec stood in the doorway while Harkness refused to acknowledge his presence at all. After a few minutes a bald man with bags under his eyes stepped forward and introduced himself.

"You'll be Alec? I'm D.S. Boyle."

They shook hands.

"Cheers. Your case gave us the 'in'."

Praise indeed and he was grateful for it. Harkness, watching on, looked sour.

"Your first high court?"

"First court ever."

A laugh.

"You've started well. Here's to more!"

Alec hadn't the heart to say it would probably be his last, but it was the present he was more concerned with.

"What happens now?"

A grunt and a shake of the head.

"We sit on our fannies while the QC's piss about. When it approaches tee-off at the country club, we get sent home."

"No trial today?"

"Unlikely. Donatelli's QC will be trying to spring him from Bar-L first."

And so it came to pass. Hours of tension and tedium interspersed by a free lunch and the two hundred Embassy Regals he passively consumed. At four o'clock a tired court usher released them into the wild and there was a dash for the exit, but when Alec reached the door he remembered Harry's instruction and pressing back through the sluice gate of humanity found the dismal court cop who stamped his citation with a sigh.

There was no sign of his Inspector when he descended the court steps. Harkness had spent most of the time cosying up to old colleagues, but there seemed little appetite to reciprocate and he'd not hung around with the group now assembled on the street.

Alec was walking towards his car when there was a shout from behind; the DS, leading his team towards the Saltmarket. A wave to follow and a shoogle of the hand. A pint? He almost turned the offer down, but there'd been another more insistent wave and he'd thought fuck it, why not. It was a decision that would provide unexpected rewards.

Epiphany

The session with the Drug Squad had been instructive. A hard life, long hours and plenty of danger, but it sounded exciting and visceral. More importantly, the drink had loosened inhibitions and the subject of Harkness had been raised. It shone a light, not only on the reasons for his transfer to Corsair Street but raised uncomfortable questions on his appearance at the Donatelli trial.

The revelation so preoccupied him on his return to work he had to stop himself from staring at Harkness at the muster, such was the new way he saw him. But useful as the information had been, the session with the squad had taken him no closer to derailing the regulation twelve.

Later that week, walking the canal in a melancholic frame of mind, thoughts drifted towards the events of the past year and to the drowning boy, his last grab at the ice as clear as the day he'd pulled him out. Passing Gillespie's house, he remembered the whisky and the old man's subtle nod towards the abandoned tenements that led to Frankie's arrest. More memories flooded in. His first day at the police college and the sense of doubt and dislocation. That first night with Harry and the prisoner in the blood-spattered van, the incident with Tommy and the stab to his arm, the tension over the money at the sudden death. The arrest of Sean Burke. The boy from the restaurant with the stolen food and the subtle way Ronnie had handled things. The faces of the dead, each indelibly stamped in his mind. The grief-stricken people he'd comforted in the dark hours before the dawn. The poverty bordering on the medieval. People who lived each day in stoic despair and the random casual violence of young men. The confrontation with Beanie. The visceral triumph of arrests won from violent struggle. Every day a Russian roulette of human failings and frailty, random events and fleeting chances. Petty rules, an archaic culture and harsh realities, small mercies and smaller achievements. As he made his way round the poverty and neglect of the reservation he began to recognise how much of it had burrowed under his skin. The abnormal had become the normal. He'd joined to escape a dead-end existence in Auchenbreoch, but now, as he paused under the tall spire of the Immaculate Conception, he was reaching an epiphany.

Gazing over rooftops that crested the folds of the land in gentle waves down towards the unseen Clyde, he pondered the world beyond the horizon. There was always Canada and opportunities in the Mounties for Scottish cops looking for a change of scenery. Maybe he'd set sail for those distant shores and start again. Maybe.

He turned towards Barnhouse, the closed ranks of tenements lit by the afternoon sun, grimy windows bejewelled with impending sunset. So many people living on top of each other, so many lives unrecorded until a random event ran their ship aground, or siren call drew them off course, all of it contributing to a grand story who's first chapter he'd barely cleared. Down on the city road, the smog of rush hour traffic diffused in the light of a late afternoon sun and he realised he needn't travel the world to find adventure. It was all here. And then Dad's words at the cafe. About self-respect and fighting your corner. He'd lost some of the former along the way. To win it back he'd have to be better at the latter, but he'd need a word with Ronnie first. The rest he'd trust to the fat lady.

Two days passed before a chance presented itself. It came in the form of a pub brawl, upon which the shift had descended with gleeful intent. There being more arrests than transport, most were frog marched the short walk to Corsair Street where the duty officer cursed all and sundry for shattering his peaceful existence. Ronnie had booked in his prisoner when Alec caught him in a quiet corridor.

"You got a minute?"

Ronnie raised an eyebrow.

"I can spare you two."

They found a room and Alec closed the door behind them.

"Why the cloak and dagger?"

Might as well be straight up.

"I need your help Ronnie, you're my only hope."

A raised eyebrow.

"Sound like Princess Leia."

"Yeah, I need to blow up a Death Star."

Ronnie placed his hat on a desk and sat.

"Right, I'm listening."

"Remember that time with Fitzpatrick outside the orange lodge? And then with McGroarty?"

Ronnie shuffled in his seat and crossed his arms.

"Yes."

"I'm going to report it."

Ronnie winced and looked out of the window. When he looked back it was with an expression of sincere sadness.

"Look. This's your fight, not mine - I'll be retired in a few months."

Alec had anticipated some resistance. It was a big deal speaking up against a gaffer and Ronnie was old school, more regimented than the new generation, but he hadn't expected such a flat out rejection.

"You won't help?"

Ronnie shrugged.

"You'll do fine without me."

At that Ronnie rose to stand, but Alec put out a hand.

"If you think you're going to walk away, you've another thing coming."

Ronnie's mouth opened to speak, but Alec pointed to the world beyond the windows.

"All those months ago you told me it was about 'us and them', us against the world. Was that just a load of shite?"

Ronnie's face flushed and he looked angry. Alec pictured the Ronnie at the viaduct. He'd need to be careful, but there was no way he was letting the old git off lightly.

"Only 'you and me'? Remember? Now you just shrug your shoulders? Fucking heroic."

He was conscious his voice was raised and he half expected to Ronnie to get up and leave but instead the old cop sat with his head bowed, hands together between his knees.

"C'mon Ronnie. If you don't help, I'm out on my arse."

Ronnie continued to stare at the floor for a while, but when he finally lifted his head, he looked resigned.

"What do you need?"

They spoke for a few minutes and when they parted Alec felt lighter of spirit. There was still a chance his dismissal would proceed regardless of the evidence of Fitzpatrick's prejudices, but it was a start. What was required, was something much harder hitting.

In the days that followed Alec had much cause to wonder how seemingly inconsequential connections would change the lives of those around him. That by accepting the offer of a drink with the drug squad he'd pushed over a domino. The thing now was to make sure it connected with the next one, and the others after that. Following the lead he'd been given by the squad, he spent the rest of the week digging and by the last day of late-shift he was in a state of nervous anxiety, worried that something in his behaviours might give him away. Ever present, was the gnawing doubt that the things he'd unearthed would make little difference in a culture where rank was everything, where there was little incentive to believe the word of a probationer with such a tainted reputation as his. But as he drove home on the Tuesday night, a stack of documents in the back seat, he hoped he'd done enough to give himself a fighting chance.

There was one more thing he had to do and somehow that felt harder. After pacing the flat for several hours, fears of rejection playing out in his head he'd muttered 'fuck it' and phoned Emma. Two weeks had passed, he'd held up his end of the bargain at least.

The phone rang out on the first attempt, escalating his blood pressure, but on the second a female voice answered and before he knew it an hour had passed and he'd to remind himself why he'd called in the first place.

"Fancy going for a coffee?"

A laugh born from inordinate patience.

"Alec, I thought you'd never ask!"

They met in a quiet West End cafe, a place he'd haunted as a student and as it turned out, so had she. It was one of the few things they had in common, but that didn't matter, it was her otherness that attracted him. She was exotic, a girl from a well to do family with a big house who'd travelled the world. He listened to stories of her childhood, amazed at how different it had been to his, so that he entirely forgot his troubles until she asked the question.

"How's things at Corsair Street?"

"Ahh. There's something I have to tell you…"

Heart in mouth, he told her of his awful start and the struggles thereafter, of Fitzpatrick and his bullying and the Regulation Twelve. She sat, occasionally stirring her coffee, but listened intently. When he'd finished, he'd waited for the polite 'it was nice to have met you' and the 'I should be going' exit, but there was neither. Just a hard intelligent scrutiny.

"Are you going to fight it?"

"Damn tootin'."

A serious nod.

"Good. I don't like a quitter."

She finished the last of her coffee and stood up.

"I could murder a drink. Coming?"

He dropped her off at her place. They'd kissed and he knew then what he'd known already; that she was a keeper. There'd been no teenage fumbles and no attempt to get an invite inside, he wanted to see her again, simple as that. While the taxi sat idling up the street he'd popped the question.

"Want to do this again?"

She'd smiled a big wide smile.

"Who wouldn't want to date a Corsair?"

Alec laughed. He was as far away from being a buccaneering pirate as it was possible. There'd been a toot from a taxi driver who's patience had finally run out and a quick kiss from her.

"Better go, tide and taxi wait for no man."

He'd walked backwards shouting he'd phone. A wave and she was gone.

He thought of phoning the following day, but keen to avoid accusations of neediness he forced himself away. In any case, he'd lots to do. Sifting through the treasure he'd found at Corsair Street, he gave silent thanks to the solid grounding he'd received from Ronnie, and for the belated camaraderie of fellow cops.

The early shift began the day after. Three days to the hearing. Fitzpatrick had taken leave and it appeared such an obvious act of cowardice Alec laughed in the muster to stares from Harkness and Andy Bell. He spent his time wandering the reservation, memorising every nook and cranny like someone leaving home for the last time. On the day before the hearing there were slaps on the shoulder in the locker room, Ronnie and Charlie walking him to the car park where Harry waited by the car. Handshakes all round, as if they weren't expecting him back, a sadness in the eyes that spoke of inevitability and the rough deal life sometimes dealt. For his part he'd thanked them. He was grateful for the friendship; it would sustain him over the next eighteen hours.

After a fitful night he rose early and armed with a thick pile of papers set off for Force Headquarters. He'd enough time to deliver a package to another department before checking in at Human Resources where he sat, stiff in his parade uniform, and waited.

A dark-haired woman in a business suit appeared and led him to a side room with a large oak desk. She invited him to sit before taking her place beside a tall elegant middle-aged man in a crisp white shirt, his epaulettes crowned and pipped. His thick white hair was swept back from his forehead and he sported a tan that spoke of luxury holidays. He introduced himself as Chief Superintendent Carmichael. The woman was Miss Brenner from HR. Carmichael raised an eyebrow and pointed to an empty chair beside Alec.

"No representation?"

"Thank you Sir. I'm happy to represent myself."

Carmichael gave him a sceptical look. Brenner clasped her hands on the desk and leaned forward.

"That's your right Alec, but we find in these circumstances it helps when it comes to disposal."

Disposal. A neat clinical expression.

"I appreciate that but I'd like to press on if that's ok."

Carmichael blinked rapidly but with an 'oh well, let's get on then' he lifted the papers from the desk began to read from them. Alec listened carefully. There was a part he especially didn't want to miss.

The evidence supporting his dismissal was covered in detail before Carmichael looked up and said the fateful words, 'is there anything you'd like to say?'

Oh yes. He'd quite a lot to say.

Alec picked up a dossier from the floor beside him and placed it on the table. Brenner looked interested. Carmichael looked irritated.

"What's this?"

Alec let his breath out and began.

"The result of my investigations into the misconduct of my supervisors. Within, you'll find evidence of criminality by Inspector Harkness and misconduct by Sergeant Fitzpatrick."

"Is this some kind of joke?"

"I wouldn't joke about something as serious as this Sir."

Carmichael's face flushed. He looked like a man who'd had a distasteful function to perform, one he'd execute efficiently so his stress-free day could continue unabated. This hadn't been in the plan and he passed a hand over the file as if wafting away a bad smell.

"What do you expect me to do with this?"

Alec had expected a blood and thunder type like Currie, but Carmichael was a bureaucrat. Someone who'd swapped the tribulations of operational life for the headquarters ladder, shuttling between departments without touching the dirty world outside. He'd pop up as an Assistant Chief some day, handing down edicts to the great unwashed. The only threat to a carefully crafted career path would be the taint of something controversial. Well, he was going to be well and truly tainted now. Alec allowed himself a smile and hoped it looked sincere.

"Sir. I expect, like me, you like to see the bad guy get the jail."

Carmichael looked ready to explode. Miss Brenner tugged the file towards her, but Carmichael reached out his manicured fingers and stopped its progress.

"If you have an allegation of criminality, it should be made through the proper channels. This is not the place."

The news he'd given was hardly going to be gratefully received. It was only right and proper that the correct channels be used. And so he had. Important though to keep the tone polite and respectful.

"This file contains copies. The original, with supporting evidence, is in the hands of the Procurator Fiscal. Another copy is with the Complaints and Discipline Branch. I've an appointment there after this hearing."

There was a pause while Carmichael crunched the gears and tried to find a way to pass an unplanned wrinkle to someone else. His eyes strayed to the file and then to Alec. Brenner pulled the file over to her side of the table and leafed through the first pages. She looked up and turned to Carmichael.

"Perhaps I could have a word?"

Carmichael, who's mouth had opened to speak, shut it again. He hadn't reached his lofty position without being able to spot a red flag and one was waving at him right now.

"Very well."

They stood to leave and Brenner gave a small smile of reassurance.

"We'll be back shortly. If you could wait meantime."

He'd replied it was not a problem, but this was the bit he'd dreaded most. There was no way of telling how they'd react. Wheels would be turning elsewhere and with that a whole set of pressures and problems would present themselves. In the meantime, his fate lay in the hands of a high-ranking chancer and an HR rep, but he'd done all he could, regardless of the outcome he'd be able to look Dad and Emma in the eye.

After a few minutes the door opened. Carmichael sat heavily and looked at Alec with the face of someone who'd discovered the look of fatherly concern and was trying it out for the first time. Alec watched carefully. With more practice Carmichael could make that look convincing.

Brenner wore a hint of a smile. Admiration? Alec couldn't be sure, but it felt as if he had a guardian angel. Did she have more influence than he supposed?

Carmichael seemed to have developed an allergy to the file for he never laid hands on it but looked askance at it from time to time.

"Miss Brenner had a brief look at the contents of your report Alec."

First name terms. Interesting.

"She's drawn attention to the nature of your allegations and the witnesses willing to speak to them. It does throw up some questions and whilst I cannot guarantee what happens next, Miss Brenner has advised that maybe it would be inappropriate to proceed with your Regulation Twelve meantime, a conclusion I'd drawn myself."

Aye right. Carmichael looked pale, but though the situation had altered he wasn't out the woods yet, something confirmed by Carmichael's next comment.

"Before I look at next steps, perhaps you could briefly tell me what investigations have taken place so far."

Alec knew a chance when he saw it. He also recognised the potential to fuck it up, but he'd rehearsed this bit, so he sat back and told them, though there were bits he'd leave out. He hadn't been altogether innocent himself.

He started with the throw away remark from the drug squad detective after the High Court. Loosened by drink, conversation had drifted to the subject of Harkness and a caustic observation that he'd engineered yet another high court overtime. Revelations about life in the squad under Harkness followed. He'd been divisive, but most of all he'd been greedy and the author of many overtime scams. One of them centred around the inclusion of his name as witness on every case whether he'd been involved or not. Word had percolated upwards, but keen to brush a scandal under the carpet he'd been transferred rather than disciplined.

Alec had expressed surprise that Harkness would then have been part of the operation against the Donatelli's. Someone had laughed and said that Harkness hadn't been part of their operation at all, but his.

He'd looked up the case on his return to Corsair Street and there it was in black and white. Harkness was listed as searching the van and finding more heroin. But, hadn't Harkness been off that day? A check of the shift register confirmed that he had. Convinced there'd be more, he'd sifted through more of his old cases, but it wasn't a crime report that provided the bombshell discovery. It was the sudden death of Mr Bannerman.

He'd been about to toss the sudden death report to one side, but the memory of Harkness collecting the money stayed his hand, so he'd looked up the details of the property seized. And there it was. Three thousand pounds, not the thirty thousand they'd counted out in Bannerman's house. Would Harkness be that stupid? Confirmation would lie in the ledger kept in the duty officer's safe, but only the Duty Inspector had the key and it was jealously guarded. There was no way he could say 'please Sir, may I investigate the integrity of your fellow Inspector?'

Some circumspection was required in describing events to Carmichael at this point, but in truth some skulduggery had been involved. No key. No ledger. Frustrated by the impasse, he'd revealed his dilemma to Charlie and Stevie. Fearful of word getting back to Harkness he'd emphasised his interest was purely speculative. Charlie, finely tuned to the possibility of scandal, had turned around in his seat and grinned.

"How much are we talking about?"

"Twenty seven grand."

"You're joking!"

"Probably a typo. If it is, I'll look a right tube."

"And if it isnae?"

That was a bridge he'd have to cross. Until then he had nothing.

Stevie had stared out the window, tapping the steering wheel.

"You need to put something in the ledger and while yer there, check it out."

"Yeah, but I'd need another sudden death."

Charlie's large head craned round the partition.

"Nope. You find some money."

Alec threw his hands up.

"Like where?"

A wink.

"Like the cash machine down the road."

"And then what?"

Charlie shook his head as if disappointed at the stupidity of his pupil.

"You find it Alec. You fucking find it…"

Was it really that simple? 'Find' money in the street, fill out a slip, lodge it in the safe? For the investment of a tenner he'd get his answer. They'd taken him to a bank and dropped him near the office. He'd sauntered into the uniform bar, paragon of virtue, and presented the ten pound note to a bemused Duty Officer. And that might've been the end of the plan had it not been for the arrival of a bucking bronco glue sniffer at the charge bar. Distracted, the Duty Officer had handed him the key with an exasperated sigh and disappeared to attend the prisoner.

He'd opened the safe with trembling hands and among bags of money and medication there was the ledger. Sick with tension, he'd flicked through the pages until finally he saw it. Bannerman. Sudden Death. And the sum of money lodged…Three thousand pounds. Holy fuck.

Harry's words had returned to him as he'd carried the ledger to the photocopier. Mother-lode right enough. In the charge bar, the sounds of shouting continued, drowning the swish-swish-drone of the copier. He'd returned to the safe and was scribbling some details in the ledger when the Inspector returned with an order to take the berserk prisoner to the cells. By the time they'd slammed the cell door on an apoplectic prisoner Alec was soaked with sweat and his heart hammering. He'd gotten further than he'd expected, but he'd much more work to do. For Carmichael's ears it was sufficient to simply say he'd been given access to the ledger and Alec left it at that.

It was much later when he got the chance to visit the Productions Room where Sam the retired cop worked as the custodian. If anyone could confirm what money had been transferred from the safe to Force Headquarters, it would be him. And Sam did.

After that he'd kept a low profile, only writing up his report once the shift had received their pay slips. Only then could he be confident that Harkness's claim for the Frankie Campbell case would've reached his bank account, though that would be a matter for someone with financial expertise to confirm.

He'd written another report about Fitzpatrick's bullying and rabid sectarian outbursts, though his discovery of Harkness's scheme had somewhat reduced his nemesis to supporting cast by comparison.

Alec concluded his briefing to Carmichael by stating he'd never sought trouble and had done his level best, but he'd been left with no options. Carmichael started at this and held up the Regulation Twelve papers.

"If you're claiming you'd have turned a blind eye had it not been for this, you'll be undoing all you've told me."

A warning shot. Fair enough.

"Sir. Sergeant Fitzpatrick and Inspector Harkness drew attention to themselves. I wouldn't have stumbled upon the facts had it not been for their actions."

There was a knock at the door. Another senior officer in a white shirt whose face Alec couldn't see. Carmichael stepped out and closed the door. Brenner leaned forward, folded her hands on the desk and smiled.

"I'd abandon this process, but I'm afraid it's not my decision."

Well, he'd convinced Brenner and Alec allowed himself a small flutter of hope, but there were no sounds of a fat lady singing so kept his own counsel.

After a few seconds Carmichael re-entered and putting on the appearance of a man considering his next steps, sat down and played with the corners of the regulation twelve report.

"The Dep is unhappy you've sent the original to the P.F., but he's instigated a full investigation. I'd give careful thought to what you've claimed, there'll be scrutiny of you and all your colleagues. You still wish to proceed?"

Hell yeah. Pedal to the metal old bean.

"Thanks Sir, I'm fully prepared."

Carmichael didn't look convinced but gave a curt nod.

"Others higher than me will decide what happens next, but in all likelihood the Regulation Twelve will be suspended until the conclusion of the investigation."

Alec allowed himself a smile. Smiles in return. There was only one more thing.

"What about my second year course at the police college?"

Carmichael looked to Brenner. It was a surprise to see him defer to a civilian, but Brenner looked relaxed and nodded.

"The investigation will take some time. I'd get prepared for eight weeks away."

She looked up Carmichael who nodded enthusiastically.

"Yes. You'll want to avoid Corsair Street for a while."

Alec left elated but exhausted, hands shaking he put the keys in the ignition and drove from Pitt Street before anyone could stop him. When he arrived home he slumped onto the sofa and fell into a deep sleep only to be woken hours later by the telephone. It was Currie, offering help and the opportunity to take garden leave prior to his course. So, he was going! And yes, garden leave would be much appreciated whatever garden leave was. Currie explained it was free time off and Alec said a lot of thank yous as the phone went dead.

Dazed, he reached for the fridge and pulled out a beer, paused and then put it back. Patting a soft middle that had expanded on a diet of fish suppers and Chinese takeaways he went to the bedroom and dug out his running gear. Time to get back in shape, he'd be doing a lot of running at the college.

The Test

After Currie's call there'd been others from Ronnie and Charlie, keen to know why all hell had broken loose at Corsair Street. Harkness and Fitzpatrick had been suspended and the station was a hotbed of rumour and introspection as cops sifted through paperwork, certain that Complaints and Discipline would call and any minor indiscretion lead to their downfall.

He told them all he could, glad he'd taken garden leave and that his course would take him out the loop for a while.

He'd then phoned Dad and gave him the news.

"So, I'm off to Tulliallan for eight weeks and we'll see what happens after that."

A grunt.

"That'll keep you away from trouble."

There was a brief pause.

"And well done son. That can't have been easy."

It was a measure of how far they'd come that he took that in his stride and thanked him for 'being there'. Corny, but at least a bridge had been mended.

But if he'd thought the police college would offer safe haven from the events at Corsair Street, he was to be rudely disabused. It was an object lesson in the interconnectedness of the police that he found himself the subject of interrogation as soon as he'd put his bags in his dorm. Two weeks had passed, plenty of time for a story to gather momentum and he spent days quelling rumours of wholesale fraud and money laundering. His explanations failed to stop the rumour factory and in the cloistered surroundings of the college he became the subject of strange looks. He was the origin of scandal and a dangerous man, for what kind of probationer would have the wherewithal to take on his gaffers. It explained the schizophrenic behaviours of the college supervisors who treated him with kid gloves on one hand, and with thinly veiled hostility on the other, for no doubt he was an upstart with an over-inflated opinion of himself and potentially a danger to them too.

None of this bothered him much. He was simply happy to be a cop. In any case he'd enough on his plate with the ongoing investigation and the prospect of facing Harkness in court, anxieties that were only calmed by the occasional phone call to Emma from a pay phone in a college corridor. It felt good to have her in his life; a hidden door had been opened and light had flooded in.

Darkness entered in other ways. The following weekend he arrived home to discover the words 'GRASS' daubed in huge white letters on his door. Heart dropping he'd opened it to find dog shit had been pushed through the letter box.

The calls began that night, the phone ringing off its hook only to fall silent as he answered. It rang throughout the night into the next morning, and it became clear that his mystery caller was in fact multiples working in shifts. Someone was trying to unnerve him, but who? Harkness had a history with the drug squad. Some of them would be caught up too. He hoped none of those who'd made him welcome after the Donatelli trial had been affected, but he couldn't shake the feeling that some would be caught in the net. He'd be deeply unpopular.

A brick came through the window the following night, glass shattering over the living room carpet. It came to rest against the far wall and he'd raced to the window in time to see a dark coupe roaring down the tree lined avenue. That had sealed it.

Exhausted, he'd called the local police who arranged for photographs of the graffiti and the smashed window. They took a report but could offer nothing other than keep a watching brief. In truth he hadn't expected much but the lack of sympathy spoke of inside knowledge and sides being picked. He was being targeted, he was certain now and it began to play on his mind. He scanned the occupants of cars in his rear-view mirror increasingly certain he was being tailed. Pedestrians outside the flat were now surveillance cops waiting an opportunity to bundle him into a van as soon as he left his sanctuary. He'd disconnected the phone, but half expected it to ring anyway and sleep became impossible as he was drawn inexorably to the living room curtains certain the car pulling up outside contained a petrol bomber or another brick hurler. Emma made dinner at her place and insisted he stayed, but fearful of pulling her into his troubles he phoned Dad who, as ever, had a succinct perspective.

"You're winning when they resort to that shit."

He'd then spent the following weekends in Auchenbreoch, worried at what he'd set in train, fearful for his future, unable stop what he'd unleashed. A fact confirmed by a phone call from Complaints and Discipline as the college course came to an end.

"Okay Alec. Case is now with Crown Office. There'll be a trial and it'll be fast tracked. Hope you've no holidays planned."

Dry mouthed and heart thumping, he'd confirmed he'd none.

"Is there a date?"

The sound of a breath being sucked in between clenched teeth.

"I'd stay close to home over the next few weeks."

He passed out with average exam results and a decent fitness score. The report card provided a middle of the road summation of a diligent officer, whose uniform had been of a high standard and who'd applied himself to the best of his abilities in trying circumstances. It was a decent enough appraisal, written by a course Inspector glad to see the back of him.

Final parade over, he'd driven back to Auchenbreoch and spent a quiet night with Tam in The Volunteer. Last bells rung, he'd waved goodbye and was walking towards the bridge when he heard the car roar up behind him. He leapt onto the pavement just as the front wing passed his legs and there it was, the dark coupe, half on the footpath and two large men getting out. It was too late to run and anyway, why should he, wasn't this his hometown? The men closed in, cops, he was sure of it, though he'd never met them before. Backing into the doorway of the butchers, he held up his hands in what he hoped was a sign of reasonableness, but they walked towards him in silence and he knew reason would play no part in what happened next.

The first, broad shouldered and bearded, looked the quintessential undercover cop and Alec realised then they were drugs squad. This wouldn't go well. He'd no chance against guys like this. He'd braced himself for the first punch, determined he'd get some in himself when there was a shout from the street and there was Tam, walking down the middle like something from High Noon. The other squad cop turned to face Tam and spoke for the first time. It was controlled and without fear.

"Fuck off wee man. This is none of yer business."

And then another voice from his left, unmistakably Dad's.

"That's my son. Anything that happens to him is my business."

Dad had appeared a few feet away, a pick axe handle in his hands. Had he been out all night like this? Had he known this would happen? There was an undeniable relief that help had come, but it was mixed with fear this would get real messy and more trouble would follow.

Dad and Tam closed the distance. It was three against two now and the squad cops looked uncertain for the first time, their sense of control gone. They looked at each other briefly and then without another word walked back to the coupe, each keeping an eye on the unexpected arrivals. As they climbed in the bearded one looked at Alec.

"You're a marked man, MacKay."

The coupe reversed off the pavement and was about to move off when Dad, with one fluid movement, brought the pick axe handle down on the windscreen, smashing a large hole in the driver's side.

"The only thing that'll be marked is yer fancy car. Now fuck off."

The driver's door half opened, but the driver was hauled back inside and the door closed. With a screech of tyres and narrowly missing the implacable figure of Dad, the car roared across the bridge and was gone.

Alec leaned against the doorway and let out a long breath. His limbs trembled with a surge of adrenaline that now had nowhere to go. He'd thought Auchenbreoch offered sanctuary, but that illusion had been shattered and for the first time he felt afraid. That dark forces would be watching him always, that revenge would come inevitably and without warning. And Dad, he'd be in trouble now. He'd smashed up a cop's car.

"Better get home before the local cops arrive Dad."

A sardonic smirk and a jut of the head towards the bridge

"There won't be any cops coming. Those two pricks have shot their bolt. Let them phone. It's them that'll get the jail."

"Then they'll be back, sometime. Just a matter of when."

Tam put an arm around his shoulder and they walked toward the bridge, Alec half expecting to see the coupe leaping back over it Dukes of Hazzard style.

"You've a lot to learn, you a cop too. A pair of cowards ran off soon as they were outnumbered. They'll not set foot in the town again."

Dad walked beside them, pick axe handle over his shoulder, a lightness of step that spoke of satisfaction and enjoyment.

"Tam's right. That was a last throw of the dice. Case closed."

Alec thought of phoning it in, but Dad counselled against it. An incident in which neither party would come up smelling of roses. He'd reluctantly agreed but endured a sleepless night plagued with dreams of faceless men in dark clothing who stalked his every move.

A local Sergeant called at the house the following morning and Alec's heart leapt into his mouth thinking it was about the night before. It was not. It was a court citation. He scanned the form. 'P.F. v Harkness. Glasgow Sheriff Court'. Monday! The Complaints investigator hadn't been kidding.

Cancelling what few plans he'd made; he concentrated on preparing for the trial. By the Sunday he'd done all he could, but wound up like a spring and convinced he was going to fuck it up, or be ambushed on the way, he'd phoned Emma who put him in his place with a piece of advice that was almost motherly.

"It's not about you anymore. Word is, there's a cast of hundreds now. Get a good nights sleep—it'll be over before you know it."

She'd smacked a kiss down the phone, told him she'd be thinking of him and wished him luck. It calmed him for a while, but back in his room the clouds of pessimism began to gather again. A gentle knock on the door and then dad's head poking round.

"Yer coming with me."

"Where?"

"The Three Kings."

He spent the rest of the evening with Dad and his old pals at their old haunt, decrying the state of politics, exchanging rumours of another pit closure and whether Celtic would win the league in their centenary year. On instructions, the elderly barman refused to supply Alec anything other than soft drinks and by the time they left he was in altogether different frame of mind.

He woke the next morning to a cooked breakfast, though his stomach threatened to return it to sender. Eyes nervously on the kitchen clock and anxious to arrive in plenty of time he'd gathered up his things and was about to leave when there was hand on his wrist and Dad shaking his head.

"I'll drive."

Worried it was a ruse to come and watch the trial, he'd protested, but the company was reassuring and when they finally pulled up outside the court, Dad declared he was driving straight back. Alec hoped the relief wasn't obvious.

"You don't need me watching. Grab yerself a beer after and get the train. I'll pick you up at the other end."

He'd said his thank yous and watched the Montego lurch around the next corner and disappear. It was down to him now. Onwards and downwards again.

If the High Court was old-time solemnity, the Sheriff Court was an altogether different beast. A modern rectangular building of smoked glass, polished stone and marble that looked part citadel, part shopping mall. Attractively foreboding.

He braced himself for a confrontation with angry drug squad detectives at the entrance, maybe even Harkness, but there were only men in cheap anoraks, some with cameras, some with notepads. He entered through smoke glass doors and was confronted instead with a reception desk and a brightly lit atrium, high walls made of the same polished stone as its exterior. It would've been a pleasant place to wander had it not been for the great unwashed who milled around, faces drawn by the expectation of imprisonment, waiting for a solicitor to promise the impossible while they chain-smoked their last cigarettes. Solicitors strutted, noses in the air, black cloaks flowing behind them, while cops keen to avoid those they were going to condemn made for lifts to the upper floor waiting rooms that offered space to get their facts straight. Alec took in the Brownian motion, the random criss-cross of humanity, the occasional meeting of 'brief' and client, occasional collisions and connections. Tannoy announcements echoed while rat-faced neds squabbled with their families, band-saw accents cutting through the sententious announcements. Alec had no doubt the architects had envisioned a contemplative monastic atmosphere in keeping with the serious business of dispensing justice, but they hadn't reckoned with Glasgow's finest.

A lift took him to the first floor where he followed signs to the waiting area for the court number listed on his citation. He'd been too absorbed by the strangeness of his surroundings to be nervous, but on opening the heavy doors to the carpeted corridor a heaviness settled in the pit of his stomach and his limbs weakened. Would he encounter the drugs squad guys here? He'd gone no further than the first witness room when one of the Complaints and Discipline officers appeared in the corridor.

"Best sit with us."

He'd hoped to see Ronnie, but the Chief Inspector led the way to a quiet area where, to his surprise, a relaxed looking Harry and Gerry sat on comfortable seats.

Harry winked.

"Morning."

Alec had no idea what to say. He was desperate to ask why they were there but was stymied by the presence of the investigators who gave the impression they were there to prevent collusion. It made for stilted conversation.

"Hi Harry...Gerry."

Gerry waved but said nothing. He was staring at the far wall, lost in his own thoughts. Harry was more animated.

"All set?

"Think so...not looking forward to this. Least it'll be over soon."

Harry cocked his head like a dog hearing a new sound.

"Soon?"

"Yeah. I'll be first on."

A laugh.

"You're not even tenth. This is day two. There were hundreds yesterday."

"You're kidding"

"Nope. Ask the Chief Inspectors."

One, an elderly officer with silver hair and a patrician face, nodded.

"Enquiry turned up a few things, you're quite a way down the list."

Alec sagged into his chair. It was going to be a long day.

The conversation drifted into banality and the odd diplomatically couched update from Harry about events at Corsair Street. Ricky was back. A fine from the Chief, but the misconduct investigation had gone no further. The others were in another waiting room, along with half the drug squad. There'd been a hard look from one of the investigators at that point, but Harry had shrugged.

"Main thing is, you're not alone, ok?"

Alec whispered his thanks and having decided that he'd pushed his luck far enough Harry shut up for a while.

Every now and again a court usher shouted an officer's name. The patrician Chief Inspector examined his list and scored it out but gave no indication how much nearer Alec's turn had come. He felt weak from strained nerves and every now and then paced up and down the corridor to loosen his cramping legs. When the call went out for lunch he looked at his watch surprised to see three hours had passed in complete limbo.

The shift were in the canteen. A thumbs up from Ronnie who sat with Stevie, Charlie and Ricky. Alec wondered what they were speaking to. Harry, freed from the presence of the complaints investigators leaned over the table.

"You kicked over a wasps nest. Complaints interviewed everybody and their granny. Harkness's name was found on just about every case the shift submitted. Same with the Drug Squad. Turns out the boss has been quite the lad, claiming court overtime he shouldn't have."

So, Emma had been right. Alec felt better and managed to finish his stodgy fish and chips. Just another cog in the big machine. But as he returned to the waiting room it was the sudden death and the missing money that were foremost in his mind. A fraudulent scheme to claim overtime was one thing but the wholesale theft of twenty-seven thousand pounds from a dead man was another. He was in for a hard time.

He'd no sooner returned to the witness room when the usher began shouting out the court numbers and the next witnesses. The Chief Inspector scored another name off his list and lifting his gaze met Alec's with a thin smile.

"You're next."

With that he nudged his colleague and left.

Alec wasn't sure what to make of the sudden departure. Harry did.

"Get yer statement out—make sure you're all squared off inside that head of yours."

"What if complaints come back?"

A smirk and a thumb slung in the direction of the corridor.

"They've fucked off. What they don't hear won't hurt them. They'll be in the court to watch you don't change yer mind."

Jolted into action, stomach churning, Alec pulled out his notebook, but though he'd studied them for days the words refused to be pull themselves into order and they swam across the pages unrecognisable. He'd never remember it all, he'd fluff his lines - be the laughing stock of Corsair Street. As panic took hold, a hand on his arm and Gerry's voice, soft and low.

"It's ok. We all think we'll forget, but every time you go in, you remember everything. Put the paperwork away, take a deep breath, and remember to keep your answers succinct. Before you know it, you'll be buying me and Harry a pint for all the shit you've put us through."

Alec felt a deep appreciation for Gerry's kindness. If he made it through this, he'd buy that pint for sure.

A shout from the corridor.

"Constable MacKay. Court Ten!"

Grabbing his hat, Alec stood up and made for the door. Harry put out a hand and looked him straight in the eye.

"Don't feel sorry for Harkness. Greed put him there, not you."

The usher shouted again and Alec followed a squat man down a narrow hallway to a heavy door that opened to a large room with white walls and oak panels. Light wooden partitions neatly separated the public gallery, the witness box and the dock. Strip lights bathed the courtroom in an antiseptic glare; a place to be forensically examined and in which there was no hiding place.

Harkness sat alone in the dock. He looked haggard and his grey hair had grown long. An average middle-aged man who'd led a hard life. Without the uniform he looked smaller somehow. He glanced briefly at Alec, then turned towards an elderly wigged man in robes who sat behind a raised dais, a relief of the crown coat of arms on the wall behind him. The Sheriff.

Alec stepped into the witness box and the Sheriff intoned the solemn language of the oath. He concentrated so absolutely on repeating the words correctly he'd no perception of who else was in the court, the spell only broken by the figure of a young PF depute rising from a table in front of him.

Mouth dry, body taught as a tow rope, he allowed himself to be guided through his evidence by a laconic prosecutor who asked him to point out the accused before stepping him through the events of the sudden death. There was no reaction from Harkness when Alec pointed towards him and he wondered if Harkness had been told not to look, or whether it was the guilt and shame.

The Fiscal stepped through the discovery of the cash, the actions of everyone thereafter and Harkness's insistence on conveying the money to Corsair Street. Did he have any suspicions at that point? No. Wasn't this an unusual turn of events? Yes. Did you ask why this sudden act of charity? No. The Inspector was the boss.

The questions moved onto the reporting of the death and the discovery of the discrepancy. Alec answered without hesitation or prevarication. The PF thanked him and sat back down.

In a legal enactment of whack-a-mole, an older solicitor sprung to his feet from the opposite side of the table, wig slightly askew. He wore the look of a man entirely at ease with his surroundings and smiled a white toothed smile as he approached. Alec felt like a seal swimming with an orca.

Speaking with a voice nurtured by a public-school upbringing, the defence solicitor began.

"Constable, would I be right in saying this is your first time giving evidence."

"Yes, it is."

Another smile. Friendly concern. A slow pacing about as if circling a hole in the floor.

"You are barely one year in service, am I correct?"

Alec nodded. The solicitor stopped his perambulation and looked stern.

"For the purposes of the court you should answer verbally Constable."

A look of slight irritation from the P.F. as if the side had been let down

Alec felt his face flush and cursed himself.

"Yes Sir. One year."

"Thank you, Constable. Now, would it be fair to say your income is considerably less than your colleagues, being so much less in service than they are?"

Alec hadn't expected this line of questioning. It was obviously leading somewhere and he'd the feeling it would be unpleasant.

"Yes. Wages go up by service."

Slow nodding, as if this was significant in some way.

"And you being an ambitious young man, you'll have invested your wages in a home for yourself, a flat perhaps?"

"Yes."

"Interest rates are particularly crippling. Must be hard to make ends meet on such a low wage."

It hadn't been a question, more of a comment and uneasy at the trajectory Alec had been tempted to say nothing, but an answer was expected and if he didn't play along it would be like poking that Orca with a stick.

"Money is tight, but I get along."

The friendly smile again.

"Indeed. For it's against the discipline code to get into debt isn't it?"

"Yes, but I'm not in—"

"—And your Inspector. He is on a substantially bigger wage is he not?"

"Of course, but—"

"—Constable. A simple yes will do."

He was being corralled in ever tightening circles with little chance to break out. Alec clasped his hands behind him and steadied himself. The solicitor returned to the table and picking up some papers began to scrutinise them as he approached again. Here we go. The questions focused on the events in Mr Bannerman's house, the time Alec arrived, who else had been there and when. Alec struggled to remember it all, but the questions went on and on until he lost track of time. He felt tired and he ached to leave a box that now felt like a prison.

"Please tell the court how much money you claim to have found."

"Thirty thousand pounds."

A frown and a purse of the lips. It was all so theatrical and intensely irritating. Alec wondered if the emphasis on claim was meant to get under his skin. He swore to keep his cool. There'd be only one winner.

"Tell me Constable. How long between counting out all that money you claim to have discovered and the arrival of the Inspector."

The emphasis on that word claim again. Arsehole.

"Just a few minutes."

A cocked head and a raised eyebrow. A look of deep scepticism. The whole range of RADA method acting was being employed.

"Can you be more precise? Two minutes, twenty minutes, an hour?"

"Can't be exact but it'd be more like twenty."

"I see."

Alec wondered just what it was the defence solicitor could see. The next question made it abundantly clear.

"Twenty minutes. Plenty of time for someone to take a portion of the money and hide it somewhere for themselves."

Alec rocked backwards on his feet. The inference was outrageous. He'd been about to explode with a retort when the prosecution stood up and faced the sheriff.

"Object your honour. This officer is not under suspicion and the inference is unmerited."

The Sheriff looked up from his notes and nodded wearily, as if this was a common occurrence.

"Please refrain from wild unsubstantiated accusations please."

A half bow from the defence solicitor in false deference. He turned back to Alec with a serene smile as if apologising, but it failed to take the form of words.

"Constable, I'm not accusing you of anything, but surely you can see the point I'm making."

"Yes, I can."

A smile.

"Then you'd agree there is an element of doubt as to whether Inspector Harkness took the sum of money you claim, to Corsair Street?"

Alec considered the fork in the road before him He was exhausted and anxious, his hands sweated in a death grip behind his back, arms and legs aching with tension. He was wrung out. Was it really worth this mental torture? Just tell the man what he wants to hear, someone else can cover this. But, no. That wouldn't be right.

"I do not."

The defence stopped his perpetual motion with a jolt and stared at Alec as if he'd been presented with a capricious witness.

"Did you not state to this court that there were twenty minutes between the counting of the money and Inspector's Harkness's arrival?"

His voice was louder now, a legal Brian Blessed and Alec came to the conclusion that it was indeed an act. That the whole circus was just that.

Cheap theatre. He'd stand his ground.

"I did, but—"

"And did you not—"

"—Sorry, I will answer this. Inspector Harkness arrived no more than two minutes after the departure of my colleagues."

There, he'd forced the answer in. That felt better. The grip of his protagonist seemed looser now.

"I see. And you're sure about that?"

He was absolutely sure. It had been twenty minutes between the count and Harkness's arrival. But this had included the time Harry and Gerry had hung around while he made his notebook entries and got them to sign. They'd in fact left just before Harkness and Fitzpatrick had knocked the door. Two few minutes not twenty, but two minutes all the same. Alec readied himself. Would there be sly insinuations over his integrity again?

There were none. In thoughtful repose, the defence looked again at his papers and having recalibrated his thoughts initiated a new line of questions. Of inconsequential things that taxed Alec's memory but led nowhere. And then, oh blessed day, the questions reached the end of their chronological order.

"Tell me Constable. Where you present when the money was lodged at Corsair Street?"

"No."

A nod.

"So, you've no idea what happened to the money after you handed it over?"

Alec had prepared for this bit.

"I know who lodged the money and who transferred what was left to Pitt Street.

A scowl.

"I'm not asking you speculate Constable, just answer the question."

He'd been rebuked but he didn't care.

"I wasn't present when the money was lodged. You'd have to ask others what happened next."

"Thank you Constable, I don't require advice on how to conduct my clients defence."

The sheriff looked up sleepily and nodded his agreement.

"Constable, you will restrict yourself to answering the question."

He apologised, he'd meant no offence, though in reality they could all go to hell. Just like Columbo, there was one final question.

"Constable. Consider this next question carefully. You are the subject of dismissal from the force due to your own misconduct, is that correct?"

Dirty bastard.

"That process has been suspended."

"Nevertheless, I put it to you, that consumed by revenge, you have fabricated a situation with your colleagues to place Inspector Harkness under suspicion and so remove the spectre of dismissal from yourself?"

Harkness looked at him properly for the first time. There was a pathetic look of hope in his eyes as if this last question would deliver a fatal blow for the prosecution and pull him from the mire. Alec composed himself. If this was the level the defence had sunk to, he'd won. Just keep it simple.

"Absolutely not. The evidence I have given has been the whole truth and nothing but the truth. I'll not be swayed from that."

The defence solicitor returned to the table and sat down. With a hand waved in the air he'd shouted 'no more questions'. Harkness sat, head bowed, shoulders slumped. The sheriff smiled and was about to say something when the prosecution stood up. Another smile. This one was sincere.

"Constable. I'm sure you're eager to leave, but I've only one question. Can you confirm that ALL the money found in the house of the deceased was indeed handed over in full to Inspector Harkness in the presence of Sergeant Fitzpatrick?"

"Yes. Every last penny."

"Thank you. No more questions."

Alec looked to the Sheriff. and hoped he didn't look too desperate to leave. Sweat trickled down his back and his legs hurt.

The Sheriff thanked him for his evidence and announced he could go. The court usher appeared like a Mr Benn character and led him from the court. It never crossed Alec's mind to look over at Harkness. It didn't matter anymore. It was over.

He came too when he hit the fresh air of the outside world, only vaguely aware of the journey down the lift and the walk through the foyer, or of the photographers pointing their cameras. Shell shocked, he wandered down to the river and sitting on a bench opposite the black and white hull of the Carrick, watched the Clyde roll by, sluggish brown waters swollen by flood tide and rain.

He'd thought no further than giving his evidence. Now it was over, he was caught between guilt for the effects his words would have on another man's life and relief he hadn't bottled it. He was exhausted, not just from giving evidence, but from the effects of the past three months and the burdens he'd carried. There was no feeling of triumph. There'd be no ticker tape parade when, or if he returned to work and he'd carry a reputation for years: the cop who'd brought down a fellow cop. And to top it off the one who'd caused him so much misery was still at large. What a life.

As he watched the gulls float past, a voice appeared behind him.

"Been looking for you."

Ronnie, and further up the path, wreathed in cigarette smoke, Ricky, Charlie ,Sandy and Stevie.

"How'd it go?"

It was hard to tell. Like those first few minutes after an exam where you hoped you'd done ok, but where mere hope wasn't good enough.

"I never want to do that again."

A snort and a hand pulling him to his feet.

"Better get used to it. Doesn't get any easier."

They joined the others and waited for Harry and Gerry to emerge from the court. There seemed to be an unspoken agreement to avoid talk about the trial and Alec wondered when they would.

"What happens now?"

Ricky stubbed his fag out with the heel of his shoe, grinding it into the pavement with two swift turns.

"What we always do. Go to the pub."

Harry appeared, cocky and casual, with no sign the experience had been gruelling in any way. Gerry followed, altogether more somber and reflective. Harry looked at his watch and smacked his palms together.

"Pub then?"

They'd all brought casual jackets and with their tunics folded inside-out they crossed over to the Saltmarket, as obvious a group of off-duty cops it was possible to assemble. Harry led them to a smoke-filled bar with thick tartan carpets and high-backed booths. It was a gloomy place lit by fake candles in antique shades that cast a soft glow. Their very own Admiral Benbow. Ronnie found a booth with a view of the street and they squeezed in while Harry brought the first round on a large tray.

"Thank fuck that's over."

Nods and murmurs of agreement. Pints lifted to mouths in silent unison. Ronnie wiped the froth from his moustache and looked at Alec with a rueful smile.

"Just get on with yer gaffers Alec, it'll save me a heart attack."

A raised glass from Charlie and Stevie and mutters of 'amen.'

Alec raised his hands in mock surrender. Having dragged them into this mess he'd expected more grief and he was relieved there was none. It was strangely comforting to be in their company again, as if all the difficult months before had been a dream. That by some form of dead reckoning and blind luck, he'd finally sailed through the fog to find there was indeed land on the other side. But what had become of Fitzpatrick?

The answer came from Charlie.

"Fitzpatrick was there. Refused to sit with us."

This was news.

"I half-expected to see him beside Harkness."

A shake of the head as Charlie sipped his pint.

"Fired in Harkness to save his skin. Misconduct hearing coming up and he needs all the brownie points he can get."

So, there would be a hearing after all. Alec wondered if he'd have to give evidence at that too.

Charlie held up his watch and tapped it at Harry.

"You making that call?"

Harry went to the bar where a sour faced barman handed over the pub phone. They all waited as he spoke to someone and then he was back, grinning.

"Right Alec, your round."

"Is it?"

"Aye. It's traditional when you've won yer first case."

Had he not been propped between the vast bulks of Ricky and Ronnie he'd have fallen over. There was a chorus of questions from around the table, but Harry raised a hand in mock patience.

"Gentlemen please."

Ronnie cried 'get on with it', but Harry would not be rushed.

"I'll have a Lagavulin."

The rest announced similar expensive whiskies and fishing around in his pocket Alec was relieved he'd enough to buy a round and still get home. Only once the drinks had been placed on the table did Harry begin.

"Harkness changed his plea after Fitzpatrick told the court he'd seen Harkness sorting the money into two piles before it was lodged. Which is good, because that's what I saw too…"

Alec sat dumbfounded.

"What?"

Harry winked.

"Gerry and I drove to Corsair Street after we left you. Gerry had a report to write so I sat in the admin office across from the Inspectors room. When the two amigos returned, Harkness had a bag of cash. After a few minutes there was an argument and the Sarge stomps out, so I took a peek and there was yer man with the money in two big piles, one much bigger than the other."

A fusillade of questions. Harry raised a hand for silence again. He was enjoying this.

"Thought it looked a bit suss, but it's when Charlie told me about the discrepancy I realised what'd happened. I cornered Fitzpatrick…told him he was an accessory unless he spoke up. Should've seen his face when he realised he'd be backing you Alec. Fucking priceless."

Alec laughed. He'd have given anything to be there. He raised his glass to Harry.

"Thank you."

"Ach. I think we're even now."

As the whisky percolated downwards, Alec listened to the talk about how the investigation had turned up frauds dating back to the drug squad and how there'd been disciplinary proceedings taken against a few. It confirmed his suspicions about the intimidation. He hoped it would stop now and that DS Boyle hadn't been one of those affected. It brought him back to the present.

"What was the verdict Harry?"

Harry shrugged as if it was inconsequential.

"Sentence deferred; but he'll get the pokey for sure."

The excitement evaporated. No-one expressed sorrow for Harkness. Alec felt what he hoped they'd all feel; Harkness had brought shame on them, but jail, he'd get a rough reception for sure. They drank in silence for a while, the bar filling with the chatter of workers newly released from a nearby construction site.

"Know why it's called Corsair Street?"

Ronnie, looked round the table for takers.

A shake of heads and non-committal shrugs.

"Then I'll tell you."

To a chorus of groans Ronnie put his pint on the table and settled back.

"You know the Corsairs were pirates?"

Nods and dismissive waves. Common knowledge.

"Well, there's Corsairs and then there's Corsairs. Different times, different places. This is about an early 19th century naval battle off Algeria and a young Captain who'd grown up on a country estate outside old Glasgow."

Alec was hooked already. He loved a well told tale. And Ronnie always told a good story.

"The Corsairs were enslaving Christians and looting ships, so the Royal Navy went to sort them out. When they arrived at the main pirate town they blasted it to bits."

Ronnie looked around the company waiting for the question. Stevie put his hands up in exasperation.

"Ok. What's the link?"

Ronnie grinned.

"The young captain, in keeping with the protocols of the day, looted the town and came home with a vast fortune. Spotting some land near the city, he built a fine house and lived a life of ease."

Alec waited for the next bit but seeing it would not be readily forthcoming took his turn.

"Where's the big house then?"

"The station stands on it."

"What?"

"The captain died, family fortune was squandered and the house fell into disrepair. It eventually burned down so the city fathers cleared it for housing and named one of the streets Corsair Street. After a while they knocked down the tenements too and replaced them with our fine police station."

Silence round the table. Charlie nodded his appreciation.

"Yer a mine of useless information Ronnie, but I like it."

There was a toast to useless information and another round bought. For Alec it was to be his last. Mentally shattered and with a train to catch he announced his imminent departure. There was a look of general disappointment, but he'd a feeling they'd all be heading home soon. They looked fucked, they just didn't know it yet.

Harry drifted into a gentle melancholy, a faraway look in his eyes.

"Maybe fits who we are. God knows there's a bit of the pirate in me. Who knows what we look like when we descend all dressed in black, scooping up the natives and carrying them off."

A snort from Gerry.

"As long as we don't descend into slavery and pillage I think we'll be fine."

Harry smirked and pulled at the ends of his moustache like a poor man's Terry Thomas.

"One more toast then."

Harry raised his glass high and passed it through the air in a circle looking each man solemnly in the eye. His voice, rich and deep, echoed around the pub. The toast was fitting and Alec grinned as they all rose to their feet, raised their glasses and shouted in return.

"The Corsairs!"

Epilogue

He stood at the water's edge, bare feet on ridged sand, cold water lapping at his toes. The wind was warm with the breath of late spring and it felt good to have his head gently buffeted for a while. Twelve miles across the firth, Arran reclined under a blue sky as white clouds chased dark shadows across its broad green flanks, the air so sharp and clear he could reach out and touch it.

He edged further in. It would be months before the sea warmed up to tepid and he remembered childhood summers and the screams of pals as they threw themselves in. Scottish seaside memories. Not for the faint hearted.

A tug at his arm.

"It's beautiful."

"Only 'cause you're here."

"Bullshit."

The wind whipped her hair so that its long strands flicked up and across his face. As she pulled it into a semblance of order she looked up and smiled.

"You're a lucky boy to have grown up here."

He was a lucky boy full stop.

They walked along the water's edge for a while, drifting in and out, arms around waists, moored fast in that slow awkward three-legged walk of young lovers. It was good to be this close, her head on his shoulder, curve of her hip next to his, and her smell. A mix of soap and perfume and shampoo. He drifted along, listening to her voice, his hand on her waist, the warmth of her skin as he slid his fingers inside the belt line of her jeans. A friendly slap on the back of his hand and a peck on the cheek.

"Down boy."

He withdrew the hand with a penitent smile and looked across the sea. After all, he'd brought her here to show her this. And his home town, a landmark occasion that only comes when the girl you date wants to hang around for a while.

He looked at his watch. They'd better get going.

"You ready?"

A nod and a nervous smile.

"Don't worry, he's not that bad."

A dig in the ribs.

"I bet he's lovely and you've exaggerated."

Probably, but there was no way of knowing. Posh girl meets Auchenbreoch Man. It would be interesting if nothing else. They walked to the car, wind chivvying them along and Alec thought of his recent past and the troubles that had so preoccupied him.

Carmichael had phoned with the news that the Regulation Twelve had been binned, but he'd be transferred 'for his own good'. The transfer was probably for the best, but he'd never travelled the easy path and it felt like running away. Carmichael had sounded incredulous.

"You want to stay at Corsair Street?"

"Absolutely."

"A desperate place, there's far better postings."

It'd been tempting. The men in cheap anoraks at the court entrance had splashed his mug all over the tabloids the day after the trial and so he'd carried some notoriety for a while. There were some at Corsair Street who'd forever regard him with suspicion. But, against all odds he'd made friends among the incorrigible old bastards and though his desire to return would seem naïve to a career man like Carmichael, what really mattered was to finish off what he'd started.

Fitzpatrick, guilty of the allegations of bullying had been transferred to an obscure corner of the force to see out the rest of his service in limbo. Harkness got two years, a sentence that rippled across the force in waves of disbelief and introspection, until everyday life regained centre ground and a collective amnesia took hold. Nobody wants to remember a bad apple in an outfit on the side of the angels.

They walked through the marram grass to the car, dusted the sand from their feet and climbed inside. A squeeze of the hand and a soft kiss on the cheek. She looked happy.

"Ok?"

A quick nod.

"Looking forward to it."

Well, he wasn't, but there was no turning back now.

Dad was standing at the front door as they pulled up. There was an upwards jut of the chin to show he'd seen them and then Emma was out and through the garden gate with a broad smile. Alec braced himself for some awkwardness but as he caught up he was forced to recalibrate his perceptions, for there stood a well-spoken charmer with a ready smile. And was that the expensive pullover he'd bought the old goat last Christmas? The one received with a grunt and never seen again? Emma made enthusiastic comments about the pullover and Dad, flushing pink, waved it off as being 'just some old thing' before leading them inside.

"Come on in, dinner's ready."

Towed in the slipstream of warm conversation, Alec passed the picture of Mum on her wedding day, eyes sparkling, laughing at a joke she'd been told, waist thickening with the child already on his way. And next to her, his course photo from the police college, in a gold frame.

Dad, basking in the glow of female company, walked toward the kitchen, gravy-stained tea-towel over one shoulder, gruff voice loud and clear.

"Hope you like steak pie!"

THE END

About The Author

The author is a proud Scot raised on that jewel set on a mystic sea, Ardrossan, in the fine county of Ayrshire.

A student of Applied Physics, he discovered atoms weren't as exciting as folk made them out to be, so he sought adventure with Strathclyde Police. He got more than he bargained for in a career that included policing Glasgow's most deprived and violent communities. He was a beat cop, plain clothes, firearms, public order and specialist search officer. He was also a crisis and hostage negotiator, and Professional Standards investigator. His career included less exciting but equally stressful posts. In 1994 he received a Chief Constable's High Commendation for bravery.

He graduated from the University of Glasgow with a MLitt in Creative Writing in 2019, has written short stories and articles for a variety of magazines and published a radio play for Hospital Radio. A resident of Glasgow he is now a proud grandparent, married with a wife, son and two daughters. He can sometimes be seen on cold rain-lashed winter nights walking Jasper their Australian Labradoodle. He never *ever* wanted a dog.

Since leaving the police thoughts have turned to the earlier years of his service and a Glasgow now changed for the better, of a style of policing that has all but disappeared and with it the attitudes that accompanied it. The squalid slums have gone. The rancid tower blocks are disappearing. But so are the distinctive communities that once characterised those areas. Not all change is for the better. In gaining something, something is lost.

The Corsairs is his debut novel.

He intends to write more…

Printed in Great Britain
by Amazon